Believable world building undergirds good fantasy. In *Masters and Slayers*, Bryan Davis takes as much care establishing the physical backdrop as he does in character development. The result is another tale that draws in fantasy lovers and satisfies the reader on a spiritual level as well as on the entertainment through adventure plane. Mr. Davis has given us the beginning of another series to put on the Keeper shelf.

Donita K. Paul
(Author of Dragon Keeper Chronicles and Chiril Chronicles)

Finally a bold tale of dragons and other worlds for a more mature Christian audience! *Masters and Slayers* is one of those rare stories that, as I delved into it, didn't merely intrigue me—but enchanted me. Uniquely imaginative, this tale of a man, his father, and a headstrong young woman as they seek the Lost Ones, is a delightful read.

Scott Appleton (Author of *Swords of the Six*)

There are two things you can count on from a Bryan Davis novel: **1)** you'll be flung headfirst into a white-knuckling adventure beyond the limits of imagination. And **2)** you're going to be challenged at the deep levels of your heart. It's a rare, satisfying one-two punch that leaves the reader exhilarated, thoughtful, and much better for the experience.

Wayne Thomas Batson (Author of The Dark Sea Annals)

Bryan Davis once again writes a novel that captures the imagination and the heart. *Masters and Slayers* is packed with colorful characters and the story moves at a good pace keeping the mind on high alert. This first novel in the adult series promises to be another masterpiece for Davis. Well crafted and beautifully written.

Aaron Patterson (Author of the WJA series)

In *Masters & Slayers*, Bryan Davis has crafted another series destined for acclaim. A brilliant mixture of both King Arthurian-like legend and futuristic sci-fi, Davis creates a believable scenario, blending fear, humility, trust, young romance, courage, rage and many other emotional ingredients. Readers beware... you are in store for a thrilling ride that begins with a father's blessing in Mesolantrum, mystery, conflicted spirits, the search for Dracon, the legendary dragon planet, and as with all of the author's novels, the clash of good and evil to the bitter end.

Eric Reinhold (Author of The Annals of Aelaina)

In his first fantasy book for adult readers, Bryan Davis takes us to a world of nobility and treachery, of freedom and slavery, of joy and despair. Serving as a companion book for his Dragons of Starlight series and as a fascinating book on its own, *Masters and Slayers* is an enthralling read, sure to please both newcomers and older readers of the young adult series.

Luke Gledhill

I wholeheartedly recommend this book to the long-time Bryan Davis fans and any new fans that are bound to crop up. Anyone expecting this Christian author to present predictable black-and-white situations with a cliché moral message is in for a shock! Expect to be drawn into a new world, weeping for the lost and abused and cheering on the heroes who would do anything to save them.

Nicole Cragin

Masters and Slayers is a page-turning read you won't want to put down. While set in the same universe as the best seller *Starlighter*, Bryan Davis has chosen to follow other characters as they are interwoven in the story. Join Adrian Masters and Marcelle the noblewomen as they meet the mysterious Cassabrie and battle to set free captive slaves. Bryan Davis's writing is getting better and better with every book of his that I read, and this one is no exception. This is one book that you do not want to miss.

Charlie Miller

Bryan Davis has created a stunning novel in which both the outward and inward struggles of life are portrayed. Adrian Masters battles against dragons in order to free the slaves of Starlight, while inwardly wrestling a spirit that challenges his thinking at every turn. This is certainly a story that Christian fantasy readers will not want to miss.

Nic Laudadio

All I can say is that I'm now a huge fan. Davis's pacing is masterful, and his story craft is on par with the greats, making him a legend in his own day. But what grips me the most are his characters. Never have I been so sad to see a story come to a close.

Davis's leap to adult fiction was no leap at all. At least he made it seem that way. Writing for an older audience comes as natural to him as Adrian parrying a sword attack. Adventure. Courage. Valor. Sacrifice. An absolute must read.

Christopher Hopper (Author of The White Lion Chronicles and co-author of The Berinfell Prophecies)

Masters & Slayers

❧ TALES OF STARLIGHT SERIES ❧

Bryan Davis

Masters & Slayers

Volume 1 in the Tales of Starlight® series

Copyright © 2010 by Bryan Davis

Published by Living Ink Books, an imprint of
AMG Publishers, Inc.
6815 Shallowford Rd.
Chattanooga, Tennessee 37421

ISBN 13: 978-0-89957-884-2
First Printing—August 2010

TALES OF STARLIGHT is a registered trademark of AMG Publishers.

Cover designed by Daryle Beam at Bright Boy Design, Chattanooga, TN.

Interior design and typesetting by Reider Publishing Services, West Hollywood, California.

Edited and proofread by Susie Davis, Sharon Neal, and Rick Steele.

Printed in Canada
15 14 13 12 11 10 –V– 7 6 5 4 3 2 1

✳ AUTHOR'S NOTE ✳

Masters & Slayers, published by AMG/Living Ink, is the first book in Tales of Starlight, a series for adults that acts as a companion series to Dragons of Starlight, a series for young adults published by Zondervan.

How to Read the Series:

You can fully enjoy the Tales of Starlight series without reading the companion series, Dragons of Starlight. If you read both series, however, you will enjoy a fuller understanding of the story world.

If you intend to read both series, here is my suggested reading order:

1. Starlighter (Dragons of Starlight book #1)
2. Masters & Slayers (Tales of Starlight book #1)
3. Warrior (Dragons of Starlight book #2)
4. The Third Starlighter (Tales of Starlight book #2)
5. Dragons of Starlight book #3 (Untitled at this time)
6. Dragons of Starlight book #4 (Untitled at this time)

You may switch the reading order for entries 1 and 2 on the above list without any problem, and you may also switch the order for entries 4 and 5.

Parents' Guide:

Although *Masters & Slayers* is designed for adults, it can be read by teenagers, especially those who have enjoyed *Starlighter*, the first book in the Dragons of Starlight series. The adult designation is due to the fact that the story follows the adventures of adult characters instead of teenagers.

The good-versus-evil violence in this book is similar to that of the young adult series, except for a few more graphic events, such as the fiery execution of a boy and the severing of a murder victim's fingers. There are no sexual scenes, but the breeding of humans by order of the slave-master dragons is mentioned. This practice takes place "off-screen" and is not described, though one character explains his dilemma when faced with an order to participate. There is no profanity or sexually provocative language.

ONE

NEVER *make a woman bleed, my son.*

Adrian stood at his corner of the tourney ring, tightening his grip on the hilt of his sword as he listened to silent echoes of his father's words.

If you draw your sword against those you were born to protect, the very ones who trust in your strength, how will you convince them that you are a shield when the dragons come to take them away?

When the dragons come, Adrian repeated in his mind. If those beasts ever returned, they wouldn't find easy prey this time. No humans would be dragged away to slavery again, not if he could help it.

He lifted *Spirit* and looked at the sharp point. As usual, the tournament officials had attached a stab guard at the end of the blade to prevent puncture wounds deeper than a half inch. Still, that was deep enough. These blood matches were more than mere displays of competitive showmanship; they were tests of courage in the face of real bloodletting.

He shook his head. The stab guard mattered nothing. No battle courage would be tested in this match, and no blood would be spilled. The only showmanship might be how his opponent would react to the decision he had already made.

At the other side of the ring, Marcelle stepped across the fighting boundary, her confident stride combining with her athletic lines to draw the usual gaping stares from men young and old. Tucked into her form-fitting gray trousers, she wore a loose, high-necked white tunic with a red dragon emblazoned over her chest. The dragon's mouth was wide open, and a sword protruded from its belly—a conquered beast, perfectly appropriate for this warrior.

Since her previous match had ended only moments ago, sweat discolored her chest and armpits, and a spot of blood stained one shoulder, her opponent's blood no doubt. Still, her slender, petite frame would have made ignorant men laugh. A woman! And a scrawny one at that!

Adrian knew better. Anyone who doubted Marcelle's skills would soon be skewered, his own blood marking her garment as a symbol of another conquered foe. Yes, she was a formidable woman indeed. She had won her earlier matches against men twice her weight. Ever since she turned twenty-one about three years earlier, every tournament swordsman in the region had learned a simple truth—no one laughs at Marcelle.

She looked his way, her shoulders not quite as square now and her dark eyes lacking their usual fire. With her auburn hair tied back in a ponytail, the hint of sweat on her brow was obvious. She lifted her elegant rapier. The hilt's ornate hand guard revealed her position in society, the highbrow nobility, a caste represented by half the audience—the well-dressed, perfumed half, separated from the peasants by an invisible wall that divided the amphitheater.

Adrian let his gaze drift around the circle of onlookers. The break between the classes was obvious—browns and grays changing over to purples and scarlets, and mops of labor-scattered hair shifting to velvet hats adorned with feathers and silk. The day's cooler weather prompted the ladies to don their autumn finery, embellished with the aroma of the season's flowers, another stark contrast with the poorer class, those who enriched the air with leather and lye soap.

While eyeing Adrian, Marcelle ran her fingers across the dragon emblem, as if smoothing out her tunic. Her gesture transmitted a message. As a secret believer in the ongoing human enslavement on Dracon, the legendary dragon planet, she desperately wanted to search for the portal to that world, and she would do anything to procure the assignment. Even wearing this draconic vesture would bring punishment to a peasant, but as a noblewoman who claimed that the design mocked the silly tale, she could get away with it. She often tiptoed on the edge of safety while exercising just enough caution to stay out of trouble.

As the buzz from the crowd grew, any thought that Marcelle was less than battle-focused vanished as her fingers flexed around her sword hilt. She was ready, more than ready.

Adrian suppressed an emerging smirk. Did she really think this contest would end any differently than the previous three times they had met in tournaments? Of course, she didn't know if she could really win. Even when they were eight years old and battled using tree branches, both weapons broke, and they fell on their backsides. He had laughed. She was furious and let him know it with a barrage of oaths, promising to cut out his heart and feed it to her cat, though the twinkle in her eye never allowed him to believe a word she had said.

"Your swords," the referee said in detached monotone.

Adrian approached the center of the ring and handed his sword to the tall, middle-aged official, and Marcelle did the same, again training her stare on Adrian.

"To your corners." While the referee examined the stab guards, Adrian backed away. Marcelle withdrew a few steps, her gaze still riveted on him.

"Shall I say it for you this time?" she asked, loud enough for everyone to hear.

Adrian squinted at her. "Say what?"

With a sparkle in her eyes, she swept an arm in front of her waist, bowed, and spoke in a sarcastic tone. "In honor of the lady's expertise, I surrender."

As laughter erupted from the nobility section, heat surged into Adrian's cheeks. Marcelle's mimicry was all too calculated. Obviously she had practiced both the bow and the cadence of speech, but her sarcasm carried more than its usual bite.

His ears burning as the laughter grew, Adrian bowed in return. "Let it be as you have spoken."

When he rose, Adrian looked beyond Marcelle into the peasants' half of the crowd. His father sat stoically, while his mother covered her face with her hands. Next to her, his younger brother Jason ran tight fingers through his tawny hair, obviously angry at yet another forfeit to Marcelle.

Adrian retrieved his sword from the referee and stalked toward his family, glancing at Marcelle as he drew near her. She caught his gaze and offered a disarming smile. "I was stupid," she whispered. "I'm sorry."

"Tell it to the crowd. Then I'll believe you." Adrian hurried across the grass separating the ring from the amphitheater's steps. As he climbed to his family's row, he tried to ignore the glares and whispers, but they pressed in on him like a vise. One remark rose above the others, obviously intentionally louder.

"Adrian Masters, master of cowards."

Then a whispered answer from nearby reached Adrian's ears. "Just like his father."

Adrian stopped. Firming his lips, he stared at the ground. *Don't even look at them. They're not worth the trouble.*

After exhaling slowly, he continued until he reached the ninth row. He found two empty spaces next to his father and sat at his side. "Where are Mother and Jason?"

His father breathed in, filling his barrel-chested frame. As a cool breeze fanned thin gray hair across his weathered scalp, he replied in a resigned tone. "Your brother is preparing for his match with Randall, and your mother went with him. She was ... well ... rather despondent."

"I see." Adrian looked at the tourney ring. Governor Prescott placed a laurel crown on Marcelle's head while the crowd on the opposite side cheered. Jason's bout was next on the schedule, the finals for the older teens, the only other division allowed to compete in a blood match. Because of the quick forfeit, plenty of time remained before that contest, so Jason and his mother hadn't departed because of the schedule.

"My son," his father said. "I see the torment in your eyes. Resist fretting over this. Rare is the man these days who understands chivalry. Be content that your sword will never be used—"

"I know. I know." Adrian propped his elbows on his knees and glared at the grass around his shoes. "I was born to use my sword in defense of women and children." He raised his head and looked into his father's gray eyes. This veteran of wars understood the tragedy of bloodshed, the reality of danger, and the duty to keep the innocent out of harm's way. After another humiliation in front of both nobles and peasants, maybe it was time to ask again.

"Father, I intend to make such a defense. You know I'm going tonight with or without your approval, so I was hoping—"

"For a blessing?" he asked, lifting his bushy eyebrows.

"Yes." Adrian lowered his voice to a whisper. "Tonight is the appointed time, so I cannot wait any longer."

His father leaned closer. "Why you, my son? An old man can take only so much grief. After losing Frederick—"

"But Frederick might still be alive! And the brotherhood believes that I am the most qualified for the mission. If I can find the portal before we complete the deal with the dragons, I will be in position to enter their world even if they renege on their part of the bargain."

"Mistrust is appropriate," his father said, nodding. "Any beast that would kidnap and enslave our people cannot have integrity."

Adrian folded his hands and stared at his intertwined fingers. "True, and if mistrust were the only consideration, then another warrior could go in my stead. But it's not that simple. I see attempts at faithfulness on the part of this dragon that no one else perceives."

Laughing, his father gave him a loving shove but kept his voice low. "Are you saying that you have met this beast? We're thankful you didn't invite him home to dinner."

Adrian grinned. "I've never seen him, but I have read his messages. Apparently he leaves them close to a willow tree near Miller's Creek, the same place we found Frederick's hat. He warns us that the portal is elsewhere, and he will reveal its location after we deliver the extane tank. He will trust us to deliver more gas later."

"Such trust indicates a faithful negotiator. Perhaps he is conflicted for some reason."

"Exactly my point," Adrian said. "I hope to talk to him when he comes into our world tonight and learn more about him. I'm wondering if …" He paused. What word would fit his thought?

"He is a rogue dragon?" his father suggested.

Adrian pointed a finger. "Yes, that's it. He is promising only access to his world, not a trade for our people."

"Because he is not in a position to offer them." His father took in a deep breath and let it out slowly. "And you're concerned that you're the only one who would treat this dragon with the respect he might deserve, depending, of course, on what you learn about his character."

"You know me well, Father." Adrian looked away and gazed at a little girl, maybe eight years old, sitting two rows ahead. Wearing a ragged sun bonnet and a work smock that revealed a neck bronzed by the sun, she slid closer to her older brother, a lad of about ten years. Her brother laid an arm over her shoulders, and the two leaned their heads together. The image of brother-sister love was beautiful indeed.

"The dragon's message," Adrian continued, "said that human children are being brutalized there, and since he demands extane in trade for our passage, I cannot but wonder at his motivations. If he has integrity and cares at all about the children, he would welcome our transport without any payment."

"True, son. Wariness is called for."

Adrian looked at his father, who was now staring straight ahead, as if in a dream. "Does that mean I have your blessing?" Adrian asked.

With a tear sparkling in his eye, he turned and set a hand on Adrian's shoulder. "Only if you swear to return. As you know, the people here can ill afford to lose another man of wisdom. It is a rare quality in Mesolantrum."

Adrian shook his head. "You ask too much. I cannot swear what I cannot control. But if you will give me your blessing, I trust that my path back to your home will be straighter than if I go without it."

"And *will* you go without it?"

"Only as a man who is dragged by chains. I must go. I have no choice. I am compelled by unseen forces I must obey, but I would rather march into battle unhindered by the worries of those I leave behind."

"I understand those forces … all too well." Edison shifted his hand to Adrian's head. Adrian bowed and covered his face. "Son, you are very dear to me, and I cannot stand the thought of losing you, but by faith in the great Creator, I give what I can." He took a deep breath before continuing, his voice trembling. "Go with wisdom, strength, and integrity. May you put an end to the oppression and set free the captives. And may you return to us safely, bringing with you a host of unshackled souls, so that we may celebrate the Creator's purpose that every man, woman, and child should be free from all shackles that bind their wrists, ankles, or hearts."

After a moment of silence, Adrian felt his father's hand lift. He raised his head, and the two locked gazes. "I will rescue the Lost Ones," Adrian said. "I will find Frederick, and he and I will restore the honor of our father's good name. Edison Masters will again pass through the lips of young and old alike as an inspiration to warriors in training."

Edison leaned close again. "Although I have given you my blessing, that does not mean I am excited about your departure. Please be kind to a poor old man and leave while I am not looking."

Adrian rolled his hand into a fist. Yes! His father had given his blessing. What a relief. " All that remains is for me to resign my post and pack one bag—"

"Shh!" Edison's eyes darted around. "Not every ear is sympathetic to our cause."

Adrian calmed his breathing. Control over his emotions was one of the reasons he was chosen by the Underground Gateway. No sense in blurting out unguarded words now.

"Governor Prescott will not be pleased," Edison said, "unless you already have a suitable replacement in mind."

"Jason, of course. He will make a perfect bodyguard."

A proud smile spread across Edison's face. "I would like that. I would like that very much."

Adrian patted his father's knee. "I have to change into my uniform. Prescott will be expecting me to sit with him during Jason's match. He also wants me to attend him at tonight's invocation of the new counselor, but I will be gone by then. Jason will have to take my place."

"Marcelle will likely follow custom and sit with the governor, so you will have, shall we say, awkward company." Edison's smile wrinkled into a mischievous grin. "Changing to your uniform is a good idea. We wouldn't want people comparing the blood and sweat on your clothes to those on Marcelle's. All the whispers would distract you from your duty."

"No worries about that. Everyone will be gawking at her crown." As Adrian shook his unruly hair, the ends tickled his ears and the back of his neck. "Who needs leaves getting tangled in this mess anyway?"

"I assume you will be keeping this journey a secret from her," Edison said.

"At all costs. If Marcelle knew I was going in search of the portal, she would hound me from one end of Mesolantrum to the other."

"My lips are sealed, but would Drexel divulge it? He is a mysterious fellow."

"I'm not sure," Adrian said, letting a smile break through, "but I do know how to handle Marcelle."

Edison laughed. "Then you are the first. She is untamable."

Adrian jabbed with a pretend sword. "I just keep her infuriated at me. She's predictable when she's angry."

✶   ✶   ✶   ✶   ✶   ✶

Now dressed in his soldier's uniform, Adrian sat at Governor Prescott's side on the nobility half of the amphitheater as they awaited the final event, the youth championship round. With his polished leather boots, dark gray trousers, sparkling sword and scabbard, and silky forest green shirt, Adrian felt akin to a traitor, a peasant in wolf's clothing guarding the head of the wolf pack. Not only that, Prescott's own son, Randall, stood at one side of the tourney ring ready to battle Jason, making Adrian a double traitor. A good brother would have been cheering with heart and soul from among the peasants, but the traitor would sit quietly amidst a sea of satin and feather caps.

Marcelle sat at Prescott's opposite side, still dressed in her tournament attire, complete with blood, sweat, and crown. She leaned forward, peered around the governor, and flashed Adrian a smile as she adjusted a trouser cuff. The material slid just high enough to expose her muscular calf.

Adrian averted his eyes. What did her gesture communicate? A woman dressed as a man had shamed him? It seemed that she had the same plan, to tame him by keeping him infuriated at her.

Taking in a deep breath, Adrian began a slow count to ten. It wouldn't work. Her theatrics wouldn't raise the slightest hint of ire, at least not this time.

After a trumpeter blew a long, shrill note signaling the start of Jason's match, the governor nodded. In response, the crowd quieted and settled into their places. While the referee announced the rules, Adrian kept an eye on Drexel, the palace's head sentry, who sat on the lowest row, about three seats to the left. This middle-aged guard, more politician than protector, had been glancing toward the governor every few minutes, as if expecting something to happen. Since he was a secret member of the Underground Gateway and the man in charge of negotiating the gas trade with the dragon, Drexel was no true friend of the ruling class. He had to be watched carefully.

A courier, tall and lean, ran up the amphitheater's steps carrying a foot-long, metallic tube. After bowing, he presented the tube to the governor and hurried away. Prescott looked through one end of the tube, a frown growing with each passing second. Finally, he lowered it and pressed a button, erasing the message. Although his face flushed red, he said nothing.

A buzz from the crowd drew Adrian's attention back to the match. Randall charged Jason, and the two locked together, blade to blade. Adrian cringed. Brute force wouldn't help Jason win this battle. Randall was too big, too skilled. It would take cunning to overcome the physical disadvantage.

When Jason finally pushed Randall back, Randall swiped his sword across Jason's arm, ripping his sleeve. The crowd stood as one, the nobles cheering and the peasants moaning. Prescott, to his credit, stayed quiet, as did Marcelle.

Adrian focused on his brother's torn sleeve. So far, no sign of red appeared. Maybe Jason's mistake hadn't cost him the match, but his strategy would have to change drastically.

Jason looked up at the royal section. Their gazes met. Adrian laid a hand over his chest and mouthed, "Listen to your heart." He then pointed at the side of his head and formed, "But use your brain," with his lips, trying hard to make the words clear. As brothers sitting through long sermons at cathedral, they had mastered lip-reading as a way to pass the time, telling jokes and riddles while trying not to burst out laughing. Now they could finally put the skill to use in a more practical way.

Jason nodded and turned to face his opponent. After a few seconds, the referee raised a hand and shouted, "There is no blood! Let the match continue!"

As he and the crowd returned to their seats, Adrian let out a breath. How long had he been holding it? The tension had wrung out his sense of reality like an old rag.

Jason used his sword to scratch something in the dirt and motioned for Randall to look. The two conversed for a few seconds before Jason, taking advantage of Randall's momentary lack of vigilance, lunged and jabbed him in the thigh. Blood oozed from the wound and darkened his pant leg.

Again the crowd stood. Catcalls sounded from the nobles' section. "Foul!" and "Bad form!"

Adrian stayed seated, now unable to see the ring. Marcelle squeezed behind Prescott and stooped next to Adrian. "Your brother tricked him," she whispered.

He kept his focus on the people standing in front of him. "I saw that. It was within the rules. Randall was bigger and stronger, and Jason had to use cunning to overcome the advantage."

Marcelle laid her hand on Adrian's cheek and forced his head around. "Look at me. Do you think I would use trickery? Do you think I care about bigger and stronger?"

Adrian let his eyes drift from Marcelle's sinewy body to her fiery eyes. "I think you care very much. The bigger and stronger your opponent, the more your head swells when you win."

Her lips drew so tight they nearly disappeared. Her face reddened as if ready to explode, but Prescott's voice doused the fuse. "Come. Both of you must accompany me to crown the champion."

Adrian leaped up and followed Prescott, staying behind by his usual three paces as he negotiated the grassy stairs. Marcelle threw her leafy crown back on, now somewhat mangled, and stalked at the governor's side with her fists tight at the ends of her stiff arms.

As they descended, Adrian caught sight of Drexel again. Their stares met for a brief moment before Drexel turned and marched away. The glimpse raised a tingle across Adrian's skin. Something new prowled in that calculating mind, a scheme that went beyond the already complex negotiations with the dragons.

"Jason Masters!" Prescott called as they walked into the ring.

When Jason turned, Prescott held out a pristine crown of laurel. Marcelle scooted close to Adrian and whispered, "Take it back."

He replied in a lower whisper. "The statement about your swelled head?"

"Yes. Take it back, or else."

"Or else what?"

With a mischievous grin, Marcelle sang her reply. "You'll see."

Prescott extended the crown toward Jason. "Bow, please."

After Jason bowed and rose again with the crown on his head, he mouthed to Adrian, "What's wrong?"

Adrian replied with a silent, "I'll tell you later."

"And now," Prescott said as he laid one hand on Jason's shoulder and the other on Marcelle's, "let us honor the warrior champions in the adult and youth divisions!"

After the crowd finished cheering, Marcelle shook Jason's hand. "Congratulations, Jason." Her eyes darted between him and Adrian. "It was a pleasure to watch a son of Edison Masters do battle in the final round. I'm glad to see that you're courageous enough to face an opponent who might be able to defeat you." After flashing a triumphant smile at Adrian, Marcelle strutted out of the ring and into the mass of people.

Adrian set a hand on Jason's back, barely keeping his fingers from clutching his shirt. "You'd better go home as soon as you can, Jason. I'm sure Mother and Father will want to congratulate you."

Jason leaned close and whispered, "Will you be home for a while, or are you going out on one of those dragon-hunting missions again?"

"Shhh!" Adrian nudged Jason with an elbow. "I'll meet you at home this evening. We have a lot to talk about."

"Okay. I'll see you then." As Jason walked away, Adrian took his place behind the governor, who was now conversing with an elderly noble. He searched the sea of heads for Marcelle. She stood near the exit path, talking to Drexel, her crown again in her tight fist and her sword at her hip. She seemed annoyed, maybe even scared.

She glanced at Adrian, a look so quick, Drexel probably didn't notice. Then, she grasped a handful of her shirt, clutching the dragon's head in a tight squeeze.

Adrian gripped his sword's hilt. Had she relayed another silent message? Had Drexel told her about the mission? Was she saying that she wanted to go with him to find the portal to the dragon world? Or was she signaling a warning? Of course she could protect herself against the likes of that skinny hack, but something had certainly spiked her emotions. What could it be?

He let out a silent sigh. No use worrying about it. She probably wouldn't appreciate his intervention, and he couldn't leave Prescott anyway, at least not for a phantom suspicion.

As if straining against a rusted hinge, he slowly turned his head away. Keeping his mind on plans for finding the portal remained paramount. The lives of countless slaves hung in the balance, and every moment delayed meant another moment suffered under the dragons' cruelty. Tonight would begin their emancipation.

*　　　*　　　*　　　*　　　*　　　*

"Would Adrian trust a dragon over his friends?" Drexel smiled, lifting his tidy mustache toward his pointed nose. "Marcelle, it seems that the ladder leading to his good sense is missing a few rungs."

Marcelle glanced at Adrian, still standing dutifully with Prescott in the tourney ring as the audience dispersed and filtered out of the amphitheater. No doubt Adrian *would* trust a dragon over most humans. With "friends" like Drexel, it was no wonder.

She squared her shoulders and stealthily looked Drexel over. Dressed in his sentry uniform, complete with battle sword, gleaming chain mail, and polished leather boots, he displayed a stately presence. Even the gray-speckled hair flowing from underneath his black felt hat and down the nape of his neck was pristine and tangle-free, and his handlebar mustache had been recently trimmed and waxed. To casual observers, he likely took on a persona of royal integrity. Yet, she knew better. This keeper of Governor Prescott's iron-clad doors guarded his darker side better than most.

"If this dragon is more than a myth," Marcelle said, lowering her voice as she crumpled the leaves in her crown, "then trusting it would be a mistake." She grabbed a fistful of her tunic and crushed the dragon's head. "If I were allowed to secretly trail Adrian, I could be his skeptical shadow and jump in to help him if the dragon proves untrustworthy."

"No doubt you could, but His Excellency has a new assignment for you that—"

"A new assignment!" She lifted a pointing finger close to his nose. "You promised if there was another attempt to find the portal—"

"Promised?" He pushed her hand to the side. "I made no promises. I merely said that I would try to persuade the powers that be."

She lowered her voice to a seething whisper. "If you wanted me to go with Adrian, you could find a way. Everyone knows about your bargaining skills."

"Then kindly control your passions long enough for me to explain. Perhaps you will get your wish."

She took in a deep breath, then, as she let it out, she answered with a growl. "Very well, but don't test my patience."

"That is the last thing I want to do." Drexel glanced both ways before continuing. "In anticipation of Adrian's resignation as bodyguard, I told Governor Prescott that I required Adrian's services, hoping to smooth the path. When Prescott agreed, I thought my plans were proceeding quite well, but then he presented an unexpected obstacle."

"And that was?"

Drexel pointed at her. "He wants you to be his new bodyguard."

"Me?" She shook her head hard. "Certainly not! I refuse to be a … a toy soldier! If he needs his posterior protected, let him wear chain mail trousers!"

"I think you lack understanding. This was not a request. It was a command. He seemed quite eager to procure you, in his words, mind you, as a lovely escort."

"That's my point. I didn't train as a warrior just to dress up for a parade. And besides, have you ever noticed how he looks at me? As a bodyguard, won't I have to be alone with him at times?"

"I have noticed his leering eyes, and that could be your way out of the assignment." A weaselly smile turned his lips. "He has quite a weakness for, shall we say, provocative persuasion?"

Marcelle whipped out her sword and set the point under Drexel's chin. "I should cut out your tongue and make you choke on your own blood." Her heart pounding, she pressed the blade, pricking his skin. "And I swear on my mother's grave that those who mourn your passing will join you in hell."

A gasp sounded from a group of four peasants, stragglers who had not yet left the tournament grounds. They spun and hurried to the exit path. Marcelle let her gaze sweep across the rest of the amphitheater. Only a few people milled about, and no one looked their way.

Drexel swallowed, his eyes focused on the blade as his voice pitched up a notch. "I assure you, Marcelle, that my comment was not intended to insult your person. In fact, I was complimenting your physique. A skillful woman knows how to use her ..."—he swallowed again—"her attributes to her advantage without sacrificing her virtue."

Scowling as she glared at his terrified eyes, she muttered, "What do you know about virtue?" With a quick swing, she thrust the sword back to its scabbard. "Or women?"

Drexel breathed a sigh. As he dabbed a trickle of blood near his chin, he reached into his tunic's inner pocket and withdrew a folded parchment, brown and wrinkled. "At the risk of raising your ire once again, allow me to explain. Our esteemed governor has been visiting the lower level of the dungeon from time to time, always insisting on going alone. I suspect that he has a secret way to access the main gas line from there. Why? I believe he is meeting someone from the gas company, but the details are not important. What is important is that you discover his access method."

When Drexel paused, Marcelle prodded for more, stretching out her words. "Okay. I'm still listening."

"I'm glad your confidence in my skills has returned. You see, during the tournament, I sent a message tube to the governor that should lure him back to the dungeon. You will follow him and see what he does. As his new bodyguard, you will have an excuse if you are caught. You were doing your duty and had no idea that he wanted to be alone."

"Then after I find his secret," Marcelle said, "I can get caught intentionally so I can talk him out of assigning me as his bodyguard."

"Allow him to hide his tracks first, or you might be terminated in a more permanent fashion." He extended the parchment toward her. "Take this and learn its contents. It describes how we are attempting to rescue the captured slaves by trading extane for passage to the dragon world. If you succeed in bargaining with Prescott, you will have to figure out a way to stay behind and access the gas lines. What you must do is described at the end of the note."

She extended her hand. As her fingers closed on the paper, she hesitated, searching Drexel's eyes for deception. This was a dream assignment, exciting and adventurous, unless he was leading her into a trap.

She pinched the note and pulled it away, keeping her stare in place. "Anything else?"

"Just a warning." Drexel looked both ways before continuing, his voice lowering to a growl. "You have a sharp blade and a sharp tongue, little lady, but take care to restrain both and heed what you find in those words. I doubt that either your sword, or your tongue, or even your virtue will keep you and Adrian alive if you fail to deliver what the dragon wants."

Marcelle glanced at the parchment but said nothing. Talking too much could ruin the opportunity. No matter what Drexel was hiding, turning down this chance to join Adrian would be stupid.

"Memorize the note and then destroy it. If Prescott finds it in your possession, your life will be forfeit, and if any of his loyalists finds out what you are doing, your mission will be short-lived."

Barely suppressing a nervous swallow of her own, Marcelle gave him a quick nod, spun toward the exit, and marched away. She couldn't let him notice her fear. So far, every battle had been fought within the confines of a tourney ring or a training class. If faced with a dragon opponent, surely she could muster the nerve to drive a blade through its heart, but what about a fellow human? What about another soldier who was just doing his duty by obeying orders handed down from his officers? If he interfered with their mission to go through the portal, could she shed his blood?

As she slowed her pace along the path toward the governor's palace, she shook her head, casting away the troubled thoughts. No matter what obstacles she faced, she would have to rely on her training and respond in a way that would complete this mission— rescue the slaves at all costs. Nothing else mattered.

TWO

W ALKING on the balls of his feet, Adrian padded into the bedroom he shared with his brother and laid a saddle pack on the pine floor. He stopped and listened. No sounds in their communal home. So far it seemed that no one had noticed his arrival. After galloping home on a palace horse, he had tethered it in the forest out of sight and earshot. Speed and secrecy had worked to this point, and now that he was safely in his room, he could take a little more time.

He leaned over and withdrew a courier's message tube from the pack. During his months as the royal bodyguard, he had kept it hidden behind a loose stone in a palace alcove, but now that he planned to resign his post, who could tell if he would again have access to it? Besides, hiding it here would allow him to carry out his plan to give it to Jason later in the afternoon.

He knelt and pried up a loose board, revealing a small cubbyhole. As he lowered the tube toward the hole, a sense of sadness dragged his spirits down. And why not? After today, he would likely never see the precious message again. Although he had long ago deciphered the hidden meaning behind most of the words, viewing it once more might reenergize him and send him off with a renewed passion.

A screen on the side of the cylinder read, *Deposit genetic material for access.*

He plucked a hair from his head and inserted it into a small opening next to the screen. The letters changed to, *Genetics verified.*

He raised the tube to his eye and looked through the end. As usual, a video played. Victor, a middle-aged man with salt-and-pepper hair and goatee, stood in the midst of the hardwood forest beyond Mesolantrum's boundary. He held a tricornered hat and said, "Adrian, you gave me this hat to analyze, and I have very little to tell you beyond what you already know. Bear hunting is perilous, and I fear that your brother has fallen victim to an especially dangerous variety. As you suspected, the blood on the band was not his. The genetic markers indicate a variety from a distant region, one that neither you nor I have ever ventured into. Yet your brother mentioned many times that he wished to go there to hunt this species."

Adrian nodded at the familiar words, coded, yet easy to translate for those who understood the mission of the Underground Gateway.

"Of course," Victor continued, "all mountain bears are intelligent, but these appear to be especially crafty. I fear that one has visited our region and placed the hat here in order to lure us to his lands. He likely wants us to come there in order to provide more captives for him and his clan. And, as you long suspected, there is a bear in our midst, one that hides his own guilt by concocting stories about other bears stealing innocent girls. If you find the bear among us, you will find his captive. The key to his secrets never leaves him, for even as he sleeps it rests upon his heart."

Adrian pondered the meaning of the "innocent girls" comment, one of the phrases he hadn't fully understood. Could Victor be referring to Elyssa, a teenager supposedly stolen from her home by a clan of bears? Yet, the bear story seemed impossible, in spite of the physical evidence that pointed to bears in the vicinity. And the key resting on a bear's heart was another mystery he had not yet solved. The key to the key, it seemed, followed Victor's brave soul to his grave, and he didn't survive long enough to offer his advice when the dragon began querying Drexel about a trade for extane.

Victor placed the hat against his chest. "Because I honor your brother so highly, I urge you to hunt the bears and rid the world of the danger."

The screen went blank. Adrian waited for the secret portion, which an intruder, thinking the video was finished, likely wouldn't see. After about a minute, another man appeared wearing the same tricornered hat, his back turned as he looked at a tall stone wall covered with thorny vines.

"Frederick," Adrian whispered. He tried to swallow, but his throat caught. Seeing his older brother always raised a surge of emotions—longing and heartbreak.

As usual, a dirty, bare-chested little boy stood near the wall. After picking up a handful of stones and putting them into a big pail, he hoisted the pail into his arms and shuffled away with it. Seconds later, Frederick turned. His face seemed narrow from loss of weight, and a few days of beard growth covered his cheeks and chin.

With wide eyes and sweat-dampened face, he spoke quickly, almost angrily. "Adrian, if every prayer of mine is answered, you will get this message. Hear me, my brother. It is all true. Every story is true. I have seen the dragons. I have met the Lost Ones. I do not have time to explain everything, so I simply beg you to come. Attempt the passage in the way I explained before I left home, and we will work together to rescue the lambs from the wolves. I cannot leave, for I fear that I will not be able to return to this world. I must stay and help them for as long as I can."

Frederick swallowed hard. A new tone etched passion into his voice. "I hope to be here to greet you when you make the passage, but if the dragons learn of my presence, you will likely not see me again. For now, I can only bring comfort to the Lost Ones. The rest will be up to you."

After the screen faded to black, Adrian wiped a tear with his sleeve. The day had finally arrived. After months of preparation, it was time to make the journey, though in a manner that differed from the way Frederick had envisioned. Frederick had learned about a way to pass through the portal and discussed it with Adrian before going on a search for the portal's location. He never returned to reveal its hiding place, and, in his hurry, he forgot to mention it in the video message. Yet, it might not matter. Apparently the dragon used a different portal to deliver the hat and this message. Finding this second portal would be Adrian's goal.

He clutched the cylinder tightly. Taking in a deep breath, he smiled. Yes, it was finally time. All that remained was to ride back to the palace, inform Prescott of his decision to resign, and then come home again to say good-bye to Mother and Jason. Of course, that last step would be the most difficult part. Father already approved, and Mother would understand his desire to go on yet another journey to find Frederick. Jason, on the other hand, wouldn't like it. He didn't believe the dragon stories and would not want his brother to go.

Adrian laid the cylinder in the cubbyhole. Father had warned him not to show Jason the message. Faith, he had said, is better rooted in prepared soil—fertile ground that embraces the seed. The soil must hope for it, long for it, though it had only imagined its presence by seeing fruit appear nearby. When soil reluctantly accepts seed that is thrust upon it, seed that it had rejected until the great farmer pushed it under the soil's skin, the seed will not germinate as readily, and the roots will likely not support a stalk strong enough to bear fruit. If Jason believes without seeing, as we all did, he will be a fruitful tree indeed.

Adrian set the board over the hole, concealing the courier tube. There wasn't enough time to wait for the soil to be ready. Jason needed to believe now, and Adrian had to force the seed down his throat. In his absence, Jason had to continue the search for Elyssa, and learning the truth about the dragons might motivate him to find his childhood friend.

Rising to his feet, Adrian stepped on the board and wedged it in place. Soon everyone would learn the truth. When the slaves returned from Dracon, every eye would see what Mesolantrum had disbelieved for so long. It was only fair that Jason's eyes be opened first.

He gazed at the wall to the right of the bedroom's only window and the mural he had painted there—the planetary system, at least all the planets the scientists had detected with the powerful sky scopes Prescott installed in his observatory.

With his eyes focused on the center of the mural, Adrian stepped closer to the wall. Solarus, of course, hovered at the focal point with orange flares streaming from its reddish surface. He counted the planets, as was his habit, and arrived at the same number—eighteen, those far from Solarus painted as frozen, blue and gray spherical rocks and the closer ones as smoother spheres displaying vibrant green and orange.

He touched the fourth large planet from Solarus, Major Four, the most verdant of the living worlds, and traced the blue line that represented the Elbon River to its mouth where it poured into the Sterling Sea. Those crystal waters yielded a wonderful bounty of fish and provided sustenance and trade for much of Mesolantrum—home to himself and ten thousand other souls who pledged allegiance, whether heartfelt or feigned, to Governor Prescott. And Prescott, of course, bowed the knee to King Sasser, the ruler of all the inhabited regions of Major Four.

As always, Adrian let his gaze jump to the opposite side of Solarus, where a black planet sat on the purple backdrop like the dark center of a bruise—Dracon, the mysterious dragon planet. Legends about Dracon described a distinct ice cap, a characteristic unseen on any visible planet. But Dracon had to be out there, likely too dark to be seen as it swept through its orbit. His drawing reflected mere speculation, a guess that it must always lie on the opposite side of Solarus where it floated like a celestial mouse trying to stay away from a pursuing cat.

Adrian smiled. Then again, maybe Major Four was the mouse and Dracon was the cat. Considering all that had happened, his own world was likely the one running from a predator.

He checked his sword and belt, positioning them in the perfect array Prescott demanded. He might as well look his part. No use making Prescott angrier than he already would be. Resigning never made sense to the pompous governor. Why would anyone ever want to leave such a high calling as guarding his person?

Adrian picked up the now-empty saddle pack and slung it over his shoulder. A high calling, indeed. Walking behind his hefty highness and watching his fat posterior swagger from one pretentious pageant to another wasn't exactly the pinnacle of a warrior's career. Still, it wouldn't hurt for Jason to use this position in order to gain some information. Maybe he could find the key Victor had talked about and solve the mystery of Elyssa's disappearance.

With a confident gait, he strode from the room. It was time to put the plan into motion—resign as bodyguard, then come back to the commune and reveal the truth to Jason.

*   *   *   *   *   *

As she hurried along the meadow path between the amphitheater and the governor's palace, Marcelle spied a column of smoke ahead and to the right. Veering toward it, she crossed into a cornfield with browning stalks, most taller than herself. After a few seconds, she broke into a clearing where a farmhand stood near a small pile of burning debris—moldy hay and dried cornstalks. Short and stocky, he jerked his shaggy head up and shuffled back a step, his fingers tightening around a garden rake. He swallowed and spoke with a jittery voice, "Marcelle?"

"Good afternoon," she said as she drew close. "I don't believe we've met."

"No, but everyone knows who you are." The man stared at the sword fastened to her belt. "What can I do for you?"

She suppressed a smile. "If you would be kind enough to fetch some water, I would be most appreciative."

"Certainly." The man dropped his rake, backed away a few steps, then turned and hurried into the cornstalks.

"Perfect." Marcelle withdrew Drexel's note from her pocket, held it open in her palm, and read the last few lines. *Turn the valve three-quarters to open the pipeline just enough to deliver the extane gas to our network. If you are successful, immediately notify the person who gave you this note so that he can arrange his part of this undertaking. You, then, must go to the collection tank and wait for a warrior we have assigned to help you. Be sure to arrive within five hours, or the collection tank's pressure valve will release gas and make a considerable noise. We do not want to attract attention, so it is imperative that our timing be precise and that you shut off the valve at the collection point. The dragon said he would leave further instructions near the tank, so when you arrive begin looking for signs of those instructions. He has provided communication in a variety of ways—a note, an etching in a tree, letters scrawled on the ground. Finding the next step is crucial, so consider every possibility.*

She closed her eyes and repeated the message from memory. Then, crouching by the fire, she dropped the note into the flames. As orange tongues licked the edges, she pictured the gas valve in her mind. This was all just too strange to be true. How long had the Gateway believers been planning this bribe? If the plan worked, would the dragon be appeased? Would they be able to bring the Lost Ones home, at least enough of them to prove to Mesolantrum that they existed?

And if the dragon granted passage to Dracon, what would prevent other dragons from coming through to Major Four and kidnapping more people in the future? Would they continue demanding ransom forever?

As the last of the note burned to ash, she rolled her fingers around the hilt of her sword. This was wrong, all wrong. The inhabitants of Major Four should fight to get their people back. Only force would teach those dragons to stay on their own planet. Accepting the fruits of extortion was the coward's way.

Taking a deep breath, she tried to calm her passion. She had an assignment to complete, an assignment that would begin in mere moments and in a most unpleasant manner. She, too, had to use stealth and deception to get her way, and fooling Prescott would be no easy task.

She searched the cornstalks for the farmhand. No sign of him. He was probably too frightened to return. This was certainly nothing new. Very few men ever wanted to be around her, whether out of fear or embarrassment.

She marched back through the cornstalks and found the path again. After a minute or so, the governor's palace came into sight. With towering marble columns, pristine white stairs leading visitors between lions of stone, and ornate carvings in the massive oaken doors, it was an edifice fit for the noblest of nobles, the most honorable of statesmen, the finest of gentlemen.

"Too bad Prescott is none of those," she muttered. With a quick stride, she marched along the grassy path that led around the palace's east side before slowing as she entered the rear courtyard's Enforcement Zone—the plaza where the pillories, burning stake, and gallows stood atop a floor of flat red stone.

She stopped and stared at the rough floor. No wonder Prescott had it painted. The blood spilled here now wore a disguise.

Although empty, each instrument of torture still provided a haunt for the ghosts of its victims—the members of the Underground Gateway who suffered under the hot sun with their wrists and ankles clamped in splintery bonds; the denounced "traitors" who swung from the noose dangling from the L-shaped post; and, worst of all, the "witches" who gave up their tender flesh to the flames of torment, all the while answering with whispered prayers the catcalls of the righteous. Even today it seemed that the smoke from the widow Halstead's burning body still billowed as her soul flew toward heaven and into the arms of God.

Tears pooled in Marcelle's eyes. How could anyone, especially the clergy, believe that Mrs. Halstead was anything but a woman gifted by her Creator to see beyond the physical? Why did the counselors preach the benefits of recognizing spiritual realities and then turn around and persecute someone who actually saw them? Such was their hypocrisy.

Marcelle swept past the noose and stalked toward the back of the courtyard where the dungeon guard rested on a flat, waist-high boulder. Clenching the hilt of her sword again, she forced her inflamed passion into submission. No sense in barking at Gregor. As a secret member of the Underground Gateway, he would never approve of Prescott's cruelties.

"I heard the governor entered the dungeon," she said. "I am his new bodyguard, so—"

"There is no need to explain," Gregor said as he rose. "I am to take you as far as the inner stairway." He bent his large frame and pulled open a door embedded in the ground, revealing a flight of stairs underneath. The hinges creaked loudly, proving their age and lack of use. Most criminals under Prescott's reign never made it as far as this door into the void. All the better for them. Even death was more tolerable than being plunged into darkness and then forgotten.

Using a pair of flint stones, Gregor lit a torch and descended the crooked, wooden stairs. Marcelle followed, treading lightly as the stout man in front of her raised loud squeaks from the two-centuries-old boards.

As light from above faded, the fire's glow spread across the walls on each side. With every step, the rough plaster felt closer, colder, as if the walls might pinch together behind her and block her escape. The air carried a musty odor intermixed with the expected smells of sweat, urine, and feces. A quiet moan echoed from somewhere below, more of an extended sigh than a cry of lament.

Marcelle tried to imagine a face to match the low voice, perhaps an elderly man with long scraggly hair and sad, bloodshot eyes. This was surely a place of precipices—life hanging in the balance, men young and old desperately clutching a shred of hope that someday they could climb these stairs, walk out with hands unbound, and feel the sun once again. Even the foul odors bore witness to each man's determination to survive just one day more.

When Gregor reached the bottom of the stairs, he turned left and lumbered toward a passageway, the center tunnel of three. Ducking slightly to keep his head from scraping the granite ceiling, he whispered, "They're probably awake. Don't listen to them. They'll tell any lie, any fable to arouse pity."

"Shouldn't we pity?" she asked as she followed.

Gregor shook his head. "If I were to allow them to prick my heart, my emotions would break out like a flood. I would unlock their cells and lead them out with a sword. I could never perform my duty."

"Your duty?" She gave him a skeptical squint. "Do you mean to Prescott or to your fellow man?"

Gregor stopped and glared at Marcelle. The torch highlighted the crags in his cheeks and chin as well as his fiery eyes. "We all compromise somewhere. Don't pretend you're excepted."

Marcelle bit her tongue. A clever retort would be easy, too easy, but what would it accomplish? Staying on Gregor's good side was essential. He represented the only way out.

She clasped Gregor's arm. "I have never stood in your shoes, my good man. Who am I to question your decisions?"

The big guard half closed one eye, but after a moment, he offered Marcelle a firm nod. "Let us be done with this task." He turned and marched into the central tunnel.

As Marcelle followed, the stench of waste and decay assaulted her nose. With no breeze to clear the air, the odor seemed to hang in the hall like a dirty curtain.

The torch crackled as Gregor walked, keeping his eyes focused straight ahead. He made a beeline for a stone wall at the end of the corridor. Marcelle stayed a few paces behind, swinging her head back and forth to get a glimpse of each barred window as she passed.

Fingers gripped the bars from inside a window on her left, and a nose protruded through the center gap. "I smell a coward," a man said.

Marcelle stopped and eyed the prisoner. With greasy stringy hair, filthy face, and grimy hands, he painted a stellar portrait of the sighing man she had conjured earlier.

"A coward?" Marcelle asked.

"As if you didn't hear me." The man spat through the bars, narrowly missing her sleeve. "You look mighty fine with a sword against your swaggering hip, but the only man who would challenge you would be a coward himself. No real warrior would fight a woman. It ain't chivalrous."

"Marcelle," Gregor said from the end of the hall. "It is useless talking to that madman."

She raised a finger. "Give me a moment." With the guard's now-distant torch barely illuminating the cell's window, she stepped closer and looked into the prisoner's wild eyes. "What is your name, friend?"

"Tibalt Blackstone, but if you're really my friend, you'll call me Tibber."

"Well, Tibber, I—"

"And you'll unlock this blasted door and let me go free."

"Really? What was your crime?"

"Believing in truth. Speaking the truth around the wrong ears, ears that wanted only to be tickled by lies. You know what they say about such ears."

"I do?" Marcelle folded her arms across her chest. "What do they say?"

"Ears of the head are like ears of the dead, they listen to nothing but air. They hear what they please, the things that appease, and the rest they pretend wasn't said."

She laughed. "That's very good. I have never heard it before."

"Figures." Tibalt spat again, this time aiming away.

Lowering her voice to a whisper, Marcelle leaned closer. "By speaking the truth, do you mean truth about ..." She glanced at Gregor to gauge his patience at her delay. "About a gateway that lies as deep as this dungeon?"

Tibalt's eyes widened. He, too, glanced in the guard's direction and kept his voice low. "Are you a believer? With your perfect hair and teeth, you look like one of the phony pheasants."

Marcelle suppressed a smile. "My hair and teeth are of no consequence, but my ears, as you say, are not dead. I wish I had time to hear your stories. You probably know a lot more than I do."

The old man's tone grew soft and friendly, though his eyes stayed as wide as ever. "If you really are a friend, and your ears aren't dead, then hear these words. The gateway to Dracon is real. I have seen it myself, but it was long ago, so long ago. My pappy showed it to me, and maybe I could find it again. Let me out, and we can find it together."

"Marcelle!" Gregor called. "If you want your timing to be right, we must not delay any longer."

She stepped away from the cell. "I will see what I can do, but I have to finish what I came here for."

Tibalt let his fingers slide down the bars. "Maybe you will, maybe you won't. When the chosen one comes, I will know it."

"The chosen one?"

"Marcelle!" Gregor called again.

"I have to go on a journey," Marcelle said to Tibalt, "but when I return, I will investigate your story."

Tibalt shrank back from the bars, disappearing in the shadows, and his voice faded with him. "If you say so, *friend*."

As Marcelle hurried toward the end of the corridor, Tibalt's emphasis on *friend* pecked at her mind. Would she really be able to investigate his story? Was he a madman as Gregor suggested, willing to say anything to escape from this hellhole, or did he really know something about the Gateway?

When she joined Gregor, he waved the torch at a downward-leading stairwell to the right. "You are to proceed alone from here." He reached under his vest and withdrew a thin glass tube and pushed it into her hand. "You will need this."

Marcelle held the finger-length tube in her palm, a glow stick. She gave it a hearty shake, mixing the elements within. Almost immediately it began to emanate a pale reddish light.

"When you get to the bottom of the stairs," Gregor continued, "turn right and go into the passageway. I know Prescott goes in that direction."

Trying her best to put on a reassuring expression, Marcelle reached up and gripped the big man's shoulder as tightly as she could. "Thank you, dear patriot. Wish me good fortune."

As she hustled down the stony steps, the torchlight from behind dimmed, enhancing the glow stick's blush. The stench decreased, giving way to stale air that coated her tongue with a bitter film. Extane gas. Although colorless and odorless, its telltale sign couldn't be missed, and its flammability was likely the reason for carrying glow sticks rather than torches. Of course, a visitor could carry a portable lamp, the kind without an exposed flame, but no one could hide a device that large under a tunic.

When Marcelle reached the landing, a ragged brick wall blocked her way. She turned right and shielded the stick with a hand before proceeding at a slower pace. The red light created a ghostly aura, just enough to reveal the down-sloping floor of uneven stone and a wall of rough plaster on each side. As in the corridor above, doors lined the walls, heavier doors with thick beams mounted in iron brackets, blocking escape. The barred windows were smaller, barely large enough for guard or prisoner to poke a nose through.

As she passed the cells, she longed to investigate each one. Who might be trapped within? What had they done to incur such wrath? Might some of them be innocent, merely imprisoned pawns in a political conflict?

She shook her head. No time to stop and ask questions. Prescott might even now be ready to give away his secret.

* THREE *

"IS that you, Knox?"

Marcelle stiffened. Prescott's voice, higher and squeakier than during his interminable speeches, seemed muffled in the thick air. She stuffed the glow stick into her trousers pocket and waited, holding her breath.

Footsteps approached. Another glow stick appeared, casting a dimmer red aura toward her. Apparently its energy was almost exhausted. "Why are you late?" The stout man walked toward her, his face not quite recognizable in the dimness.

Marcelle swallowed. It was too late to do anything now but go into her act. "Governor," she said as she withdrew her glow stick. "It is I, Marcelle."

He stopped at her side. Even in the dimness, the anger lines on his face were clear. "What are you doing here?"

She touched the hilt of her sword. "I heard that you requested me as your new bodyguard. As you know, I am not lax in any of my duties, so when I heard that you had entered the dungeon, I, of course, followed. His Excellency should not walk unguarded in the darkness among such vile criminals. One might reach between the bars and grab you, or perhaps pelt you with spittle."

Staring at her, Prescott let out a low "Hmmm" before continuing. "Who told you that I was here? Gregor?"

"No, Governor. As a matter of fact, he strongly challenged me, but I convinced him that the blame would all be mine should you protest."

"Very well, then who did tell you?"

"As you entered, one of the maids saw you from the window. She later heard me asking of your whereabouts and reported what she saw."

"I see." Prescott glanced around nervously. "I suppose you want to know why I am here."

She straightened her body to attention. "Not at all. Who am I to question the Governor's decisions?"

"It is clear that I made the correct choice. You will be an excellent bodyguard." He set a hand on her elbow. "But we must go now. It seems that your presence has dissuaded my contact from coming to meet me, and besides, if my wife learned that I was down here alone with you, she would have my head."

"Wait." Marcelle set her feet, not allowing him to push her along. "I beg for the opportunity to appeal."

"Appeal? What do you mean?"

"I …" She cleared her throat. She had to be direct without offending him. "I am appealing your decision to assign me as your bodyguard. I am not the best choice."

"Why not? Everyone knows you are the finest swordplayer in the land, so it seems fitting that you be assigned to attend me."

"Perhaps, but wouldn't some consider it odd that you are being guarded by a woman? Think of the whispers, the secret taunts by fools who don't know any better." She lowered her voice, hoping to sound humble. "Wouldn't Jason Masters be a good choice? He's strong and gifted."

"True, but I think I have had enough time with a peasant guarding me." He stepped closer and extended his hand. "I prefer a touch of class and a garland of beauty near my person."

She shifted to the side, avoiding his touch. "Please hear me out. Appoint Jason as your bodyguard and give me leave to find a traitor in your midst."

"A traitor?" He drew his head back. "What traitor?"

Marcelle bit her lip. Warning signs flashed in her mind. Prescott was obviously suspicious, but it was too late now to back out of her plan. "I have reason to believe that a member of the Underground Gateway is plotting to steal extane gas from the supply line."

"Oh, really? How did you come by this information?"

"I'm sure you know that the Gateway conspirators have long hoped to raise funds to conduct a real search for the portal to the dragon world. Selling extane would be quite lucrative for them. We need to expose the traitor, and I could be your investigator."

"No doubt you could." The glow stick coated his stare in crimson. "What evidence do you have that a Gateway member is behind the scheme?"

She averted her eyes and paused for a moment. Showing reluctance and hesitation would make her more believable. "I know someone in the group."

"And you haven't reported him to me?"

"It wouldn't be wise until I learn more. I assume you want to catch more than one bird in this trap."

"Indeed. I already have a bird walking into a trap. My spies tell me that one of the fools has been commissioned to search for the portal this very night. My people will follow him and, if he should pass beyond the boundary, remove his head." He slashed a hand across his throat. "One less fool means one less headache."

Marcelle steeled herself. Of course, that "fool" had to be Adrian. Her next words might mean the difference between life and death for him. "I have often wondered why you have such a vendetta against those lunatics. Did one of them harm someone close to you?"

"If you really want to know …" Prescott opened the top of his shirt, revealing a glowing patch of skin on his chest. It pulsed with yellow light as if mimicking the rhythm of the underlying heart. "Have you heard the myth of the litmus finger?"

As if drawn to its light, she edged closer. "No. Never."

"It is supposed to be a guide to the dragon portal. The person who wears it under his skin will feel a guiding force, but that never happened to me. It is as useful as a one-legged stool." He left his shirt open, scowling in its glow. "I, too, once believed in the dragon myth, and it consumed my thinking to the point that I allowed this wretched device to be implanted."

"Then why don't you have it removed?"

"The physicians believe that it has somehow attached itself to my heart, and removing it might jeopardize my life." He touched the glow with a finger. "So there it stays, a painful reminder of my idiotic obsession. It is my passion to rid this land of that foolish tale once and for all."

"Why are you revealing this to me?" She backed away a step. "Why now?"

"There are many secrets that beg to be revealed, and this one is the beginning of a puzzle that I will help you put together. Yet, I have already heard that there is a traitor in our midst, perhaps in my inner circle. Until I flush him out of hiding, I must keep the other puzzle pieces concealed."

"Then allow me to help you. Let me join your strike team. We will rout this portal chaser and find the thieves all in one evening. Perhaps they will lead us to the traitor." She drew her sword and set the edge near Prescott's cheek. "Who better than I to do battle on your front lines? The bodyguard position is window dressing, purely ceremonial. My sword would be of better use in the field."

He pushed the blade aside. "My spies tell me that there is also a conspiracy to take my life. Such is the desperation of the Gateway dogs. That is why I want you at my side."

"Why not take this opportunity to trap the assassins? Jason's youthfulness might embolden them to come out in the open, and you will learn their identities. My presence would keep them in hiding."

"True, but could Jason stop an attacker? Perhaps even two attackers?"

She lowered her voice, as if making a clandestine offer. "If I could prove his capabilities, would you grant my request?"

He matched her volume. "And how do you propose to do that?"

"First, assign Jason as your bodyguard for tonight's invocation. Then bring your son to the lobby just before the invocation. I will need him as a second attacker. We will plan our theatrics so that Jason can prove his mettle."

"I think I am beginning to understand," Prescott said, again stroking his chin. "If your test is successful, only then will I allow you to join the soldiers I am sending to capture the wayward bird."

Marcelle nodded. He had taken the bait. It was time to reel him in. "For my part, I will need a photo gun."

"A photo gun? Why?"

"For insurance. The Gateway's portal searcher might have weapons we don't expect." Cocking her head, she lifted her eyebrows. "Did you not consider that possibility?"

"Very well. I will supply the gun, but, again, only if Jason passes the test in a convincing manner. If he does not ..." He extended his hand and caressed her cheek. "You will be my bodyguard."

She firmed her jaw, refusing to cringe. Her arms begged to swing the sword and whack off his head, but she just strangled her hilt and forced her muscles to relax as she whispered, "I thought you were concerned about being alone here with me."

Prescott jerked his hand back. "Come, then. There is no need to stay in this dismal hole any longer." He held his shirt open and let the litmus finger's glow guide him toward the stairs. "At least I can use this evil device for one purpose."

"If it pleases you," Marcelle said, "I prefer to wait here until you are well away from the dungeon gate."

Prescott stopped and turned. "Whatever for?"

"To protect you, of course. If the two of us are seen leaving together, tongues will wag. It would not do for the governor to have such a cloud hanging over his head."

"I see your point. But perhaps you should leave first, as if you were unable to locate me."

Marcelle shook her head. "At this moment, I am still your bodyguard, and a good bodyguard never precedes the one being guarded."

"Very well. Just don't stay long. There is an extane pipeline nearby, and it leaks into the dungeon. With your smaller frame, even a brief stay here could raise your blood level above acceptable limits. If you feel your heart racing, chew manna tree shavings to detoxify."

She nodded. "Manna shavings. Got it."

"I will meet you in the lobby with Randall." With the glow from his skin patch painting a yellow aura around him, he hurried up the sloping floor and disappeared.

Marcelle leaned against the wall and let out a breathy whisper. "I hope I didn't get us all in trouble."

A woman's voice sounded from the cell at the opposite wall. "That was a fine acting job."

With her sword still drawn, Marcelle padded to the door and peered through the small window, but darkness shrouded the inside. She cleared her throat and called out, "Who's there?"

"Who's asking?"

Marcelle squinted. The woman sounded young, maybe her own age or younger, and her voice came from a far corner. "I am Marcelle, daughter of Issachar, the—"

"The Royal Banker. Yes, I know him."

"You know him? How?"

"You get to know people well when you do their laundry. Six pairs of purple stockings, one pair of pink for Cathedral, and his trousers have been taken in twice this year."

A sudden wave of sorrow shook Marcelle's voice. "He … he has been ill and has lost a lot of weight."

"Yes, I know. The stains on his tunic indicate severe nausea. Perhaps he should reside outside the palace. It seems the royal dining room has not served him well."

Marcelle grasped a window bar. What could she have meant? Had he been poisoned? If so, did this prisoner have something to do with it, or was it just a flippant remark? "So were you a scullery maid?"

"You are a sharp one, Marcelle. Most actresses I know are one step below a stump in intelligence."

"Actress? What do you mean?"

"You weren't concerned about Prescott's reputation. It's a good thing he isn't skilled in detecting deception."

"Well, I'm not an actress. I am a warrior and a trainer of warriors."

"Oh. I see. Most warriors I know are dumber than actresses."

Marcelle suppressed a laugh. This feisty girl had a lot of spunk. "Let me guess. Your sharp tongue pierced Governor Prescott a little too deeply, and now you're here until you learn your lesson."

"Hardly." Her voice took on a bitter tone. "I am not the one needing a lesson, and I expect that I will stay here until His Stubbornness learns humility and wisdom."

"Then you'll be here a very long time." Marcelle pushed her nose between the bars. The odor of human waste grew stronger. "What is your name? Your voice is familiar."

"My name is Elyssa. My voice is familiar because you have heard me ask about laundry instructions for your bloodstained shirts, but since I'm a peasant, I am invisible to uppity nobles like you."

Marcelle smirked. No doubt she and this girl would get along very well. Either that or they would try to kill each other. "Come closer, Elyssa. I want to see you. I'm sure your face will spark my memory."

Metal jingled at one corner. "I am chained to the floor. I cannot come."

Marcelle drew a picture in her mind of a half-starved teenager sitting in chains with her own refuse scattered about. "How long have you been here?"

"A couple months. Why?"

"Perhaps we can help each other. After I finish my task here, I will do what I can to get you released."

After a moment of silence, Elyssa's voice sounded again. "I'm listening."

"I'm looking for a gas line. Prescott said it was close, and my source tells me Prescott accesses it from this dungeon level."

"He does. I can hear him scratching the wall at the end of the corridor, so I think that wall is probably a façade. I know it's him, because he talks to himself, usually about the bitter film on his tongue. Fortunately, the gas doesn't seep into my cell, so it's not a death trap for me, at least not yet. In any case, he usually mumbles something about finding the right hole, so that must be the key to opening the wall."

Marcelle licked her lips, again tasting the bitterness. "Why all the secrecy?"

"My guess is that the line leads to the gas company's office. While Prescott makes pretense of visiting the poor wayward prisoners, he is actually committing a crime. He promotes policies that help the gas company, while he takes a share of the profits from invisible hands."

Marcelle nodded. "My father mentioned doing an audit of that company, but when he became ill, it was all he could do to keep up with his routine duties."

"As I said, the royal dining room has not served him well. It is safe only for friends of the regime."

Marcelle regripped the window bar. So that was it! Her father would have discovered the graft and exposed Prescott, so they made sure he was unable to do the digging. "For a scullery maid, you certainly know a great deal."

"I have my ways," Elyssa said. "I am here because of my snooping."

The girl in Marcelle's mind slumped her shoulders, and her head dipped toward her chest. How sad! No, it was tragic! This poor girl was just a nosy maid, and here she wasted away in chains and filth. Something more had to be going on. Even Prescott wasn't so cruel that he would cast a child into the lower level of the dungeon to rot.

Marcelle pushed as much confidence into her voice as she could. "Now it's my turn to snoop. When I'm finished, I will do everything in my power to get you released, even if I have to steal the keys and break you out myself."

A youthful laugh filtered out from the dark cell. "I believe you will try," Elyssa said. "Maybe good fortune will be our friend. Even if you fail, at least I might have a cell mate. I have enjoyed our conversation."

"As have I, Elyssa." Tears crept into Marcelle's eyes. "Until we meet again."

She brushed away the tears and marched into the darkness. This was no time for weakness. She had to think like a warrior and get to that gas line.

When she arrived at the end of the corridor, she passed the glow stick slowly from left to right. Several holes had been drilled into the wall in a random pattern. She pushed her finger into one of them, but nothing happened. She then did the same for one hole after another until finally something clicked. A brick at her waist level slowly pushed out a few inches before stopping. She grasped it and pulled. Acting as a doorknob, the brick swung out a section of the wall that began at her ankles and reached to about chest level.

Again extending the glow stick, she ducked down, stepped through the hole, and emerged into yet another corridor, this one with a ceiling so low, she had to stay bent at the waist. A metal pipeline, sitting on the floor and rising to thigh level, took up most of the space in the passage. The long tube ran parallel to the wall and extended into darkness.

After following the pipe for a dozen or so paces, a Y-junction appeared in the glow. She touched a vertical metal wheel attached to the side. This had to be the valve mentioned in Drexel's note, but the instructions didn't say which way to turn it. She sheathed her sword, gripped the wheel with both hands, and pushed the top side toward the right, grunting as she set her feet and drove her body into the effort. The wheel wouldn't budge.

"Okay," she whispered to herself. "We'll try the other way."

Again setting her feet, she placed both hands on the right side of the wheel and thrust herself forward. The wheel turned slowly, making a high-pitched squeal as it rotated. A few seconds later, she had shifted it three-quarters of the way around.

She released the wheel and brushed her hands together. Five hours to get to the collection tank and too much to do beforehand. Time to get going.

After exiting the pipeline corridor and sealing the wall, she gave Elyssa another encouraging word before hurrying to the dungeon exit, the glow stick again lighting her way. When Gregor opened the door embedded in the ground, she emerged into failing daylight and blinked at the brightness. He held out manna bark shavings in his meaty palm. She pinched some and pushed them between her cheek and gum, preferring to allow her saliva to leech out the healing chemicals. Years ago, Mother made her chew it whenever she got a rash, and the stuff always left splinters between her teeth.

About a stone's throw away, Drexel stood on the gallows platform, inspecting the dangling noose. "It is important," he called, "to make sure executions run smoothly, don't you think?"

Marcelle approached but stopped a few paces short of the steps leading up to the platform. "I assume that rope will carry traitors both large and small."

He pushed the noose, making it swing. "Which is precisely the reason I prefer to watch others carry out my plans."

As the noose passed back and forth, she eyed the cowardly conspirator. "I opened the valve, and I convinced Prescott to let me join some men he is sending out to kill an unnamed portal hunter. I'm pretty sure he doesn't know it's Adrian. I think the two of us will have no trouble defending ourselves."

"An interesting development." He glanced at the palace behind him. "Perhaps the good governor has not been as forthcoming as I would like him to be. I assume, however, that he will soon alert me to the hour this mission will begin. He always wants his head sentry to know about the comings and goings of the soldiers."

"I would tell you myself if I knew. I have other obligations to meet before Prescott will give me leave to go."

His brow lifted. "Oh, really? Other obligations?"

Her cheeks burning, she gripped her sword's hilt. "Need I remind you—"

"No. You need not. I merely want to ensure proper timing. You and your skeptical spirit must be in place before Adrian makes the delivery. You being in the company of soldiers who are not dedicated to our cause will result in an unfortunate delay, but it is unavoidable if we wish to help Adrian. You will either have to send them on a tangent away from your destination or else disable them. Either choice could delay you too much." Drexel wrinkled his nose. "Yet, I suggest that you take the time to change your clothes."

Marcelle looked down at her tunic, still bloodstained, marked with sweat rings, and emblazoned with a skewered dragon. "I will arrive before the five hours elapse and without Prescott's men. If the dragon doesn't keep to the bargain, Adrian and I will persuade him with the point of a sword."

Drexel grabbed the noose, stopping its swing. "You had better be off to your obligations. I will be at the front entry for the invocation, and I have to supervise some cleanup and polishing details well before it begins. Apparently, His Excellency wants to show off tonight, so I have been given the honor of standing at the door and ushering in the peacock parade."

"I know what you mean." Marcelle took in a deep breath. Should she tell Drexel about Elyssa? Maybe he could aid in her release. "There's something else. I met a girl in the dungeon. She seems to be innocent of any real wrongdoing, a political prisoner I suppose."

"Yes," Drexel said in a matter-of-fact tone. "Elyssa. I know about her. She is innocent of any evil. She just learned more about Prescott's schemes than he could tolerate."

"Can you use your influence to get her out?"

Still hanging on to the noose, he looked toward Gregor who stood like a brawny boulder at the dungeon entrance. "I already have. She is an integral part of my plan."

"Because she can expose Prescott's corruption?"

"The reason matters nothing to you. She will be released soon. If all goes well, this very night."

"And there's another prisoner," Marcelle said, raising a finger. "Tibalt, I think."

Drexel laughed. "That old geezer is so addled, even if he was released, he wouldn't know how to take care of himself. He would become a beggar, a wild man haunting the streets."

"I think it's an act. He seemed quite sharp to me."

"Are you asking me to empty Prescott's dungeon of every whining puppy you met? The price for your services is far too high."

"Okay." Marcelle breathed a sigh. At least Elyssa was taken care of, but there was something else. Oh, yes. The finger. She touched her shirt just below her clavicle. "Have you seen the glowing patch of skin on Prescott's chest? He called it a litmus finger."

Drexel's jaw tightened, and his voice rose. "A litmus finger? Are you sure?"

She nodded. "He said something about it being able to guide someone—"

"To the portal. Yes, I know what it is." His eyes rolled upward, and he loosened and tightened the noose several times before speaking again. "It seems that I can use this neck-stretcher in a productive way."

"How so?"

A crafty smile spread across his face. "Never you mind, my dear. I think I have devised a plan that will make all your wishes come true. I will persuade the governor to send the traitor-hunting party out under my command. When you are finished with your obligations, come to the front gate to join them."

Marcelle gave him a long, hard look. Could he be trusted? Probably only to do what was best for himself. Obviously planning the return of the Lost Ones would make him a hero, and he would use that for political gain. Rising to loftier seats was likely enough for him, but if not, who could tell what he might try to do?

She withdrew her sword. "When I return, if I find that you have deceived me, I will feed your body to the vultures."

He waved a hand of dismissal. "Your perception will change soon enough. When you and Adrian return with the Lost Ones in tow, the adulation we all receive will confirm everything I have done. I will let nothing stand in the way of this rescue attempt, neither dragons, nor Prescott, nor a suspicious warrior maiden."

Marcelle grumbled under her breath. "I have good reason to be suspicious." She stalked by him, purposely flashing her blade as she passed. Trusting this self-seeking backstabber seemed like a fool's gambit, but for anyone who wanted to make a real effort at rescuing the Lost Ones, Drexel stood as the gatekeeper. His status gave him access to resources no one else had.

After shoving her sword in place, she ran up the stairs toward the palace's back entry, nodding at the mustachioed guard as she neared the tall double door. Grasping a curved handle that resembled a thick fishhook, the guard opened the right half, his face stoic but not unfriendly.

Keeping her gaze low, she hurried to the spiral staircase on the left, relieved that no visitors roamed the rear foyer. Soon, with the invocation of the new counselor, the palace would likely be crawling with nosy nobles who loved wandering in the public-accessible rooms. Later they would gossip about cracked marble tiles, dust on the sills of the stained-glass windows, and the lack of shine on brass doorknobs and banisters.

As she scrambled up the stairs, the wagging tongues played their poorly hidden venom in her mind. *"The palace has seen better days, has it not? Try as he might, our good governor has not brought in sufficient revenue for upkeep. You would think with the new tax rates, fair as they are, he would be able to hire decent help."*

Then a counterpart would say something like, *"You have identified the real problem. Who can find good help these days? The peasants have become such an ungrateful lot. We graciously provide employment, and they work as if entitled to their pay. I had to release one woman who constantly wanted time off to care for her father. I told her she had to decide between being a dying old man's nursemaid or working a decent day for the generous wages I provide. Why should I pay for her personal choices?"*

And so the clucking biddies would continue, having nothing better to do than to complain about nothing—cutting down those higher than they and building themselves up, though they did so with bricks of manure. That was all their self-compliments were worth.

At the top of the stairs, she turned left and strode along a dim hallway, bordered on one side by a railing that provided a view of the foyer below, and on the other by a wall filled with framed art—portraits of past governors, smiling in the midst of powder and blush; murals of battle scenes with horses rearing and their riders raising swords while enemy combatants cowered beneath the hooves; and a few sketches depicting recent scientific discoveries.

Marcelle paused at one of the sketches. Prescott loved boasting of the advances in technology that had taken place in Mesolantrum during his rule, and this particular diagram always piqued her interest. It showed a summary of the human genome, a smaller and abbreviated version of the enormous chart hanging downstairs. Although kingdom scientists had long understood basic genetics, they had solved some of the deepest mysteries only recently and used their discoveries in many applications, so Prescott was only too glad to take credit.

She stared at the complex code. The seneschal had employed it many times to identify criminals during the past twenty years. If only the worst of scoundrels, the one who had ruined her family's life, had left behind a traceable genetic clue, maybe her obsessions would finally ease.

Shaking her head, she turned and hurried on, passing Drexel's quarters as well as those of the counselor, the seneschal, and the head chef. Prescott wanted his trusted officials indebted to him, so he purchased their favor by providing opulent housing, free food, and high status.

She stopped in front of the door to her family's rooms. How little Prescott knew. Drexel plotted against him constantly; the counselor announced his retirement, citing age, though everyone else knew he hated Prescott's prying into religious affairs; and the seneschal ignored any legal edicts that interfered with his personal vendettas. Such was the flavor of the hand that fed them.

She turned the brass knob and pushed the door slowly open. Father would be resting. With the counselor's invocation promising to keep him up late, he needed to sleep, but how could she depart on a dangerous mission without saying good-bye? And, of course, she had to warn him about the food. If he really was being poisoned, eating at the palace was out of the question, and until he could prove it one way or the other, he had to take precautions.

After tiptoeing into the room, she unbuckled her belt and laid the sword gently on the floor. Across the way, Father reclined on his bed, his back and head propped with pillows. His eyes were closed, and his hands rested on his wasted-away stomach, riding up and down with his uneven breaths.

She glided closer. Perhaps he was asleep, but he rarely slept soundly. Nightly eruptions of nausea saw to that. And now, as she replayed his symptoms in her mind, the evidence pointed again and again to poisoning, like slaps in the face accusing her of negligence. How could she have been so stupid? So naïve? Knowing what a scoundrel Drexel was, witnessing the counselor's hypocrisy, and hearing stories of the seneschal's corruption, how could she have overlooked the possibility that the chef might dirty his hands by polluting the soup?

Speaking of dirty ... Marcelle looked down at her tunic. Presenting herself before her father in such array would be less than respectful. She turned and stepped quietly into her own room, using a narrow door that opened to the quarters she had called home for the past nine years.

Ever since Prescott appointed Father to his role as banker and elevated him from peasant to noble because of his keen mind and unparalleled mathematics skills, they had shared this two-room domicile. Although it wasn't any larger than their previous space in the commune, Prescott allowed them free access to the library, ballroom, dining hall, and courtyards, making this home seem as spacious as outdoors.

She looked at her bed—four ornate posts of rich dark wood surrounding a feather mattress covered with freshly washed sheets and a velvety purple comforter. Luxurious. Rich by any standard. Still, it never replaced her old bed in their real home. When Mother died fifteen years ago, the place they called home died with her—the smiles, the songs, the smells—every detail that brought warmth and joy melted away. And, try as her father might, his own songs never carried the same joy, his smiles wilted on the vine, and, of course, he could never fill their two-room living space with Mother's gentle aromas—the perfume from flowers she often wore in her hair, and the scents embedded in her clothes when she had cooking duty. Ever since she passed away, the lilacs never seemed to bloom with the same glory, and every meal tasted like sand. Such was the curse when the heart of the home stopped beating.

Marcelle stripped the dirty shirt over her head and tossed it into a corner near her closet, a shallow cubbyhole across the room from her bed. No time for neatness. She would have to tidy up when she returned.

As her thoughts bounced around in her mind, the final three words echoed. *When she returned.* She looked at a mirror on the wall, an oval glass framed in mahogany, large enough to reflect her head and chest. Looking into her own eyes, now gleaming with tears, she breathed out a replacement. "*If* I return."

After changing into black trousers and a clean black tunic, perfect for the tasks ahead, she spat out the manna bark, washed her face in a basin, dragged a brush through her hair, and tiptoed back to her father's bed. She slid up onto the mattress and sat cross-legged at his side, angling her body to get a good look at his aging visage. With hair now gray from temple to temple and thinner than ever, and with deepening creases in his narrow face, he looked very little like the robust man who would dance with Mother on rainbow nights, those magical evenings when showers watered the garden, and the setting sun transformed the droplets into a magnificent spectrum in the sky.

The sages always said that rain in the midst of sunshine foretold of a double blessing, a promise of good tidings that would be delivered in short order. The peasants celebrated with song and dance that lasted well past the sun's disappearance below the horizon. At the age of nine, Marcelle had already become proficient with the pipes, so the adults always chose her to play for the dancers while Adrian pounded out a rhythm on a deerskin stretched over a barrel. With smiles, giggles, hugs, and kisses passing around the room like a fresh breeze, this celebration of peasants topped any party the nobles ever tried to manufacture.

Oh, yes, the *peasants*. Marcelle smiled at the term she had come to use herself, though never with the spitting punctuation most nobles added when speaking it. To her, the word would forever be a kiss, not a curse.

She grasped her father's hand and rubbed a finger over the wedding ring he had never removed. "Father?" she whispered.

His eyelids twitched.

As her nine-year-old self reentered her mind, she reverted to the name she preferred during those days of joy, a name she still spoke from time to time when the occasion seemed appropriate. "Daddy? Can you hear me?"

This time his eyelids fluttered rapidly. Soon, he gazed at her, a weak smile emerging. "Marcelle. Is it time for the invocation?"

She shook her head. "But it's time for me to tell you something. I have to go on a journey, perhaps a very long one."

"Is that so?" His voice was low but distinct. He looked at her expectantly, as if wanting an answer to an unasked question.

Marcelle chewed on her lip for a moment. Father wouldn't like the answer. "I ... I am joining a company of soldiers, perhaps three or four, who are being sent to track someone in the forest."

His brow lifted. "Soldiers? Palace guards, or rank and file?"

"The palace guards will be on duty for the invocation, so probably rank and file. Drexel will be arranging it. I don't have details."

"Drexel?" He shifted his body higher against the headboard. "Why would he send a woman into the forest with scoundrels? Is he out of his mind?"

"Daddy, they're not scoundrels, they're—"

"Soldiers, scoundrels," he said, very nearly spitting. "The words are different only in their spellings."

Marcelle averted her eyes from his reddening face. "I can take care of myself."

"Against one, yes, and perhaps against two, but if three men decide to give in to their bestial lusts ..." As his face flushed an even darker red, his voice trailed off.

"No one lusts after me. I have never given anyone reason to."

"Reason?" His voice spiked. "A scoundrel needs no reason. Just because you cover your cleavage and decline to wear dresses, don't think that stops a libertine from probing you with his mind. You are a desirable woman, and that's all he cares to know. Your fiery spirit might be an exciting challenge rather than a repellant, and in his eyes your trousers would merely accentuate your posterior. He will view your willingness to traipse out into the woods with him as a handwritten invitation, sealed by a sensuous swagger. No virtuous woman would dare do such a thing."

Marcelle looked down, unsure how to answer. Of course she had noticed how some of the trainees had looked at her, but a grasp of her sword instead of a batting of her eyelashes made their passions wilt in a hurry.

"So," her father continued, his voice calming, "you will decline this assignment. I will speak to Prescott myself and—"

"No, Father." As she looked at him, she clasped her hands together to keep them from shaking. "You cannot trust Prescott. There is something else I have to tell you, something you will not like."

"Not like? I have liked nothing you have said since you awakened me. Will this news be even more petulant?"

The word felt like a dagger reopening an old wound. "I am not petulant, Father. It is because of love and respect that I awakened you. I heard from an informant that someone might be poisoning your food."

His brow lowered. "Poisoning me? Why?"

"To make you too sick to audit Mikon Industries. Prescott is skimming profits."

"Nonsense. I have known their officers for years. They would never allow him to—"

"Daddy! Think about it. When did your sickness begin?"

"This is absurd. You know as well as I do when my sickness—"

"Almost six months ago. And when did you first schedule the audit?"

"A mere coincidence." A deepening scowl bent his features. "I take my food from the plates that are passed around, just as you, the governor, and everyone else does. It cannot be poisoned. And my drink is poured from a common pitcher."

Marcelle imagined a servant moving from place to place, pouring the wine into each vessel as he passed. Her mind's eye focused on her father's unique goblet, hand-carved with a rainbow on one side and the sun on the other. "Your cup is your own, Father."

"Ah!" he said, raising a finger. "So now the cupbearer is my assassin. My suspicious daughter leaves no servant without accusation."

"Better to be suspicious than dead."

"Better to be dead than to be friendless because of the never-ending conspiracies you conjure in your brain."

The two stared at each other. For a moment, his expression flashed with anger, but it soon settled into a wash of uncertainty and confusion.

She touched his knee tenderly. "Don't you see? Who told you that ulcers are causing your problem and that you shouldn't take on stressful projects? Prescott's own doctor, that's who."

"But the medicine he gave me helps. It—"

"It masks your symptoms. Nothing more."

Redness crept its way back into his cheeks. "So now you're a doctor? Wearing a man's sword and trousers wasn't enough? Now you're wielding a surgeon's scalpel?" Looking away, he shook his head. "Your mother must be weeping with the angels."

Marcelle winced. There was the dagger again, this time plunging directly into her heart. Years of experience had taught her that ignoring the stab was the only way to keep him from twisting the blade.

She let her tone rise to a desperate plea. "Daddy, just take your goblet with you after your meals and wash it yourself. Then watch for any attempts to give you food that isn't from a community plate." She enfolded his hand in both of hers. "Will you do that for me?"

Still looking away, he took in a deep breath and let it out slowly through his nose, raising a quiet whistle. A tear spilled from one eye, and his voice fell to a whisper. "You are surely your mother's daughter."

Marcelle caressed his knuckles with her thumb. "No, Daddy. Mother was everything that I'm not. I am far more stubborn and colder and aggressive and—"

"And irresistible." He turned toward her, both eyes now brimming with tears. "Your beautiful eyes and comely face make your entreaties impossible to refuse. I was never a match for her, either."

She compressed his hand. "Then you'll do it? You'll wash your goblet and watch out for poisoned food?"

"Of course, my dear." His expression hardened slightly. "If you will decline this absurd jaunt into the woods."

She released his hand and pulled back. "But ... but I cannot decline. It is my duty to—"

"Duty?" His voice grew to a shout. "Where is your duty to your father? Where is your respect for my experience? If I say that the scoundrels will rob you of your maidenhood, you pretend that you know better, that somehow these soldiers whom you have never met will be less vicious than the vile creature who pierced your mother with flesh and fangs."

As she stared at her father's enraged eyes, a sob tried to emerge from deep within her chest, forcing her to take a quick breath. "I ..."

She couldn't speak. Her throat had tightened far too much. She swallowed, but it didn't help. It would have to loosen on its own.

Her father turned away and looked at the wall, quiet, yet flushed redder than ever.

Marcelle sighed. At least he understood a woman's need to ruminate. He didn't mind gaps in conversation. In fact, he often caused them himself.

The comment about her mother's death brought a new stabbing pain, this one worse than the others. She imagined the terror once again.

Sleeping with Mother in her bed while Father was away one night, a stranger intruded and set a sword blade across both their throats. His growling voice scraped her senses to this day. "If you stay quiet, I will let you both live."

Little Marcelle stiffened. Even with a full moon casting a strong glow through an open window, the blade looked dark, and the intruder's face stayed in shadows.

"What do you want?" Mother whispered.

"I have been at the battlefield for months, and I must return by dawn. I care not who provides what I need." He said nothing more.

Marcelle swallowed, feeling the cold metal against her skin as it pressed closer. Mother glanced at her before answering. "Take me. But not here, I beg you."

"Very well." He lifted the sword and looked straight at Marcelle, his bright brown eyes clear in spite of the shadow over his face. "Stay quiet, or you will find your mother's heart lying next to her body." He clutched a handful of Mother's hair and shoved her toward the window.

The moment they disappeared outside, Marcelle ran from the bedroom and dashed into the commune's shared living area. Trying not to sob, she looked at the three corridors leading to the sleeping quarters of the other families. What could she do? All except the older men were off to war, and if she told anyone, that intruder might hurt Mother. But maybe he would hurt her anyway. She had to get help.

She ran into a room Adrian shared with his two brothers. Standing at his bedside, she whispered breathlessly. "A man ... took my mother ... and went out the window."

Adrian, also nine years old, leaped from his bed. "We have to tell Grandfather!"

The vision faded away. Only scant snippets remained. After searching for nearly an hour, Adrian's grandfather found Mother's body in the forest, but he refused to report any details. When Father returned the next day and heard the news, his frame seemed to wither, as if every drop of blood drained from his body. Surely every shred of joy had been ripped from his heart.

And all the while, a terrified nine-year-old sat in stunned silence, watching a parade of mourners weeping and rending their garments. Nothing like this had happened in the region in anyone's memory, and from that day for the next three years, the windows in the commune stayed closed and locked, no matter how hot the night. Although no similar attack had been reported since, the specter still lingered. The wars were over, so the killer had returned to his home, perhaps satisfying his violent urges with those who were too frightened to report his cruelty. Still, fear of the potential never eased. Whatever happened once could happen again. The village had lost its innocence forever.

No doubt life as she knew it had come to an end. Yet, a new purpose was born. That very day she swore that no one would ever take them by surprise again. No one would dare enter their abode with evil intent. When she became the greatest sword maiden in the land, even the male warriors would tremble when she drew her blade.

And she had marked that day in her mind. When she won the great tournament, she would be ready. She would begin hunting down that monster and have her revenge. Reliving that nightmare once again had left its mark. Now her mission would have a twofold purpose—rescue the Lost Ones and pry information from soldiers. Someone, somewhere, knew the truth. She just had to find its hiding place.

Finally, as tears flowed, she whispered, "You know what I have vowed, the words I cry out with every nightmare that throttles my breath."

He kept his eyes averted, saying nothing.

"Now I am able to seek Mother's killer," she continued, "and I cannot conduct that search while staying home, parading around the palace in silk dresses, exchanging pleasantries with tea sippers about how too cold or too rainy it is, about runs in their hosiery, or about how men have ruined their lives by not paying attention to their feminine pouts and puckers. And all the while I would not be listening to a word they say, nor they to my words, because our brains will have become numbed by superficial trivialities.

"If you want me to live a lie and be one of those pitiful caricatures of femininity, if you want me to continue waking up with a scream every night because the murderer's blade has again fallen cold upon my throat, then by all means forbid me from infiltrating the ranks where the true scoundrel might still be hiding. Prevent me from stripping him of the disguise that makes others think he is a protector of the innocent. Turn me back from keeping that monster away from other mothers who lie peacefully in bed with their daughters, not suspecting that an evil madman is creeping into their window ready to ravage them with brutality and never-ending torture.

"Perhaps even now he oppresses daughters of his own, satisfying himself while they suffer under the weight of his dominating presence, silenced by threats of a fate worse than ultimate betrayal and humiliation.

"Yes, that is likely why we have heard no new reports of such crimes. With the wars at an end, this ravisher feeds his lusts in the laps of those who should sit protected in his, while their muffled cries reach only his deaf ears rather than those who are willing and able to disembowel the villain and hang his carcass in the public square."

Shaking her head, Marcelle let out a loud sigh. "But I will not be able to rise up and protect these innocent ones. Why? Because of fear, fear of the dark woods, fear of a company of strangers, and fear that some foolish hens of nobility will cluck about a banker's daughter cavorting with soldiers when she should be scratching in the dirt with them in search of reputations to besmear with their sharp claws."

Father kept his stare on the wall, his chin shaking with his frail whisper. "Your speech is well practiced."

"Passion has honed my prose, Father, but every word is from my heart."

"I believe you." He looked at her, his entire face trembling. "What can I do to help?"

"I need every detail. You told me Mother was stabbed, but how wide were the puncture wounds? How deep? Were there any suspects? Was anyone questioned? And did the fiend …" Her throat tightened again. Could she even utter the next question? After taking a breath, she continued. "Did he leave any … any genetic evidence?"

A tear dripped down Father's cheek. "To answer your last question, yes, but not in the way you imagine. We believe your mother coerced him to go into the forest, hoping to ensure your safety, and then she fought the devil. Perhaps he was so badly hurt, he staggered away after killing her. We found a considerable amount of skin under her … well, under her nails. So we searched the soldiers for someone with a fresh wound."

"Deep scratches?"

He nodded. "We thought it might be easy, considering the amount of skin your mother gouged. We saved a large sample for genetic testing, including a few hairs on her body that were not her own."

He lowered his gaze to his lap, letting his tears fall into his open palms. Spasms interrupted his lament. "I still … see her face … her final expression … terrified, mortified. … She died in despair, perhaps knowing her murderer's identity but unable to warn her loved ones so that they could defend themselves upon his return from the battlefield."

Marcelle's stomach knotted. As a sob erupted in her own chest, she had to swallow it down to speak. "You think she knew him?"

His lips trembling, he just nodded.

She looked at his handful of tears. How many similar handfuls had he wept through the countless lonely nights? The days of rainbow dances had surely ended forever. "So ... so what did you do about the evidence?"

He took a cleansing breath before continuing. "When we searched the soldiers, we even stripped several down who could not prove their whereabouts during the night."

"And?"

"We found three men with recent scratches, and all explained their wounds with clarity and precision. The seneschal ordered genetic testing just to be sure, but none of them matched. Whoever the beast is, he wasn't among the soldiers we had access to."

"Access? Didn't you interview everyone?"

He shook his head sadly. "At the time, I had no influence with government officials, so getting a list of all the soldiers was impossible. The seneschal assured us that we had seen well over ninety percent of the men, so that should have been satisfactory. And since all were cleared, he refused to order any more genetic testing.

"I had no way of pursuing the matter any further except to look at every soldier who crossed my path. Did he have a scratch? Did he avert his gaze? Yet, I was unable to locate him. Even after becoming banker and having access to the list, many of the soldiers had died or were no longer in service, and his wounds would have become scars, and who could discern scars earned through courage on the battle-field from scars incurred while committing a crime? And who would take pity on me and order a genetic test on a war hero who had suffered a wound for the cause of keeping the peace for our good king?"

His voice pitched higher again and shook with emotion. "To this day I look for old scars on the faces of friends and foes alike, but it serves only to inflame my hatred and sink me deeper into despair."

"Oh, Daddy!" Marcelle rocked up to her knees and threw her arms around his neck. They swayed in place, now no longer weeping, though their trembling continued. She cast away all the horrible thoughts from the past and just focused on her daddy. This poor, grieving man had lost so much, and the stab wounds from that day still festered in his heart, an infection that never stopped leaking poison into his mind. Somehow she would find this foul beast who had plunged his sword into their family's bosom and excised their soul. Her father would never find peace until the day the murderer swung from Drexel's noose.

She pulled back, this time with her muscles flexing. "I will not rest until I find him, but I need those details."

"I have something that will help." He nodded toward his closet. "In the far corner, you will find a lockbox. The key is under the mattress. Once you open the box, you will understand."

She caressed his cheek for a moment before sliding off the bed. After finding a small silver key under the mattress, she walked toward the closet, glancing back at him with every step.

He nodded. "Go ahead. The time is right."

She found the box, a heavy, leaden container about the size of two bread loaves, and carried it to the bed. After unlocking it, she flipped the lid back. Inside lay a courier's tube.

As she lifted it out, her father spoke softly. "Fortunately, the undertaker at the time was my friend, and he had access to video. In addition to other disfigurements, you will see six stab wounds, each one close up and in detail, and you will hear his commentary as he measures and catalogues them."

The tube grew heavier. Her hands trembling, Marcelle set it on the mattress, imagining the horror that lay within. She had heard of this role the undertaker sometimes took for peasants, since the official coroner rarely cared to record such details except for those of nobility. Now she would have to witness it for herself.

"I ..." She swallowed through a painful lump. "I will have to do this later."

"It has waited fifteen years. It can wait a few more hours or days." He squinted at her. "How long will you be gone?"

"I'm not sure." The details of her mission roared back into her mind. If she managed to get to Dracon, who could tell how long it might take to bring the Lost Ones home? "I'll carry it with me, in case I'm delayed."

"But if you lose it—"

"I'll have a copy made," she said. "A courier will bring the original back to you."

"Very well." He rubbed his palm along his bed covering, taking several seconds to make it smooth. "So this is good-bye, I suppose."

She climbed back onto the bed and kissed his cheek. "I will return as soon as I can. I promise."

"It is foolhardy to promise what you cannot control." He dropped his gaze as if ashamed of his words. "But I understand."

She slid down and ran to her room, talking while she grabbed a pack and stuffed it with a change of clothes. "Remember, keep your goblet with you. And wipe your plate and utensils. Try to think of any way someone might be poisoning you."

His voice filtered in from the front room. "I am not a child, Marcelle. I know how to heed a warning."

When she returned to his bedroom, she picked up the tube and pushed it in with her clothes, making sure it had plenty of padding. She then straightened her shoulders and looked him in the eye. "And I will heed your warnings, as well, but finding Mother's killer is more important than my own safety."

He gazed at her lovingly. "Not to me, my dear. That's why I was being such a stubborn goat about your assignment."

"No need to apologize," she said. "I understand."

"I wasn't apologizing." He nodded toward the door. "Now go. Before I change my mind."

She took his hand into hers and kissed his knuckles. "I will hold your other hand when I return, while we watch the hanging of Mother's killer together."

✱ FOUR ✱

CARRYING a few essentials in his duffel bag, including the courier's message tube, Adrian marched from his home and toward the forest path with Jason following close behind. Earlier, they had talked about Jason's new bodyguard assignment, and Adrian had given *Spirit* to him with its scabbard and belt. For himself, he had chosen to strap on his old battle sword, a much better option for the task that lay ahead. It was time for them both to embark on exploratory journeys, Adrian to find the portal to the dragon world, and Jason to find the key and perhaps even Elyssa.

As they drew closer to the forest, a man cried out. "Adrian!"

Both brothers turned back. From the field near the woods behind their communal home, their father hurried toward them. Carrying a thick-handled axe against his shoulder and favoring a leg wounded in the great war, his face contorted, yet he continued a resolute march.

"Come," Adrian said, pulling Jason into a trot. After a few seconds, the trio met near a head-high woodshed, where the coming winter's store of firewood grew each day, mainly due to the muscular arms holding the axe.

Breathing heavily, Edison set a hand on Adrian's shoulder and leaned his stocky frame against him. A slight tremble passed from his roughened fingers into Adrian's body. Anxiety? Probably. How could a bereaved father ever shake the pain of a lost son?

"I wanted to tell you something." As Edison paused, his shadowed eyes grew wide and tear-filled. The trembling increased, as did the weight on Adrian's shoulder.

Adrian grasped his father's forearm, trying to push strength into the grieving warrior. But could he say the right words to provide inner strength as well? Father always loved oratory. Maybe a bit of eloquence would help now. "You have nothing to fear. I will honor you in all I do, your wisdom, your vision, and your legacy. We are not saying good-bye, for even more certainly than I carry a sword at my side, I am taking your heart and your passion with me. I will find the Lost Ones and restore them to our world."

For a moment, they stared at each other in silence. Adrian tried to read his father's eyes. Something changed. What was once a shadow of gloom transformed into a spark of confidence, as if the warrior within had awakened for a moment, ready to take up a sword and fight. The vision sent a ripple of strength through Adrian's muscles. What a joy it would be to march into Dracon with his father at his side! The Ram, his fellow soldiers had called him, was a warrior, indeed, a man who charged into battle with his head down and his sword swinging, not caring about the arrows that flew over his battering-ram body.

The flicker, however, quickly faded, and the tired old man returned. Adrian relaxed his arms. It was all for the best. Edison Masters had long ago sacrificed his body for the good of those less able to fight. He deserved to rest from the wars of yesteryear. Yet, he never seemed to rest, not with the shadow of doubt hanging over him. One of his fellow soldiers had accused him of treachery. Of course, the charges were never proven, but the cloud of guilt followed him ever since, even among his fellow peasants. Still, he never once mentioned the name of his accuser. He preferred that the story die and be forgotten.

But Edison Masters never forgot. Though his desires remained unspoken, all three sons knew that he longed to redeem himself in the eyes of his friends, a desire that could never come to pass. With its neighbors no longer rebelling against King Sasser, Mesolantrum lay at peace, and Edison's wound kept him bound to labors in which he could use his powerful arms. Without good legs, the old soldier would never rise again.

Edison laid down his axe and pulled both brothers into a tight embrace. Then, staying quiet, he marched alone back toward their home. Although his limp was less pronounced now, his head hung low, and his shoulders shifted in rhythmic heaves.

"Come," Adrian said, pulling Jason by the arm. "We must not watch his grief."

While they walked along the path through the forest, Adrian gave Jason the courier tube and explained his mission, to listen to Victor's message, solve the mystery about the key, and find any record of what really happened to Elyssa. The arching branches of the ever-present manna trees seemed to provide a veil of secrecy, as if laying a muffling hand over the sound of their voices.

When they reached a glade where the trees thinned to expose the late afternoon sky, Adrian set his feet in the soft loam that fed a carpet of lush grass. A mere three steps away, Miller's Spring bubbled up from the ground, providing cover for their conversation.

He laid a hand on Jason's shoulder. "My brother, I know you have doubted the stories Frederick and I have taught you all these years, and I have offered you no solid proof. But you have honored your family by working with us as if you were a true believer. Soon, however, you will reach a crossroads that will force you to decide to either believe in or betray our cause. You will find that you can no longer stand outside the tourney ring."

Jason averted his eyes for a moment. He seemed pensive, unsure. Did those words act as a stinging rebuke or rather as flint stones set against a well-oiled torch?

"You're right," Jason finally said as he grasped Adrian's wrist. "Even though the legends sound like storybook fables, I will keep my mind open. But as long as I live, I will never betray you or our family, no matter what happens."

Adrian gazed at his brother. Oh, yes, the torch was well oiled. Now the message would be easily received, and his fire would ignite with a passionate blaze. He pulled Jason close and kissed his forehead. "Good. Because if you betray us, I'll walk all the way back from Dracon and introduce you to a mama mountain bear who has lost her cubs."

Hiding a grin, he gave Jason a hearty pat on the back, then marched away, following the shallow stream into the woods. Again manna trees drew thick shadows on the soft carpet, and the grass thinned, making the newly forged path muddier. Yet, even more difficult paths lay ahead. The place where his compatriots had found Frederick's hat was dangerously near the boundary to the Forbidden Zone. Since the hat provided the first clue that helped Victor prove the existence of the dragon planet, and since the extane-seeking dragon had left more messages in the vicinity, Adrian had to explore the entire area once again.

After an hour of hacking through the underbrush with his sword, he broke into a clearing. He took one step into the open and sniffed the air—damp, slightly musty, and sprinkled with the scent of wildflowers. Although not as well-developed as his father's, his own sense of smell was acute.

Clouds flowed from the horizon to his left, darkening the sky further. Evening approached, and a storm brewed, a violent one if the sudden rise in humidity had anything to say about it.

His mind drifted to a communal house near his own and a cramped bedroom where the Underground Gateway's inner circle of five men stood around Victor as he lay on his deathbed. "Feel the air," Victor had said. "Take in deep draughts. You will find the dragon's meeting place through all your senses—tension at the tips of your fingers, sharpness in your nostrils, and a presence in your mind, a phantom that stalks but cannot be seen. When all these come together, know that you likely have already been discovered by the dragon, and he will summon you to his presence."

Adrian took in a deeper breath. Now that he had passed the boundary and entered the Forbidden Zone, new sensations filled the air. The odor was different, sharp in a way, but it also carried a hint of human perspiration, a dirty, oily sweat, obviously not his own. Someone lurked nearby, not real close but close enough for the hidden man to realize that he had to stay silent or be discovered. Adrian expected a pursuer, but hacking through the underbrush had likely masked any noise the man had made.

The approaching storm kicked up a breeze at his back, fanning the mixture of pines, beeches, and manna trees and stirring up a cacophony of noises. Would the commotion be enough to give the tracker courage to draw closer? Whoever it was likely had no idea that the breeze would reveal his presence. Being upwind, his odor would allow Adrian to sniff out his angle of approach and identify where his body created a slight buffer for the breeze. He would not be able to launch a surprise attack.

Adrian resisted the urge to turn and show his sword, choosing instead to hold it steady at his side. If his pursuer believed himself equal to the task of attacking the son of Edison Masters, then he likely would have made his move by now. Perhaps he was a scout who awaited his opportunity to flee and report his findings to others.

A crackling sound rose over the random bustle of wind and branches. About fifty paces into the woods, a man wearing a soldier's uniform leaped out and dashed away, charging back on the path Adrian had blazed.

Adrian stayed put. Short and lean, this scout scooted like a jackrabbit, obviously too fast to catch, and he carried no weapon to slow him down.

Sliding his sword away, Adrian strode to the other side of the glade and crouched in the shelter of two leafy bushes—ironwood bushes, the older folks called them. He searched the branches for any berries the birds had left behind. As expected, only a few remained, and the tender bark had turned orange and was flaking away, similar to rust on an iron bar. Once stripped for winter, the bush would lose every leaf but one, a leaf at the top of the focal shoot that would stay green until spring when it would finally wither and fall, signaling that new buds would appear the next day.

Since this bush grew wild in the forest, no one had picked it clean. He grabbed a berry and popped it into his mouth. The sweet juice carried a stinging bite, a reminder that eating too many would make his stomach bitter. The flavor also brought an aroma, another biting sensation as it flared his nostrils. Was this the sharp smell Victor had mentioned?

He peeled off a strip of the failing bark and rubbed it between his fingers. Its ridges dragged along his fingertips. Tension. Was this Victor's meaning? In his death throes had he fashioned a riddle, thinking that perhaps he would keep the secret safe from fools or infiltrators?

Still, no phantom stalked this glade. No sense of a looming presence entered his mind, and that scout was certainly neither phantom nor dragon. Maybe the dragon would show up later. It was a little early yet.

Now hidden for the moment, he settled down to think. When would the scout return with his company? How many would be with him? Adrian glanced at his sword. He might be able to take on two trained soldiers, but not three or more.

Could he risk leaving this spot? The dragon might show up at any minute, and if the beast seemed to be dealing with integrity, Adrian would have to go to the extane collection site and bring the tank here, along with the help of whomever Drexel had chosen for that task. Yet, this might not be the right place at all. Victor's riddle could have many meanings.

As the breeze again whipped through the forest, the damp air moistened Adrian's cheeks. Maybe the storm would come first.

Heavy rain and high winds would give a hidden warrior a supreme advantage over his pursuers. Besides, even if the storm passed him by, no company could sneak up without raising a lot of racket. Staying put had to be the best option.

After eating three more berries, Adrian kept his eyes trained on the clearing, a circle about ten paces across. Lightning flashed far away, brightening the dimming sky. It wouldn't be long before the storm arrived. This portal-finding mission would become a chilling nightmare with or without a dragon. These autumn storms sometimes carried quite a punch—cold wind, flooding rains, and even sleet.

Again the sky lit up, but this time the brightness lingered. An aura appeared in the center of the clearing, dazzling white and shimmering. Roughly the shape and size of an adolescent female, yet without details of face or form, the aura spun slowly.

Feeling a chill, Adrian rose to his feet and, drawing his sword, took three steps closer. Particles of even brighter light swirled in the midst of the feminine shape, like excited fireflies buzzing in a tornadic frenzy. Still, the form itself maintained a slow rotation, a graceful dancer spinning on her toes. She seemed to be wearing a skirt that fanned out with her motion.

He extended a hand, expecting to feel warmth from the glowing visage, but frigid air surrounded it, as if the ballerina had been sculpted from ice. Dirt swirled up into the vortex, thickening from bottom to top as it rose. Soon, the feet took on color, the flesh tones of a barefooted girl. The legs solidified. Two slender limbs protruded beneath the hem of a flowing dress that seemed to fabricate its own snowy white array from the upwelling soil—a calf-length skirt, silky sleeves that extended just past the elbows, and a high, lacy neckline. Then a cloak materialized, fanning out around her as she spun.

With every rotation, the remaining light took on substance, and details drew themselves in place—shining green eyes on a thin, alabaster face; streaming red hair that fell past her shoulders; and a scant frame that told of malnourishment or perhaps illness. In one hand, she carried a small leather bag, tied at the top with string, while the other hand clutched a parchment.

As the spinning form slowed and her cloak settled around her, Adrian cleared his throat and called out, "Hello? Can you hear me?"

After a final twirl, she stopped, and her aura began to dim. A girl no more than fifteen years old staggered at the center of the clearing, setting and resetting her feet to keep from toppling.

Adrian grabbed her forearm, steadying her. "Are you all right?"

Her soft voice broke through the gusting breeze, weak and fragile. "I am well."

Releasing her slowly to make sure she could stand, he looked at her wrist where his fingers had grasped. In the failing light, the imprints in her tender skin seemed blue. Adrian stared at his own fingers. Was she really as cold as she felt?

She gazed up at him, a smile on her lovely face. "Who are you?"

Adrian stepped back and bowed. "I am Adrian Masters."

"Pleased to meet you, sir," she said, offering a curtsy. "I am Cassabrie."

Adrian couldn't resist smiling with her. This girl had appeared out of nowhere from a spinning halo of light and now acted as if materializing in the middle of the forest was as natural as the wind and rain. Apparently a portal lay here in the center of this clearing, exactly what he had been searching for, but how could one pass through? Time would tell. "May I ask why you are here and where you came from?"

"You may ask," she said, her expression turning serious, "but I cannot tell you anything until I contact the people I have come to meet. My business is a matter of life and death."

She opened her bag and withdrew a white stone. "I have work to do, so if you'll excuse me, I must go, and I can't have you following me."

Now that the aura had faded, leaving the evening's storm-darkened sky as the only light, Adrian had to squint to examine the stone in her palm. Smooth and even, it looked like it had been polished by running water, perhaps a stream. He glanced at the parchment. Something had been scrawled on one side, but the light was now too dim to allow for reading. Could it be a note from the dragon?

"I think I understand now," he said. "You're the dragon's representative."

She sucked in a quick breath, her eyes wide as she pointed at him. "Are you the gas merchant?"

Adrian bowed again. "I am here to facilitate the transaction."

"But …" She turned her head from side to side. "But you're not supposed to be here yet."

"I'm not?"

She lifted her bag. "The plan was for me to lay down these stones in a line so you can follow them from the gas line to this place, and … and for me to leave a message explaining what you must do. Arxad didn't tell me you would already be here."

Adrian formed the strange name on his lips before repeating it out loud. "Arxad? Is that the dragon?"

Backing away a step, Cassabrie swallowed. "I … I'm not allowed to tell you. I shouldn't have said that name at all."

"No one will report your mistake to him." Adrian held out his hand and lowered his voice. "Come. We need to leave. Some people will be here soon who won't be friendly to our cause."

She stared at his hand, her own hands quivering. The gusting breeze tossed her hair, making it fly behind her, and she blinked at the droplets of rain spitting from the sky. Her eyes reflected fear, uncertainty, perhaps concern that her well-planned mission had been scuttled.

Finally, she reached out and slid her fingers over Adrian's palm. They felt cold, almost like icicles, and the ring finger was missing on each hand; not even a stub remained. "We have to come back here," she said. "The portal is my only way to get home."

"Don't worry. After we get the gas tank, we will bring it to this spot, as planned." He led her to the path he had cut through the woods. With the storm brewing, maybe his pursuers wouldn't be back soon, or at all. Still, if Prescott learned that his former bodyguard had stolen into the woods to carry out this treasonous mission, he would send two dozen spearmen to hunt him down, even in the midst of a rollicking tempest.

"There is a storage shed near the tank," he said as heavier rain began to fall from the dark sky. "When we get there, we can talk."

*　　　　*　　　　*　　　　*　　　　*　　　　*

Marcelle crouched between two stone columns that lined the interior wall, waiting for Prescott and Jason to enter the palace's vestibule. Shadows covered her body. With black stockings, black trousers and tunic, and a black hood over her head, she felt like a squatting strip of licorice. Although the failing light of evening filtered into the center of the room, the darkness in her hiding place was so complete, even the tiny pebble in her open palm was invisible. This pebble would come in handy later.

To her left, about three columns away, Randall stood, also veiled by darkness. Even from this distance, his breathing carried across the still air. Although certainly imperceptible to any casual passerby, Jason would hear Randall's rattling breaths and be alerted to an attack.

Marcelle nodded. All for the better. When Jason passed this test, he would be the new bodyguard, and she would be released to join the soldiers assigned to track Adrian. But she had to put on a good show. Randall, still stinging from his earlier defeat in the tournament, would likely try to hurt Jason if he had the chance, so his attack would require no acting skills. Yet, with Randall wearing protective armor, he would be too slow, too cumbersome to get past Jason's sword.

She, on the other hand, would have to fly at Jason like a rabid bat while making sure to do him no harm. That wouldn't be too hard, but keeping herself safe at the same time might pose a problem. Jason was good, very good.

A door at the rear of the vestibule creaked open. Footsteps clicked on the marble floor. Marcelle listened. Yes, two people approached, one closer than the other, likely Prescott leading Jason. Soon, they appeared in the dimness. Jason glanced all around, his hand on the hilt of his sword. Being the brother of Adrian Masters, his suspicions were already aroused. He knew the governor shouldn't enter a darkened room without a source of light.

Still, even with Jason's skills, it wouldn't hurt to give the boy fair warning. With a flick of her thumb, Marcelle flung the pebble toward Randall. It clicked once before settling to the floor.

Turning toward the sound, Jason slid out his sword. He then jumped ahead, grabbed Prescott's arm, and pulled him behind a statue at the far side of the vestibule. They whispered something between them, too far away to hear.

Walking on the balls of his feet, Jason returned to the middle of the dim chamber, his eyes wide, his knees bent, and his sword ready. After flashing a glance at Randall's position, he turned away, as if searching for an intruder at the adjacent wall.

In spite of her role as a slimy ne'er-do-well, Marcelle allowed herself a smile. This young man was as cool as a frosty morning. He had already identified Randall's position and now feigned ignorance while waiting for his attacker to show himself. Randall didn't stand a chance.

Like a cat, Randall leaped from between his columns, shrouded in black, swift and silent. Jason ducked underneath Randall's swinging sword and tripped him up as he passed by. Randall tumbled, heels over head, and the sword flew from his hand.

Jason hustled over and ripped the black hood off with the tip of his sword. "Randall?"

Gasping for breath, Randall stared at the blade. "Don't kill me. I was just—" He clamped his mouth shut and closed his eyes. "Just don't kill me!"

Marcelle rose and slinked from her hiding place, her sword out in front. It was time to put on a show.

As she drew closer, Jason stared at Randall, apparently deep in thought. Marcelle kept her gaze fixed on him. Yes, he would figure it out, but he had better hurry. If he didn't soon discern that the governor's son wouldn't hatch a plot against his own father, she would have to fake a miss in a convincing fashion.

Marcelle swung her sword. Like lightning, Jason spun and met her blade with his own. The two swords clanked. Using her legs, she pushed forward, bearing down on him with all her might, forcing him to crouch to compensate. Then, springing up, she vaulted over his head, flipped in the air, and landed on her feet. Glad to have her hood on to hide her smile, she charged again.

Jason lunged to the side. She swiped her blade close to his face, close enough to shave his beard if he had been of age to grow one. He thrust his own blade, low and hard. Just before the sharp edge cut into her calf, she leaped over it and hustled out of his reach.

As he straightened, she spun back and pointed her sword at him, trying to calm her breathing and her racing heart. That was too close. Another split second and her severed foot would have been kicking her in the backside. Justice, to be sure. Making this deal was stupid at best.

His fingers flexing around his sword's hilt, Jason stared at her, as if sizing her up. She stared back at him. By now, he realized how small and agile she was, a tough target. He would have to devise a strategy to combat her strengths. That was good. As soon as he executed his plan, she could counter it to a stalemate and retire with grace, the test complete.

Jason stepped to the right. Marcelle did the same. He stepped again. She matched his moves, step-by-step, and the two slowly orbited the center of their makeshift battle ring.

Eyeing him closely, Marcelle tried to calculate his next move. If he resorted to typical tourney maneuvers, it would be hard for her to fake a nontraditional counter. Prescott knew enough about one-on-one combat not to be fooled by anything phony.

After a few more steps, Jason backed away until he stood only inches from one of the walls. With his sword out in front, he seemed to be daring her to attack.

She stalked toward him. Maybe a bold approach would scare him from his defensive perch, but without a passing lane, a direct assault would be perilous. His blade was too fast, too precise. Looking up at her headless body from the cold marble floor wasn't the best way for her to prove his worthiness.

She halted, staying well out of his reach. Just a few more seconds of acting ought to do it. "Are you a coward?" she called. "Come out and face me in a fair, head-to-head battle."

"You talk about fair," Jason barked, jabbing the air with his sword. "You sent a scared puppy ahead of you and attacked me from behind. It seems that *you're* the coward."

"I see." Marcelle glanced Prescott's way. He peeked out from behind the statue and gave her a nod. She blew out a long breath. Good. The test was over. Reaching up with her free hand, she stripped off her hood, letting her hair fall to her shoulders.

Jason's mouth fell open. "Marcelle?"

She couldn't resist a smirk, but this young man had performed so admirably, she had to find some way to boost his spirit. "You should teach your brother some of that bravado." As soon as the words spilled out, a surge of warmth blistered her cheeks. *That was stupid. Why don't you cut off your own foot, Marcelle, and stick it in your mouth?*

Prescott emerged from his hiding place, clapping his hands. "All three of you performed with excellence!" he said. "And Marcelle, you were right, as usual."

As Randall rose to his feet, Prescott laid a hand on Jason's shoulder. "Merely a test, young man. Adrian recommended you, but, because you are so young and inexperienced, I wanted Marcelle to take his place at my side. Yet, Marcelle assured me that you would be a fine bodyguard."

Jason glanced at Marcelle. His eyes blazed. Avoiding a wince at his angry glare, she attempted a kind smile and a friendly nod. He certainly *would* make a superb bodyguard.

"I suggested a test," Prescott continued. "And you have passed brilliantly. Both Randall and Marcelle knew not to harm you, so there was no danger."

A growl spiced Jason's reply. "Not to question your idea, Governor, but I could have hurt your son."

Prescott pulled Randall's tunic back at the shoulder, revealing a sheet of metal. "He was well-protected, and the suit made him heavier, which explains your easy victory over him. Marcelle, of course, required no such protection.

"We needed Randall to distract you in order to test your warrior's sense and your reflexes. My son, of course, is just as qualified to be my bodyguard as you are, but since he is so dear to me, if he were captured by an enemy, he could be used to bend my will."

This time Marcelle had to wince. Prescott's arrogance wouldn't allow him to admit Jason's superiority, and a verbal stab at his new bodyguard proved his stupidity. It was time to step in and smooth things over.

She touched Jason's arm, trying for the sweetest tone possible. "Fret not. Your skills have been approved. You will make a fine bodyguard for His Lordship."

Jason gave her a friendly nod and whispered, "Thank you."

"Now …" Marcelle turned to Prescott, forcing a sharper edge to her smile and her voice. "You will adhere to your part of the bargain."

"Of course. Of course." Prescott reached into an inner pocket and withdrew a ring of keys. After pulling a long, brass key away, he handed it to her. "You will find what you are looking for in the weapons cache. After you secure it, you may keep the key. I have another." His eyebrows lifted. "Do you know where the cache is?"

"I do." Resisting the urge to snatch it, Marcelle grasped it daintily and turned toward Jason. Once again hoping to communicate kindness with her tone, she whispered, "I meant no insult to your brother. I made this bargain to save his life."

After giving Prescott a final glare, she thrust her sword back to its scabbard, picked up the pack she had left in the shadows, and ran toward the exit. Shoving with her free hand, she flung the door open and stalked down the stairs. The arrival of evening dimmed the area, and billowing dark clouds spreading toward the palace hastened the coming darkness.

When she reached the gate, wide open for invocation attendees, she slowed to a stop at Drexel's sentry station. He was talking to a tall, muscular man, perhaps forty years old. Dressed in loose dark green trousers and an equally dark waterproof jacket, he looked ready for a stealth search in the midst of the brewing storm, especially since a short close-combat sword hung from his hip and a crossbow sat cradled in his arm.

"Ah!" Drexel said, turning. "She's here."

Marcelle pushed her hair back and nodded at each man in turn. What would this stranger think of her, dressed all in black and carrying a sword? No other woman in the region would dare look like this.

Drexel extended a hand toward each of them. "Marcelle, this is Darien, the captain of the company charged with intercepting the conspirator who seeks the mythical portal. Darien, this is Marcelle, daughter of Issachar, the banker."

"And champion sword fighter of the realm," Darien said, bowing. "Your skills have been proven time and again; your presence will be a boon. Yet, having you on this detail will be like squashing a roach with a ten-ton hammer." He let out a snort. "Whoever this portal-seeker is, he's just a Gateway peasant."

Marcelle gave him a coy smile, searching his face for any sign of a scar. Nothing. But skin could be clawed loose from other parts of the body.

"Yes," she said. "I know."

His eyes moved up and down as if surveying her. A hint of a smile broke his stony face. "Perhaps watching you perform will be, shall we say, a pleasurable lesson in physical contact?"

Keeping her own smile intact, she slid her hand around the hilt of her sword. Darien, with his dark curly hair, strong chin, and charming smile, was as handsome as they came, especially for someone his age. His pretty head would look dashing impaled on a stake.

She pursed her lips into a comely pose. "I am looking forward to teaching you whatever lessons you require."

"Lessons?" Darien smirked. "Do not be surprised if the lessons you wish to teach are lessons you end up learning yourself. The point of the sword is a sharp tutor for any who fail to keep their guard up. I am well practiced at divining the secrets of the heart."

Marcelle eyed him. That little speech was practiced, a stealthy word of warning. Did he know more than he was letting on? Had his suspicions been aroused?

As she studied his face and eyes, a new realization dawned. Maybe he was even older than he appeared. Fifty? Sixty? His eyes said so, though his body cut the figure of a man in prime physical condition. In any case, considering his current rank, he was likely a battlefield soldier that fateful day fifteen years ago. And what was he now? Since she hadn't seen him around the palace, he was probably the lead officer at a field outpost.

Drexel nodded toward the darkening sky. "You should leave immediately. A vicious storm is brewing. From the looks of the clouds, it might be raining within minutes. Darien has sent scouts to follow three men who have ventured toward the Forbidden

Zone. Two are likely decoys and will veer away before they reach the boundary. When one returns with news of a violator, you will begin pursuit."

Marcelle lifted the key Prescott had given her. "First, I need to get a photo gun from the cache."

"A photo gun!" Darien said. "Now you want to burn the cockroach after you squish it?" He drew out his sword, a wide-bladed black viper. "This will be all I need."

Marcelle stared at the blade. Wasn't it a dark blade that lay across her throat that night? She folded her arms over her chest and took on a skeptical pose. Maybe she could learn more. "I haven't seen a viper since ... well, since I was a little girl. An archaic weapon, is it not?"

"It is old, to be sure, and it is too heavy for a weakling, but in the proper hands, it is an excellent sword for night battles." He waved it from side to side. "Opponents are unable to see the blade until it's too late."

"Good," Marcelle said. "Carry it well. But I will get the photo gun. You never know what weapons the Gateway thugs might have stolen."

He bowed again, this time with a condescending smile. "Whatever pleases the lady."

Tossing her pack over her shoulder and hanging on to its strap, Marcelle strode through the gateway, but Drexel grasped her arm and pulled her close. With a sharp tone, he whispered, "Do what you must to him, but leave no evidence."

She looked down at his grip, tightening with every second. "If you don't let go of me ..." Shifting her gaze to his face, she drilled a stare into his eyes. She didn't have to finish her threat. Drexel was a coward among cowards.

He jerked his hand down and glanced at Darien. "Just be wary," he said, lowering his whisper further. "He has never entered the tournament. He says such juvenile showmanship is beneath the dignity of a true swordsman. He has been in many battles. Perhaps his boasting is more than hot air."

Marcelle backed away and replied with a loud voice, laughing. "Oh, Drexel, I fear no snakes. Just because my dear mother is dead, you need not take her place on the worry seat." She hooked her arm around Darien's. "Come, soldier. Let's visit the cache, and we will get what we need to make war with the cockroaches."

✳ FIVE ✳

HEAVY rain poured from the thundering sky. Although Adrian now walked far from Miller's Spring, its swelling flow had spread throughout this low-lying area, forcing him and Cassabrie to splash through ankle-deep water.

Soon the current grew swifter. Adrian scooped Cassabrie into his arms. Still frigid to the touch, she shivered. Was she frightened? Worried? Somehow he had to transmit confidence and warmth into this slave of dragons.

"Do you get much rain on your world?" he asked as he pulled her closer to his chest.

Cassabrie shook her head. "Only light sprinkles. I have never been in heavy rain. We see it falling in the mountains, and the water flows to us in shallow rivers, but only the woodcutters who travel into the higher lands have actually stood under its blue curtain, and they tell us stories about it." She covered her mouth and giggled. "One of them said it felt like the Creator was sprinkling the hills with a watering can!"

Adrian tried to smile, but the laborious trudging kept his face taut. "The Creator? I see that you slaves never lost your faith, even after all these years."

"Some have, and I am thankful that I am not a slave."

Adrian glanced at her earnest face, brow arching up and eyes wide. He would ask more soon, but with the gas tank in sight and shelter only seconds away, his questions could wait.

He stopped in front of an old tool shed, head high and deep enough for only a modest collection of digging tools. He set Cassabrie down and pulled the door handle. The door swung open and fell off its rusted hinges, splashing into the muddy wash. Inside, the shed appeared to be empty. With the pipeline construction at a halt, maybe the workers had taken all the picks and shovels with them.

With a nod, he guided her inside, and the two sat on the dirty wood floor. They had just enough room to lean their backs against the rear wall and cross their legs to keep their feet out of the storm. Adrian unbuckled his belt and leaned the scabbard against the side wall.

The wind blew over the roof and cast an arching drip line in front, keeping the water out of the shed. About thirty paces away, a metal tank sat at the end of the pipeline collecting gas. At least it should be collecting gas if someone had managed to turn the valve at the source line. If not, this mission would be a dangerous waste of time.

Shaped like a barrel, the tank stood as high as the tallest of men and at least as big around as Jesse the butcher, all five hundred pounds of him. Obviously they would have to roll it to the portal site.

"Is that my gas tank?" Cassabrie asked, pointing. "The dragon described something like that."

Adrian nodded. "It will be yours if all goes as planned. So far, every step has been a misstep. I was supposed to talk to the dragon at the portal, but you showed up instead. And it's too dangerous to be there now, especially for you. It's better to wait here for one of my people to arrive. It shouldn't be long."

Cassabrie hugged herself and shivered again. "It is certainly cold in your world."

"We're in our autumn season. It will get even colder." Adrian looked at her trembling body and the droplets falling from her hair. The poor girl needed some warmth.

He slid his arm around her and pulled her close to his side. Leaning her head against him, she sighed through her words. "You remind me of my brother."

"Your brother? How old is he?"

"Oh, he is dead. He died of old age a few years ago."

"Old age? How could you have a brother that old? What are you? Fifteen? Sixteen?"

She snuggled closer. "Let us talk of other things."

"Okay," Adrian said, stretching out his reply. "How about the slave issue? You said you aren't a slave."

"I *was* a slave, but not now. I was promoted, at least in a sense, not like how other slaves are promoted. I went to the Northlands to be with the great dragon king. We are not slaves there, not really. We are the dragon's servants, to be sure, but we serve him gladly. Even Arxad serves him, one dragon bowing to a greater one."

Adrian looked down at the young teen nestling in the crook of his arm, barely visible as lightning flashed split-second portraits of her wide-eyed face. She had just rattled off an explanation that raised a handful of new questions. Promoted? Northlands? A dragon king? Slavery versus servitude? Obviously it all seemed so natural to her, yet it sounded like a foreign language.

Thunder rumbled, shaking the ground. Another peal joined it from the opposite side of the sky, sounding like an echo of the first angry call. With new flashes illuminating her face, Cassabrie's eyes darted from one boom to the other, her smile expressing pure delight. This visitor from another world feasted on discovery.

"Why does Arxad send you to leave messages?" Adrian asked. "Wouldn't it be safer for him to make this transaction? After all, a dragon can certainly protect himself better—"

"He cannot come."

Cassabrie's reply was terse, sharp. A new flash revealed a knitted brow and a slight frown.

Adrian blew out a long breath. That question had pierced a soft spot. Was the dragon so callous and cowardly that he would force a defenseless girl to venture into an unknown land? He couldn't know what perils lurked. Maybe the dragons looked upon their slaves as dogs, useful for dangerous tasks, yet expendable if the worst happened.

"Since Arxad didn't come, that means you must have delivered the hat to this world."

"I did." Her tone still carried a hint of irritation, but not as much as before.

"Did you meet its owner?"

She shook her head. "Arxad brought the hat to me from the southern regions. He didn't tell me anything about whose it was."

"Hmmm." Adrian stayed silent for a moment, watching the driving rain in the light of staccato lightning flashes. While waiting for either the gas tank assistant or an attack from Prescott's goons, he could ask a hundred more questions, but Cassabrie seemed reticent now, as if annoyed by her own presence here. This cold, blue-skinned girl remained a mystery beyond words.

For now, patience seemed to be in order. Soon he hoped to step into her world and learn the answers to all the questions that ached to be asked. But would he have to pass into that realm with his sword swinging? Since Arxad had guaranteed only entry into his world and not freedom for the slaves, it seemed that this dragon lacked both the authority to unchain the captives and the power to protect his human guests. And perhaps he was also a coward.

As another lightning bolt lit up the shed, Adrian caught a glimpse of his sword, still leaning against the wall, and a hatchet in a belt holster in one corner, apparently left behind by a worker. Soon he would be able to use his training for something other than guarding the rear quarters of a pompous governor. Being the tail feathers of that prideful peacock had provided a lot of opportunities, and now the step for which he had prepared for years lay only moments away.

Cassabrie let out a quiet sigh and nuzzled close. Adrian slid his hand into hers, again feeling her unnaturally cold fingers and her increasing tremors. Her unusual trust, unguarded affection, and trembling frail body blended into an arrow that plunged through his heart.

Sympathy flowed and with it a flood of words, giving substance to his passion, as if his own inner voice echoed what his father had taught so many times. *You draw your sword for one purpose, to defend those who trust in your strength. And let your arms provide more than the swing of a blade. Give love to the weak. Give them warmth. Whisper words of comfort to those who keep your heart strong.*

As cold rain continued to whip around in the stormy wind, Adrian embraced Cassabrie with both arms and kissed her on the head. "Fear not," he whispered. "You're safe with me. No matter what happens, I will never forsake you. I will do whatever it takes to set every captive free."

*　　　*　　　*　　　*　　　*　　　*

Marcelle followed Darien as he marched near the edge of Miller's Creek. While windblown rain pelted their bodies from the left, they trudged along the right side of the flooded bank. With the sky growing darker as evening progressed, she stayed within three steps of the splashing boots in front of her. Of course she could keep this up for hours; her training had seen to that. But Darien wouldn't recognize her abilities. In fact, he had already made a stabbing comment.

"Let's step lively, men," he had said only moments ago. "With her short legs, Marcelle will have to jog to keep up, but such is the liability of traveling with a woman."

As she forced herself to keep pace without accelerating into a running gait, she tightened the strap that held her bag in place on her back. Darien would find out soon enough what his liabilities really were, *soon* being the operative word. By her reckoning, they had less than half an hour before the gas-collection tank would fill up and begin making noise. The bad weather had slowed their progress so much, she had thrown her planned timetable into the scrap heap long ago.

Barely visible another ten paces ahead, a short, thin scout led the way, carrying a coil of rope over his shoulder and retracing the route he had taken when trailing the Gateway rebel past the boundary. To her rear, four other soldiers kept pace, each one almost as tall and muscular as Darien. The number in the planned company had started at three and had swollen to seven, but Darien, in spite of Marcelle's chiding about squishing a cockroach, refused to explain the reason, citing "customary practice in stormy weather."

As they marched in verbal silence, ways to subdue all six floated around in her mind. The scout wouldn't be a problem. He would likely flee at the first sign of violence. Darien was the obvious first target. A blast from the photo gun—accidental, of course—would fuse his feet together, and when the others bent over to give him aid, a few quick slices across their legs would render them immobile. Since Darien's crossbow hung in a harness at his side, he wouldn't be able to load and aim before she disarmed him. Still, even in her imagination, the task seemed impossible. They would have to be total buffoons to allow themselves to be fooled like that. But what else could she do?

She patted the photo gun, tucked away in her waistband and under her tunic to keep it out of the rain. Would it stay dry enough? Should she time her mutiny to coincide with their approach to Adrian's location? With his help, subduing all six might be possible, but it would be better if the soldiers didn't know the whereabouts of the portal or the plan to deliver extane. If they learned the truth, merely immobilizing them wouldn't be enough. They would have to die.

Marcelle gripped the hilt of her sword. Waiting until they found Adrian seemed to be the only option. If she killed the scout too early, she could never pick up Adrian's trail in this running wash. In that case, she would have to go straight to the gas line and hope to arrive in time to complete the deal with the dragon, but darkness and floodwaters had erased her mental map. Could she find the tank now? Probably not in this storm.

As her previous plan reentered her mind, she shivered. Could she really kill the soldiers? What had they done but obey orders? They were fools to march under Prescott's banner, to be sure, but should death be the penalty for lack of wisdom? Would the grieving widows and fatherless children lament any less if told that the man they wept for shouldn't have put on his uniform? Of course, if evidence came to light that revealed Darien as her mother's murderer, she could kill him with pleasure, but that would be little solace if the others had to die with him.

Shaking her head, she trudged on. Maybe the solution would become clear soon, but, to this point, it seemed that the rain symbolized bad luck, and all her plans were washing away.

Soon, the scout slowed. He pushed aside a branch, exposing a clearing. As rain continued to pour, Darien signaled for her and the trailing soldiers to come closer. Drawing his black sword, he peered into the opening, waiting, listening. With the wind rustling the trees and a cascade of droplets pattering the swollen creek behind them, any sound Adrian might make would surely be drowned out.

After nearly a minute, Darien turned and slid his sword away. "He is not here, nor anywhere within range of our voices, so we may converse freely."

"How do you know?" Marcelle asked.

"If I am allowed to stand still, I can detect the presence of a man from a hundred paces away."

"Even if he is downwind?"

"It is not his odor that gives away a man's location; it is his thoughts, his attitude, his fear. I assume he left this place in search of shelter."

Marcelle laughed. "So now you're a mind reader as well as a soldier. Were you raised by gypsies, or did you run off with the circus when you were a boy?"

He nodded at the soldiers. "Take her."

A soldier grabbed her elbow and held her arm in place, and a second did the same while the other two drew swords and stood at her back. Marcelle tried to jerk free, but her captors held her fast. Glaring at Darien, she kept her voice in check. "What are you doing?"

"Ensuring the success of our mission." Darien lifted her tunic, pulled the photo gun from her waistband, and slid it inside his own clothes. "I told you that I am well practiced at divining the secrets of the heart. Your loyalties are not with the governor."

Marcelle jerked again, but the soldiers pinned her arms to her sides. "What are you talking about? I am a noble, the daughter of a noble. My father is Prescott's personal accountant. We eat at the head table every evening. I am not one to bite the hand that feeds me."

"Perhaps. Perhaps not." Darien slid her sword from its scabbard and set the point against her throat. "I must, however, trust my instincts, and disarming you for the remainder of this quest will allow me to keep my head from being impaled."

Rain pelted the blade, sending a rivulet against her throat and down her chest. As the point pricked her skin, she resisted the urge to swallow. How could he have known her thoughts? Was he truly a mind reader? Rumors had long swirled about Diviners, people who could feel trouble riding on the wind, but weren't they always female, the witches Orion had burned at the stake?

Again forcing her voice to stay calm, she looked him in the eye. "I was never a threat to you, and now that I am disarmed, your gorillas can let me go."

Darien pulled back the sword and nodded at the soldiers. When they released her, she rubbed her wet sleeves, trying to restore circulation to her stinging arms. She ached to give him a tongue-lashing, warning him of certain demotion once Drexel learned of his insult, but without blade or gun, giving him another reason to kill her would add to her growing pile of stupid moves. "So," she said, her tone quiet and submissive, "what are you going to do now?"

"There is a shelter not far from here, a shed, really, but enough to keep out the storm. If our prey knows about it, we might find him inside, already trapped in a snare." He slowly rotated, searching through the angled curtain of rain. "It's at the end of the gas line, but finding it in these conditions will be difficult. The rain probably washed away his tracks, and I'm not sure of the pipeline's exact direction."

"And complete darkness will be upon us in mere moments," the scout said. "We could use our lamp, of course."

"Not yet. Being seen by our prey before we see him is not a good hunting maneuver." He looked at the scout. "Do you know the way to the gas line?"

The scout pointed back the way they had come. "I know where it emerges from the ground. We could follow it, even in the dead of night."

Darien shook his head. "It branches from that point. Even if we chose the right path, it would take too much time."

A high-pitched whistle penetrated the storm's din. Marcelle cringed. It was the collection tank. The stupid thing picked the worst possible time to sound its alarm. It might as well have shouted, "I'm over here! Come and ruin the freedom fighters' plans!"

"What's that noise?" Darien asked Marcelle.

She shrugged. "How should I know? A bird, maybe?"

He stared at her, his eyes probing. "You know better, don't you?"

She scowled. Maybe a dose of anger would shield her thoughts. "If I know better, then read my mind. Maybe you'll learn more than you want to know."

"Impudent wench!" He slapped her savagely across the cheek. "If your father was half a man, he wouldn't allow you to play with swords."

The slap stung, but Marcelle refused to grimace. With her mind unguarded, she hurled a string of vile insults his way, each thought punctuated with a silent snarl.

Darien laughed. "I cannot read your thoughts, my dear, but I can read your malice. You have stripped your façade and stand naked, so you can lay your pretense aside."

Marcelle wrapped her arms around herself, covering her cold, wet chest. This monster's gaze seemed to pierce through anything. "The storm is getting worse," she said, forcing a hard shiver. "We should return to Drexel and allow him to judge who is and who is not loyal to our land."

"I will not return without completing my mission," Darien said. "Putting an end to this idiotic conspiracy will be a feather in my cap."

"No cap will ever fit that swollen head of yours, but a feather is appropriate for your plumage."

He used Marcelle's sword to cut a strip of cloth from the hem of her tunic, exposing her side to the cold wind. "Your tongue is sharper than your blade." He wrapped the strip around her jaws, gagging her, and tied it in the back. "And I prefer to avoid its fury." He then took the rope from the scout and tied her wrists together behind her.

She grunted through the gag. If only she could say what this self-worshiping dung beetle deserved.

Darien handed the sword to the scout. "Use this to cut through the underbrush. We will head straight for the whistling sound and learn what bird calls us to its nest."

✳ SIX ✳

ADRIAN peered through the veil of rain, but darkness allowed only a blurry view, nothing visible beyond three feet in front of the shed. Water seeped from the cobbled floor, soaking his trousers and Cassabrie's dress and cloak. No matter. They had dried very little anyway, and she didn't seem to mind. At least her chilled body wasn't getting any colder.

As he listened to the competing noises—peals of thunder in the distance, rain splashing in deepening pools, and whistling wind tossing the trees into a rustling fury—another sound drifted in, a constant whistle that pierced the chaos, like a flute playing its highest note while the rest of the orchestra tuned their instruments.

Adrian gave his head a mind-clearing shake. How odd that he would construct such a comparison. Music had never been his forte. Rhythm, yes, but sweet melodies and harmonies had always been someone else's role.

"What is that noise?" Cassabrie asked.

The shrill note grew louder, giving away its direction. Adrian pointed into the darkness. "It's coming from the collection tank."

"What does it mean?"

"It's probably a warning mechanism telling us it's full of extane. Whoever was supposed to help me deliver the tank should have arrived by now. The storm must have delayed him."

"Him?" Cassabrie repeated. "Do you know the person's identity?"

"No. My group didn't tell me who it would be."

"Then how do you know your helper is a man?"

Adrian shrugged. "It's a man's job. Since we have powerful opponents, the journey is dangerous. And the tank is heavy. I assume it will take two strong men to roll it into place."

"Assumptions are often wrong." Shivering once again, Cassabrie smiled. "Remember, you thought I would be a dragon."

"Your point is as sharp as any sword, but why would you think my helper might not be a man?"

"I have a gift." Cassabrie gazed upward and spoke in a slow, mysterious cadence. "A woman is out there, suffering in this storm, oppressed, troubled, perhaps in danger."

Adrian stared into the rain again but to no avail. "How far away is she?"

"Not close enough for me to tell." She looked up at him, gesturing with her hands as she shifted back to her normal tone. "You see, I am able to tell stories that recount events, some of which I have never seen. I reveal secrets whispered in dark places. I shout hidden thoughts. I resurrect history that myths and legends have corrupted by their skewed retellings." She laid a hand on her chest. "I am a Starlighter."

"A Starlighter?" Adrian glanced in the direction of the whistling tank. It likely posed no danger, at least not yet. Who would hear its alarm in this storm? He could risk probing for more information. "Can you show me what you mean?"

"Here?" she asked, touching the floor of the shed. "Now?"

"Why not?"

"I have not tested the full extent of my gifts here, but I can try." She rose to her feet and extended her hand into the rain. Water quickly filled her palm and spilled over the sides. "I need more room, so I will have to stand out in the storm."

Adrian rose and gently grasped her arm. "Never mind, then. You shouldn't—"

"I don't mind getting wet." She pulled free and walked into the ankle-deep water. "I want to enjoy this new experience."

Adrian stepped out and joined her. The lightning had eased, now flashing intermittently far away. It seemed safe enough.

"What story would you like to hear?" she asked as she turned her hips, twirling her water-laden cloak around her legs.

Adrian's heart raced. For some reason, this girl's claim seemed truer than the wetness of the rain. "Can you tell me about my brother Frederick? Is he alive? If so, where is he?"

She set a finger against her chin. "I have never met him, so that will be very difficult, especially since I feel weaker here. But I will see what happens as I begin the part of the story I know."

As lightning provided split-second glimpses of Cassabrie's slight body, she lifted her hands and spoke with a haunting cadence. "Frederick, beloved brother of Adrian, ventured into another world in search of lost souls. These souls, captured in the prime of life by a sinister dragon, have been enslaved for a hundred years, and good Frederick sacrificed his own comfort and safety in an attempt to bring them home to this land of freedom."

Her eyes grew wide, unblinking in spite of the wind and rain. An aura took shape around her body, not as expansive as the one that ushered her into this world. It was more like a soft glow covering her hair, skin, and clothing, as if an artist had painted her in muted starlight. Her tone shifted, taking on a resonant, almost echoing nature, though her voice stayed sweet, feminine, and melodic.

"Frederick," she called into the wind. "I need your help. The dragons have doubled my quota, and I am too ill to carry so many stones."

A bucket appeared at Cassabrie's feet, semitransparent in her ghostly glow. As she picked it up, its weight tilted her body to one side. "Will you help me, Frederick?"

A phantomlike man materialized, though not completely. As he knelt in front of her, the glow shone through his body. When his lips moved, Cassabrie gave him voice, changing her tone to a deeper register. "I will help you, little girl, but not to collect stones." He took her hand in his. "Come, and we will escape this place."

Cassabrie dropped the bucket, and it crumbled to dust. She trotted in a tight circle, following Frederick. Although every fall of her bare feet raised a splash, her ghostly leader hurried on in silence. When she finally stopped, a stone wall covered with thorny vines appeared next to her, double the height of a grown man, though it, too, allowed Cassabrie's glow to pass through.

She panted, holding a hand against her chest and staring at Frederick as he knelt again in front of her. "We will scale this wall together," he said through Cassabrie's altered voice. "And I will take you to the enclave in the wilderness. Do you understand?"

As she nodded, her eyes shot wide open. A shadow penetrated her glow, a black form with sharp claws. Frederick leaped up and drew his sword in one motion. "Back!" he shouted. "Or you will feel my blade in your gullet!"

A roar erupted from Cassabrie's throat, so deep and rough, it seemed impossible that such a sound could come from her frame. "Foolish human! Your pitiful weapon is no match for me. Surrender yourself, or die!"

Frederick's face drew taut, but he showed no signs of fear. "I will defend this girl to my death. You have no right to keep these little ones as cattle, forcing them to do your labors. Your laziness and cruelty expose your cowardice, so I have no fear of you."

A pop sounded. A stream of fire shot into the scene, but it looked real, a blue streak with a long jagged tail. Adrian focused on it. A photo gun?

The streak zipped in front of Cassabrie's nose and continued into the darkness, sizzling in the rain. Finally, it struck a distant tree and raised a splash of fire.

Frederick and the wall crumbled. Cassabrie's shroud of light disappeared, leaving her in darkness. Adrian lunged, grasped her arm, and pulled her toward a stand of bushes, navigating the blackness by memory. His legs felt stiff, his brain foggy, as if he had just awakened from a deep sleep.

Now crouching in the brush, he stared into the clearing. Something moved out there, dark and fuzzy. Lightning flickered in the distance but too far away to illuminate anything close by. The whistling to the left continued, marking the collection tank. The shed stood somewhere to the right. His sword still lay inside. Could he leave Cassabrie and grope toward it without being discovered? Would their attacker be able to locate either one of them? Obviously he had a photo gun. The telltale blue fireball gave it away. Might he use a glow stick to light his path? No. That would reveal his own location, a foolish move.

Adrian flexed his fingers. If only the hilt of his sword were already in his grasp. Since the attacker didn't know that his prey was unarmed, they were at an impasse. With the storm's noise shield, maybe he could find the shed. Better to prolong the impasse with something more than his opponent's assumption.

He set his lips against Cassabrie's ear and whispered as quietly as possible. "Stay hidden. I have to get my sword."

She pulled his sleeve and drew his head close to her mouth. "The woman is here, but she is not alone. She is angry, very angry."

"Can you tell how many are out there?"

"Not with certainty. Maybe five others. All are men. I sense hostility toward the woman. Yet, I sense another man not among the others. He is distant, lost and searching, and he seems friendly."

Adrian stared again into the darkness. If the closer men felt hostility toward the woman, then apparently she wasn't on their side. Her anger might mean that she was their prisoner. But why? Had the Gateway sent a woman to help deliver the gas tank? If so, who could possibly be brave or strong enough for the task?

He nodded at his own question. Marcelle, of course. But she didn't cry out a warning. One of the men likely held a dagger at her throat, or perhaps she was gagged. In any case, if Marcelle was out there, she would be the most uncooperative prisoner possible. She would find a way to help.

After touching Cassabrie's shoulder, signaling his departure, he tiptoed into the clearing. While the tank continued to whistle, he used its noise as a beacon, keeping it as a landmark in his mental image of the surroundings.

As he padded through the streaming water, anxiety pricked his senses. The attackers wouldn't be sitting still, doing nothing. They had come to squash this plan, and waiting for their target to escape made no sense.

Something flashed in the corner of his eye. A bright yellow light erupted from a stone between him and the tank. He crouched, but it didn't help. A gas lamp atop the stone cast a powerful glow all around, exposing him to whatever eyes cared to look his way. He felt naked, unable to see past the covered flame to identify the shadows undulating close behind it.

Another blue fireball shot from one of the shadows. Adrian dove toward the shed. As he slid through the water, pain ripped through his leg, a burning torture that ate into his skin. He rolled, dousing the burn, then leaped back to his feet and stumbled as he groped for the shed. His injured leg gave way, forcing him to crawl. He had to get to his sword. It was his only hope of protecting Cassabrie. Surely they would find her now.

With each splash, he cringed, waiting for the next fireball. Photo guns took some time to reenergize, but not that long. Maybe the rain had choked its mechanism.

He rolled into the shed and grabbed his sword. Now shielded by a wall, yet partially exposed by the doorway, he looked toward Cassabrie. Although she crouched low behind a bush, the white lining in her cloak could still be seen by someone looking in that direction. Since the attackers had no idea she was there, maybe they wouldn't notice.

"Adrian Masters," a man called. "Surrender. You are no match for our numbers and our weapons."

Adrian peeked around the door frame. A man strode in front of the lamp, but with the light at his back, his face stayed in shadow.

"You are the most despicable of traitors," the man continued. "His Excellency trusts you enough to keep his back turned to you as you wield a sword to protect him, yet you plot against his rule in secret. Your father would be proud. You are truly a son of the Ram."

The Ram? Adrian studied the voice. Very familiar. Everyone knew about his bodyguard position, but only retired soldiers knew his father's battle nickname. And who among them would think of Edison Masters as a traitor but the man who accused him of treachery long ago?

Drawing his head behind the wall again, Adrian shouted, "A plot against the governor's rule? What are you talking about? I am here at the behest of one of his own."

"Oh, really? Who gave such an order?"

"Since you don't know, I must assume that you're an enemy." Adrian peeked out again. "I will give you no more information until you identify yourself."

The man picked up the lantern by a handle on top. As it swung, the light passed back and forth across his face.

Adrian squinted. He had seen this soldier a number of times, one of Prescott's highly ranked officers.

"I am Darien, head of the governor's military council." A cocky smile bent his lips. "Any further questions?"

With the light now shining into his sanctuary, Adrian searched for another weapon, a rope, a net, anything that might help him in battle. A broken shovel leaned against one corner, and the old hatchet and its leather sheath still lay in another. Adrian grabbed the sheath and tried to open it, but the metal fasteners had rusted. Would he be able to pry them loose in time?

He quickly unbuckled his belt and attached the sheath. While yanking on the fasteners, he kept glancing outside. Since Darien and his company hadn't already attacked, they might believe he had dangerous weapons in the shed, maybe a photo gun he was keeping dry. It wouldn't hurt to enhance their fears.

"I have other weapons in here," he shouted. "Since you have a photo gun, you know its power. I suggest you leave and allow me to complete my mission."

Darien stared into the shed, his brow low. "You hide the truth. I can tell when a deceiver is playing games with his words."

Adrian rebuckled his belt. The hatchet's fasteners stayed locked in place. "If you're so confident, then come a few steps closer, and you'll find out."

Darien advanced a foot but drew it back. He set the lantern down and stalked toward the shadows. "I have another way of forcing your surrender."

A few seconds later, he returned with two men and a woman. The men held the woman in place between them, her hands apparently bound behind her. A gag covered her mouth, but her identity was unmistakable.

"Marcelle," Adrian whispered.

One of the soldiers shouted. "I see someone in the bushes!"

In a flash of white, Cassabrie dashed deeper into the forest.

Darien waved two fingers. "Go check it out."

Sloshing footfalls headed toward the woods.

Adrian clenched his sword. He had to help Cassabrie, but how? They already had a head start, so chasing them in this storm would be impossible. And if he left, who would help Marcelle?

Darien withdrew a dagger and sliced away Marcelle's gag and bonds. "If you try to help her," he said, "I will cut her throat. But if you surrender, I will allow you both to stand a fair trial in Prescott's court."

"Idiot!" Marcelle barked. "I have nothing to do with this nutty conspiracy. Why would this peasant give up anything for the likes of me?"

Adrian gritted his teeth. Marcelle's courageous denial gave him an opening he might be able to use. "Is that Marcelle?" he called out. "I hardly recognized her without the trappings of her fancy nobility or the swagger the sword adds to her hips."

"I recognized you," Marcelle shouted through the storm's continuing patter, "even without seeing your face. You're hiding, as usual, afraid to fight like a man."

Darien swung his head back and forth as they argued, his eyes narrowing.

Adrian threw back a verbal volley. "If I fight you, I can't win. If I draw blood, I'm the beast who skewered the little princess. If you draw blood, then *I'm* the princess. If I can't beat a little girl, then I might as well wear a dress and tiara."

"Oh, now I see how it really is. Some people tried to tell me you were too chivalrous to fight me, that Adrian is too much of a gentleman to cross swords with a lady. But, oh no, he fears for his own reputation."

"My reputation? Do you think forfeiting every time I had to face you helped my reputation? Listen, Miss Too-manly-to-wear-a-dress. Bowing out caused me more shame than winning or losing to you."

"Well, I hope when you bowed, your tiara didn't fall off, you—"

"Silence!" Darien shouted. "You sound like urchins from the schoolyard!"

Marcelle pressed her lips together and kept her icy glare on the shed. Adrian blew out a breath. Either she meant every word, or she was the best actress in the land. Did she have a plan in mind? If not, he would have to make a run for it, somehow try to save her and Cassabrie. But how?

Darien looked Marcelle in the eye. "We shall soon see whose side you're really on." He pressed the photo gun into her hand, jerked a crossbow and arrow from the harness, and set the loaded arrow against her neck. "Shoot into the shed. It will either kill him or flush him out."

"If you had half a brain," Marcelle growled, "you'd be dangerous. He would have attacked us by now if he possessed the means."

"He is wounded. If he has photo guns, his only chance is to stay where he is. And, as I said, this will reveal your allegiance." He prodded her with the arrow. "Shoot! Now!"

Marcelle pulled the trigger. With a telltale pop, a flash of blue rocketed out and blasted through the shed's open doorway, missing Adrian and splashing across the rear wall. Flames erupted and spread throughout the interior.

His sword in hand, Adrian leaped out and rolled through the water. Crawling on hands and knees, he scrambled toward the spot Cassabrie had last crouched. Maybe he could get away and find her somehow.

"Take him!" Darien yelled.

As Adrian tried to climb to his feet, slipping and sliding, he tightened his muscles, expecting an arrow in his ribs at any second. If Marcelle had a plan, she had better hatch it now.

Another pop sounded, and a flash of blue lit up the area. A man screamed. Adrian flipped over to his back and looked. How could Marcelle have recharged the gun so quickly?

One of Darien's soldiers, now ablaze, dove to the water and slid close to Adrian's side. A second soldier slipped and fell. Marcelle ducked under Darien's arrow, thrust a knee into his groin, and, with a backhanded slap, knocked the crossbow from his grip. As he staggered backwards, Darien reached for his scabbard.

Adrian leaped to his feet and shouted, "Marcelle!" He slung his sword, forcing it to slowly rotate as it flew. Surely she had practiced this maneuver, but the heavy rain, along with skewed lighting from a lantern and a burning shed, made the sword seem nearly invisible as it whipped toward her.

With a quick flick of her hand, she snatched the hilt from the air and slashed at Darien. Like black lightning Darien's dark blade whipped out and parried her attack. Adrian grabbed the burning soldier's sword and hobbled toward them, but the other soldier swung out his leg, tripping him. Adrian fell headlong and slid face-first through the mire.

While Marcelle and Darien fought, swords clashing in the clamor of beating rain and the gas tank's continued whistling, Adrian jumped up and faced the soldier, who had risen, wet and muddy, but ready with a sword. With every limb trembling, the soldier seemed hesitant, scared, giving Adrian a chance to watch the other battle for a moment and glance around for any sign of Cassabrie.

Marcelle dodged Darien's thrust and glided by him. When she tried to slice his torso as she passed, in what seemed like an impossibly agile move, he blocked her blade again and shoved her away. She backpedaled, splashing and sliding, but managed to stay upright. As they faced each other once more, Marcelle's jaw tightened. She seemed surprised at Darien's skill, yet determined.

Adrian stepped forward to help. Out of the corner of his eye, he caught a glimpse of movement. His opponent lunged with his sword. Adrian blocked him. As the two blades slid together and intersected near the hilts, the combatants met eye to eye. Adrian scowled and spoke with even, measured words. "If you give up now and leave immediately, I will let you live. This is your only warning. Drop your sword and run."

For a moment, the soldier's features stayed stony, but as rainwater poured down his face, the droplets seemed to melt his bravado. He snapped his hand open, letting the sword drop, then turned and ran into the darkness.

Adrian picked up the sword and, with two weapons now in hand, spun toward Marcelle. She and Darien had again engaged in battle.

Although dripping wet, her blade whipped in time with her sinewy arm, thrusting and parrying with power and precision. Darien's blade whistled through the air in reply, almost invisible in the darkness.

Jumping into a limping run, Adrian rushed toward them, but the mud and water slowed him down.

Darien slammed his blade against Marcelle's and wrenched the sword from her grip. She dropped to her knees and searched the dark water with her hands. Darien lunged, slashing his sword. She ducked underneath and tried to roll, but he kicked her in the side, pushed the sword tip against her thigh, and shouted, "Stand back, Adrian, or I will cut her to shreds!"

Adrian slid to a halt only four steps away, let the sword drop from his left hand, and hid the one in his right in his own shadow. In the glow of the lantern, Marcelle lay still on her side. Her heavy breaths bubbled in a puddle at her cheek.

Tightening his grip on the hilt, he glared at Darien while again using his left hand to loosen the fasteners sealing the hatchet. "What now?"

"I'm contemplating whether to take you both prisoner or kill you immediately."

"Darien! Look what we found!" Two soldiers emerged from the bushes, each holding one of Cassabrie's arms as they carried her toward the lantern. Her legs dangled limply, and her head lolled to one side, her skin and lips bluer than ever.

As they drew closer, Darien squinted. "She looks dead."

"She is. No breathing. No heartbeat." They dropped her to the mud. "We were chasing her and she just collapsed, stone dead."

Adrian swallowed. *No! Not Cassabrie!* But he kept his mouth shut. He had to stay calm and look for a way to escape.

"Are you sure?" Darien asked. "I want to know why she was out here."

"I'm sure." One of the soldiers withdrew a sword and drove it through Cassabrie's back. She didn't flinch. "See?"

Cassabrie's body dissolved and blended with the mud. The two soldiers gasped and staggered back. His mouth gaping, Darien leaned closer. "What in the name of …"

Like a volcano, Adrian erupted. He slapped Darien's blade away from Marcelle's thigh. She swung a leg and swept Darien's feet out from under him. He landed on his back, somersaulted, and leaped into battle stance, his sword ready.

Marcelle grabbed her sword and lunged out of the way, then rose to her knees and pointed the blade at Darien, now several steps in front of her.

Leaping again, Adrian flew at Darien. Their swords clashed and locked in place. The black blade sparkled in the lantern light, like coal embedded with crystals. Heaving breaths during their stalemate, Adrian glanced at the two soldiers. They approached slowly, both extending their swords.

Marcelle jumped to her feet and waved her blade. "Stay back if you want to keep your heads!"

Adrian pushed with all his might, thrusting Darien away, and rushed at the soldiers. Marcelle charged with him, and both swung simultaneously. When the soldiers parried, Adrian spun to the side and slid his blade across his man's throat, slicing it deeply. He crumbled in a heap.

While Marcelle battled her opponent, Darien charged. Adrian picked up the second sword, swung around, and halted Darien's blade again.

Another figure jumped into view, grabbed Marcelle from behind, and dragged her away. "That's a dagger you feel!" a man barked. "If you move, you're dead!"

Marcelle spat out, "I feel the hands of a spineless weasel. Who but a lowly scout would attack from behind?" She kicked backwards. The man yelped, but a sharp cry from Marcelle and the sudden arching of her back proved that the man had pushed his dagger point a bit deeper. She quieted and slid away with her captor.

Her former opponent attacked Adrian, forcing him to use both swords while pivoting his head back and forth madly. He blocked blow after blow, sometimes two at the same time. With Darien constantly making lightning-fast moves, and the other soldier slashing from the opposite side, he couldn't break off this fight, but with his arms weakening, he would have to change tactics soon.

Thrusting his legs out in front, Adrian fell to his seat. Darien's jab swiped over his head, but the other soldier lost his balance and stumbled forward. Adrian stabbed him in the belly, then, using his other arm, shoved him toward Darien.

Darien danced out of the way and attacked again. Adrian rocked into a backwards somersault, leaped to his feet, and, shouting a guttural cry, threw a sword. The blade cut into Darien's right arm and splashed into the mud.

As blood poured from the wound, Darien shifted his sword to his left hand. With rainwater spewing through his heavy breaths, he set his feet. "I'm not done yet, traitor!"

Adrian transferred the second sword to his right hand and lunged. Darien blocked his swing, again locking their blades, but Darien's arm bent under Adrian's pressure. Adrian's blade edged closer and closer to Darien's face. His eyes widened, and his teeth began to chatter. Finally, Adrian broke through, slashed Darien from forehead to nose to chin, and shoved him to the ground.

Darien writhed in the mud, a hand covering his bleeding face, but he made no sound.

The scout shouted, "Throw your sword at my feet, and drop to your knees, or she's dead!"

Adrian extended his sword with one hand, shaking it as if scared, hoping to distract the scout while he once again worked on the fasteners at his left hip. Finally, they popped open. The hatchet was available. He tossed the sword. As it splashed close to Marcelle and the scout, Adrian lowered himself to his knees.

The scout eased the dagger back, allowing Marcelle to straighten. As muddy water streamed down her face, she glared at Darien. "You couldn't beat us, so your toady had to take the coward's way out."

Darien rose slowly to his feet, his sword still in his grip, and stumbled toward Marcelle. His face now divided by a bloody gash that split his nose and chin, he set the point of his blade against her throat. "A vixen and her tongue are easily parted."

Still on his knees, Adrian slid closer while easing his left hand toward the hatchet's handle. He couldn't save Cassabrie, but he would rescue Marcelle … somehow.

Stepping back, Darien, now using his left arm while his right dangled at his side, set his sword's edge against Marcelle's waist where his earlier cut had exposed bare skin. "Before I remove your tongue," he said, breathing heavily, "I want to hear you cry for mercy. My face is ruined, and I want you to share the pain I feel."

He sliced into her waist, drawing a stream of blood. Marcelle grunted but, biting her lip, didn't cry out.

"Ah!" Darien crooned. "I should have known you would be brave. Let's see if you stay silent when I cut a finger off."

She twisted, but the scout held her fast, again pressing the dagger against her back. As Darien shifted his blade toward her hand, her eyes widened in terror.

Adrian jerked out the hatchet, regripped it in his right hand, and slung it at the scout. The blade whipped past Marcelle's cheek and embedded in the scout's jaw. Groping for the handle, he staggered back and toppled over.

Adrian and Marcelle dove for his sword, but Darien stomped on it and set his blade against Marcelle's neck. Adrian rolled and shot back up to his feet.

"Stay where you are!" Darien shouted.

Adrian froze in place, now within two steps of Marcelle. She lay on her stomach, one hand on his sword's hilt and one inching toward Darien's boot.

The scout lay motionless near the lantern. The rain, now easing to a light drizzle, allowed Darien to speak without raising his voice. "You leave me no choice but to—"

A burst of light made every head turn. At the point where Cassabrie vanished, a swirl of radiance rose from the ground. As before, it seemed to collect the soil and draw it into the vortex, changing the swirl into a turbid whirlpool.

The spin slowed, and Cassabrie appeared, her cloak saturated and much dirtier than before.

Darien's jaw dropped open. "What sort of devilry is this?"

Adrian kept his face like stone, though his heart pounded. "You'd better surrender. Now that she has returned from the dead, you can't imagine what will happen next."

Darien kept his sword against Marcelle's neck. Droplets of blood sprayed as he spoke. "What vile demoness have you called up from hell?"

An aura dressing her in an eerie glow, Cassabrie stepped through the slurry, her bare feet squishing the mud. With her cloak clinging to her thin body, she looked like a walking corpse. She joined Adrian and stood at his side. "He is near," she whispered.

Adrian repeated the words in his mind. Who could be near? The soldier who ran off? Why would she mention him?

Darien pushed the sword tip into Marcelle's neck. She cried out, but the muddy water muffled her voice.

"Back away, you foul creature," Darien said to Cassabrie. "Go to the blazing fires where you belong."

Marcelle grabbed his ankle and pulled, but he jerked his foot away and stomped on her hand, pinning it.

Adrian lunged, but Cassabrie grasped his wrist and held him back. Her powerful grip belied her stature. "All is well," she said. "He is—"

A guttural yell sounded, followed by a loud splash. A man leaped out of the darkness and swung a sword, cleanly slicing off

Darien's hand. As blood spewed, the hand and blade dropped to the ground. Darien screamed and stumbled backwards, gripping his hemorrhaging wrist. He tipped to the side and collapsed. After writhing for a moment, his body slowed to a gentle, rhythmic twitch before falling still.

The rescuer—stocky, gray-haired, and soaking wet—helped Marcelle to her feet.

Adrian limped forward. Could it be? He whispered the word blaring in his mind. "Father?"

Edison looked up and offered a grim smile. "You're hard to track in the rain."

"I know, but ..." His thoughts crumbled. The sight of his father wielding a sword so skillfully took his breath away.

Marcelle wiped mud from her face and arms. "Is Darien alive?"

"If he is," Edison said, "he won't be for long."

She picked up the viper, splashed over to Darien, and sliced open his tunic, exposing his chest. With quick, jerking movements, she stripped his torso bare and scanned his chest, then, after turning him over, she looked at his back. With a huff, she threw the sword on the ground.

Adrian lifted his brow. "What was that for?"

"A personal matter." With her hair plastered across both cheeks, she glowered at him. "I will say no more, except that the scoundrel is dead. Good riddance."

After sheathing his sword, Edison crossed his arms over his chest. "In light of what I have seen and heard, including this pitiful maiden and that infernal whistling, I think you should explain what's going on. I thought you set out to find the portal to the dragon world."

"First," Marcelle said as she limped toward the tank, "let me stop this racket." She turned a valve between the tank and the pipeline, silencing the whistle.

Adrian reached for Cassabrie and took her hand. With the rain ended but the wind still whipping, he pulled her close, hoping to radiate some body heat into this feminine icicle. "Okay, I'll tell the story, but let's gather at the shed. The remains are still hot."

Grunting softly, Marcelle hobbled toward the shed. Edison pushed a shoulder under her arm and helped her the rest of the way, while Adrian guided Cassabrie. She seemed weaker now, somehow more fragile.

They stood as close to the dying flames as possible, warming their hands and drying their clothes. Marcelle examined the cut on her waist, while Edison used a handkerchief to clean the puncture in her neck. Both injuries looked painful, but neither seemed dangerous.

Using strips of cloth cut from Darien's uniform, Edison fashioned a bandage and wrapped it around Marcelle's waist. After tying it snugly, he brushed his hands together. "I never trained as a battlefield medic, so that will have to do."

"It will do fine," Marcelle said, offering him a kind smile.

After making another bandage and binding one of Adrian's wounds, Edison surveyed the carnage. "Battle is an ugly business, is it not?"

"Ugly, but too often necessary," Adrian said.

"Heroism is never ugly." Marcelle limped close to Adrian and looked into his eyes. "If I had my crown, I could give it to you, but I think you'd rather have something else."

Adrian glanced at his father before answering. "What might that be?"

"My humble apology." She bowed. Then, as she backed away, she added, "You are the better swordsman, and I appreciate your chivalry and your heroic character."

Adrian returned the bow. "And I humbly accept the garland of your kind words, but I hope we never learn who is truly the better swordsman. I was driven by passion. Something inside me exploded in a way that I could never replicate in the sanitized atmosphere of an arena."

As she smiled, her mud-smeared face seemed lovelier than ever. "Keep it up, Adrian. I could get used to your chivalrous ways."

Adrian's cheeks grew warm. Her words felt good, a balm of affirmation. He peered at his father, but he showed no reaction. Surely he heard. His wisdom had been proven once again.

A dozen replies came to mind, but each one seemed inadequate. Maybe it was better to stay quiet, let the words of peace settle between them. They were no longer combatants; they were friends and allies. And this union of hearts and swords felt good, very good.

"Okay," Edison said, clapping his hands, "let's move past the sentimentality and on to your story. In other words, what's going on around here? And who is this young lady with the cloak?"

Adrian turned to his father and laughed. "You're right. Besides, one of the soldiers got away. We can't stay around here much longer."

Adrian explained their mission and Cassabrie's presence, then Marcelle told her story, including her deal with Prescott and Drexel.

When she finished, Adrian nodded at the smoldering shed. "How did you manage to recharge the photo gun so quickly?"

She shrugged. "Simple. It has a setting to fire only part of its charge. Most people want to shoot with all of its power every time, but if you plan ahead, you can get up to three effective shots on one charge."

After they had dried out fairly well, Adrian pointed at the tank. "So now all we have to do is roll the tank to the portal."

"I see," Edison said. "But how will Cassabrie carry it through the portal to the dragon world?"

"I thought we would go with her." Adrian gave Cassabrie an expectant look. "Right?"

"I am able to transport it through the portal myself," Cassabrie said. "And I cannot take you with me now. He who sent me wants to ensure that the gas is what the dragons need before he allows you to come. Once he verifies that it is really pheterone, I will come back and get you."

Marcelle raised a brow. "He who sent me?"

Cassabrie shifted from foot to foot, apparently unsure of what to say.

"A dragon named Arxad," Adrian said. "He set up the exchange."

Marcelle waved a hand at Cassabrie. "Oh, no! That's not the deal. He gets the gas, and we're allowed entry. If we let him take the tank and leave us behind, we have no leverage."

"Leverage?" Cassabrie repeated, her head tilting. "I don't understand."

Adrian pushed a lock of hair out of her eyes. "It means she doesn't trust Arxad to provide what he promised. Once he has the gas, we have nothing with which to force him to keep his end of the bargain."

"And why should we trust him?" Marcelle said. "The dragons stole our people and enslaved them, and Arxad is a dragon. We would be fools to trust him."

Cassabrie's eyes widened. "No, Arxad is good and noble. He is against the slavery. That's why I'm helping him. Since he opposes the other dragons in secret, he needs me."

"In secret?" Marcelle laughed under her breath. "Maybe he has you fooled, but he's not fooling me. Tell him he gets no gas unless we come with the tank."

Cassabrie looked up at Adrian. "Is that your will? Are you the leader of your clan?"

Adrian glanced at Marcelle. Her cheeks flamed, and likely not because of the shed's warming embers. "Now that my father is here, according to the Code, I must defer to him." Shifting to a softer voice, he added, "Right, Marcelle?"

She lowered her eyes, matching his tone. "That would be in keeping with the Code."

Cassabrie turned to Edison. "I assure you, my lord, that Arxad is of the highest character. At great risk to himself, he saved my life, a worthless slave. Even as I was being executed, he spirited me away, and now I am safe from all harm and no longer in slavery."

Edison took Cassabrie's hand and looked into her eyes. "There is something very different about you, young lady. Your body is that of a cold cadaver, yet you are alive and youthful, and your eyes are those of a prophetess. What are you?"

"Please, kind sir, I beg you to ask me no questions about myself. Arxad is surely already concerned about my delay. Allow the tank to accompany me, or give me leave to return to him without it."

After staring at her for a few more seconds, Edison nodded at the tank. "We will let you take it, and we will wait for your return."

Cassabrie clasped her hands together. "Oh, thank you! You won't regret this!"

Marcelle glared at Adrian but said nothing. She picked up hers and Darien's swords and stalked toward the gas line.

After disconnecting the tank, Adrian, Edison, and Marcelle worked together, with Adrian in the middle, to roll the head-high cylinder through the muddy water. The deeper areas helped buoy their load, but bushes, roots, and stones slowed their progress. Along the way, Marcelle picked up a bag and strapped it to her back, explaining that she had stealthily "lost" it, but she refused to say why a change of clothing needed to be kept secret.

Cassabrie led the march, not offering to help with the pushing. With her gaze fixed straight ahead and the lantern in her hand turned to its brightest setting, her surrounding halo made her look like a glowing ghost.

As they rolled the tank through a denser part of the forest, Adrian watched the strange girl out in front. With her cloak drier now, yet still dirty, it fanned out in the wind. The ghost transformed into a storybook angel, albeit a soiled one. So much mystery! Somehow, she convinced the soldiers that she had died—no heartbeat or breathing. Then, when they stabbed her, she crumbled and later reconstituted herself.

What kind of creature might she really be? Father noticed a strange spirit within. She seemed filled with inner strength, yet her body was so fragile. Maybe that's why she didn't offer to help. As thin as a wafer, she might have broken a bone.

When they arrived at the clearing, Cassabrie stopped. "We are here," she said quietly.

The three pushed the tank toward the center. The water had receded, leaving soft, grassy turf that bent under the weight of the tank as they dug in to roll it the last few feet.

When they finally stopped, Edison leaned against the tank, mopped his brow with his damp sleeve, and looked at Cassabrie. "Now that we are here, little maid, what will you do?"

She handed Adrian the lantern. "Please move to the tree line and watch from there. I will return as soon as I can."

"Minutes?" Marcelle asked. "Hours? Days?"

Cassabrie laid a palm on the tank. "I truly do not know, my lady. Arxad must test the gas, and I have no idea what that involves. I assure you, however, that I will beg for a speedy trial and return."

"Let's just do as she asks," Adrian said as he backed away, motioning for Edison and Marcelle to follow.

When they had gathered near the base of a fir tree, Cassabrie spread out her arms and looked into the sky. "Arxad? Can you hear me?"

For a moment, she tilted her head, as if listening. Adrian craned his neck, straining to hear a whisper, but the wind made it impossible.

"I know," Cassabrie continued. "We encountered some obstacles, but all is well now. The people of Darksphere have given me leave to deliver the gas for your inspection, and I promised to return to them right away." Again she listened, this time with her head bowed. "I realize the danger, but for the sake of my friends, I will accept that risk. It is mine alone to take."

With arms still spread, she closed her eyes. An aura shone again, enveloping her and the collection tank. Flakes appeared on her exposed skin, as if the light had absorbed all moisture. The breeze peeled them away, layer after layer, and tossed them into a cyclonic spin around her body. Soon, every particle of her frail form lifted into the swirl and blew away.

A silhouette of rotating light remained, still feminine, still recognizable as Cassabrie, and her glow, a sphere of radiance, expanded beyond the tank, taking up most of the clearing. The tank slowly faded, as if ingested by the light.

Marcelle stepped away from the tree and walked slowly toward Cassabrie's shining form, her eyes focused straight ahead.

"Marcelle!" Adrian called. "No!"

"Someone has to make sure the dragons keep the deal." She ran into the glow and instantly began fading.

Adrian leaped from the tree, but with a quiet pop, the aura vanished, taking Cassabrie, Marcelle, and the tank with it.

Lifting the lantern high, Adrian ran into the clearing. Not a trace remained.

Edison joined him and set a hand on his shoulder. "Marcelle possesses an independent spirit."

"I just hope she's all right. If Arxad's dangerous ..." Adrian let his voice fade. Even if Arxad was a nobler dragon than the rest, he still might be angered by Marcelle's appearance. The dragon made the deal, and he had not yet broken it. Distrust and trespassing weren't exactly the best ways for the humans to keep their part of the bargain.

Edison interrupted the silence. "Let's just pray for Marcelle to be, shall we say, less assertive than usual."

"My thoughts exactly." Adrian walked to the indentation left by the tank and looked up into the dark sky. "Cassabrie!" he shouted. "Can you hear me? Arxad?"

Bryan Davis

"Shhh!" Edison warned. "Remember the soldier who escaped. Following our trail from the pipeline to here will not be difficult."

"You're right. If he goes back for help, we might be surrounded in less than an hour."

"Come. We have some time before we have to douse the lantern." Edison laid a hand on Adrian's back. "Let's conceal ourselves among the trees and have a talk."

Adrian gave way to the gentle push and walked back to the forest, allowing for his father's limp, more pronounced now. All that laborious pushing had taken a toll.

After finding a stand of trees packed tightly together, Edison leaned against a wide trunk of smooth tortoise green bark, his head angled toward the sky. Only a step away, Adrian rested against a twin trunk and crossed his arms. Father surely had a speech ready. His pose proved that. With so much time alone in search of his son, and with the amazing sights he had just beheld, he had to be brimming with thoughts.

"Son," he said in a low tone, "the moment I blessed your journey, it felt as though a logjam broke open. All my doubts and fears rushed out, and I realized what a fool I have been. The loss of my integrity in the eyes of the people made my confidence waste away, and losing Frederick filled my heart with terror. I wanted to gather all my possessions into my arms and hold them close, for fear that another treasure might slip from my grasp."

Tears glistened in the sage's eyes as he continued. "Then, when you and Jason left together, seeing you ready to risk your life by marching into the unknown and dangers unimaginable for Frederick's sake ... well, that was like a flint stone that relit a torch long ago discarded. My final doubts drained away."

He patted his chest. "Frederick is *my* son, and to build walls of fear around our family, monuments to faithlessness and betrayal, would be to dishonor everything he stands for. I would truly become the traitor that Darien made of me, and perhaps that has been my failing. Every whisper, every askance look, every snicker whittled away my courage until I allowed the opinions of others to shape me into the coward they believed me to be. But, one event changed that course forever."

As Edison looked up again, his gentle smile trembled. "That event," he said, his voice shaking as he gazed again at Adrian, "was today's tournament final. I witnessed an act of courage that only a scant few comprehended. Knowing that his reputation would be crushed and his courage would be castigated, one of the combatants bowed and humbly backed away. And why? Because he believed in a higher calling than that of mob approval. He cared not for the applause of men or a crown of perishable leaves. Oh, no. He sought after the crown that never withers and the blessing that never ends, the pleasure and fellowship of his creator."

Edison set a fist against his chest. "And that, my son, was the spark, the first glimmer of light from the opening door that set my soul free from the dungeon I had constructed for myself."

He stepped away from the tree and set a hand on Adrian's cheek. "Now, I wish to march at your side as the fellow warrior I should have been all along. I wish to honor our creator by taking up arms to set his people free, knowing that we will be successful only as we keep in step with his code and call upon him in times of trouble."

Adrian wrapped his arms around his father and kissed his damp cheek. Drawing their bodies into a tight clasp, he wept as he spoke. "You are my hero, and you always will be. It was your wisdom that taught me to seek heaven's applause, and I take that wisdom with me everywhere I go. That's why I was able to leave home without fear, because I knew, even without hearing your marching footsteps at my side, I would be able to hear your words in my heart. Edison Masters is my constant companion."

After a moment of silent embrace, Adrian patted his father on the back and pulled free. "We'd better concentrate on watching for Marcelle."

"Yes," Edison said, "which raises another thought. With a woman such as her in our company, one who will insist on risking every danger we do, we will have to keep one precept constantly in our minds."

"What precept is that?"

"In assaying the value of blood, hers will always outweigh ours, and anyone who displays a differing opinion is never to be trusted."

✳ SEVEN ✳

DREXEL stood at the palace's front door, watching, waiting. Jason, the youngest of the Masters brothers, sat on the marble steps that descended toward the front lawn and the main gate, closed now and soon to be locked for the night. His head hung low as the approaching storm darkened the grounds and cast peals of thunder their way, and his fingers clutched his sandy brown hair tightly, as if vexed by the worries of the world.

Unable to suppress a grin, Drexel nodded. All performers had executed their parts perfectly. With Jason so young and inexperienced, they had maneuvered him like a piece in a game of chattels, the peasant-pawn whose wisdom was nothing more than a list of platitudes, too naïve to guess the motivation behind the forked tongues.

Drexel chuckled. Watching the plan unfold had been like sitting in the audience while a masterful production took place on stage. Jason played the unwitting fool, thinking he was a real bodyguard on duty for the Invocation Ceremony, while a parade of Prescott's friends followed the script like award-winning actors.

First, the new counselor, Viktor Orion, intentionally flaunting his ceremonial silk, glided up to Prescott and Jason like a waltzing flower and said, "He is a handsome lad, to be sure, Your Lordship. Perhaps he will help us find the Diviner. It is said that the sultry witches are always on the lookout for a callow catch."

Then later in the evening, former Counselor Darmore said to Prescott, "I see you have chosen another peasant for your bodyguard. I suppose if he dies defending you, it will be no loss. There are many more rats in the sewers who can handle a blade."

And, as Drexel had hoped, Governor Prescott had laughed at each line, a most spiteful laugh, the perfect poison to weaken the spirit of a boy who wanted nothing more than to be seen as a man. Now he was a humiliated pup, ready to be goaded toward the final step.

Drexel cupped a hand around his mouth to call for Jason, but a rumble of thunder made him pause. Yet, Jason rose to his feet and marched toward the door, a firm resolve in his gait.

"I forgot to give something to Governor Prescott," Jason said when he ascended the final step. "It's very important."

Drexel gazed at the boy's sincere brown eyes. Now he had to play his own part, even without a script. "What could a peasant have that His Lordship would want at this time of night?" he asked, forcing a scowl. "Bodyguard or not, it had better be urgent."

"Oh, it's urgent." Jason pulled a sheet of parchment from his pocket and smoothed out the wrinkles. "I took this from someone in his inner circle. It appears that one of those crazy conspiracy theorists is within his ranks. Of course, I couldn't interrupt the ceremony, but I forgot to tell him afterwards."

Drexel kept his staged frown in place. "You forgot? What kind of bodyguard are you?"

"A new one," Jason said, offering a bow. "I beg your indulgence."

Drexel eyed the page. Of course he knew what it was, a copy of the Underground Gateway's newsletter, but feigning ignorance would likely be the best approach. He reached for it, but Jason pulled it back.

"I must speak to him privately," Jason said. "It is up to His Lordship to decide what to do with this information. It would be a shame if I had to tell him tomorrow who prevented my access to him tonight."

Drexel barely kept a laugh in check. This boy had a lot of spunk, and he would need it. He was walking right into the trap.

"For a new bodyguard," Drexel said, "you are a quick student of political maneuvering." He inserted a key into the door's lock and released the bolt. What should he say now? This opportunity was so perfect, could he risk a jest that the others could laugh about later? "Take care that you don't maneuver yourself into a dangerous corner. There are people in the governor's employ who are far craftier than you realize."

Jason nodded. "I will leave through the rear door. It's closer to my path home."

"Very well. You will find a lantern in the vestibule."

Drexel watched Jason enter and pick up the lantern. Apparently he didn't wonder why it was already there, trimmed and lit. Being so inexperienced with the ways of the palace, he wouldn't know any better.

As soon as Jason walked out of earshot, Drexel entered and locked the door behind him. With a wave of his hand toward a side corridor, he summoned Bristol, the interior night watchman. It was time to execute the most difficult step yet.

When Bristol, a tall, muscular lout, emerged from the darkness, a sword in a scabbard at his right hip and a dagger sheathed at the left, the two followed Jason from well behind, the glow of the lantern guiding their way. They had to be careful not to let their shoes squeak or weapons rattle, or even to breathe heavily. Although the boy was surely green in the ways of politics, his ability to sense someone's presence was legendary.

After passing through a corridor and into the governor's private wing, Jason turned down the lantern's flame and stopped at the bedroom door.

Still in the corridor, Drexel halted and extended his arm, blocking Bristol. This was the crucial moment. When Jason entered, everything would fall into place, but nothing would be certain until he walked in. If he heard Prescott's snoring from the anteroom, he might turn around and go home. Still, he might enter anyway, thinking he could leave the newsletter where the governor would see it in the morning, perhaps with a note attached. Drexel and Bristol just had to stay quiet and hope the darkness would keep their presence a secret while the boy decided what to do.

Jason set the lantern on the floor and lifted the latch. Pushing the door open a crack, he peered in. A dim light from inside washed over his face, illuminating his anxious expression. After a few seconds, he pushed the door fully open. Leaving the lantern, he tiptoed in. The door closed behind him, but not quite all the way.

Drexel skulked to the door, picked up the lantern, and waved for Bristol to join him. Drexel handed him the lantern and signaled for him to enter.

Bristol withdrew a dagger from his tunic and showed it to Drexel, a grin emerging as the metal gleamed in the lantern light.

Rolling his eyes, Drexel set a hand on Bristol's back and pushed him toward the door. The oaf had the intelligence of a warthog, but this part of the plan didn't require brains.

Bristol held the lantern out in front and walked in while Drexel waited in the anteroom, listening. Perhaps Jason would hide, thinking a night watchman had entered to check on the governor, but Bristol had no intention of finding him. He would complete his grisly assignment and leave immediately.

Soon, Bristol returned, the lantern in one hand and a bloody handkerchief in the other. Drexel grabbed the handkerchief and wiped off its contents, Prescott's keys and a piece of metal with two bends that made it look like a finger. It pulsed with yellow light, as if infused with burning extane, the litmus finger.

When they were free of blood, he pushed them back into Bristol's hand, stuffed the handkerchief into his pocket, and took the lantern. He then stood in front of the door, pulling the hem of his tunic down and smoothing out the wrinkles. It was time for another acting performance.

The door flew open. Jason appeared, his eyes wide with alarm. Drexel blocked his way and lifted the lantern. "Have you finished delivering your message to the governor?"

Jason raised his sword, his tremulous voice matching his quivering body. "I have to catch a murderer! Someone has killed the governor!"

Raising a hand to his lips, Drexel let out a low moan. "Oh, dear! The governor has fallen! And it seems that the only person who entered his bedroom was a certain peasant boy who spoke petulantly to the palace's sentry. Obviously he was an Underground Gateway conspirator who sought revenge on the great governor who forbade his nefarious practices."

Jason set the sword's point against Drexel's chest. "You're the murderer!"

"Oh, not I." Drexel gestured with his head, signaling for Bristol to join him. The guard walked into the lantern's glow, the keys in one hand and a sword in the other. "I have already entered my suspicions in the official log," Drexel continued, "so killing me would only double your crime. Perhaps you would like to reconsider your offensive posture and join us."

"Join you?" Jason's sword arm wilted. "What do you mean?"

"Bristol," Drexel said, "show us what you retrieved from our dear governor."

Bristol extended the key ring and the glowing finger.

"Take them." Drexel kept his voice calm and reassuring. "You will find what you're looking for in the lowest level of the dungeon at cell block four."

Bristol laid the key ring and cylinder in Jason's palm. The boy stared at them, his eyes dark and somber.

"Before today," Drexel said, "we dared not take this bold step, but now that you have come, we have the means to proceed. You see, when you leave, we will blame you for the murder, and you will be forced to carry out the mission. We have both a warrior and a scapegoat."

Jason's cheeks flushed. He looked at the sword at his side, then at Bristol's sword, but he seemed rooted in place, unable to decide what to do.

"And your answer?" Drexel prompted.

Jason slid his sword back to its scabbard. "I guess I have no choice."

"Ah! Very good! You *have* learned the art of political maneuvering." Drexel pulled Jason into the anteroom and closed the bedroom door. "You have two hours to flee before I alert the new counselor of your deed. The dungeon guard is one of us, and he will allow you to enter. When you find her on the lower level, you will learn what you must do."

"Her?"

Drexel pushed him toward the hall. "Just go!"

Clutching the keys and the finger, Jason hustled toward the rear of the castle, darkness enveloping him, leaving Drexel and Bristol alone in the anteroom.

"Come quickly," Drexel said.

The two hurried into the bedroom. Drexel withdrew the handkerchief from his pocket and rushed to the bed. A dagger protruded from Prescott's chest. Blood covered his nightclothes and dripped to the sheets. His wife, Lady Moulraine, snored at his side, her mouth wide open.

Using the handkerchief, Drexel slid the dagger out of Prescott's chest and wrapped it up. "Get rid of it in the way we discussed," he said as he handed it to Bristol. "Then summon Orion. I will wait for him here."

After Bristol left and closed the door, Drexel looked at Lady Moulraine. The potion he had put in her cup would keep her asleep even if a quake shook the palace.

He pulled a small leather book from an inner pocket and opened it to the first page. In neat block letters, it read, *The Journal of Uriel Blackstone.*

The extane channels in the walls had been turned down to their nighttime setting, but they provided enough light for reading. He thumbed through the pages, probably for the thousandth time. Although he had very nearly memorized it, maybe another perusal would raise a subtle point that might help him massage his plan. Every detail had to be perfect, or else *he* might be swinging from the gallows instead of Jason.

Soon, he was again experiencing Uriel Blackstone's tragic story. He had written his letters boldly and neatly on the opening pages, announcing his intentions to tell the entire tale and tuck the journal away for his son, Tibalt. The governmental authorities were chasing him, calling him a disturber of civil society, so he would have to finish the journal as quickly as possible.

Indeed, on the following pages, his penmanship suffered. With hastily scrawled characters, his story began.

More than one hundred years ago, a most foul dragon by the name of Magnar transported to Major Four from another world. The dragons called their planet Starlight, but that is a lie. Nothing exists there but the darkest of deeds. It is better to call it Dracon, for dragons rule there with cruelty. Oddly enough, they label our world Darksphere, a malicious twist in reality.

While on Major Four, Magnar captured me in the prime of life along with four other males and five females of similar age, none of us related by blood or by marriage. Bound by chains, the dragon took us to a transportation portal deep underground where a river flowed that had apparently cut the tunnel through the centuries.

We waited on a dry floor, facing a bare wall while Magnar inspected its surface. I stood with my shoulders square and my head straight, though my companions whined and wept as they hunched in fear. They clutched burning torches, but I declined to carry one, choosing instead to bear a new copy of the Code, the greatest light of all. Who could tell when we might return? Surely we would need the holy instructions within its pages.

When Magnar announced that the transport would commence, I stepped toward him and said, "No matter how distant your world, I swear to you that I will escape and return here. We have courageous men, and we will mount an army you cannot withstand. We will not rest until every soul you have stolen returns to its homeland."

Magnar laughed and replied with a deep throaty voice. "Uriel, you are a fool. No one in Darksphere knows of the portal, and I will be back to take more of your kind, for we need many to dig deep in search of pheterone."

"You are the fool!" I shouted. "When I return, I will lock this portal so that no one can pass through from either side, and I will not unlock it until our army is ready to invade and destroy you slavers." The moment I uttered those words, I regretted them. What a fool I was to reveal my plans. Such was the state of my passion.

"You overestimate your comrades," Magnar said. "I have half a mind to release you to prove your error. You are one of the few who care for more than his own bread and porridge. Your fellows would not believe you, and even if one could be persuaded, he would be frightened, unwilling to risk being thought of as insane. Even if you escape, no one will join your army. No one."

I stared at him for a moment, trying to invent a courageous response that would not further reveal my purpose, but I had not the chance. With a wave of his wing, Magnar interrupted my thoughts. "Enough of this prattle. Move to the wall."

We shuffled toward the wall, our chains making a racket with every sliding step. Using his foreleg, Magnar touched a peculiar dark oval embedded in the stone. It appeared to be black glass. A light glowed behind his claw, yellow at first, then red, and finally blue. Like a heartbeat, it pulsed. It began rather dim, but its energy increased until it spread out and bathed our chamber in radiance. The blue light swept away everything in sight, the wall, the river, and even ourselves. For a few moments, I could see nothing, only the bright blue light. Then, the light faded. The wall holding the glass disappeared, and new light illuminated the chamber from a source beyond where the wall had stood. It seemed as if the wall simply vanished, opening a way into a second room.

I glanced around at my companions. The cowards had crouched and covered their faces with their hands. I, however, stood tall. I couldn't let this dragon cow me into submission.

"You are now on Starlight," Magnar said, "and here you will stay. If you work for us, we will treat you well. In order to provide us with more labor, you will populate our world as quickly as possible. If you fail to obey, we will kill you and return to your world to capture others to replace you."

He stared at me, his fiery eyes red and throbbing, but I stood my ground.

"This one is strong," Magnar said, his voice now quieter. "We will break him soon enough."

I wondered to whom he was speaking, for no other dragons seemed to be present. I thought perhaps that he might be possessed by an evil spirit.

The dragon looked down at the floor, so I looked as well. A row of crystalline pegs made a line from one side wall to the other. He plucked the middle peg with his clawed hand. A moment or two later, as if by magic, the river vanished, replaced by what appeared to be a continuation of the room in which we stood.

With a wave of a wing, he turned and pointed at an upward sloping tunnel, the source of light I mentioned earlier. "Come. You will no longer need your torches."

As we marched toward the exit, I moved to the end of the line and glared at Magnar. I wanted him to know that I was not a beaten man. Somehow, I would escape and return with a legion of soldiers to rescue our people and destroy the dragons.

We marched under a dreadful hot sun. It looked like our own Solarus, reddish orange with an occasional flare, though perhaps bigger. After we hewed some trees with a primitive saw, giving us our first taste of slave labor, Magnar took us to a stream that ran near a cave. He forced us to undress and wash in the water. Two of the women were especially hesitant, their natural modesty protesting such exposure while men were around, but a shot of fire from Magnar's nostrils encouraged them to obey. I turned my back, but one of my fellows leered at them. I scolded him, of course, reminding him of the Code's conduct for gentlemen, but he paid me no mind.

Later, my own resolve was sorely tested. Magnar herded us into the cave, divided us into pairs, male with female, and guided each couple to separate, private areas, dim and cool. He ordered us to do what was necessary to reproduce, warning us that failure to comply would result in our deaths, and then left us alone.

The poor young lady in my company, Laurel by name, was one of the more modest lasses. She laid herself on the stone floor, curled into a fetal ball, and wept—for a return to her mother, for preservation of her virginity, for rescue from this darkest of nightmares.

What was a gentleman to do? Look away from her uncovered body? Comfort the frightened young woman, who appeared to be no more than eighteen years of age? Protect her from death by encouraging her to obey the dragon, in spite of our great misgivings? The last option seemed the vilest. I had a wife at home, a most lovely and loyal woman, whom I left pregnant with our own first child, a son, my wife had predicted, citing how her belly distended in a certain way. And though she would likely forgive me for forced adultery, I would rather have died in the dragon's river of fire than betray our vows of fidelity. Yet, Laurel would suffer death as well. Would I be a villain to force my view of the Code on her so that she, too, would burn in the very same river?

Speaking tenderly to her, I suggested a pact. We would lie to the dragon, which we both agreed would be a holier option than the alternative, and pretend to have completed the act he had demanded, hoping the dragon knew too little about human physiology to seek evidence. Then, we would try to escape that very night.

As we waited for the dragon to return, we prayed together, asking the Creator for rescue, both for ourselves and for the eight others who faced the same choices that had beset us. Later, we were allowed to dress, and Magnar announced our labors, a drilling project through the planet's crust in search of a gas he called pheterone.

Drexel flipped past several pages and stopped near the end. So far, nothing had drawn his attention. Maybe Uriel's final entry would spark something new.

Yes, those days passed at a tediously slow pace, inventing and manufacturing tools based on our recollections, and drilling, chiseling, and digging in dark tunnels under a mesa in the midst of a sun-baked plateau. Because of my success in stealing the crystalline peg Magnar had used to open the portal, he was never able to venture back to our world to capture more humans, so he grew more agitated about Laurel's apparent inability to conceive. With the other four women already pregnant, Magnar's patience with us was growing thin. And since he suspected that I had taken the peg, though he could not prove it, I endured frequent chastisement by means of his whip.

Now that he had learned more about how we procreated, Laurel and I had to devise creative ways to fool him, and each private encounter and each secretive plot drew us closer to each other. We became friends, though still not lovers, but guilt blossomed in my heart along with my affection for her. It felt so wrong to be the friend of another female while my dear wife likely longed for my presence.

In spite of our apparent infertility, Magnar kept Laurel and me together, even forcing us to sleep shackled to one another in the night cave, warning us that he would give her to a more virile man should she not soon conceive.

The one man of low character, who earlier stared at the vulnerable women while they washed, often cast his lustful eyes at Laurel. Allowing this beast to have her in his clutches was a thought I could not bear. We would escape. Somehow I would get past the dragon guard and open the portal.

Then the blessed night came. I finally managed to purloin a file we had fabricated to sharpen chisels. Laurel and I pried open our sleep shackles and sneaked out to the portal cave. Because my previous escape attempt had come many days prior, the dragon guarding that cave had become less than vigilant and eventually fell asleep.

We stole into the portal cave, and I inserted the crystalline peg into the empty hole. When the underground river appeared, we walked together through the portal and into our world. Of course, I took the crystal with me. When I removed it, the portal stayed open for a short time, but it eventually closed, once again sealing Magnar in his own world.

Our escape raised another dilemma. Should we risk going back for our enslaved brothers and sisters? Or should we rather muster an army and return with the weaponry needed to enforce our wishes?

After deciding on the latter plan, we hurried to our homes. Oh, but tragedy upon tragedies! We both learned of great loss. My wife had died giving birth to you, Tibalt, and Laurel's mother, a widow, had died of heartache. Laurel now had no one else in her home.

Grief-stricken and enraged at the dragons for taking me away from my beloved, I told my story to the authorities, but when I was unable to decipher the black ovular glass in the underground wall and open the portal, they thought me mad and threatened to lock me up in the lunacy ward. I urged Laurel to keep her journey to Dracon a secret, so that she would not suffer the same humiliation.

During the passing days while I studied the dark glass, which seemed to be the key to opening the portal from the human world, I slowly recovered from the pain of my loss. Laurel and I secretly wed in the presence of a kindly minister and two trusted witnesses, and we decided to stay in separate abodes to ensure her safety. She lived in a remote area, while you, Tibalt, and I kept a residence in the village, so the fact that Laurel became with child was never discovered by anyone save for the midwife who kept quiet about the new little girl in the rural cabin.

After a few years, I finally learned the secrets behind the glass. Because of its strange properties, I dubbed it an Eye to the Sky, an intelligent window to other worlds. It can be programmed to respond to certain influences, so I proceeded to teach it to respond only to me and my genetic progeny.

Once I was able to control it fully, I renewed my efforts to publicize the existence of slaves on Dracon, but now no one would follow me to the underground river. When it became clear that further efforts to raise an army would cost me my freedom, I returned to Dracon on my own and hid the crystal in a safe place, but there is no need to tell you about that, dear Tibalt, for I trust that the humans there will soon follow the instructions I left for them so that they can find the crystal themselves and escape. I also left the Code at one woman's bedside, a green-eyed redheaded lady who seemed to be of higher character than some of the others. I hope she has preserved it well.

When I returned to our world, I devised and constructed the intricate obstacles to locating and opening the portal, which I will fully describe on the last pages and also show to you before I again attempt to raise an army. With my instructions fully revealed to you, I can have confidence that, even if imprisoned, my passion to rescue the captives will carry on to the next generation.

And now, my son, I bid you good-bye, hoping, of course, to see you again, but, considering what happened the previous time I reported my story, I fear that our reunion might not come to pass.

Drexel turned to the last page and studied the portal notes. An amazingly intricate set of obstacles lay in front of any seeker of the portal—a field of flowers with a sleep-inducing aroma, a pit that dropped the unwary into an underground river, and wandering ghosts who guarded the entry. And yet, Uriel had also provided measures to avoid each one, including a recipe for an elixir that counteracted the flowers, an alternative entry to the portal that avoided the pit, and poems that would appease the ghosts. Only the possessor of the journal would be able to survive the ordeal. Obviously, Uriel was much more than a confident gentleman of unyielding principles. He was a genius.

Unfortunately for the poor man, the seneschal of the time accused him of murdering the missing people and concocting the story about the dragon planet. The authorities threw him into the dungeon, and when his rantings grew too loud and absurd, they committed him to the insane asylum. He stayed there for decades, making friends with the younger men, even dubbing some of them Tibalt, after his own son. He died at the age of seventy-seven, alone and forgotten.

After closing the journal, Drexel rubbed its leather cover. It never reached Tibalt's hands. No, Laurel found it among her late husband's effects and hid it well, but not well enough to keep it from those with passion to learn the truth about the Lost Ones. Nor was she able to hide her own progeny. Laurel's little girl grew up to birth another girl, who later became the mother of Marcelle, making Marcelle Uriel's great-granddaughter.

This meant, of course, that Marcelle carried Uriel's genetics, which made her capable of communicating with the Eye to the Sky and perhaps opening the portal. Yet, the obstacles described in Uriel's journal presented other great dangers she might not be able to overcome. Commissioning Adrian to locate the portal the dragon used to leave behind Frederick's hat and courier tube seemed to be a better way to benefit from Marcelle's talents.

The door opened again. Drexel pushed the journal back into his pocket and stood up. "Counselor Orion?" he whispered.

A tall, lean figure strode toward him, still dressed in his invocation vestments, dark and silky. "Lady Moulraine is here?"

"She will not awaken. A strong potion has seen to that."

Skepticism wrinkled his brow, but it soon eased. "Let us proceed."

Drexel altered his voice to a formal tone. "I have long admired your quest to rid the land of sorceresses. In my opinion, the pyre is used far too infrequently. There are many witches among us whom the flames should taste. So I was gladdened when I learned of your ascendance to the position of counselor."

"Do not be tiresome, Drexel. Come to the point."

"Gladly." Drexel cleared his throat before continuing. "The Diviner you seek. At what age would you have been allowed to take her from her parents?"

"Sixteen years. If a girl is really a witch, she cannot hide it when she reaches that age."

"And Elyssa was ..." Drexel paused, waiting for Orion.

"Fifteen when the cave bear took her, only days from her birthday, a most frustrating circumstance."

"Oh, yes ... I think I heard about the upcoming birthday. So tragic."

"Get on with it, Drexel. You are testing my patience."

Drexel stroked his chin. "I apologize. I am simply contemplating the idea that Elyssa was spirited away just before you were able to legally take her by force."

"I am a man of the law. Everyone knows that. I would never violate one law in order to enforce another."

Drexel glanced at Prescott's dead body. "Yes, I know. I learned from you the art of delegating the more, shall we say, unsavory jobs."

"I did not agree to our little charade with Prescott in order to be strung along for time interminable."

"Is not becoming governor enough of a reward for your participation?"

Orion's voice deepened to a growl. "It will be enough when the Diviner burns at the stake, and I will see to it that you are included in the kindling if you continue to exasperate me."

"I will trouble you no more, Excellency. My delay was caused by this revelation about Elyssa. Now I know why Prescott hid her in the dungeon's lower level."

Orion's brow arched. "The witch is in the dungeon? At this moment? *Prescott* had her taken there?"

"Yes. I thought she was imprisoned for snooping in his affairs and Prescott made up the bear story to prevent sympathizers from seeking her release. But now it seems clear that he determined to hide her from you."

Even in the dim light, the redness in Orion's face shone clearly. "Well, his charade has ended in an appropriate manner. Do you have the keys?"

"I had them, but I gave them to Jason, Prescott's bodyguard."

A vein near Orion's temple throbbed. "You did what?"

"Shhh!" Drexel looked at Prescott's wife. She groaned once, turned to her side, and snored on. Leaning closer to Orion, he lowered his voice further. "Jason will let her out. Your first order as governor will be to assemble a search party, an army if need be, to track her down. When you catch her, she is yours. Then I will need command of your search party in order to conduct business of my own. Her temporary freedom is essential to my purposes."

Orion shook a finger near Drexel's nose. "If this plan fails, and the little witch escapes, I will personally hang you from the gallows by your wrists, slice you open from sternum to navel, and stuff a nest of hornets into your open belly."

Drexel kept his eyes focused on Orion, resisting the urge to hold a hand over his queasy stomach. "You told me yourself you wanted the governorship, and I have delivered it to you."

"I wanted the office only to have free reign to investigate witchcraft. Again, if this fails—"

"It will not fail if you follow my plan to the letter. If the litmus finger doesn't lead Jason to Blackstone's portal, then the Diviner will. You will follow their trail and wait. Of course, since they lack the genetic material, they will not be able to open the portal. The Diviner will be yours to feed the pyre, and Jason will be hanged for the governor's murder. Carrying out both executions simultaneously would create quite a spectacle, would it not?"

"Yes … it would." Orion stared in silence for a moment, giving Drexel an opportunity to touch the journal inside his tunic. Once Jason and Elyssa found the portal for him and were then taken out of the way, he would be free to use the genetic material he had collected to open the portal himself and enter Dracon. Then he would return with the Lost Ones, and his fame would spread beyond Mesolantrum. He wouldn't bother settling for the governor's office. He could be king of the domain and reside in luxury in the capital city.

Finally, Orion spoke in a low monotone. "How will Jason escape the dungeon?"

"Since we will lock the front entrance behind him, we expect the Diviner to lead him through the maze and out the back gate, which is why we left it unlocked for the time being."

"So you expect him to walk right into the forest with the witch at his side."

"Yes, Your Excellency, Governor of Mesolantrum." Drexel grinned. "You must enjoy the sound of it."

"Your sycophancy is naked, Drexel. Just make sure the plan works. That alone will garner my favor." Orion looked at Lady Moulraine again. "What are you going to do with Prescott's body?"

"I will let his wife decide. When Bristol returns in mere moments on his normal patrol, he will discover the murder and awaken her."

"And Prescott's son?"

"Bristol will take care of everything. Randall will be coaxed into joining a hunt for Jason, his father's presumed killer, and meet his own death in the process, which, of course, will also be blamed on Jason.

Randall will never reach the age of ascendancy, and you will remain governor."

Shaking his head, Orion sighed. "I am uncomfortable with all these deaths, Drexel. I just wanted one soul cast into hell, and now the toll is mounting. What if that madman's portal is just a dream? Maybe he deserved to be put away in the lunacy ward."

Drexel clasped Orion's shoulder. "If I may be so bold, Governor, I ask you to look me in the eye. You are a shrewd judge of a person's inner soul. I am risking everything, so I am either certain of the truth of these legends, or I am as mad as the one who concocted the wild stories."

Orion stared at him for a moment before looking away. "You are not mad. You are simply evil. And I see that you truly believe this, whether it is true or not. Yet, with all that you have learned of these legends, it seems strange that Blackstone never revealed the portal's location."

"He was counting on his son's memory, and failing that, the litmus finger is here to guide us."

"Yet the litmus finger is not part of the original legend." Orion stared toward the rear of the palace, as if looking beyond the wall. "What is your theory about the madman in the dungeon, the one who goes by the name Tibalt? He seems to know quite a lot about the legends. Wasn't Tibalt the name of Blackstone's son?"

Drexel laughed. "What crazy idea did he put in your head? That he knows where the portal is? He will say anything to get out of the dungeon."

"Yet, he makes me wonder. He recites intriguing poetry that belies our madman theory."

"Madman or no, I checked his birth records. He is not really Uriel's son. The elder Blackstone named at least six of his disciples Tibalt, and they all swore by that name until the day they died."

"Still, before I call up a search party, I would like to pay our Tibalt another visit. If he does know something, a bit of painful persuasion might convince him to provide some information."

"If it pleases you, Governor." Drexel gestured toward the door. "Now that we are in agreement, and I have your trust, shall we proceed?"

Orion sighed. "Trust is a fragile flower, Drexel. If I find that any part of this plan has gone awry, I will withdraw my support and go after the Diviner in my own way."

* EIGHT *

MARCELLE grasped her tunic. Particles of sparkling light clung to her and then spread out, like ice melting and forming pools of radiance. The pools transformed her skin and clothes into transparent blotches, and each one tingled, not painful, but buzzing, like the numbed sensation of a sleeping limb. Soon, the blotches merged, and her entire body disappeared.

Yet, her eyesight stayed clear. Only three steps away, Cassabrie's shining frame continued to spin slowly, and the collection tank, also covered with spreading blotches, remained in place, though the ground beneath it vanished, leaving a dark void.

Marcelle lifted her hand and set it in front of her eyes, but only the slightest glimmer appeared, an appendage with barely discernible fingers, each one just a two-dimensional outline drawn by strokes of light.

Soon, patches of skin grew on her hand, dirty and bloody, and sleeves covered her arm, still damp from rain and sweat. The tank rematerialized, as did the ground, but instead of muddy grass, a layer of white supported the metal cylinder from underneath.

Cold air filtered into Marcelle's senses, much colder than the stormy wind she had left behind. She turned and looked for Cassabrie, but she had not yet reembodied. Something was there, an outline, much like her light-sketched hand and fingers, nothing more than a wisp, yet it resembled Cassabrie's slender frame.

A few seconds later, Marcelle's surroundings came into view—a forest populated by firs and spruces, though considerably less dense than the previous woods. As she lifted and lowered her feet to test her legs, a blanket of snow crunched underneath. Ah! That explained the cold. But where was Cassabrie? Even the outline had vanished.

It was daytime here, perhaps midmorning or late afternoon. No surprise, really. After all, this was a different planet. Who could tell how its rotation compared to Major Four? The residents here might have very short or very long days compared to those back home.

Shivering, she pulled her bag from her back, set it on the snow, and opened it. With no one around, now would be the perfect time to add an extra layer, but she would have to put the dry tunic underneath.

She stripped off her shirt, threw on the fresh one, and buttoned it from bottom to top while bouncing in place. It was cold, too cold to do the same with her spare trousers. This would have to do.

After putting on the damp shirt, she reattached her bag and surveyed the area in more detail. Crystalline stakes encircled her, driven into the ground like tent pegs. They glittered in the scant sunlight, cast by a reddish ball floating above the horizon, a sun much like Solarus. Was it rising or setting? Time would tell.

Perhaps an hour's walk in the distance, a castle lay nestled in the recesses of a snowcapped mountain, apparently constructed from ivory-colored stone, except for three turrets on the third and highest level. From her vantage point, these appeared to be red, but the sun's rays might have skewed her perception.

A shadow passed overhead, large and winged. She looked up. A dragon flew toward her, diving down with its wings beating furiously.

Marcelle whipped out her sword. The dragon shifted to one side and smacked it away with his tail as he passed by. The sword flew into a snowdrift, and the dragon landed just beyond the circle of crystalline pegs.

As soon as his wings settled, he glared at her, gray smoke pouring from his nostrils. "Who are you?" he asked in a throaty rumble.

Marcelle glanced at her sword, too far to make a run for it. She set her hands on her hips, letting a finger touch the scabbard that held Darien's viper on the other side. "My name is Marcelle, and I am from Mesolantrum on Major Four."

His scaly brow bent downward. "Did Cassabrie allow you passage?"

"No. I forced my way through. We had a deal—"

"Do you often barge into abodes uninvited?" He took a step closer and extended his neck, bringing his head within five paces. "Or is your rudeness today reserved for a special occasion?"

Marcelle grasped the viper's hilt. "Come no closer, dragon, or—"

"Or what?" He took another step. "Has a great dragon slayer come to this land? Is the best Darksphere could send a dirty little woman who shivers like a frightened lamb?"

She glanced at her filthy clothes. "I am not just—"

"Are the men in your land all dead? Sick? Crippled? What plague or pestilence has brought about this devastation?" Two new lines of smoke burst from his nostrils. "Or are they all cowardly?"

She drew the dark blade and pointed it at the dragon. "Some are cowardly, to be sure, but those who are not, no matter what their gender, will do what it takes to secure freedom for all."

The dragon let out a low chuckle. "I will give you credit for verbal confidence, but it will take more than mere words and that little blade to slay me."

"I did not come here to slay you." She set her hand on the collection tank. "I came here to make sure payment for this gas tank is made in full."

"And I have come to ensure that what you delivered is what I purchased."

"So you're the dragon who arranged the gas deal."

"I am."

"And you sent Cassabrie to make the transaction?"

"I did."

Marcelle looked him in the eye. Obviously this was Arxad, but was she supposed to know his name? If he wanted her to know, he likely would have introduced himself when she told him hers. Maybe it would be better to stay quiet about it. "Where is Cassabrie now?"

A toothy smile spread across Arxad's maw. "Are you saying you cannot see the young maiden standing at your side?"

Marcelle tightened her grip on the hilt. The dragon's smile might have been designed to make her feel at ease, but it sent a wave of chills across her body. Still, her fear subsided. If Arxad wanted to kill her, he would likely have done it by now. "We tell jokes in our world," Marcelle said, "but they are usually accompanied by a wink or a nudge to the ribs."

"After watching humans, we dragons adopted the wink, but I am not telling a joke. I assure you, Cassabrie is near you at this moment."

"That's nonsense. She is as tall as I am, has red hair, and is wearing a white dress and blue cloak, or at least the dress was white until—" She thrust the viper back to its sheath. "Oh, I don't know why I'm telling you this. Of course she's not here."

"Very well. Believe what you wish. I must be about my business." He shuffled past her and stopped at the tank. As he studied it with his flashing red eyes, the end of his tail flicked back and forth, and his ears flattened.

Marcelle resisted shivering. The shed's remains had dried her pretty well, but the biting cold still penetrated her inadequate tunics and trousers. She would need to find shelter soon, and a thousand questions demanded to be asked. What is this place? What are those crystalline pegs? Where are the slaves? But it would probably be better to wait for this dragon to finish what he had come to do.

Arxad's head drifted back and forth in front of the valve—a three-foot-long pipe that extended from the tank's end and curved at a ninety-degree angle before ending at a nozzle. A small wheel was attached to the pipe at the bending point. "I assume I should turn this wheel to release the gas."

"Yes. Are you able to do that with your ... uh ... hands?"

"*Hands* is an adequate term for the clawed ends of my forelegs. We call them something else in our language."

"Your language?"

"Of course. Are humans on Darksphere so arrogant that they believe all creatures speak only their language?"

"I just thought—"

"No, you did not think. That is your problem." Arxad set his hands on the wheel and wrapped his claws around it. Grunting, he tried to turn it but to no avail. "It seems that my claws do not allow for a firm grip."

"Here," Marcelle said, reaching for the valve. "It was designed for human hands."

While Arxad kept his head hovering close, Marcelle grabbed the wheel and pushed her body into the effort. The valve turned, and a slow hissing sound emanated at the nozzle. Arxad set his snout close and sniffed the escaping gas.

"Extane is odorless," Marcelle said. "It is—"

"To humans, I suppose it is, as is pheterone." Arxad shot a tiny jet of flames from his mouth. The extane ignited, sending an orange and green plume of fire rocketing from the tank.

"Stop!" Marcelle lunged and shut off the valve, snuffing the fire. "What are you trying to do? Kill us?"

"I assumed you could close the flow." Arxad took in a long breath through his nose and exhaled. "It is definitely pheterone. The color of the flame, the distinctive flavor, and the invigorating effect prove it."

"Good!" Marcelle slapped a palm on the tank. "We did our part. Now you do yours."

"You mean allow your entry?"

"Exactly."

Arxad gave her a quizzical look. "I find your demand rather odd. You are already here."

Marcelle crossed her arms over her chest. "Not just me. I hope to bring two others."

"I see, but I fail to understand how they will help. Unless you can bring hundreds of warriors of larger stature, you are better off by yourself. In fact, your size and gender are beneficial for a stealthy operation."

Marcelle fought back an emerging scowl. The dragon's words were likely true, but his tone seemed condescending rather than helpful. "I left my compatriots in a dangerous situation. If they stay where they are, they will likely be captured or killed."

He averted his eyes, as if studying the sky. "That is not my concern."

"It should be. If they're captured, we won't be able to deliver any more gas."

Arxad let out a long humming sound. "I see your point."

"Then send Cassabrie back with me, and we'll bring them here."

His pointed ears flared and stood at attention, as if listening to a distant sound. His long neck carried his head slowly around until he looked directly at the castle. After a few seconds, he nodded and turned back to Marcelle. "I will send Cassabrie, but you must come with me."

"With you? Why?"

Arxad stared at her for a moment, his red eyes dimming for a brief second. "Because you will soon freeze to death. Your lips are already turning blue, a poor sign for human health."

Marcelle let herself shiver. Her teeth chattered as she replied. "How do you stay warm? I mean, you're … well …"

"Naked?" Arxad laughed. "Human modesty is charming. You even hesitate to say *naked*. I have always enjoyed that about humans, yet I have not fully understood the inconsistencies you display. Young children sometimes run around naked without shame, while adults stay fully clothed in public, and in the breeding rooms they often show great shame when exposed to one another."

Marcelle furrowed her brow. Breeding rooms? That would be another question to add to her list. For now, she had to press on. She really was about to freeze to death. "You didn't answer my question about staying warm."

"Oh. Yes. We dragons have a furnace of sorts within our bodies. We can create heat, even fire, and that keeps us warm. But, as you might expect, the price is a rapid consumption of energy. In cold weather I must take food quite often. That is why dragons live in warm climes."

"Warm climes?" she asked, her chattering now interrupting her words. "Do you … consider … this place warm?"

"When you come with me, you will understand." He lowered himself to his belly. "If you are as bold as you present yourself, I assume you will not be afraid to ride on me."

Marcelle surveyed the dragon's scaly back. With sharp, protruding spines, it looked like a thorny but manageable obstacle course. A flight, on the other hand, would be a breathtaking adventure, especially in the cold wind.

Forcing her teeth to stop chattering, she nodded. "I would find it exhilarating, but I have to be sure that Cassabrie is on her way."

"Very well." Arxad directed his gaze past Marcelle. "Cassabrie, you have my permission to fetch the other two humans. Tell them that I have taken their companion to the castle."

A glimmer of light appeared in the snow near the tank, as if reflecting the sunlight. The glimmer spread over a circular section about the size of two handbreadths, sparkling like diamonds. Then, in a flash, the light disappeared.

"She is gone," Arxad said. "Come. Climb up my scales. We must take flight."

Marcelle glanced back and forth between the dragon and where Cassabrie had been. "Can't we wait?"

"No. I do not wish for the other humans to see me. The fewer who know my identity, the better."

Marcelle looked him in the eye again. This was her proof. Obviously he didn't want her to know his name, so telling him that she, Adrian, and Edison already knew it might well cost them their lives.

After collecting her other sword, she grasped the edges of two scales, each the size of her hand, and, thrusting with her legs, vaulted up. She dodged the sharp forearm-length spines rising from the ridge down the center of Arxad's back and settled between two of the spines near the base of his neck.

"An excellent leap," Arxad said. "You are quite fit. I did not expect a free woman to be so strong."

Marcelle held on to the spine in front of her, hoping she wasn't violating dragon-riding protocol. As Arxad spread out his wings, she pondered his words. A free woman. That was what her mission was all about. The distractions with getting the gas tank, fighting Darien and company, and leaping into another world had squeezed the goal out of her thoughts. It was time to focus. She was here to rescue slaves, and by sword or by stealth, she would do it.

*　　　*　　　*　　　*　　　*　　　*

Adrian crouched with his father just behind the tree line and looked into the clearing. With the lantern off and the moon peering around the intermittent clouds, the grassy area came into view at intervals. Every few seconds a water-laden twig or a bristle cone fell, making Adrian snap his head toward the sound. Marcelle had been gone only a few minutes, not enough time for a new company of Prescott's soldiers to arrive. Still, that lone soldier might have chosen to follow and wait for a chance to strike while they weren't looking. They had to be cautious.

"Father," Adrian whispered. "I figured out who Darien was. Are you willing to talk about him?"

Edison just nodded, barely visible in the moonlight.

"How did it feel to cut his hand off?"

"Wicked." Edison drew in a long breath and let it out slowly. "Revenge was not my motivation, son, but it felt like revenge all the same. I had no remorse for the blow I inflicted. It felt wicked, indeed."

"He was a liar, a scoundrel. He deserved to die."

"No doubt, but I would have preferred that he not die by my hand. Revenge is not mine to deliver, and I regret it deeply."

Adrian let out a sigh, loud enough to communicate his sadness. Words were no longer necessary.

Edison pointed into the clearing. "I see something, a spark of light."

A lengthening glimmer emerged from the ground, as if a beanstalk of pure light had sprouted. As white as newly fallen snow, it expanded rapidly, forming a spinning aura.

Adrian set a hand on Edison's back and guided him into the grassy area. "Come with me," he said. "This is a sight you'll never forget."

As before, the aura took on a feminine shape, and excited particles buzzed within. Her cloak fanned out, and once again soil swirled into her body, thick and moist. When she had fully solidified, still barefooted, wet, and dirty, she looked around, her eyes blinking and her feet shifting as she regained her balance.

Adrian ran to her and pulled her into a brief embrace. Again she felt cold, too cold. When he pushed her back, he held her shoulders. "Where is Marcelle?"

She looked at him, still blinking. "Arxad took her to the king's castle. She is safe."

"And the gas?"

"It is pheterone. Arxad seemed very pleased. He is allowing your entry."

"Good." Adrian checked his sword and belt. "Let's go."

Cassabrie touched his shirt. "Marcelle seemed very cold there. Be prepared for a chill." With that, she spread out her arms and closed her eyes. The aura reappeared, expanded throughout the clearing, and swallowed all three of them.

Adrian laid a palm on his chest. The light felt warm and soothing, like bathing in a freshly filled tub. Again, flakes formed on Cassabrie's cheeks and forehead, but his closeness revealed more this time. Instead of debris from her surroundings, the flakes were composed of skin. As each one peeled off in the wind, her face thinned. Her hair pulled away from her head and joined the flakes in the growing swirl. Soon, her body dissolved completely, and only the aura remained.

Glancing between himself and his father, Adrian felt his mouth drop open. Their surroundings were disappearing, not crumbling as Cassabrie had, but rather fading away.

After a few seconds, only light stayed visible, so bright he closed his eyes to shut it out, but it wouldn't go away. Then, as quickly as the light had appeared, it fractured like glass and evaporated. Cold wind knifed through his clothes, making him shiver.

He scanned the area. His father still stood at his side, and the gas tank sat just beyond him, but Cassabrie was nowhere in sight.

Adrian swung his head from side to side. "Where did she go?"

Edison glanced around. "Could she have arrived before we did and run away?"

"I don't think she had time." Adrian looked at the ground. Snow lay in a thick blanket that stretched into a thin forest. "I see footprints, but they're not from bare feet. Maybe they're Marcelle's."

Edison followed the trail to the tank. "They end here. I also see animal tracks, something very large with claws."

"The dragon?"

"Perhaps. If the dragon took her to a castle, as Cassabrie said, then they must have flown. I see no sign of prints leading away."

Adrian looked toward the horizon. A mountain loomed about an hour's walk away, the sun gleaming on its snowy cap. A castle sat within a deep cleft, white with reddish trim, apparently an enormous structure, though the size of the mountain likely skewed the perspective.

"Well, I don't know what happened to Cassabrie," Adrian said, "but we had better start for the castle. We'll freeze if we wait."

A warm sensation crawled along Adrian's skin, like a summer wind. It penetrated deeper and deeper, funneling toward his chest until it seemed that his heart had caught on fire. He gasped and fanned his face with his hand.

"Son!" Edison called. "What is it? Your cheeks are as red as tomatoes."

He panted through his words. "I don't know. It's like I ate ten lava peppers, only worse." He pulled open the front of his shirt and let the air cool his body.

Edison drew closer. "There is something on your chest."

"Where?" Adrian looked at his skin. A dim light, about the size of a tithe coin, pulsed yellowish orange, like a summer firefly from the southern regions. As he watched, it grew until it doubled in size, as big as a hen's egg. The warmth in his body seeped toward that point and focused the scorching pain. The patch of skin emanated heat, warming his entire chest.

"A bee sting?" Edison asked. "I remember no such allergies in our family."

Adrian blew on the spot. Nothing seemed to help. "There's no swelling, and I didn't feel a—"

"Adrian!"

He swiveled, searching for the source of the voice. It sounded like Cassabrie.

Edison turned. "Did you see something?"

"Heard something." Adrian scanned the snowy blanket. No sign of Cassabrie. "Did you hear a voice?"

Edison shook his head. "Once when you were bitten by a spider, you said you heard ringing in your ears. Maybe it's—"

"No, I heard someone call my name."

As he concentrated on every sound—the wind rustling the laden firs, the ploof of snow falling onto deep drifts, and the twittering of distant birds—Adrian caught the melody of gentle laughter.

"Adrian," a voice broke in. "This is Cassabrie."

He searched the area around his body. It sounded as if she were standing right in front of him. "You heard it that time, didn't you? Cassabrie called my name."

"No, son. Birds and wind. Nothing more."

Cassabrie stretched out her words. "Adrian. I am speaking to you. Just talk to me."

"Cassabrie?" Adrian kept his gaze away from his father, feeling less than sane for addressing someone who wasn't there. "Can you hear me?"

"Better than ever," she replied. "I am now inside you. That's why you feel the warmth. It is my spirit, and I have taken residence in your breast. The glow is my mark."

Adrian looked at the glowing patch of skin. "Say something else, louder this time. I want to check something."

"Son," Edison said. "Are you talking to me?"

Adrian set a finger to his lips. "No, Father. Just a moment."

"Oh, Adrian," Cassabrie said in a motherly tone. "What must I do to get you to believe me?"

As she spoke, the patch grew brighter, as if measuring the volume of each word, or perhaps the passion in her mood.

Adrian pointed at his head. "Father, Cassabrie is speaking in my mind. She says she's inside me, and this glow is a sign that she's there."

Edison stared, his mouth ajar, then, with hesitant fingers, he touched the patch. "It seems that this world is full of surprises."

"Cassabrie," Adrian said. "What do we do now? Where do we go to find Marcelle?"

"Arxad flew with Marcelle to the castle. Should you choose to go, our journey will be more difficult than hers. We have no wings."

"And no suitable clothing," Adrian added.

"Son," Edison said. "Perhaps you could give me a short summary of her words. It is difficult to guess what she is saying."

Adrian looked at his father. "Marcelle is at the castle. We're talking about how to get there."

"Is that so?" Edison took a few steps toward the valley between the forest and the mountain and gazed at the castle. "Very difficult, I think."

Adrian joined him. Snow and ice covered the low-lying area, possibly concealing any number of obstacles. Lakes? A river? Ditches?

"Yes," Adrian agreed. "We could fall through the snow and end up at the bottom of a canyon."

"What does Cassabrie say about the terrain?"

Cassabrie's voice entered Adrian's mind again, this time in the tone of a teacher. "I am able to glide on top of the snow, so, of course, I cannot stumble. You, however, might have more trouble. I have seen the valley in seasons of thaw. The snow never completely melts, but those seasons allow a better view of what lies underneath. A narrow yet deep river winds like a serpent through the center of the valley. In these conditions, you will not know you have reached it until its waters chill your feet. Once you have passed this obstacle, I will tell you about another."

Adrian nodded slowly. "She says there's a river in that valley, a deep one."

Setting a fist on his hip, Edison studied the scene. His scant hair whipped across his scalp, and his gray eyebrows scrunched together. "I have an idea." He strode to the tank and set his palms behind it. "Give me a hand."

Adrian hurried to his father's side. They rolled the tank to the edge of the forest at the point the slope gradually turned steeper as it descended into the valley. After giving it a final shove, they watched it roll, pressing down the snow, bumping over rocks, and finally crunching through ice and splashing into the river. The tank turned on its end, like a ship ready to sink, but it stayed put, apparently locked by the surrounding ice.

"That worked perfectly," Adrian said. "Assuming you were trying to blaze a trail."

"That was exactly my intent." Edison snatched up a long branch and stripped off its protruding twigs. Then, using it as a walking stick, he marched ahead, calling back as he made tracks across the smooth path, "And now the tank is our way of crossing the river."

Smiling, Adrian followed in his father's footsteps. Having him along was a gift from above. His wisdom and experience would likely be a blessing time and again. Yet, how could the tank help them cross the river?

"You are both fine men," Cassabrie said. "Arxad will like you."

The warmth spread again throughout his body, this time a soothing warmth that carried no sting. He stayed a few steps back, hoping to keep his end of the conversation with Cassabrie private. "What I am, I owe to my father and the Creator."

"I'm glad to hear you speak of the Creator." Cassabrie's voice grew animated. "I heard you mention the Code earlier. What do you know about it?"

"Well … it's a book that tells us how to live life, and it was written by the Creator himself." He rolled his eyes upward, as if trying to look at her in his mind. "How do you know about the Code?"

"We have a copy of it, and we pass it around from family to family. Each person of age is assigned a passage to memorize. That way, if it gets confiscated by the dragons, we will be able to write it again."

"That's an excellent idea. I wish we had been so careful to guard its value. A full copy would be a treasure, indeed."

"Really? Your people are free. Why wouldn't everyone on Dark-sphere have his own copy?"

Adrian sighed. "Not as free as we would like. The governing authorities in our land gathered them all and burned every page. They sent armed soldiers who ransacked homes in search of them. I assume a few are still in existence, those that were hidden well, but if they are, no one breathes a word about it. Our governor has many spies. I have a partial page that I keep hidden, but even that would be enough to put me in the stocks for three days if he found out about it."

"Your governor fears the Code that much?"

"To be sure. He is loyal only to our nation and himself. Anything that might hold a greater authority than his own is certainly a threat."

"If you have no copies of the Code, then how do you follow its precepts? Do you have it all memorized?"

"Not so that I can quote it. I have listened to my father for so many years, it seems that it's ingrained in me, not the words, but its spirit." Smiling again, he touched the glowing patch on his chest. "I assume you can understand that."

A soft laugh rippled across his skin, again warming his body. "Being inside you is a pleasurable experience. I feel your nobility, your integrity, your love, especially every time you gaze upon your father. The spirit behind the Code has certainly made you a clean vessel."

This time heat radiated from Adrian's ears and cheeks. Having someone inside felt warm and good, but also more than a little bit uncomfortable. If she could feel his emotions, what might she think if something happened that aroused his anger, especially if he had to draw his sword for battle as he did against Darien and the other soldiers? If someone was in danger, holding back his emotions just to keep from offending her wouldn't be a good idea, but could he forget she was there and go to war with an unguarded mind?

After another minute or so, Edison reached the edge of the river and stopped in front of the tank. When Adrian caught up, he looked at the broken ice and the castle beyond, now a half hour away, assuming, of course, a path without obstacles. About three feet from the bank, the cylindrical tank sat upright with one flat end protruding from the water, its output valve visible at the top.

Jagged lines carved the ice between the shoreline and the tank, making the path appear fragile. Adrian stepped on the ice with one foot. A piece twice as long as his foot broke away and sank under his weight, forcing him to pull back. "It's too thin, and it's likely to be even thinner in the middle."

A cold breeze tossed Edison's hair again, but he didn't shiver. With his shoulders square, his cheeks red, and his eyes wide, he seemed alive, energized, animated. He was having the time of his life. "Think, son. The solution is staring right at you."

Adrian grinned. His father never failed to take advantage of a learning opportunity. "Okay, but we can't keep Marcelle waiting, especially in the company of a dragon."

✳ NINE ✳

AS Arxad descended toward the castle's front entry, Marcelle held on to the spine in front of her, hugging it with both arms. Even with her bag strapped on her back and two layers covering her torso, the wind still bit through, chilling her skin. Her bare hands felt like blocks at the ends of her arms, numb and stiff, and her feet had long ago lost any feeling. Teachers in training classes had warned of frostbite conditions and the need to amputate frozen toes to prevent a deadly infection. Could these feelings be a precursor to such on-the-field surgery?

She shuddered. Although accustomed to the sight of blood, lack of any experience as a battlefield soldier had left her squeamish about some things. Cutting off her own appendages was one of them.

The view below drew closer, a castle unlike any other she had ever seen. Every window stretched higher and wider than those in her own world, and, behind a gap in a row of ivory columns, the massive entry lay open to the outside air.

Stretching out his wings fully as he passed under the opening's arch, Arxad sailed inside, and the air suddenly turned warm. He landed in a brisk trot on a wooden floor, apparently designed for such draconic arrivals. Scratches marred the otherwise smooth surface, likely a soft wood designed to allow claws to dig in.

When he came to a stop, he spoke brusquely. "Get down." His words echoed in the cavernous hall.

Marcelle released the spine and slid down the dragon's scales, bending her knees to absorb the impact. She staggered for a moment as her numb feet responded to the weight, but she soon righted herself. She checked the two swords and the pack. Everything was in place.

Tilting her head upward, she surveyed the massive chamber. Ivory beams curved across a domed ceiling, leaving space between them for leaden glass embedded with colorful designs that made up an intricate work of art. Could it be a display of planets revolving around a central sun?

A giant fresco covered the wall opposite the entryway, composing an illustration of an empty throne—gold and bejeweled with red, blue, and purple gems. Even in the absence of direct sunlight, or any apparent source of light at all, the gems sparkled.

"Wait here," Arxad said. "I must inform the master of this house of your arrival. His servants will see to your comfort."

With a beat of his wings, he flew into an expansive corridor to the left, staying close to the floor, though there was plenty of room between him and the high ceiling. Again, light shone from somewhere, making his progress clear as he passed more illustrations on either side of the hallway.

A similar corridor lay to her right, darker and apparently just as large. Someone obviously designed this castle for dragons—plenty of room for wings and long necks.

She rubbed her hands together, trying to generate heat. Although the air was much warmer, her fingers had not yet recovered.

Walking while rubbing, she edged closer to the arched entry. With no doors to close, how did the room stay so warm? Wouldn't the breeze sweep in the wintry chill?

She stood under the arch and reached a hand across the boundary. Cold washed over her skin and ran up her sleeve, as if her arm acted as a conduit for the frigid air. As a stronger draft blew in, she jerked back, shutting off the flow.

How strange! An invisible barrier to the wind, yet easily penetrated. What other wonders might she find in this fascinating place?

"I assume you are Marcelle."

Marcelle stiffened. Who had spoken? A girl? Yet, no one was around. She turned toward the source but found only empty floor space.

"Hello?" Marcelle called. "Who said my name?"

"Oh, yes. I forgot. I have to be in motion." Like a shimmer on a pond, light rippled at the center of the wood floor, drifting in a tight circle. Although indistinct, the waves of light, soft and yellow, filled out a woman's shape. Her height and gentle curves made her look young, perhaps a teenager. "Can you see me now?" she asked.

Marcelle squinted. "I see a light in the form of a girl, but your face isn't clear."

The girl stopped. The ripples faded, making her disappear. "If I were to run or dance, you would see my face more clearly, but for now, maybe you will be able to recognize me by my voice."

As she spoke, a flow of sparkling light emanated from where her mouth should have been. The sparks vanished almost immediately, but their split-second presence gave away her location.

"What is your name?" Marcelle asked.

"Deference."

"Deference? I have never heard that name before."

The girl's voice inflected as a question. "You do not know what deference is?"

"I know the word, but I have never heard it used as a girl's name."

"I assumed it was a girl's name, because none of the boys wanted it. But if you think it's too masculine, maybe I should—"

"No, that's not what I mean. I haven't heard it used as anyone's name, neither male nor female."

"Oh." Deference stayed quiet for a moment. "Peaceable was my second choice. Do you like that? I will change it if it pleases you."

Marcelle sighed. "Deference is fine. I think it suits you perfectly. I hope you will pardon my ignorance of names here. I am from a faraway land."

"Yes, I know." The ripples of light returned, dipping up and down as if Deference had curtsied before vanishing again. "I am here to welcome you."

"Thank you." Marcelle offered a slight bow. Learning to curtsy wasn't part of her warrior training. "Where I come from, I am called a human. What might your species be called?"

"Oh, I am also human. I have merely lost my body."

Marcelle cocked her head. Deference had said this as if it were the most normal occurrence in the world. *I lost my body* was somehow the same as *I misplaced my hairbrush*. But if she really was human, might she be a slave here? Were the servants in this castle the humans they had come to rescue? This one didn't seem bothered at all by her servitude.

"So," Marcelle said, hoping the question in her mind wasn't too ridiculous, "do you know where you were when you misplaced your body?"

Deference laughed. "That's very funny. Misplaced my own body! Imagine that!"

As warmth flooded her cheeks, Marcelle decided not to explain her belief that *lost* and *misplaced* were practically synonyms. Being a visitor on this world meant that every step might introduce a new reality she couldn't possibly understand. She would have to learn slowly, be patient.

"I trust that you are warm enough now," Deference said. "Are you hungry? Thirsty?"

"Thank you for your kindness, but I am warm and not in need of food." For a brief moment, Marcelle wished she had asked for something, just to see how this being of light would serve it, but it was too late. "May I see more of this castle?"

"I wish I could show you everything, but I can't." Her voice stayed as cheery as ever. "Arxad said that you must wait here until he returns."

Marcelle nodded. "That's fine. I understand."

"You look very tired." Deference reappeared, walking into the darker corridor. As soon as she entered, the room brightened, as if illuminated by her presence. She set her hands behind a chair and pushed it into the vestibule, though her body never really touched the chair at all. Her hands seemed to hover behind the chair's back, maybe an inch or so of light waves separating it from her touch.

"There," she said, stopping the chair near Marcelle and disappearing once again. "We have only a few chairs for humans, and we keep them close to the entryway."

Marcelle pulled the bag from her back and sat down. "Thank you. Thank you very much." The chair's wooden seat was hard, not comfortable at all, but at least her legs would get a rest.

"If you have no need of anything else," Deference said, "I should be going. My king is waiting."

"Your king? Who is he? Arxad?"

"Arxad?" Her merry laugh sent a flurry of sparks into the air. "You really are a very funny person."

Marcelle laughed with her. Another joke. Who could have guessed that coming to this world would transform her into a comedienne? "I do have another question. If I am to be traveling soon, I need to understand your days and nights. Will it be dark soon?"

"Dark? It never gets dark here. We are on top of the world, always pointing toward the sun."

"I see," Marcelle said, tapping her chin. "An axis tilt. Major Four has no such tilt, but our astronomers have located other planets that do."

"Major Four?"

"Yes, that's the name of my planet."

"Oh, I see. Ours is called Starlight."

Marcelle's throat caught. "What did you say?"

"Starlight. That's our planet." Deference's tone shifted to one of concern. "Are you well? Your face has turned pale."

Marcelle laid a hand on her forehead. "Just a little dizzy. I'll be all right."

"Well, I hope I have answered your question."

"You have. Thank you."

Deference walked into the brighter corridor, waving her rippling arm. "Farewell, Marcelle." She laughed again. "That rhymes. Wonderful!"

"Farewell … Deference." Marcelle followed the girl's progress down the hall. Soon, she disappeared, as if swallowed by the light.

"Starlight," Marcelle whispered. A song from her childhood mentioned that name. Could it be a coincidence?

She set her bag on the floor, leaned back in the chair, and let out a long breath. Her legs ached, but her brain ached even more. What had she gotten herself into? Of course traveling to an alien planet was bound to bring surprises, but these mind-benders had caught her off guard. Even asking for explanations seemed a waste of time.

She looked at the bag. Inside lay the video tube that might lead to her mother's murderer, but it would surely drain her soul. Just imagining lifting it to her eye and turning it on brought a wave of nausea. It seemed impossible.

She closed her eyes. Just rest. It would all make sense soon, and her body needed to be ready for the next task. No use missing the opportunity to let her limbs regain a bit of energy.

Soon, a dream entered her mind, a replay of her recent battle with Darien, but this time when she stripped off his shirt and flipped him over, a series of long scratches striped his back. She looked at her fingers. Bloody skin caked each fingernail, red and dripping.

Nausea boiled again. She sat up, pressing a fist against her stomach and blinking away tears. She couldn't vomit. Not here. Not now.

"We have medicine for cramps."

Marcelle looked up. Arxad stood in front of her, his head bobbing at the end of his extended neck.

"I don't have cramps," she said. "I'm just feeling a bit queasy."

"Ah! Flight will do that, even to some dragons. Yet, you will have very little time to recover before your next journey."

"Next journey?"

"You came to liberate the human slaves, did you not?"

"I did, but the only human I have seen, at least she called herself human, didn't appear to need liberating. She's happier than most humans on my world."

"Deference is human, but she no longer has a human body. Her situation would take much too long to explain now, but she is not one of those you have come to set free."

"Who is this king she serves?"

"Again, I cannot take the time to explain. You do not need this information in order to complete your mission." Arxad unfurled his wings. "In order for you to find the people you have come to liberate, you will have to fly to lands south of here, to a warmer climate that you will likely appreciate. If your queasiness is not serious, we should go immediately."

Marcelle rose slowly from the chair. "What was the extane trade all about? Why did you want it?"

"Extane, as you call it, is a gas that dragons need to survive. Knowing that you have an ample supply on your world is beneficial. That is all I will tell you."

She gave him a skeptical stare. "I don't like the sound of that."

"I do not seek your approval." He lowered his body to the floor. "Now climb on again, and I will take you to your people."

"What about my traveling companions? Aren't we going to wait for them?"

"I have spoken to the king, and he said that you must go as soon as possible, and they will make the same journey later. Perhaps you will reunite in the southern region."

"Perhaps? That's not exactly comforting."

"Did you come here to gain comfort?" Arxad glowered at her. "I suspect that you will find none. In fact, I doubt that you will even survive. The forces against you are far stronger than you can imagine, and your puny poking sticks will be of little use against most dragons. If you escape our realm with your skin intact, I will be very much surprised."

Marcelle glanced at her swords. "Do you have a suggested strategy? Do we secretly bring the slaves here to transport them home?"

"This land is too distant. Such a journey would kill the young and the feeble. There is a second portal in the Southlands, but it is no longer operational. If you can restore its function and clear the obstacles in your way, you will have easy access to your world, but every step will be dangerous, as you will soon learn.

"Your friends will have a guide, and you can hope they find you later. Then you can decide on your course of action. But, no matter what you do, one part of the stratagem is crucial. You must never divulge that I have helped you. If any other dragon knew what you were doing, he would kill you without a second thought and without mercy. If it were known that I have brought you here, then my own life would be in jeopardy."

"I understand," she said, nodding. "You are our only dragon friend."

"Friend?" His eyes flashed, and a sharp growl punctuated every word. "I am *not* your friend."

A tremor rode up Marcelle's legs, but she steeled herself, keeping her stare fixed on the dragon's eyes. Something in his countenance gripped her heart. Passion? Resolve? Whatever it was, it carried no malice, just a steadfast purpose that would not be thwarted.

"Very well." She restrapped her bag to her back and climbed up the dragon's scales. After settling in her seat, she hung on to the spine with one hand. She closed her eyes for a moment and took in a deep breath. Could she really do this? If the slaves were unable to free themselves, what made her think she could do it with, as the dragon put it, poking sticks?"

Finally, she exhaled and said with the strongest voice she could muster, "I'm ready."

✳   ✳   ✳   ✳   ✳   ✳

"All we have to do," Edison said, pointing at the tank, "is to jump on and ride it to the other side."

Adrian studied the tilting cylinder. "Ride it? Are you sure it floats? Maybe it's just stuck in the ice."

"A gas tank like this will float when filled with air, and extane is slightly lighter than air."

Adrian touched his sword's hilt. "The ice is thin, but cutting it with a blade to make a path across the river could take all day."

"We're not going to cut it." Edison withdrew a pair of stones from his pocket and showed them to Adrian. Flint stones. "A good soldier never goes on a journey without a way to build a fire."

"You mean you're going to light the gas?"

"We'll tip the tank so that the valve shifts forward and points down." He tossed the walking stick toward Adrian. "Just push from the back with this."

Adrian caught the stick and looked at the tank again. "Are you sure it will support both of us? Balancing will be tricky. And besides, you can't swim. If you fall in, you'll sink like a stone."

"We'll go one at a time. If I fall, I can hold on to the tank." Edison pointed at him. "You cross first and shove the tank back to me.

With the ice cleared, it should float that far. If you can't throw the steering stick across this stream, then you're not the son I trained."

Adrian looked at the stick. This plan sounded feasible in theory, but nearly impossible in practice. "If you say so, but won't Arxad be upset if we use so much extane?"

"Perhaps. I'm not sure how much we will use, but I got the impression that he just wanted to sample it."

Cassabrie spoke up. "Your father is correct, Adrian. Arxad has already tested the gas and found it satisfactory. He requested the delivery for sampling only, so he has no further need of this tank."

"You're right," Adrian said. "Cassabrie tells me the dragon is finished with it."

Edison rolled the flint stones into Adrian's palm. "Good luck, son."

Adrian stared at the angular reddish stones, each about the size of two knuckles. This idea sounded impossible, but what other choice did they have? With Marcelle in that dragon castle, they had to cross the river somehow.

Gripping the stones in one hand and the walking stick in the other, Adrian ran and leaped onto the tank. With a loud crunch, it broke through the ice and sank to within inches of the top where he stood. Using the stick to balance, he rode out the bobbing motion. When it finally settled, he lowered himself to a crouch, tucked the stick in his lap, and turned the valve wheel.

A hiss rose above the sound of wind and crunching ice. Adrian pushed the stones into the extane flow and struck them together. A spark flew from the contact point and instantly ignited the gas. A bright orange and green flame shot out, pointing to his right.

Now all he had to do was spin the tank about ninety degrees toward the front and shift his weight just enough to push the flame close to the ice. He and Jason had balanced on logs floating on the Elbon River, sometimes on the same log as they tried to throw each other off, but this oddly shaped tank wouldn't be as predictable … or stable.

Standing fully and taking in a breath, he looked at his father. Edison's gray eyebrows twitched, and his chapped lips moved silently. Was he nervous? Praying?

The wind blew harder, making Adrian cold for the first time since Cassabrie entered his body. His ankle throbbed, worse than ever. This idea now seemed more impossible than ever. What had possessed him to believe that crossing the river in this way made any sense at all?

"Adrian," Cassabrie said. "What is this feeling I detect? Fear? Doubt?"

He mumbled his reply. "A sudden burst of common sense."

A frigid gust knocked him off balance. He teetered, waving the stick wildly with one hand.

"Son!" Edison shouted as he waded in. "Reach the branch toward me!"

Adrian toppled to the far side of the tank and crashed through the ice. As soon as he sank, the ice shifted and trapped him underneath. He shivered so hard, his teeth ached. Cold! Mind-numbing cold!

Flailing, he thrust his body upward and hit his head on the solid roof. A death trap. Pain shot through his spine. His limbs numb, he sank deeper.

"Adrian!" Cassabrie shouted. "Do not despair. I have called for help."

As his feet touched bottom, a thin stream of thoughts trickled through his mind. *Hold your breath. Father can't swim. Don't try, Father. Don't try. Cold. So cold.*

A veil of blackness flooded his mind. Holding his breath no longer mattered. His chest seemed frozen, unable to draw in anything. Was he still underwater? Yes. So wet. So cold. How long had he been here?

A sharp pain in his neck sent a jolt from head to toe. A sudden upward pull seized his body, followed by a splash and a blaze of light.

He opened his eyes. The blistering wind snapped his mind awake. He was flying! Below, his father lay on his back in the snow, shivering, and the extane tank sat beside him, blowing its flame just over his body.

Adrian looked up. A huge white creature carried him, too big and close to see clearly. A pair of clawed forelegs curled under its chest, but its head stayed out of sight. Wings whipped the air, and, flying in a slow circle, Adrian descended toward his father. His feet touched the ground gently, allowing him to stand. Seconds later, a white dragon landed in front of him.

Adrian pushed his stiff legs and staggered toward his father. After getting what appeared to be a safe distance from the dragon, he stopped and called out, "What … what do you want from us?"

"Get close to the fire," the dragon said. "I will gather wood for you."

"Are you …" Adrian could barely push words through his frozen lips. "Are you the dragon who wanted the extane gas?"

"I am not." The dragon waved a wing toward the tank. "Warm yourself, or you will soon perish."

Adrian set his hands on his father's soaked and shivering chest, allowing the jet of flames to warm his fingers. His teeth chattered so hard he could barely speak. "You … you rescued … him?"

"I did. Although he was valiantly trying to save you, he would never have survived. And when I tried to snatch him from the river, he fought me. That is why you had to wait so long for your deliverance."

"Th … Thank you!"

As the dragon nodded, his blue eyes shone. He lifted effortlessly into the air and flew over the forest.

"Father!" Adrian called. "Can you hear me?"

With his eyes tightly shut, he sputtered, "You're … you're alive!"

"Shhh." Adrian brushed ice crystals from his father's brow and began stripping off his shirt. "We'll be warm soon."

From the corner of his eye, movement caught his attention. He looked toward the castle. A dragon flew from between the center columns and lifted high into the air. As Adrian's body shook, his vision shook with it. Could that dragon be Arxad? Someone rode on its back. Was it a woman? In the blur, it seemed that long hair streamed behind the rider, but nothing was clear. After a few seconds, the dragon and its rider faded in the distance.

As soon as Adrian managed to get his father's arms out of his sleeves, the white dragon returned, clutching a bundle of sticks in each of four claws. He deposited them next to Adrian and landed several paces away. "You must work quickly," the dragon said. "Your father's light is dimming."

Adrian rose on his aching legs and picked up a handful of sticks. As he set them in the gas flame, he looked at the dragon. "Can't … you use … your fire breathing?"

"I do not breathe fire."

The dry sticks caught the flame. Adrian staggered to the pile of wood and set the ignited sticks underneath. Slowly, the flame crawled from one twig to the next. Adrian held the kindling sticks in place until the pile began to crackle greedily. Then, he shut off the gas and dragged his father closer to the growing blaze.

With his chest bare and his shirt and arms dragging underneath, his father felt like a corpse, except for his constant shaking. Once Adrian laid his father as close to the fire as he dared, he stripped off his own shirt and lay with him chest to chest. Ice crystals in his father's nest of gray hairs popped and melted, wetting their contact point, and the aging man's body continued to shake violently.

Adrian pushed his arms around his father, pressed close, and breathed heavily, trying not to cry. Father couldn't die. He just couldn't.

Cassabrie's voice entered his mind. "You are a noble son, Adrian. I will see what I can do to add to your love."

The patch on his skin throbbed, again spreading heat across his chest. Adrian cringed. The stinging pain bit hard, but it didn't matter. Cassabrie's warmth helped.

The fire began to roar. Warmth radiated across their bodies, a glorious sensation that dried their clothes and drew sweat from their pores.

After a minute or so, Adrian rose to his knees and grabbed a pair of sticks that had not yet caught fire. He plunged their ends into the ground and hung his and his father's shirts on them to dry.

Again Cassabrie spoke. "It is time to speak to the king, is it not?"

"The king?" Adrian sat down and looked at the dragon. He had backed away several more paces from the fire but still sat close enough to listen.

"Yes. He is Lord of the castle and King of the Northlands. When I called to him, he rescued you."

Adrian glanced at the castle. "How could he hear you from that far away? And how could he get here so quickly?"

"The king watches. He knows. He waits for our call, a shout from the heart, a cry from the bosom. The appeal ignites his fire."

"But he said he has no fire."

"Not so, Adrian. He said he doesn't *breathe* fire. There is a difference."

He lowered his voice to a whisper. "Can I ask him questions?"

"Whatever you wish, but I have learned that he doesn't always answer in the way I expect."

"What is his name?"

"He reveals his name only to those he chooses, but you may call him 'my king' or 'gracious king' or whatever suits you."

Adrian looked at his father. His body had stopped shaking, and color had returned to his cheeks. His chest rose and fell in a steady rhythm.

Turning to the dragon, Adrian offered a polite nod. "O King, may I ask you something?"

The king nodded in return. "You may."

"Do you know why we are here?"

"I do."

The dragon's head tilted, and his triangular ears rotated. He seemed to be asking his own silent question, something like, "Why wouldn't you know that I know?"

Staying seated, Adrian shifted his weight from side to side. He felt like a child asking questions of a scholarly professor. "So do you understand that I intend to rescue my people from your own kind, even if I have to engage them in battle?"

"I know your mission better than you do, and what I consider my *own kind* likely differs from your interpretation of those words."

Adrian let the dragon's reply percolate in his mind for a moment. It was obviously meant as a riddle of sorts, something he would have to figure out later. "Arxad told us to go to the castle, but I think I saw him flying away a little while ago."

"You did. Yet, I wonder how you learned his name. He did not want you to know it."

Adrian looked down at the melting snow. The dragon didn't really ask how Arxad's name was revealed. Maybe he wasn't expecting an answer. "So," Adrian said, drawing a line in the slush with his finger, "what are we supposed to do now?"

"Ah! An excellent question, but one that is best answered after you learn more about this land."

Adrian waited for the king to continue, but he just stared with his flashing blue eyes.

"Well," Adrian prompted, "what do we need to learn?"

"I will tell you only the essentials now, and you will learn much on your own later, for experience is a far better teacher than words alone." The king looked in the direction Arxad had flown. "The souls you wish to rescue live to the south. I cannot leave my realm at this time, and Arxad will not return for a few days, so you have no air transport. Therefore, you will have to devise your own method of getting there." He let out a merry chuckle. "I advise, however, that you refrain from riding on gas tanks, though I am gratified that the incident brought about our meeting."

New warmth flowed in Adrian's cheeks. This mission to find the Lost Ones was proving more embarrassing than exhilarating. "My father is still unconscious. Do you know if he will be able to make the journey?"

The dragon extended his neck, bringing his head closer to Edison, but still several feet away. "He is feverish. I have servants who will nurse him back to health, but it will likely take more than a day or two."

"But Marcelle is already gone. I need to—" Adrian bit his tongue. Did this dragon already know about her?

"You need to help your friend right away," the dragon said. "I agree. If you set out immediately and leave your father with us, she and the Lost Ones will benefit greatly."

"You know we call them the Lost Ones?"

The dragon's white scales seemed to brighten, as if his emotions shone through them. "Your passionate thoughts are particularly loud, human from another world."

Cassabrie giggled.

Again Adrian's cheeks flushed hot. Having an indwelling girl and a huge white dragon reading his mind was more than uncomfortable. He had to shake it off and concentrate on the task at hand. "How will I find my way?"

"Cassabrie will guide you. She has not been in the Southlands for a long time, so she is eagerly anticipating the journey. Is that not true, Cassabrie?"

She spoke into Adrian's mind. "It is true, O King. Although it is a pleasure to serve you, I long to see my people again."

As the dragon nodded, Adrian focused on the source of Cassabrie's voice. Since it seemed to come from inside his brain, how could the dragon hear what she said?

"And Cassabrie," the king prompted.

"Yes?"

"Remember the reason I have commissioned you as Adrian's guide. It will be difficult and heartrending, but you are the only one who is capable. No matter what happens, you must never forget your purpose."

"I understand." Her voice seemed quieter, more somber. "I will obey."

"Now, Adrian," the dragon continued, "I will take you to my home. My servants will feed you and your father, and they will provide you with all you need."

Adrian raised his eyebrows. "Will we ride on your back?"

"Do you have other means?"

"No, but I was wondering about something. If there really is no way to reach the castle without air transport, then why did you not send Arxad to come and get us?"

The dragon drew his head closer and gave Adrian a piercing stare. "Why do you think?"

As Adrian looked into the dragon's eyes, odd questions bubbled in his thoughts. Did the crazy river-crossing scheme come to his father's mind for a reason, an idea devised by the king to bring about this meeting? Was Cassabrie's ability to enter a person's body similar to this thought infusion? Maybe that was the way things worked in this world—influences and voices could meld into the minds of willing listeners.

Not only that, a new realization merged with his questions. For years, dragons were the demonic enemy, the evil captors of innocent humans, slave drivers who needed to submit or die, and now the first dragon he had ever met seemed to be kind and trustworthy, a far cry from the dark visage the legends had painted.

"I think," Adrian said slowly, "that I have a lot to learn."

"You are a wise young man indeed." The dragon waved toward his back with a wing. "Please climb on, and I will carry your father underneath. Since he is unconscious, he will not be uncomfortable."

Adrian rose again. This time, his legs felt more limber. After putting shirts back on himself and his father, and warming his hands again near the dwindling fire, he scaled the king's ivory body. Delicate streaks of red ran across his scales, like a network of thin blood vessels, invisible until examined at close range.

Once on the dragon's back, Adrian looked around for something to hold, but the scales lining the backbone pressed so close together, the gaps between them were too small. He would just have to lean against the dragon's body and ride out the bumps, but after the tank ordeal, his confidence in his balancing abilities had sunk pretty far. Still, excitement surged. After all the stories about dragons, actually riding on one was like a dream come true.

Of course, the legends said that dragons had spines along their backs as well as fiery breath, so the fact that this dragon had neither came as a surprise. Yet, that didn't matter. The talebearers of today had no way of knowing the truth, and battling the dragons that enslaved the Lost Ones would be easier this way. No fire-breathing meant no incineration. Who could complain about that?

As they rose into the air, Adrian watched the fire, now shrinking in the distance. With an alabaster wing beating at each side, and snow and ice blanketing every inch of ground, the scene looked like a white canvas with a spattering of paint here and there. Splotches of blue appeared along a serpentine line where the river's ice had broken, and the tops of green trees protruded in forest pockets. What a beautiful sight to behold!

He leaned over, trying to see his father, but with nothing to grasp, he quickly straightened, again locking his palms against the scales. He would just have to trust the dragon, a concept that seemed improbable only minutes ago—a dragon with integrity and nobility.

Cold wind tore through his clothes, raising a chill and a bitter bite. As if on cue, Cassabrie spoke into his mind. "Would you like some heat?"

"If it causes you no pain or discomfort."

"On the contrary, providing warmth for you is a pleasure."

Starting with a mild sting at the center of the skin patch, heat spread across his chest again. Ahhh! It felt so good, like a steaming bath after hauling firewood on a winter's day. Yet, there was more. There was Cassabrie. Her presence. With every pulse of warmth, it seemed that she breathed with him, as if his body fed her sustenance, and her emotions bled into his. Her love flowed with her warmth. She infused his being with her passion for life, as if her loss of a body no longer mattered. Her spirit now had a place to reside, and all her longings—walking, dancing, and basking in sunshine—could be realized in the muscles, bones, and skin of another. Maybe that's what she meant by pleasure.

"Cassabrie?" he whispered.

"Yes?"

"What would you like to do? I mean, what would you like to do through me?"

For a moment, she stayed silent. Then, as the warmth pulsed ever hotter, her voice returned, broken by emotion. "Can we ... can we spread our arms and feel the glory of the wind?"

Adrian looked at his hands, still pressed on the scales. As he lifted them and stretched out his arms, heat radiated to the tips of his fingers, and with it, pleasure—pure joy, exhilaration. Cassabrie was flying.

He closed his eyes. Tears flowed. He laughed out loud, not his own laugh but rather hers. Soon, his own joy blended in. He and this lovely girl flew together, she on the back of her beloved king and he on a newly found trust. Both had discovered the joy of fusion—hearts and minds once separated, now acting as one. And the ecstasy could be expressed in only this way—tears, laughter, and outstretched arms.

✴ TEN ✴

MARCELLE looked down at the scene below, interrupted every few seconds by the dragon's slowly beating wings. Mile after mile of landscape flew by. The blanket of snow thinned and vanished, replaced by an artist's masterpiece—high ridges of green trees and amber stone spilling blue waters into valleys of emerald grass, sprinkled with flowers of gold, crimson, and sapphire. Breathtaking!

The air lost its biting cold, allowing her to enjoy every moment. What change the last hour had brought! She had leaped from her familiar world and landed in a realm of strangeness. She had come with two swords, ready to skewer dragons, and now she rode atop one of her targets. She expected to find humans much like herself, but instead met a shining vapor of a girl. Such oddities belonged in dreams, not in waking reality.

An hour passed, then two. The sun hovered low, casting the sky in dimness. Had evening arrived, or had they simply passed into lower latitudes where darkness had already begun falling? Arxad flew on, never changing direction. Below, the vibrant colors faded, leaving only hints of the spectrum in stony outcroppings and thin forests.

Near the southern horizon at a somewhat higher elevation, a wall snaked from one side of her view to the other, too far away to tell how high it rose, especially in the waning light, but it had to be massive to be seen from such a distance. Beyond that, a river ran from somewhere out of sight down to the wall, but there was no sign of it exiting on the near side.

"Hold on," Arxad said. "Secrecy demands that we descend quickly. You will feel a sudden loss of weight, and the lower air levels will become increasingly warmer."

Marcelle wrapped both arms around the spine. During the flight, she had gained the courage to ride without hanging on at all, but now it was time for a different kind of courage. The real adventure was about to begin.

As Arxad folded in his wings, he tipped forward and dropped. Marcelle's bottom lifted from his back. She squeezed his body with her legs and swallowed as her stomach rose toward her esophagus. The warm air buffeted her face, whipping her hair and clothes. The bag with the video tube thumped against her back, and the swords flared out like a pair of wings, making her belt ride up her waist.

She reached back and held the bag in place. The tube had to survive, at least until she had a chance to view it.

As the ground zoomed toward her, Marcelle blinked away tears. The wind's friction stung terribly, but at this rate, the ride would be over in seconds.

Finally, Arxad fanned out his wings. They caught the air and billowed. Marcelle slammed against his back, making her grunt, and the swords clanked against his scales.

When he hit the ground, a series of thumps shook her body. Finally, Arxad slowed to a halt near a copse of gnarled trees and rested on his belly. "Dismount quickly on my left side." His voice was low, though not quite a whisper.

Marcelle moved the swords to safe positions, slid down his scales, and landed upright. Her knees buckled for a moment, but she managed to keep her balance. "From whom are we hiding?" she asked, trying to match his volume.

His head swung toward her. "Did you see the wall?"

She nodded.

"The wall surrounds the dragon empire, and we are on the outside. Sentries are stationed there, dragons selected for their keen eyesight. They are charged with not allowing anyone, dragon or human, to cross the boundary from either direction. Although evening is descending and detection is less likely, I wanted to conceal you by landing at this distance."

"If no dragons are allowed, then how will you—"

"A dragon priest is the only exception," he growled, his red eyes flashing. "Now I must go. Even if they cannot see you, they might be able to see me, and I do not wish to explain why I have tarried here. Although I have permission to come and go, this liberty is tenuous."

"But how do I get across?"

As he drew his head back, his long neck formed an S shape. "I assumed your people would send skilled trackers and warriors. Freeing your people is your purpose, not mine. I kept my promise to allow your entry into our world, and now you will have to manage on your own."

"How do I find the other portal?"

"How, how, how," Arxad said, his tone growing irritated. "Again, they are your people, your mission, but I will tell you that you must search the mines. If you are skillful enough to pass the wall safely, you will soon learn what I mean." He waved a wing toward the trees. "Now hide there until you decide what to do. I must leave immediately."

As he unfurled his wings, Marcelle ducked low, ran into the copse, and huddled among the short, stubby trees. She watched the dragon from behind a skinny trunk with multiple bends, not exactly a good hiding place.

Arxad pushed off the ground with his rear legs and vaulted skyward, his wing beats sending gusts of air and sand into her face.

She blinked away the grit. The reddish brown dragon lifted higher and higher, rising in a tight circle before straightening and heading toward the wall. Soon, he appeared to be no more than a paint splotch, an artist's mistake on the canopy of pristine violet.

After backing deeper into the copse, Marcelle stood upright, set her hands on her hips, and stared in the direction Arxad had flown. Now what? Should she wait for Adrian and Edison? Arxad had said they would be told about her drop-off point, but they could be delayed by hours, maybe longer. Wouldn't it be better to scout the wall to see where its weaknesses might be?

To her left lay a broad open expanse—stony ground with sparse vegetation, a few solitary trees here and there and some tufts of wiry grass—certainly not a good choice for a stealthy approach. To her right, the wooded area widened into a forest, still somewhat sparse, but likely enough to cover her.

A slight tinkling rose above the diminishing breeze. Running water? She followed the sound, glancing in all directions. Leaves and needles littered the ground, preventing any footprints, but every step raised a crunch. If anyone haunted this desolate region, surely her noise would alert him ... or it ... to her presence. Approaching nightfall wouldn't hide her if she kept raising a racket.

After a minute or so, the sound led her to a stream spilling from a fissure in a cliff face. The stair-stepped wall of dark rocks rose to at least three times her height, and water poured from about halfway up, cascading to the level where she stood and down a pebbly creek bed, about as wide as a running leap.

Using her hands along with her feet, Marcelle scrambled up, bypassing the water's exit, and peered over the top of the cliff. A meadow of dry grass began here and extended to the wall, too open to walk across without being seen, except maybe by night, but the darkest hours had not yet arrived.

She rotated, then sat on the cliff's second step from the top, now facing away from the wall. Could the sentry dragons see in the dark? Probably. What good would it do to guard a wall that could be approached without notice during the night hours? Still, with darkness as her ally, a low crawl through the grass might work.

She looked at the sky. Evening was giving way to night. Maybe it would be better to rest here and see how dark this world's night would get.

She took off her bag and belt and lay on the rocky step. As tired as she was, falling asleep would be easy, yet potentially dangerous. The sound of running water could mask the approach of an enemy, or she might roll off the step as she dozed. Her battle training had made her a light sleeper, but exhaustion could easily hold sway, even if a hundred roaring dragons descended from the sky.

Closing her eyes, she let out a sigh. She would have to take the risk. She was a warrior, and warriors took risks. Still, taking a risk by leaping out and going with Cassabrie to this world seemed pretty stupid after the fact. Now she wandered alone in a world of dragons with only a shadow of a hope that Adrian would join her. She couldn't rescue the slaves by herself. Who would rally behind a woman, especially a woman in trousers who too often let her sword speak for her? She was foreign to her own people at home, probably much more so to the slaves here.

She slid her hand over the hilt of her sword. How many times had she acted on passion? How many times had she chosen boldness over caution? Glory over incognita? Would she ever change? Would she ever learn to be more like Adrian?

As his name came to mind, the image of their recent non-battle came with it. He stood in the tourney ring, his face beginning to flush as he made ready to forfeit once again. Surely he must have battled within his heart far more fiercely than in any tournament bout. He gave up any hope of glory and instead chose shame, not only for himself but also for his family. Would he have won? Probably. His victory over Darien proved that. He was stronger and quicker, and they both knew it. Yes, even before tonight.

Yet, why did he forfeit? Chivalry wasn't that important, was it? Adrian and his family were the only men in Mesolantrum who practiced it. Well, there was also Noonan, the barkeeper's son, but he did it to steal hearts, not to protect them. Since the Masters family practiced chivalry in isolation, no one understood, so no one scolded those who laughed at them. The Masters were just those old-fashioned folk who lived in days-gone-by, taught by a stubborn old soldier who never escaped from his past.

She exhaled loudly. Lying here under a foreign sky seemed to change everything. Two Masters men stood as her only hope. Now they appeared to be far more than relics. They were true warriors— men of valor who protected both body and heart.

Marcelle let her thoughts drift away from her troubles. For now, she had to sleep. Maybe it would be dark when she awakened, and maybe a new chance to make the right decision would present itself. Either way, rest had to come first. The slaves needed her body functioning properly even if her brain coughed and wheezed. At least she could give them that.

As she lay still, an image appeared in her mind, her mother's face, pale and with eyes closed. Her dead body lay on a wheeled table, wrapped from neck to feet in white linen. Family members stood around, including herself at her mother's side, each one holding a long candle with greenery encircling the base. With her hair down to her shoulders, clean and shiny in the light of the candles, she wore a long black dress with sleeves reaching to the heels of her hands.

Although half asleep, Marcelle recognized the scene, her mother's funeral day. As the dream played out, her mind entered the girl's body and saw everything through her eyes.

The candle's wax dripped through the leaves and stung her skin. Marcelle dared not flinch. Let it stay there. Let it burn. Let God punish me for my slowness. If I had chased after her instead of running for help like a scared kitten, I could have stopped him … that man, that wicked man. I would have scratched his eyes out, and he would be the one wrapped in sheets, not Mother.

The mortician laid a white cloth over her mother's eyes. Father handed Marcelle his bamboo pipes, the mouth organ he had crafted as a boy. She stared at it for a moment, the holes at the ends of the reeds, the cloth strap for draping around the neck, and the insignia engraved in the band holding the reeds together, their family emblem, a dove in flight.

She glanced at Adrian. He stood with his family in the line of mourners, bravely holding back tears. He wouldn't provide a rhythm this time. She had to do this alone.

As she raised the pipes to her lips, a song flowed into her mind—*the* song—the melody and words that called her to play for this occasion. Her father had encouraged her not to burden herself with such a heavy weight, but she had insisted. The world must listen to Mother's tune once again. Although no one would hear the words she always sang while rocking Marcelle gently in front of the communal fire, she and Father would hear them in their hearts, and today, that would be enough.

She played the beginning note. Immediately, Father began to hum along, and the lyrics flowed freely through her mind.

Starlight I see at night beyond my mortal view
Daylight revives my sight and wakens me anew
O let me dream of homeland's shores awaiting my return
O let me fly in skies so high and let my passion burn

The chains of death I toss behind and run to catch the wind
The chains of breath I now embrace and fill my lungs again
To sing of starlight, take me back to set my people free
So they can breathe the air I found, the love 'tween you and me

When she lowered the pipes, she looked at Father. Tears rolled down his cheeks. She checked her own. Dry, as she expected. No more tears. She was empty, just a shell.

Two men pushed the table out the door and into the evening air. Holding hands with her father, Marcelle followed, feeling the dress brushing against her legs as she stepped in time with the men in front.

After several minutes, they arrived at a grassy field. A hole lay open at the nearer end, too wide for leaping across and much too long, a communal plot Mother would share with several others. The men halted the table at the edge of the hole and stood at each end, their hands folded at their waists.

"We must say good-bye," Father whispered. He removed the covering from Mother's face. "Take as much time as you need."

Marcelle stood over her mother's body. She gazed at her pale, gray face—stoic, yet peaceful, as she always looked when she was asleep.

As she stared, the color returned to Mother's cheeks. That was it. She was asleep, swooned after a long illness that had drained her blush. Now she would awaken and take her loved ones into her arms again. She would sing in front of the fire about starlight and freedom and the chains of breath. Rainbow twilights would return in all their joy.

She laid a hand on Mother's cheek. "Wake up, Mother," she said out loud. "This nightmare is over. Father and I want to go home now. I will cook dinner, so you can rest a while longer. And soon we will sing together and laugh again. We will—"

"Marcelle."

She turned. Father stood behind her, his cheeks again wet. She gave him the biggest smile she could. "Father, see? She was sick, and now we need only awaken her. We can take her home and—"

"Marcelle, no!" Father took her hand and pulled her gently away. "Mother is dead," he said softly. "We talked about this already. She will not awaken until the angels call her name."

Her lips trembling, she looked at him hopefully. "Let us try to awaken her now, and we will see. She always called me her little angel."

He grabbed her upper arms and looked her in the eye. "Listen to me! A wicked man murdered her. You were there. You saw him drag her away to her death. She will not awaken for you or anyone else in this world. From now on, you and I will have to live without her."

He pulled her close to his chest. His body quaked, and his hands trembled as they rubbed her back. "Dearest one, you and I will again hear her song, but until that day, we have to live in this world. We have to let them put Mother into that hole. We have to say good-bye."

With her cheek pressed against his body, she glanced at Mother out of the corner of her eye. The color in her face had faded back to ashen. Tears trickled down the cheeks of the two men as they continued waiting. She turned her head to see Father's sister and three brothers. They, too, wept.

Marcelle pulled back and looked up at her father. "You say good-bye. I have something to do." Then, she grabbed Adrian's hand and, running as fast as her legs would carry her, she dashed with him toward the commune. Along the way, he mumbled a half-hearted protest but kept up without further prodding.

Once inside, she led Adrian to his bedroom and set her hands on her hips as she panted for breath. "Do you have any trousers that no longer fit?"

He looked at her, his eyes wide. "I think so. Mother is saving them for Jason."

"Get them. When Jason's old enough, I'll give them back."

Adrian hustled to a closet, rummaged through it, and came out again with a pair of trousers. "Here."

She snatched them out of his hand and ran to her family's side of the commune. Now in the bedroom she shared with Father,

Marcelle yanked the dress over her head and threw it to the floor. She pulled the trousers on, buttoned the fly, and looked in an oval mirror propped on a stand. Wearing a camisole for a top, she flexed her bare arms, skinny and pale.

Anger boiled within. Like a cooker loaded with steam, the pressure built up, higher and higher. Finally, she picked up the dress and threw it at her reflection, shouting, "No!"

Marcelle shot to a sitting position. The mirror disappeared along with the bedroom. The darkness of twilight had returned. It was all a dream.

She grasped her bicep, muscular and tight. She moved her hand to her thigh, toned and strong. Then, she touched her cheek. Dry.

Lying back, Marcelle looked up at Starlight's darkening sky. The tune she had piped at the funeral played again in her mind, and she sang the final words.

To sing of starlight, take me back to set my people free
So they can breathe the air I found, the love 'tween you and me

As the last word trickled out, a sob followed. Tears flowed, dampening both cheeks. "Mother," she whispered, "when I find your killer, Father and I will sing your song again."

✳ ELEVEN ✳

STANDING at the river's edge, Adrian looked back at the castle. Father lay inside on a feather mattress, warm and cozy. Apparently, he had struck his head on the ice, and the dragon didn't know how soon he would be well. Still, he breathed easily and displayed no obvious signs of trauma. Not only that, three unusual attendants saw to his comfort, among them a delightful young lady named Deference who spoke of Marcelle's brief visit.

Conversing with a person who became visible only with motion took some getting used to, but after she followed his suggestion to sway as they talked, their discussion became rather entertaining. Also, learning that Marcelle had gained airborne conveyance to the Southlands made him feel at ease. Now he just had to find her.

After drying himself and his clothes in front of a roaring fire, he bundled together a thick cloak the king had bestowed. It felt good to be so warm.

"So, Cassabrie," Adrian said, pressing a toe into the riverbank's icy surface, "shall we be on our way?"

"At your pleasure, Adrian." A soft laugh flavored her voice. "As the king instructed, I am to be your guide, not your mistress, so the departure time is yours to decide."

"Is downstream that way?" he asked, pointing. "It's too frozen to tell."

"Yes, but we will not follow this river for more than a few minutes. Another one will come into view that will guide our way."

Adrian marched in that direction, watching his steps to make sure he didn't accidentally meander into the ice. The waterproofing his mother had applied to his boots worked perfectly, but it wasn't designed to withstand a tumble into a river. Although his feet and toes still suffered from cold, at least they would stay dry.

As he trudged through the snow, Cassabrie's warmth spread through his limbs. She was walking with him, apparently enjoying the feeling of physical motion. "Now that we have some time," he said, "would you like to tell me about how you lost your body? Were you a slave?"

"Oh, yes. I was a slave. All humans in the Southlands are slaves, but some of us get what the dragons call Promotions."

"Promotions? We have those in our military."

"I am not familiar with your military, but they are likely not at all similar. I can't imagine that any human organization would create such a system."

"Then tell me about your promotions."

"Not mine. I never received one, but other slaves did, Deference, for example. I am in my state for another reason, which I hope to explain later rather than sooner. Since the king sent me to be your guide, I prefer to fulfill that purpose before I explain my presence in this state."

"Very well, one explanation at a time." Adrian scooted down a gentle slope that led into a forest of snow-laden spruces. "What happened to Deference?"

"All she knows is that she was awarded a Promotion. She didn't understand why, because her exam scores were the lowest in her class. As you might expect, since you spent some time with her, she received outstanding marks for conduct and demeanor, so I think that's why she was Promoted."

"She is a sweet young lady, to be sure."

"Indeed. Anyway, she remembers very little of her Promotion day. Arxad took her to a place called the Zodiac where they gave her a syrupy drink that made her groggy. He is a priest among the dragons, and that's the place he watches the heavens, looking for signs of future events. She stood in the middle of a room with a dome ceiling, but in her dizziness she couldn't tell if anyone else was there.

"Suddenly, she felt a surge of heat. She thinks she might have cried out, but she isn't sure. For a while, everything went black, and she felt the sensation of floating. Then, she woke up in the castle in the state you witnessed. And all the others reported the same experience."

Adrian nodded, mentally counting the promoted servants he had seen—Serenity, an adult female; Vigilant, an adult male; and Deference. "So," he said as he reached the top of a snowcapped rise, "Arxad knows exactly what happened."

"He does, but neither he nor the king will tell the Promoted slaves the details. They say there is no need. We are content now, so why resurrect the past?"

"Then maybe you are like pets in the castle, something to entertain the white dragon." When he reached the bottom of the slope and walked out onto a flatter area with fewer trees, he looked back. It seemed that the castle sat at the center of a plateau, like a bastion atop a frozen fortress. "Do humans have pets here?"

"I have heard of pets in old fables, but I never had one, so I cannot say whether or not I am one. Some human children in the wealthier dragon homes feed crumbs to the birds, but adult humans scold them, saying that all scraps should be saved for the children in the cattle camp."

"The cattle camp?"

Cassabrie sighed. "I would rather not tell you about that. When you see it, you will learn that it is impossible to describe how bad it is. Yet, I beg you to see the camp, for it will surely confirm that we must sacrifice everything to free our brothers and sisters."

"Then I will see the cattle camp." Adrian looked at the region to the south. The snow extended only a few hundred feet before thinning and giving way to a lush, colorful meadow. It seemed that the cold plateau acted as a wintry cap atop a man wearing a springtime sweater. The abrupt change from an ice cap to a temperate zone seemed strange. Did that mean Dracon was a small planet? How much farther might it be to a tropical climate?

Another river, this one slightly wider and flowing freely, bent to the southwest. Adrian mentally drew a line that stretched due south and, following that line, marched forward with a rapid pace. "Keep me going in the right direction, Cassabrie. I have a good inner compass, but I have no landmarks to go by."

"I have only a feeling that guides me, a pull upon my heart that leads me to the place where I died."

"Died?" The memory of Cassabrie's appearance in the forest brought a chill in spite of her warmth. With cold, pale skin and bluish lips, she had seemed cadaverous. Had he been comforting and cuddling a corpse?

He shook off a building shiver. "I think it's time for you to tell me your story."

"It is long and complicated, and it grieves me to tell it. Perhaps I can simply answer your questions."

"Very well. Let me think." Still looking southward, Adrian inhaled the crisp air. The sky seemed darker in that direction, as if the sun had already set in the lower latitudes. "If you're dead, how could you breathe and walk on our home planet?"

"When I passed through the portal, I gathered material from the ground that I generated into a lifelike representation of myself. I animated it with my life energy, but without any real blood, it carried no signs of life. I was able to simulate breathing, which was necessary for speaking, but if you had listened for my heart, you would have heard nothing."

Again, Cassabrie's dead body came to mind along with the soldier's announcement that she had no heartbeat. "Could you do that now? I mean, could you create a body here?"

"I have tried, but here I am able to conjure only phantasms when I tell stories. I think it's because Starlight somehow cripples my abilities."

Still striding quickly, Adrian pointed at the ground. "So you call this place Starlight, and my planet is Darksphere."

"Correct."

"How did you die?"

Adrian detected a mood change. Cassabrie's usual joyful infusion depressed to a melancholy burden, and the warmth she shed cooled to a tepid flow. "The dragons feared me, so they sentenced me to death at the cooking stake. I suffered for days before I finally died, but somehow Arxad was able to capture my spirit and take it to the Northlands."

With each word, an image coalesced in Adrian's mind. Chained to a pyre, Cassabrie writhed in agony as she slowly roasted to a charred corpse. He shook his head, casting away the thought. "Why would the dragons fear you? You're what? Five feet four inches tall?"

"I … I prefer not to discuss this any further. My heart is breaking, and I wish to enjoy our time together."

Adrian pushed his hand under his cloak and laid it over the glowing patch of skin. "Then enjoy, Cassabrie. I will ask you nothing more about your trials. Walk with me. Tell me what delights you. Talk to me about what brings you joy."

After a few moments of silence, heat reignited and surged throughout his body, and her voice spiked with energy. "I love vibrant colors, both when they blend together in a lovely tapestry and when they clash as if in battle for chromatic supremacy in a mosaic of strife. I love music, the melodies, the harmonies, the way the rhythm commands them to march together."

Adrian passed the snow boundary line and entered the meadow he had seen from the higher elevation. Flowers scattered a million colors in a sea of green, some with petals so large they appeared to be dangling tongues of pink and purple, others with cottonlike heads of blue, and still others with hundreds of spindly hairs, each having no apparent color. When combined, however, they shimmered with crimson.

A breeze swept across the field, brushing the grass and flowers into a sway. Like waves on an ocean, the colors undulated, as if inviting him to wade into the flow.

Adrian sucked in a breath. It was all so beautiful. Surely this was the tapestry Cassabrie had mentioned. "Do you see it?" he asked.

"Oh, yes! It is the spectral season. Now all we need is a song. When music and visual art combine, the ecstasy is beyond compare."

Adrian drank in her words. Even her natural prose seemed poetic. How could a former slave girl be so eloquent? "I would love to hear you sing."

"Once you learn the words, will you sing with me? Then I will add a harmony. Your marching footsteps have already given us an excellent rhythm."

Adrian glanced at his boots as they brushed through the grass one after the other. "I'll do my best."

Cassabrie began a sweet, lilting melody, perfectly in time with his steps. Then, she added words to match.

> A splash of rainbows, colors splayed
> Across a sea of emerald grass;
> O let this season never fade,
> Forever bloom and never pass.
>
> And now these colors live in me
> The spectrum stage of holy art;
> I give these hues and shades for free
> To paint your grace upon each heart.
>
> The grace of mercy, love on high,
> Creator's blessings, splendor's splash;
> Where rainbows end, the flame draws nigh,
> Creator's winds disperse the ash.

Replacing red with eyes of blue,
Replacing scales with wings of love;
And shedding all his gifts of hue
The dragon king becomes a dove.

Cassabrie repeated the stanzas twice, and when she started
yet again, Adrian picked up the tune and joined in. After the first
line, she switched to singing a harmony that blended in beautifully.
Then, when they came back to the beginning, she added a descant,
high and sweet, like a piper's call flowing in the wind.

After the fifth repetition, Cassabrie sighed. "Your singing is
lovely, Adrian Masters. Thank you for giving me such joy."

"The pleasure is all mine." Adrian couldn't stop smiling. It seemed
that Cassabrie's elation fed his own, and then his brimming happiness
circulated back to her, a cycle of upwelling emotion that made him feel
like he was about to burst, or at least break out into song again.

After a few minutes of silent marching, Adrian looked out over
the expanse before him. It seemed endless. Before they left, the king
didn't say how long the journey would last, only that travelers could
decide to take risks that might speed them along. So far, no such
options had arisen, at least none he could detect.

Soon, the river came into view again as it bent back toward
them. With the meadow now declining in elevation, the flow had
transformed into rapids, churning and white-capped. The sun had
disappeared behind the tree line, signaling the approach of evening.
Soon it would likely be too dark to continue.

When Adrian reached the water's edge, he stopped and studied the surrounding trees. Many were small enough to chop down
with a hatchet, and thick vines hung in others, low enough to reach.
Building a raft would take a while, but it would probably save many
hours in the long run, especially if they could drift at night. "Will
the river continue flowing south?" he asked.

"For quite some time," Cassabrie replied. "In fact, it will continue in the general direction for most of the remainder of our

Bryan Davis

journey. It will eventually join a north-flowing river at a point where both tumble into a steep waterfall that turns them west."

Adrian mentally sketched her description. Could someone riding a raft get off in time to avoid the falls? Surely Cassabrie would be able to warn him in time. "You enjoy exhilarating experiences, right?"

"Indeed, I do. So far, the delight has been beyond description."

He opened his cloak, revealing the hatchet on his right hip and the sword on his left. "Then get ready for another one. I'm going to build a raft."

"Do you intend to ride the rapids?"

Adrian cocked his head. "Is that ill-advised?"

"There are rocks. You might get cut or pummeled."

He withdrew the hatchet from its harness. "I have to find Marcelle, the quicker, the better."

"One adventure in the river wasn't enough? This one is not frozen, but it is still dangerous."

Adrian wrinkled his brow. Why was Cassabrie probing him with such questions? Was she trying to discourage him for some reason? Did she want to slow their progress so she could spend more time enjoying the flowers? That seemed far too selfish. It didn't match her character. "If you mean the gas tank," he replied, "there wasn't any other way to cross."

"You could have chosen not to cross."

"True, but then I wouldn't have made it to the castle."

"Who said you had to go to the castle?"

"I thought you did."

"No, Adrian. I merely told you that Marcelle was at the castle. It was your decision to try to find her, and if I had known the river crossing was impossible, I would have done more to dissuade you, but I can go only so far. Remember, I am your guide, not your mistress. You choose where you wish to go and by what conveyance, and I will do my best to help you get there."

Adrian looked out over the darkening landscape. "I see only two conveyances—on foot or by the river. On foot is slow, and it will soon be too dark to see any ditches or other hazards. The river is also risky, but I don't mind taking risks if they're beneficial."

"Ah! The faster the conveyance, the bigger the risk you are willing to take in order to use it."

He nodded. "I think that's a fair statement."

"Then how do you gauge when the speed is worth the risk, or otherwise when it becomes too risky?"

Adrian gazed at the sky again, now purple and filling with stars. This conversation had grown complicated, philosophical, and time consuming. Was this the same Cassabrie who enjoyed the simplicity of riding the wind? "I'm not sure," he said, looking at the river again. "It's more of a guess than anything."

"Ah! You act on faith. If you are willing to take a risk that will speed along your sacrificial mission, you assume that all will be well."

Adrian nodded again. "That also sounds reasonable."

"But …" Cassabrie paused. As the river rushed past, it seemed that the rhythmic splashing of water against the rocks counted the seconds. "If Marcelle stood at the bottom of a chasm," she continued, "about to be slashed by a swordsman, would you jump down to get to her quickly?"

Adrian glanced at his side as if to address his inquisitor. "How deep is the chasm?"

"Let's say two hundred feet."

"Of course not." His voice sharpened, his new tone unbidden. "That would be suicide."

"Oh, please don't be angry with me, Adrian. I'm not trying to expose flaws in your character. I'm just trying to see if there are limits to your faith."

"Limits to my faith? Isn't that the same thing as flaws in my character?"

"No, Adrian. You have already explained why a limit is not necessarily a flaw. If the reason for your risk does not warrant taking it, then who would fault you for declining? Surely you wouldn't risk your life to save a grasshopper, would you?"

He furrowed his brow. "Marcelle is *not* a grasshopper."

"And that's exactly my point. The greater the value of your goal, the more risk you are willing to take. If the goal is valuable enough, even if the risk rises above reasonable limits, your faith will incite you to act."

"Even a two-hundred-foot jump?"

"Perhaps. I cannot tell you. You have to decide if the goal is valuable enough, and if your faith is strong enough. Who can tell where the line should be drawn between a faithful risk and suicidal foolishness? My guess is that a mother trying to save her baby would draw the line at one place while a warrior trying to save a fellow warrior would draw it at another. Faith seems to grow along with the value assigned to the goal."

Adrian shook his head, feeling very strange, alien, even insane. He was standing on a planet an unfathomable distance from home, speaking out loud to a dead girl dwelling inside his body, all the while planning a raft ride down a dangerous river, risking his life to save people he had never seen.

After a few seconds of silence, he let out a sigh. "Okay. Marcelle is a fellow warrior, so my risk should be in keeping with that goal, saving a fellow warrior."

"I am merely asking questions, Adrian. I don't know where your faith begins and ends regarding her or anyone else, nor do I pretend to be your teacher on the matter."

"But there is a purpose to your questions."

"My purpose is to help you consider how your heart speaks to your circumstances. As you sojourn here, this lesson will likely be crucial, because, quite frankly, your mission is very nearly impossible, and learning where great faith and brutal practicality meet might be your only hope."

As he gazed at the water splashing against the rocks, he let her words sink in. They were eloquent, piercing. "How did such a young woman learn so much wisdom?"

"I am not as young as I appear, and the king has taught me a great deal. I am communicating the kinds of questions he asks. He believes that one of the greatest treasures is learning how to think, and pointed questions plant seeds that sprout and grow into wisdom."

"I think I understand." Adrian stripped off the cloak and lifted the hatchet. "I have constructed rafts and ridden them on many a wild river. I think that risk is well within reach of my faith."

"Then so be it."

For the next half hour or so, Adrian chopped down small trees, stripped their trunks, and cut down vines to fasten them together. Since the trunks were relatively slender and uneven, he constructed a craft with three vertical layers to close every gap while making the layers long and wide enough for one person to stand or sit upon without capsizing.

Evening faded into night, forcing him to work in the dim glow on the horizon, perhaps a rising moon. When he finished tying the last knot, he slid the raft into a quieter section of the river and set a foot on the center, pressing down with most of his weight. It floated well, quite well in fact.

He slid the hatchet back to the harness and wiped sweat from his brow. Yes, this would work fine.

After collecting a few extra vines, grabbing a leftover branch to use as a steering pole, and laying the cloak on the wood for padding, he stepped fully onto the raft and sat facing downstream. It sank for a moment before lifting again and floating with the current. Ahead, the river exploded into a sea of white splashes flying into the air and glittering in the brightening moonlight.

Gripping the pole with one hand and the side of the raft with the other, he took in a deep breath. "Are you ready for a really wild ride?"

"I am with you heart and soul, Adrian."

The raft hit a sudden dip and then an upsurge that sent the front of the raft flying. The rear kicked up, and the raft flew through the air for a few seconds before splashing several feet downstream. The momentum sent the raft's front edge knifing into the water, swamping the surface.

Adrian let out a whoop and hung on, riding out the dips, bumps, and eruptions. The raft sped along, sometimes smacking against rocks, but it held together. Of course, he became soaked, but with every mile the river carried him, the air seemed to get warmer, bringing comfort to his wet skin.

Cassabrie added warmth as well. With each surge and fall, heat pulsed through his body, as if expressing her emotions in exclamations of feverish delight. When she gasped, he sucked in the cool, wet air. When she sighed, he expelled her breath, warm and saturated with pleasure. Her spirit had crept into his, and the two had become one.

Hour after hour, the river drove them southward, and three moons rose high into the sky, giving light to their surroundings. Mile after mile of dimly lit scenes passed by on each side—meadows bursting with flowers, forests brimming with lush evergreens, and deciduous trees dressed in muted autumn colors, making him wish he could see them in daylight.

The current eased in places, providing more casual views of violet sky, rocky beaches, and densely packed woods. Here, Adrian pushed his pole against the riverbed to overcome the lack of current, but these doldrums never lasted long. The land soon dipped down again and sent them into another surge of white water and exhilaration, and each time they regained the rush, the ecstasy very nearly burned his skin.

As the night hours passed, the forests thinned, and grass replaced the flowers. The air seemed drier, almost crackly, as if they had moved into a region that lacked regular rainfall. The river slowed again, this time with no rapids in sight.

Adrian pushed with the pole. His hands and arms ached. After a few minutes, the river's bottom dropped out of reach, and the raft drifted slowly along. Quiet descended, as if in concert with the loss of color in the landscape.

He set the pole down and heaved a sigh. "I suppose you have no idea how much farther we have to travel."

"I don't, but the feeling that draws me is much stronger now. We are certainly going in the right direction."

"I hope so. I'm getting tired."

"When did you last sleep, Adrian?"

Adrian blinked. How long had it been? The mission began at nightfall, and when they finally passed through the portal it was likely past midnight. He had stayed awake ever since entering this world, working hard nearly every moment. "I think I last slept about the equivalent of a day and a half ago, but I'm not sure."

"Then we must sleep now."

"Where? On the riverbank?"

"That should be fine."

"Are there any beasts in this region who might think of us as a nighttime meal?"

"I don't know. I never lived in this area. The dragons drove out many human-eating beasts in our region. Slaves were too valuable to lose to predators."

"So the predators had to go somewhere. We have no reason to believe they aren't in this area."

Cassabrie laughed. "I love your logical mind, Adrian. You are again weighing risks versus goals."

He picked up the vines and began tying them together. "We'll make an anchor and spend the night on the river."

"Will we go on shore and find a rock to use as the anchor's weight?"

"We might not have to." After fashioning a long rope, he doubled it, letting the loop on one end hang loosely. As he reeled it out into the water, it sank into darkness. "I'm hoping to catch something, maybe a sunken log."

"Very interesting. Is this something you have done on our home planet?"

Adrian smiled. *Our* home planet. Cassabrie was learning to adopt an alien world as her own. "Something like this," he said. "Jason and I used to fish on the Elbon River. There were plenty of logs on the river bottom, so it never took long to snag one."

"Who is Jason?"

"My younger brother. Frederick, my older brother, is the one who owned the hat you brought."

"Oh, yes. The hat. I never finished the story."

"Can you tell me more? I must find Frederick."

After a moment's silence, she replied. "I have no more to tell. It seems that the story ended when the shadow appeared."

Adrian felt a pull on the line, but whatever snagged it immediately let go. It seemed that he was fishing for two catches—a log and answers from Cassabrie. "Frederick mentioned a wilderness enclave. Do you know what that means or where it is?"

"The wilderness is a forested area that lies within the boundaries of the great wall. Some slaves have tried to escape there, but none has ever returned. The optimistic among us think they have found safe refuge and don't want to risk coming out, while others believe that they drowned in the swamps, became food for the beasts, or died of starvation."

Adrian drummed his fingers on the raft. Frederick was a survivalist. If anyone could create a haven for slaves in the wilderness, he could. "If there is such an enclave, are there any rumors about its location?"

"I am not aware of any, but I have not been in the company of the current slave population for quite some time. If runaway slaves have established a refuge recently, I would have heard about it only if the new arrivals to the Northlands had mentioned it, but none has, and I have not had a reason to ask them."

Adrian nodded. "Then I will have to ask the current slaves about it when I get there."

For the next few minutes he sat, feeling the vine's tension and waiting for any change. The gentle lapping of water against the raft played a lullaby that eased his mind toward sleep. But he couldn't sleep. Not yet.

"Cassabrie, keep talking. I need to stay awake until I secure the raft."

"Very well." She hummed for a moment before continuing. "I was asking about your family. Do you have sisters?"

Adrian shook his head. "Just us three boys. My parents wanted more children, especially a girl, but Mother became ill for several months. They never said if her illness contributed to infertility, but Frederick and I guessed that was the case."

"Oh. No sisters. How sad."

"True. I think I am worse off for not having that experience."

"Is there any female in your life?"

"My mother, of course, and there are a few girls in the commune. They aren't really like sisters, though. We eat together and sometimes work together, but they aren't as close to me as my brothers are."

Cassabrie hummed again, this time taking up the tune she had sung during their romp through the field of flowers. Finally, she spoke softly. "And what of Marcelle? Is she your friend or merely a fellow warrior?"

"Marcelle is—" Something pulled on his line and held fast, stopping the raft. "Ah! I think I have it." He tested the anchor with several strong tugs, then tied the vine's loose ends to his ankle.

After putting on the cloak, he lay back on the raft and looked up at the sky, nearly black to the west, dark purple toward the east, and violet within the influence of the three moons rising in an arc toward the top of the dark ceiling. Shadows veiled the shorelines, masking the widely separated trees. Any beasts prowling about likely wouldn't notice a potential prey floating on the river. He and Cassabrie would be safe.

"Good night, Cassabrie," he said as he closed his eyes.

After a few seconds of silence, she whispered, "Adrian?"

"Yes?"

"You were going to tell me about Marcelle."

"Oh, yes. Marcelle." He stretched his arms and yawned. "What do you want to know about her?"

"I asked you if she was your friend." Her voice carried a hint of anxiety.

"We were friends at one time. When we were children, we lived in the same commune and played together. She acted more like a boy than a girl, so she roughhoused with the best of us."

"And now?"

"When she and her father went to live in the governor's palace, we drifted apart. We have been rivals in battle tournaments, but our rivalry has been respectful. She is a superior swordplayer and a champion of the cause to find and free the slaves here."

A few seconds of silence ensued, broken by a quiet, "Oh. I see."

"Do I detect a question in your voice?"

"I thought there might be something more between you. The way she looked at you made me think so."

"The way she looked at me?"

"It was likely my imagination. I was just concerned that I might be violating a covenant."

"A covenant? What do you mean?"

"Adrian, you and I are intimately united, sharing a body and a bed, hearts and spirits bound as one. If I were your intended, I think I would not appreciate such an arrangement with another woman."

Adrian yawned again. "I see what you mean, but Marcelle and I are not each other's intended, nothing like that at all. As you said, she is a fellow warrior."

She sighed, and her voice settled into a contented whisper. "Then all is well. We have broken no covenants."

Warmth oozed across his skin and deep within, as if Cassabrie had crawled over him and nestled on his chest. He instinctively crossed his arms over his torso as if to hug her, but no one was there. Cassabrie was a wisp, a phantom, not a woman. He could no more violate the moral precepts of the Code with her than he could with a gust of wind. Yet, something felt wrong—this intimate union, this sharing of a body, as she called it. Was this any less a union? If an intended would not approve, should he, himself, approve?

He opened his eyes and looked again at the sky. "I meant to ask you about the moons. We have two on Major Four, but one is so small we can barely see it with the naked eye."

"The three always rise and ride the nightscape together. We also have a fourth, Trisarian, which sometimes rises as the others set."

Blinking his tired eyes again, Adrian murmured, "It looks so different, I could stare at the sky for hours."

"Sleep, Adrian. The moons will rise again, and our stars will be no different tomorrow night."

"You're right. As usual."

"If you will not be disturbed, I will sing while you slumber. I need only your body's rest, so I will stay awake and listen to the sounds of the night."

"Singing is fine. It might make for better dreams." He let his eyelids fall closed. Froglike peeps rose from both riverbanks, a soft breeze brushed his ears, and the current's gentle waves slapped against the raft's edges.

Soon, Cassabrie's voice joined in as she sang a soft melody.

The moons that cross the sky tonight
Can tell my tale, my fatal flight;
The end of life, the end of chains
Allow the moon to now explain.

Pariah, dim, the smallest moon,
Its withered face, a pockmarked prune,
Withstanding rocks the others hurl,
Like insults cast at red-haired girls.

Adrian floated with her song, sleeping now, dreaming of three
moons in a line across a violet sky. Near the horizon, the least of
the three shone a pale yellow light, revealing a craterous surface, as
if pummeled nightly by meteors. Pariah. Sad, lonely Pariah.

As he watched the moons glide across the apex of the sky, Cassabrie continued her song.

Though favored by the dragon race
For tales we tell, hypnotic grace,
A fellow human softly stirs
A jealous plot disguised by purrs.

For just as moons reflect the light,
Possessing none, they're falsely bright,
A traitor smiles with lips that lie
And sends the red-haired girl to die.

While Cassabrie's song faded to a hum, Adrian slept on, aware
of his slumber as well as his dreams. He ran across the sky, caught
Pariah, and swallowed it. Its light shone through his eyes and
through a small hole in his chest. A woman dressed in black stalked
toward him from the horizon, a sword drawn. Soon, her identity

became clear—Marcelle, an angry glare on her face. She stabbed Adrian through the hole and ripped it wide open. The light spilled out. His eyes dimmed, and his entire body deflated. Then, everything faded to black.

✳ TWELVE ✳

REXEL lowered himself to one knee in the midst of a field of yellow flowers. Two people—Randall, Prescott's son, and Tibalt, the madman from the dungeon—lay sleeping within his reach. Apparently, Randall survived Bristol's attempts to kill him, and Tibalt convinced Randall to take him along.

Rising to his feet, Drexel gave Randall a nudge with his boot. No response. Sound asleep. Obviously, Uriel's first obstacle, the sleeping flowers, had prevented these two from proceeding, but where were Jason and Elyssa? With Adrian and Marcelle not returning from their mission, it seemed that four travelers had either perished or else succeeded in finding a portal.

He looked to his right where a pit led deep into darkness— Uriel's second obstacle. Could they have fallen in?

On the far side of the pit, about an athlete's leap away, two columns of mist swirled, human-shaped but indistinct, without face or gender—snatchers, as a few townsfolk witnesses had dubbed them. Uriel had brought them from Dracon, though his journal never explained their origins.

"Did they fall?" Drexel asked.

One of the shapes hissed its reply. "The boy and girl fell into the water's rush and were swept away."

Drexel recalled a poem from the journal, a code the snatchers would recognize. "Another question I will ask, and you'll submit to do this task."

"Very well, friend of Uriel Blackstone," the second snatcher said. "What is this task?"

Drexel pointed into the pit. "Go to the portal. Tell me if they survived. If they have found the portal, don't let them open it."

"We can only persuade," the snatcher replied, "but our persuasion skills are rarely thwarted." The two snatchers stretched out into ribbons of fog and streamed into the hole.

When they disappeared, Drexel scanned the field, empty except for flowers and the two sleeping bodies. If the plan had not gone awry, he would have had a company of soldiers at his disposal, but Orion's lust for the Diviner's blood had spoiled everything. Tibalt's disappearance likely saw to that, causing Orion to worry that Elyssa would escape to the dragon world.

Drexel looked at Tibalt, snoring peacefully under the influence of the flowers. Could he really be the son of Uriel Blackstone after all? Maybe Uriel altered his son's birth records to hide his identity. Did Tibalt provide Jason and Elyssa with genetic material for opening the portal? His fingers were still intact. Perhaps they could use his hair somehow.

He turned toward Mesolantrum. Now outside the boundary, he stood in a land forbidden to the citizens. With Orion on a maniacal crusade, it seemed safer here. He had sent fifty soldiers in search of Elyssa, but the fools had no idea which way she went, and in their superstitious ignorance they had stayed within the confines of the boundary, fearful of ghosts and poisonous flowers.

Drexel laughed quietly. As well they should be. Some old wives' tales carried more truth than myth, and finding Bristol and his search dogs torn to pieces near the border likely steered them away from proceeding in the most sensible direction. Whether Bristol had succumbed to myths or mountain bears mattered little now. Drawing a line from the palace to where his mangled body lay provided the clue Drexel needed to find the portal's opening. Bristol had done his job.

"Time to move on," Drexel muttered. "I can't wait for those hellish snatchers forever."

He checked his sword on one hip and a photo gun on the other, then withdrew the journal from his tunic and turned toward the back pages. The secondary entrance was supposed to be exactly a thousand paces due east of the pit. Getting there and finding it might take some time.

After counting off the steps, he searched the ground for an embedded door, supposedly much like the entry to the dungeon. It was impossible to know if his own stride matched that of Uriel, so he would have to comb a considerable area. According to Blackstone's notes, a hole larger than the other pit once scarred this field, allowing Magnar to fly from the underground river into the open. It must have taken Blackstone years to fill it in while keeping the cavern intact underneath.

Pacing back and forth, he scuffed his boots, hoping to rip up turf that might have collected over the past century. Finally, a strip of grass flew loose, exposing a wooden plank. Using his sword, he cut through the grass around a small door. Then, after finding a metal ring near the middle, he jerked it open.

A strange light emanated from below, glittering in a variety of colors. He dropped to his hands and knees and peered in as far as he could. It looked like a chamber with a wall of light on one side, and water had risen to within a few feet of the opening. According to the journal, that wall held the portal, and a flood indicated that an intruder was within, apparently trying to transport without going through the proper steps.

Drexel looked across the field at the pit. Someone was walking around, too big to be Tibalt. Randall, maybe? Had Tibalt jumped into the pit? Perhaps Jason and Elyssa had returned and revived them, now realizing that hair wasn't enough of a genetic key. If Tibalt really was the son of Uriel Blackstone, they needed his fingers.

After lowering his legs into the hole, Drexel, pulling the door closed above himself, dropped in. As he swam toward the wall, the water level dropped rapidly, revealing a mosaic of light that sketched two roaring dragons. With every second, new details appeared, matching the description in Blackstone's journal. Facing each other, the dragons' outstretched forelegs reached for something, and when the level dropped far enough, their target became clear. A young male bobbed in the water, his fingers wedged in holes in the wall just above the dragons' claws.

Drexel, finally able to stand, grabbed the victim's shoulders, pulled him from the wall, and laid him on the stone floor, now covered by only a few inches of water. The lights in the wall began to fade, but not before Drexel caught a glimpse of the young man's face. It was Jason, apparently drowned.

Drexel knelt next to Jason and listened to the underground river rushing past. Maybe Elyssa had gone alone to revive Randall and Tibalt. If so, she might be back soon. As clever as she was in nearly every discipline, perhaps she could revive Jason.

Standing again, Drexel looked at the wall and found the holes, barely visible in the dimness. Jason had failed. Adrian and Marcelle would fail. But Drexel, head of the palace guard, would not. Soon, everyone would realize his worth. After being drummed out of the army for his lack of fighting skills, he would prove to the world that brains and courage counted for more than brawn, and such a hero deserved to rule the land.

And if they didn't agree? Drexel smiled. They would agree. They wouldn't want Magnar and the other dragons to find their way back to Mesolantrum.

He reached into his tunic and felt for the genetic keys that would fill the holes in the wall, the keys to the portal lock that Uriel had installed a hundred years ago. With or without soldiers, it was finally time to enter the dragon world and bring the Lost Ones home.

*　　　*　　　*　　　*　　　*　　　*

Marcelle opened her eyes. Where was she? She lay on something hard, perhaps stone, and the freshness in the air meant she had slept outdoors. But where?

Like thunder from a distant storm, her memories rolled back in. *Dracon. The Lost Ones. Flying on a dragon.*

She sat up. A dawning sky greeted her eyes. Had she slept all night? Oh, no! She was supposed to sneak up to the wall under the cover of darkness. She had missed her chance.

She rose to her feet and stretched her stiff legs. What now? Apparently Adrian hadn't come yet, unless he had passed this point without seeing her in the dark. Either way, waiting for him didn't make sense. She would have to go alone.

The sound of water called her attention to the fissure one level below where she stood. After reattaching her bag and belt, she leaped down and, leaning close, looked into the waist-high hole. As water poured out of the three-foot-wide opening, a warm spray moistened her face. The stream filled the gap from side to side, but at least eight inches of airspace lay above the water level, though a strong gush flooded it every few seconds.

Where did it lead? Could this be the outflow of the stream on the other side of the wall? Maybe it went into the ground, split into smaller channels, and exited in several small waterfalls like this one.

Marcelle looked down at her body, then at the hole. Yes, she would likely fit, though not with swords at her sides or a bag on her back. But how could she journey into such a dangerous place without a weapon? How could she leave the video tube behind?

She loosened her bag's strap and let it slide down her arm. She could hide the bag. Who would bother to steal it? Apparently no one ever stalked this area, certainly no human. But how could she take that chance without at least looking at the video? As horrific as the images probably were, checking for clues that only she could detect was her duty.

She pulled the video tube from the bag and looked through the viewing lens. After taking a deep breath, she pushed the view button and waited. As if replaying her nightmares, the video showed her mother's pale face, a close view that made her appear to be sleeping, perhaps merely sick, explaining the wan aspect.

As the view enlarged, her body appeared, naked and punctured, except for a sheet that covered her from her waist down, including her hands.

A man stretched out a tape measure from one end of a gash to another. He spoke in monotone as he rattled off his findings— length, depth, and organs affected. He seemed callous, uncaring, just doing his job. Did he know that this woman was a beloved queen? Did he realize that her death destroyed a home? Yet, not one tear spilled from his eyes, and not one tremor altered his voice. He must have left his heart at home.

As the examiner continued, the camera zoomed in on the wounds. Marcelle studied them closely. They didn't look like anything Darien's viper would inflict. The slices appeared to have rough edges, as if torn, perhaps indicating a duller blade. Whoever did this used a weapon that had not been sharpened, but the battlefield soldiers surely kept their blades bright and honed. Their lives depended on it.

Marcelle blinked away tears. Could the murderer have been lying? Maybe he hadn't been on the battlefield at all. Had he planted a diversion? Father searched for him among the soldiers, but if he had never been one, that path could not have led to his capture.

Swallowing, Marcelle concentrated once again on the video. The examiner lifted one of her mother's arms, pulling her hand from underneath the sheet. It ended in a bloody stub, save for a single thumb.

Marcelle gagged. She gasped for air. How could this be?

The examiner lifted her other arm with the same result, the exposure of a fingerless hand, and crossed her arms over her waist while casually commenting on the wounds.

"Augh!" Marcelle jerked the tube away and hurled it at the waterfall. It smacked against the rocks and tumbled down with the water, its frame bent and its lens shattered.

She grabbed a fistful of hair and pulled. Her body quaked. She dropped to her knees and, covering her mouth, screamed into her palm. Then, she set her hands on the ground and heaved a series of hard convulsive spasms that yielded nothing but an upwelling of burning bile.

Finally, she crawled to the stream and scooped up a handful of water. After a rinse and a swallow, she rose to her knees and wiped tears from her eyes. She was still in the dragon world, still far away from the man who butchered her mother, still unable to track him down and make him pay in blood for his crimes.

She picked up the courier tube and her clothing bag and climbed to her feet. After finding a dry cleft in the rocks, placing the tube and bag inside, and plugging the gap with a stone, she stood in front of the stream's exit hole again, her feet now in the water. She unbuckled both scabbards from her belt and laid one next to the creek bed. After covering all except the butt of the hilt with pebbles, she used the bag's strap to attach the viper's scabbard to her back, then pushed her hands and head into the hole, keeping her nose above water.

As soon as a gush splashed her face, she began to count. *One, two, three …* When she reached seven, another surge filled the hole. Again, she counted. When she reached seven, a third gush interrupted.

Pulling with her hands and pushing with her feet, she crawled in. At least the water was warm enough, like a tepid bath. Within seconds, darkness veiled her eyes. From here on out, her fingers would be her only guide to the tunnel's size and direction.

As she squirmed along, she repeated her count to seven again and again, holding her breath and closing her eyes in anticipation of the surge and accompanying splash. At times, the space above her head dwindled, forcing her to keep her nose under water, but never for too long.

The tunnel gradually expanded. After about twenty minutes, she rose to her knees and then to her feet, standing in knee-deep water. She set her fists on her hips and listened. The sound of running water echoed, signaling a vast chamber. Now, instead of following the surrounding walls, she would have to feel the current to continue upstream.

That plan, however, had its problems. The flow had grown sluggish, carrying swirls that posed a foreboding question. Did a deep pool lie ahead? If so, might there be dangerous creatures in its depths stirring the current?

Marcelle reached to her back and drew the sword from its scabbard. She would soon find out.

*　　　　*　　　　*　　　　*　　　　*　　　　*

"Adrian!" a familiar voice called.

He blinked open his eyes. "What?"

"I hear something in the water, a splashing noise."

He sat up. The sky gave hints of dawn to the east, while to the west, the three moons hung low over the horizon.

When the splashing sound registered, he searched for the source. A huge creature swam toward them, maybe twenty feet away, but it was still too dark to tell what it was.

Adrian reached for the knot in the vine and tried to untie it. It wouldn't budge. The splashes drew closer. He grabbed the hatchet and chopped through the vine, setting the raft free. The current pushed it along, but would it move quickly enough?

Something heavy sloshed onto the raft. It tipped to the side, throwing Adrian into a pair of furry limbs. As it squeezed him close to its body, he slashed at it with the hatchet, not seeing where his blows landed. The beast let out a squeal and released him. He tumbled into the water and immediately dove underneath.

In the darkness, underwater pulses gave away the attacker's position, allowing Adrian to swim in the opposite direction, perpendicular to the current. Would it follow? Likely yes, if it wasn't wounded too badly. Should he turn and fight? The beast could be enormous. Yet, with his ankle still sore, outrunning it might be impossible, even if he made it to shore.

Finding the bottom of the river, he turned downstream and pushed off the sandy bed. His only hope was to find the raft and defend it with sword and hatchet. The cloak and his weapons weighed him down, but stripping them off was out of the question. He would need them later.

As he swam, he looked up. The dawning sky cast shadows on the surface above, including that of the floundering creature behind him. Ahead, a rectangular object floated slowly along. It had to be the raft.

He surged toward it, grabbed the edge, and hoisted himself aboard. About three body lengths back, the beast roared and lurched toward him, his hairy limbs slapping the water. It looked like a cross between a bear and a beaver, as large as the mountain bears in Mesolantrum. Yet, those bears didn't swim well at all, and this creature seemed right at home. It glided toward the raft, its jaws snapping as if devouring the water in front of him.

Adrian chopped the hatchet's blade into the raft's surface. The pole had fallen into the water. There was no way to propel. He drew out his sword and jammed it into the river. Too deep. His only paddle would be a prayer.

As the beast drew closer, Adrian smacked the water with the sword. "Stay back!"

The beast hesitated, but only for a moment before swimming again, now even more quickly. A swifter current kept the raft out of its reach, at least for the moment.

Adrian shouted, "Do you know what it is, Cassabrie?"

Her voice breathless, she spoke quickly. "Storybooks tell of a similar creature called a vog, but I can't be sure. I have never seen one."

"Do the stories tell of any weaknesses?"

"They are very intelligent, and they are strictly nocturnal. They fear the light."

He glanced at the horizon. Sunrise was near, but not near enough. As the vog drew within a few strokes of catching him, Adrian pulled off his cloak and ripped open his shirt, exposing the patch on his skin. "Give me all you have, Cassabrie!"

"I understand!"

Heat blasted into his chest. His skin cast a pale orange glow, like a covered lantern with a hole cut into its shield. Just as the vog reached out a meaty hand to slap the raft, Adrian aimed the light at its face. It drew its arm back and stared, its black gleaming eyes narrowing.

"Give me more!" Adrian yelled.

"I'm trying!" Cassabrie cried. "We're still tired!"

Adrian stretched out with the sword and nicked the vog's snout. "If you want a fight, I can give you one! I won't be an easy breakfast!"

As battle passion surged through his muscles, the light burst into a pulsing blaze. The vog squeezed its eyes closed and let out another squeal. Then, after smacking the water angrily, it submerged and swam away.

Adrian fell back to his bottom and exhaled heavily. The raft rocked with his weight but soon settled into an even keel and drifted with the current. The patch on his skin cast a glow across his tight fist, still clutching the hilt of his sword. As it gradually dimmed, he whispered, "Thank you, Cassabrie."

"You are most welcome, dear friend, but the energy surely came from both of us, not me alone. That proves my concern."

He touched the hatchet's handle but left the blade embedded in the wood. "What concern?"

"About the possibility of breaking a covenant. Our union is very nearly complete."

"Nearly complete? What do you mean?"

"Did you not feel it? Your energy combined with my own. The closer we draw, the more easily we will act as one. When the sliver of separation finally ebbs away, we will be inseparable."

"Do you mean …" He grasped the hatchet fully. "You'll be inside me forever?"

"Only if you wish this to be. Your will is the only barrier."

"My will?"

"I have been given to you as a guide, and that is my purpose. Yet, when our journey is complete, you will have the choice to keep me or expel me. If you want to keep me, you need only to let your desires be made known."

He released the hatchet and reached for his ankle. The vine was still attached, still knotted tightly. "Is that what *you* want?"

"It is all I have dreamed about for many years. I have no body of my own, so living and breathing through another is the fulfillment of that dream. And, oh, Adrian, to wake up and be alive in the body of a man such as you is … is …" Her voice faded away.

Adrian swallowed. A man such as him? Inseparable? "I … I don't know what to say."

"Say nothing. Our journey is far from complete. Then and only then will you have to make a decision, and by that time you will know me well enough to decide."

Adrian set the sword down and rebuttoned his shirt, shutting off the glow. The rising sun shed enough light to provide a view of the river, wider now and flowing at the pace of a sluggish march. Yet, it seemed that events hurtled through his mind like a raft on the rapids. "I don't have a way to steer."

"Perhaps the current will guide you safely. Sometimes we have to trust in an invisible hand."

Adrian shifted around and looked at an upcoming bend in the river. What might they find around the corner? Rapids that would send them on another wild ride, this time without a pole? A waterfall that would plunge them into sharp rocks and certain death? Who could know? That invisible hand had better be a kind one.

He reached for the edge and hung on. At this point, that was all he could do.

After an hour of riding at the same pace, Adrian scanned the landscape. The meadow to the left was clear of trees, and walking, even with a sore ankle, would likely be faster than drifting on this lazy river.

"This is too slow, Cassabrie. Do you have any ideas?"

"We have come a great distance, and my sense that we are closing in is overwhelming. If we are within sight of the great wall, then we have another option."

"The great wall? A fortification of some kind?"

"Yes, it surrounds the dragons' home region. I'm not sure why they live in that area, except for the fact that the pheterone mines are there. I would prefer the meadows to the north. In any case, they have built a wall that prevents slaves from escaping, and dragons patrol it constantly."

"How does being close give us another option?"

"If you are willing to risk harm to your body by taking the rapids, then maybe you would be interested in another risk that might provide the fastest way into the heart of the Southlands. You see, even when you find the wall, getting past it without detection is probably impossible."

Adrian looked again at the shoreline. A long-legged bird, gray and blue with a yellow crest, stalked the shallows, its long neck curled as it sought minnows or bugs. Even at its slow hunting pace, it kept up with the raft. "Okay. What's your idea?"

"First, paddle to shore and climb a tree. If the wall is not in sight, then there is no need to explain the rest. The option won't be available."

"It's better than crawling along at this pace." Using his hands, Adrian paddled toward the western riverbank. After sliding the raft up on shore, he found a tall tree with low branches and scrambled up as high as he could. Fortunately, pain from the photo-gun burn had eased, and sleep had rested his muscles.

He set a hand on his brow, shielding his eyes. To the south, the meadow's grass thinned, exposing bare rock and pebbly soil. Beyond that, barely in view, a wall stretched from one side of his field of vision to the other with no end in sight.

"I assume that's the wall," he said.

"It is."

"So what do we do?"

"We can signal the guardian dragons. They will capture you and take you to the Southlands."

"But then I'll be a prisoner."

"An armed prisoner. If you don't resist, they might be unaware of the weapons you possess, and they will carry you to the wall. Once there, you can choose whether or not to fight for your free-dom. As I said, the risk is high, but it's the fastest way to your des-tination ... and likely to Marcelle."

Adrian climbed down and walked back to the raft. His ankle throbbed again, forcing him to limp. After pulling the hatchet from the wood and returning it to its harness, he picked up the sword and sheathed it. "How many dragons will be at the wall?"

"When I was a slave, I heard reports from those who tried to escape, but I believe some to be exaggerated. I think since the wall is so long, they cannot concentrate more than two in one place. Unfortunately, they would probably take you to the top of the wall at the river gate, where there might be more guards to keep slaves from trying to use the river to escape."

Adrian put on the damp cloak, concealing both sheaths. Now he had to weigh another huge risk. Everything likely depended on the intelligence and experience of the guardian dragons. Would they search a human for weapons? Had they ever faced an experienced swordsman? Besides that, would there be a way down from the top of the wall that didn't require wings?

"Do runaway slaves have weapons?"

"No, Adrian, just the clothes on their backs. Some try to swim in the river at night, hoping to make it to the underground channel. You see, the river runs to the wall and then goes underground."

"Where does it go after that?"

"We don't know. The slaves are so desperate when they try to escape, they are willing to rely on hope that they will find an opening. The risk is high, but the goal is a valuable treasure. Since the dragons guard it so carefully, we think it must lead to freedom."

The patch on Adrian's skin grew warmer again, as if punctuating *freedom*. No doubt that word meant everything to her. Not only did she long for freedom for her fellow slaves, it seemed that she craved the freedom that dwelling inside his body provided. She relished feeling the wind and stretching her arms and legs, even if through the animation of another.

Yet, she was willing to allow him, her host, to be imprisoned and enslaved. Why? Because of his friendship with Marcelle? Cassabrie offered a way to get to her more quickly at the potential of great cost to her own freedom. Why would she be willing to sacrifice so much?

Adrian looked at the endless expanse in front of him. It might take most of the day to cross on foot, especially with his sore ankle. How would Marcelle fare among the dragons while he tarried?

Finally, he let out a sigh. "How do I signal the guardians?"

"Build a fire. When they see the smoke, they will come. They have keen eyesight and will notice a rising column of smoke."

Adrian reached into his trousers pocket and withdrew the flint stones his father had brought. As he shook his loose fist, letting the stones tumble within, he searched the area for other trees. Several green saplings stood here and there, plenty of wood to create a smoky fire, but starting them would require something older and drier.

"Okay," he said, nodding. "I'll do it."

After chopping down eight saplings and collecting fallen leaves and needles, he piled them on the river's pebbly bank. Then, he gathered handfuls of grass and pushed them underneath the pile. It took a few minutes to ignite the grass with the flint stones, but the flames finally caught and began to spread. Soon, a blazing fire erupted, creating plumes of white and gray smoke.

"Do you think that will be enough?" he asked.

"It should be."

Adrian put the hatchet in its sheath and refastened his cloak with its leather belt, still damp from the river. As the wind whipped the fire into a frenzy, he stayed close, hoping to dry out a bit more as he watched the sky to the south. A single white puffy cloud interrupted the sea of deep blue, nothing to prevent the dragons from detecting his signal.

While he waited, Cassabrie hummed a new tune, this one more melancholy than the others, perhaps a dirge for a funeral. It seemed appropriate for the occasion—flames calling for a potential executioner. His shoulders sagged. The wordless song's influence weighed him down. This Starlighter was powerful indeed.

Soon, a reddish brown figure took shape, a dragon bobbing with the beat of its wings. "Do you see it?"

"I do," Cassabrie said. "He is a guardian, not the most powerful of dragons, but also not the least. He is dangerous."

"What should I say when he gets here?"

"Tell him that you surrender to the mercies of Magnar, and you request representation from Arxad."

Using his foot, Adrian shoved the raft into the river. No sense in giving the dragon a clue as to how he had arrived or where he had come from. "What kind of representation?"

"Arxad acts as legal counsel for slaves who break the law and ask for his help. Usually they are guilty, so Arxad does little to protect them, but if we make the appeal, the guardians have a legal obligation to acquiesce."

"But couldn't he just kill me? No one would ever know that I made the appeal."

"Yes, he could."

"I see. Another risk."

"You guessed correctly, but many of the guardians are sticklers for the law, so your chances are good if they fail to notice your weapons."

Adrian watched the approaching dragon. With a sword and hatchet at his disposal, his arms yearned to reach for them and make ready for battle. But that would ruin everything. This dragon meant fast transport. Battle would have to wait.

The dragon stormed down from the sky and landed in a flurry. "What are you doing here?" it bellowed.

Cassabrie spoke up. "Tell him you intentionally signaled him. Show humility."

"I made the fire to signal you," Adrian said, bowing low.

"Tell him you're surrendering to him and you appeal for Arxad's protection."

"I humbly surrender to you, good dragon, and I appeal for Arxad's protection."

"Oh, do you now?" The dragon looked Adrian over, his head swaying from side to side. "How long have you been wandering? You are too well-fed to have been gone long."

Adrian raised his hands to tighten the cloak's belt again but quickly lowered them. Even though it had loosened, drawing attention to it might be a bad idea. "Your observation skills are keen. I have been here less than a day, and I soon realized that I need to be with my people."

"How did you escape? Where did you breach the wall?"

"Well ... you see ..."

"Tell him you will explain everything to Arxad," Cassabrie said. "He is your counselor, so to him alone you will confess your actions."

"I beg your pardon, good dragon, but I must appeal again to Arxad. He is my counselor, so I will make my confessions to him."

The dragon looked him over again for a moment before rumbling, "So be it."

"Ask him his name," Cassabrie said. "It might help you later."

Adrian repeated his bow. "By what name may I address you, good dragon?"

"Zerath. Why do you ask?"

"So ..." Adrian had to think fast. No time to wait for Cassabrie's advice. "So that I may tell my fellow humans about your merciful ways."

"Uh-oh," Cassabrie said. "That was a mistake."

Zerath reached out with a wing and slapped Adrian across his cheek, knocking him on his side. "Tell your fellow humans about that!"

Adrian dabbed his cheek with a finger. Blood. Not much, but the wound felt like fire.

"Get ready," Cassabrie said. "Fasten your cloak tightly."

With another flurry of wings, the dragon rose into the air and flew in a low, tight orbit. Just as Adrian refastened his cloak, the dragon snatched the back collar with his rear claws and lifted him into the air.

Adrian held his cloak against his body, making sure it couldn't flap in the wind and expose his weapons to any dragon watching from below. If several of the beasts patrolled the wall, surprise would be his only chance for survival.

As they flew higher, the wall came into view on the horizon. It stretched out of sight to both east and west, but at this distance there was no way to tell how tall it was or how well guarded. Below, the river tumbled into a waterfall, meeting a north-flowing stream that did the same from the opposite side of a canyon. A brown rectangle appeared in the flow—their raft. It eased toward the brink of the waterfall. After pausing for a moment at a protruding rock, it bent toward the shore and beached itself, at least for the time being.

Adrian imagined falling off the raft and plunging into the canyon with the roaring water. He shuddered. For some reason, that picture raised more terror than did the reality of being dragon prey.

"Are you warm enough?" Cassabrie asked. "Don't answer verbally. Raise a finger if you would like more heat."

Adrian shook his head. The cloak was warm, and the combination of the fire and the encounter with the dragon had brought plenty of heat.

He raised his hand to his lips and kissed his ring finger, hoping that would communicate his feelings. Since she was missing that finger on both hands, surely she would understand as he shouted his thoughts. *I love you, Cassabrie. I'm glad you're with me.*

THIRTEEN

DREXEL walked up a flight of stone stairs and emerged into a new world, a rocky, desertlike land, mostly flat, except for a mesa in the distance and a forest in another direction. A hint of light just above the tree line grew in brightness, signaling the approach of dawn.

Turning, he examined the structure he had exited, another mesa. Perhaps forty feet in height and a couple thousand in circumference, it stood out in this vast flatland like a wrinkle on otherwise smooth skin.

He checked the photo gun at his hip. It was wet, but it would probably dry before he needed it. And the journal? He reached into his tunic's inner pocket and withdrew the leather-bound book. The cover was moist, but the pages seemed unharmed. The instructions leading to the crystal remained intact. Soon, he would use it to reopen the portal and take the Lost Ones home.

He let his gaze run across the brightening sky. No dragons. If they really did fly, maybe they had not yet awakened. Perhaps soon they would fill the air and begin their slave-driving ways. But where were the slaves?

Something moved far away, a line of activity near the distant mesa. Slaves heading to work? There was only one way to find out.

Drexel jogged in that direction. Getting there before the dragons showed up might be his only chance to talk to the slaves.

After wading through a shallow stream and covering about two miles of terrain populated by dry grass, stunted trees, and an occasional lizard, he arrived. A small girl walked through an arched entryway into the base of the mesa, her head low and her bare feet shuffling, apparently the last of the line, a water carrier perhaps. Surely she was too small to drill for gas.

Drexel followed her into the cavelike tunnel, staying far enough behind to keep out of sight. As he skulked behind the girl, the tunnel, narrow and dark, concealed him in shadows. Soon, she stepped over a low shelf of rock, signaling the end of the tunnel, and walked into a more brightly lit chamber.

Stopping at the shelf, Drexel peered into a cavern. Six men and five children, three boys and two girls, all wearing torn and dirty trousers and tunics, sat on the floor in a circle. Various tools lay strewn about—hammers, chisels, ropes, pails, and drills. A hole in the ceiling directed a shaft of light to the stony floor behind them.

He licked his lips. A familiar bitterness coated them. Extane.

One man spread out his arms and said, "Are we all agreed?"

The other men nodded, a few murmuring, "Yes," or "We are." The children, most kneeling, nodded as well.

"When a patriarch dies," the first man said, "the Code tells us to weep for a day, but to celebrate the life he lived here and his new life hereafter."

"And the prophecy," a girl sang out. "It's another day closer to coming true. The Starlighter will come back."

The man reached out and rubbed her mop of scattered dark hair. "Yes, Cassandra. Thank you for another reminder. It is one day closer. Maybe even today she will come, and the man in whom she dwells, whether a warrior, a prince, or a beggar, will lead us to freedom at long last. Today we will weep, so let us maintain silence throughout our labors. But keep in mind that our dear friend is already free. While we weep for ourselves, let us celebrate for him. His chains have already been torn asunder."

"Are we going to have lessons?" Cassandra asked. "I memorized all my vocabulary words."

He patted her on the head. "Good girl, but not this morning. We will pick up where we left off tomorrow."

While the slaves rose to their feet, Drexel drew back into the entry tunnel and pressed against the wall. A Starlighter dwelling within a man? What could that mean? Clearly they were expecting a rescuer, a man carrying the spirit of a woman, and they didn't know what he was supposed to look like. Could the situation be any better?

He touched his photo gun. A prophecy. A rescuer. Might he be the prophesied one without even knowing it? But what about this Starlighter person? Who was she?

Slowly reaching into his tunic's pocket, he felt for the genetic keys. Pinching one, he withdrew it and set it in his palm, a finger, still well-preserved by the druggist's chemicals and closed off at the base by a cauterizing seal.

The night he collected the fingers reentered his mind. When he crawled into Marcelle's bedroom and set the sword over her and her mother's throats, he had hoped to take Marcelle. Killing and dismembering a little girl would require less effort, but when her mother volunteered, fear and a desire to finish the job had overtaken him. It would be better to snuff out an adult witness and trust that a little girl's memory would never be able to identify him. How many times had he regretted that the two were sleeping together that night? The fear of being found out had haunted him ever since.

Yet, this time, a new thought came to mind. A Starlighter? Even as Marcelle's mother begged for her life, trembling on her knees, a strange light glowed in her eyes. Hands clasped and skin slick with sweat, she had cried, "Please. Do to me what you must. I will cooperate. But do not return to my daughter. Spare her life and her innocence."

Drexel scowled. Stupid woman. He wouldn't commit such a revolting act. Adultery? Child rape? Despicable. The very thought was beyond nauseating. She would be the sacrifice, the lamb who would lose her life to save countless others. How could he violate a holy vessel in such a base way?

Yet, as she begged, her eyes continued to glow. What was it? At the time it seemed to be a reflection of the moon in her tears, but now ...

"A Starlighter," he whispered. Didn't the moon shine even more brightly as he plunged the dagger into her heart? Even as each finger broke away from her hand, hadn't her blood sparkled? When she gasped her final breath, didn't the glow in her eyes radiate, so much so he had to close her eyelids to keep the beams from signaling for help?

As he gazed at the finger, he smiled. The timing of this epiphany had to be Divine Providence. Like the guiding stars, everything was lining up. Not only were the eight jewels the key to entering Dracon, they would be the sign for the slaves that he was the anointed deliverer, and with the Starlighter's fingers pointing the way, he and the Lost Ones would march home in triumph.

Drexel peeked into the chamber again. The laborers had dispersed, leaving only the children in sight, each one carrying a pail. They stood in a line as if waiting to take a turn looking at a big hole about twenty paces away.

He walked in and stooped next to the closest child, the little girl they had called Cassandra. With tangled dark hair and tattered trousers and tunic, she looked like one of the street urchins in Mesolantrum. "Where is the man in charge?" he asked.

Cassandra let out a little gasp. "Who are you?" She quickly covered her mouth with a dirty hand, apparently remembering her vow to stay silent.

The other children turned and stared, but they didn't make a sound.

"I am a very special friend." Drexel gestured for the children to gather around. When the five had made a tight circle, he spoke in a hushed tone. "It is noble of you to honor your departed patriarch with silent prayers, and it seems that your grief will soon transform into joy. You see, I am the rescuer you have prayed for. The Starlighter is within me."

Cassandra's eyes widened, but she stayed silent. The tallest of the children, a bare-chested boy who appeared to be about twelve years old, whispered, "What do we do?"

Drexel rose to his full height and extended his hand. "What is your name, son?"

The boy shook Drexel's hand. "Orlan."

"Well, Orlan, if you will take me to the man in charge, we will begin our plans to end your slavery and take you to freedom."

Orlan looked at the sword on Drexel's hip. "How can you defeat the dragons with that?"

"Shhh." Drexel set a finger to his lips. "Maintain your silence for now. Just take me to your human master."

Orlan gestured with his head for Drexel to follow. The boy stopped at the edge of a pit, perhaps a hundred paces in circumference. A ledge skirted the pit, wide enough to allow two people to walk abreast between the hole and the surrounding wall.

Drexel looked down. No voices rose from the darkness, only the sound of clinking metal and soft grunts. Six greenish lights floated far below, like fireflies, though jerking, usually in time with the staccato sounds.

As he lowered himself to his knees, Drexel looked around. The hole in the ceiling cast a light that angled against the wall, not providing enough illumination below. The miners likely carried a flameless source of light they could discard later in the day when the sun's position in the sky provided a better angle for natural lighting.

He licked his lips again. The bitter film was thicker now, more intense. Extane likely saturated the air, explaining their need for keeping flames away.

As he set a hand down, lowering his body to call for the men, his fingers touched a tube that led into the pit, parallel to a long ladder that faded into the depths. Made out of twisted cords of fibrous plant material, it snaked in the other direction through a hole in the wall. In fact, five other tubes ran along the ground and fed through the hole.

Drexel lifted one with a finger. An air tube. With the extane so dense, the miners likely couldn't breathe without a fresh supply from outside.

Orlan knelt next to him and gave the air tube a gentle tug. A louder grunt sounded from below, and a few seconds later, a man appeared, climbing the ladder. A dirty gray mask covered his mouth, with the end of the tube attached at the side. Wearing a three-day beard and a kerchief around his sweaty neck, he stopped with his hand on the second rung from the top.

He took off the mask and nodded, his features tense. "Greetings, stranger. My name is Jacob."

Drexel took note of Jacob's apparent anxiety. After all, how often did strangers visit a slave operation? The friendliest tone possible was in order. "Greetings to you, as well. I am Drexel."

As the children gathered around, Jacob stepped out of the pit and set his hands on his hips. "Orlan, why are you not carrying stones? Ghisto will be furious if you don't make morning quota."

Orlan hustled to a large basket at the edge of the pit and began transferring rocks to his pail. The other children did the same, but they kept looking at Drexel, wonder in their eyes.

After smiling at the children, Drexel turned back to Jacob and looked him over. He appeared to be a no-nonsense sort—stern and clear-eyed. Perhaps he would be sensible and agree to the plan.

"I'm pleased to meet you," Jacob said, now more at ease. "Your name is unfamiliar. Are you a village worker?"

Drexel set a hand on his sword's hilt. "Not exactly. I have come from a faraway land, and I hope to be of service to you."

When Jacob's gaze shifted to the sword, his brow dipped low, and his muscles flexed. "Why have you brought a weapon? What is your intent?"

Drexel cleared his throat. "As I said, I am from a faraway land. Wild beasts populated my path, so I needed a weapon for safety's sake."

"You speak in a strange manner, so I believe you're from far away, but how can you be of service?"

"I think I can help you with this operation. I assume you're mining extane gas."

"Extane?" Jacob shook his head. "We mine for gas, to be sure, but it's called pheterone."

"Just a matter of synonyms. I recognize the bitterness in my mouth." With a casual glance toward the hole in the ceiling, Drexel raised his brow. "How many other mines are there?"

"Just one other, but this is the more productive of the two by far."

"Is it also in the heart of a mesa?"

"It is." Jacob nodded toward the hole where the air tubes exited. "Besides shade, the covering allows us many options for support mechanisms, and since the tunnel is too narrow for dragons to enter, we are able to converse without them hearing us."

Drexel pictured the cave where the portal brought him into the dragon world. Perhaps that mesa housed the other mine. "Then the dragons would be in trouble if this mine became unable to produce."

"Of that, there is no doubt," Jacob said. "In fact, the dragons are talking about opening a third mine. If they lost this one, they would likely suffer greatly."

"Well, then, I think I have all the information I need." Drexel withdrew his sword a few inches, then slid it back in place. "I am here to set you and the children free. I have the power of the Starlighter with me."

"What?" Jacob grasped Drexel's arm and pulled him close to the wall. He lowered his voice to a bare whisper. "What is this nonsense you're babbling?"

Drexel looked at Jacob's tight grip. "Why are you so surprised? I overheard you confirming Cassandra's faithful confession. The rescuer is not a prince or a beggar, but a warrior who will lead you to freedom."

Jacob gazed at him in silence, blinking.

"Have I misinterpreted your words?" Drexel asked.

Jacob shook his head hard. "No. No, that's not it. Cassandra believes in that tale, as do many of the children, but it is only a tale, something we tell the young ones to give them hope in the midst of their labors. No one of age really believes in it."

"Then what happens when the children learn that you have told them something you don't really believe?"

Jacob's grip eased. "When they're old enough, they can understand that it's a fable with a moral … a … a spiritual reality, if you will. Death is the real rescuer, and we will be transported to the next life where the Starlighter dwells. So we're not lying to them. We're just telling the truth in a way they can understand."

"Then how do you respond to someone like me who bears a sword and claims to be your rescuer?"

Flashing a nervous smile, Jacob pulled off his kerchief and swabbed his forehead. "Pardon me for saying so, but I am concerned about your state of mind. I assume you know the legend about the last man who fashioned a weapon such as yours."

"Let's say I don't." Drexel tapped a finger against his head. "Remember, I might not be of sound mind."

Jacob nodded toward the mesa's exit. "Well, the man's charred bones still lie in a heap in the Basilica courtyard as a reminder of what will happen to anyone who rebels against dragon authority."

Drexel looked that way. "Interesting. And do the children know the truth behind the bones?"

"The older ones do, but we prefer not to frighten the younger ones. Since they aren't aggressive, there is no need for the warning."

Drexel studied Jacob's expression—nervous, unbelieving. "So you would need proof that I am the rescuer."

Jacob laughed under his breath. "My deluded friend, let me make the matter plain to you. There is no proof you could show that would convince me that one sword-bearing man is able to defeat a hundred dragons. We have no other weapons, save for a few picks and shovels, so you would be charging into battle alone. It's impossible."

Drexel glanced into the pit. "And the other men? Do they believe the same way you do?"

"Of course. It is difficult to kick reality out of bed."

Drexel turned toward the tunnel exit. All the children had left with their filled pails. "Is reality persuaded to leave the bed if a person comes bearing the Starlighter?" He reached into his tunic and withdrew a finger. As he gazed upon it, it seemed to glow. Yes, it was, indeed, a fulfillment of prophecy. Surely this man of reason would understand now.

Jacob's mouth dropped open. He withdrew a step, his voice altering to a rasping whisper. "What did you do? Murder someone and dismember the body?"

"Murder?" Drexel blinked at him. "She gave herself to me. In fact, she begged me to take her. Such is the sacrificial nature of a Starlighter."

Glancing at Drexel's sword, Jacob backed toward the pit. Offering a tremulous smile as he picked up his air tube, he nodded multiple times. "I ... I had better tell my fellow workers that our rescuer has arrived. They will be overjoyed." When he set a foot on the ladder rung, he raised a hand. "Now stay right there, and we'll all be up to discuss our battle strategy."

Jacob hurried down the ladder, skipping rungs along the way.

Drexel followed his progress until he disappeared in the darkness. "Battle strategy," he muttered as he slid the finger back into his inner pocket. "What kind of fool does he take me for?"

He removed the photo gun from its holster and examined it. It seemed dry enough. After switching on its energizer, he aimed into the pit. When the indicator showed a full charge, he pulled the trigger. As soon as the fireball punched out of the barrel, he spun and sprinted toward the exit.

With a loud *Phoom*, a wave of heat shoved him through the tunnel and into daylight. He rolled across the ground, his sword clanking, until he hit something solid—Orlan's legs.

Drexel climbed to his feet. Orlan and the other children stood with their mouths agape, each one carrying an empty pail.

Spinning, Drexel looked behind him. The mesa erupted in a fountain of fire, spewing green and orange flames from the hole at the top, and a stiff breeze blew from the exit, hot and dry. Then, like a candle snuffed out by a breath, the flames disappeared.

A load roar rumbled from behind the children. About a hundred paces away, a dragon stomped toward them, beating its wings to give it lift.

Drexel waved his arms. "Hurry, children! Back to the tunnel!"

As he ran with the children, he checked the photo gun. The energizer had not yet recharged. When he reached the entry, a blast of hot air from within blew back his hair and clothes, but it wasn't scalding, merely uncomfortable. Surely these children were accustomed to discomfort.

While Orlan herded the children inside, Drexel stayed at the entrance and aimed the gun at the approaching dragon. "Go in as far as you can," he shouted. "It's hot, but the fire has died down."

Orlan called from within the tunnel. "We're out of the way. Ghisto can't come this far."

"Excellent." The energizer light flashed on. With Ghisto now in range, it was time to show the dragon population something they likely had not seen before. He pulled the trigger. A blue fireball shot out and zoomed toward Ghisto. It smacked against his chest and splashed in an arcing array of blue sparks.

Ghisto lifted his head and screamed. Then, beating his wings again, he half ran and half flew to a nearby stream and dove into the water. As he flailed, plumes of steam shot up all around, masking the sound of his continued shrieks.

Drexel pushed the gun into its holster, dashed out of the mesa, and ran toward the fallen dragon, withdrawing his sword along the way. He waded into the knee-deep water and hacked at the dragon's wriggling neck. With the first swing, the blade clanked against a scale, but the second struck between two scales, creating a bloody gap. While the dragon continued to squeal and flail, Drexel aimed at the wound and slashed again and again. Finally, with the neck half severed, the dragon flopped into the stream and jerked in rhythmic death throes.

With the sword at his side and his chest heaving, Drexel set his feet and glared at the defeated enemy. Too easy, much too easy. Obviously this dragon had never faced a warrior with a photo gun. Perhaps it was a weak female assigned to guard children and men who had the hearts of children.

He looked up at the sky. Would other dragons respond to this one's cries for help? Would blood in the water send a signal to guards downstream? Even if they were all as weak as this one, facing two or more would likely pose an insurmountable obstacle, even for a Starlighter-empowered warrior.

Sliding his sword back to his sheath with a triumphant thrust, Drexel marched back into the tunnel. When he found the children, huddled and sweating in the hot breeze, he stooped beside them, smiling. "Did you see what I did out there?"

"I saw," Orlan said with a scowl. "Now when Yarlan comes on patrol, he will kill us all."

Drexel flipped on the photo gun's energizer. As it hummed, he pointed it at the exit. "If Yarlan comes alone, I will do the same to him."

"You act like you've never seen a guardian dragon." Orlan shook his head sadly. "He is powerful, very powerful."

"I will trust your appraisal, young man. That means we have to leave as quickly as possible."

"What about Jacob and Broderick and the others?" Cassandra asked.

Drexel turned off the gun and pushed it back to its holster. "I will check on them." Easing past the tunnel's shelf, he closed in on the mining pit. Hot air assaulted his face, stinging his cheeks. He peered into the hole. The odor of burnt flesh poured into his nostrils, making him choke. No one could have survived.

He returned to the tunnel and, putting on a sincere expression, he grasped Cassandra's arms and spoke softly. "There has been a terrible accident. Something lit the gas and ignited a huge explosion." Adding a sigh, he lowered his head. "I'm afraid the miners were all in the pit when it happened."

Cassandra covered her face with her hands and sobbed. "Oh, poor Jacob! Poor Broderick!"

As she continued naming and lamenting over the fallen miners, Orlan squinted at the photo gun. "Did that thing cause the explosion?"

"This?" Drexel touched the gun. "Possibly. I was unaware of the volatility of the gas, so a spark might have triggered the explosion."

"So *you* killed our miners?"

"Of course not! Jacob asked what it was, so I showed the photo gun to him. He caused the spark."

Orlan pointed toward the mine chamber, his voice cracking with emotion. "I thought you said they were in the pit."

"They were. Jacob fell in with the force of the explosion. The others were already down there."

Orlan shifted his finger to Drexel. "Then how did *you* survive? And how did you get the ..." He took a moment to recall the name. "The photo gun back?"

Drexel looked Orlan in the eye. "Young man, if you are going to lack faith in me, then perhaps you should leave now. I cannot lead you to freedom if you're going to spread doubt among the others. We will go without you."

"I'm sorry. I was just—"

"For your information, the explosion was confined to the pit. Jacob fell into it, and I did not. That's how I survived. And I never fully released the gun into his hands. I kept my grip on it the entire time." Drexel forced a scowl. "I hope that satisfies your faithless questions."

"It does." Orlan lowered his voice to a whisper. "I won't ask any more questions."

Drexel relaxed his expression and studied each face. Two children were openly crying, perhaps grieving over lost friends or family. The other three were pensive, worried, probably about the power of the guardian dragons and the likely punishment they would have to endure. Maybe their fear would play into his hands.

"Because of this unfortunate series of events, we will have to flee for our lives before Yarlan gets here." Drexel slid his hand into Cassandra's. "You must maintain silence and hurry with me to the other mine. There, we will be able to escape."

"We don't have time," Orlan said. "Yarlan will be flying by at any minute. Nothing escapes his sharp eyes." He lowered his head. "That was a statement, not a question."

Drexel looked at the exit, then at the pit. The dragons would be unable to enter the tunnel and investigate. Maybe they wouldn't risk sending any other humans in until they were confident the mine had stabilized. "Then we'll wait here. If no one comes out, they will assume that everyone perished, and we can leave under the cover of darkness."

"But once we go to the other mine, how do we escape? It's just another mine."

"That was a question, Orlan." Drexel laughed and mussed the boy's hair. "Fear not, my valiant skeptic. I have everything under control. We will walk out of here and into the arms of freedom before night reaches its midpoint."

FOURTEEN

WITH her head above water, Marcelle swam in darkness, using one arm to paddle and the other to hold the sword in front of her as a feeler. She kicked as noiselessly as possible. If something dangerous lurked in the depths, better to let it sleep. She would be a minnow passing by, a missed lunch.

She jabbed with the sword, always hitting empty water. Was she going in the right direction? With the stream so calm, she might be swimming in circles.

She stopped and tried to stay as stationary as possible, feeling for the current. No. She had drifted off course. Upstream lay twenty degrees to the right.

A cold appendage slithered up her ankle and held on. She let out a yelp and jerked her leg up, but the creature pulled back, dragging her down.

She dove and hacked with her sword, aiming just below her foot. She sliced through something. A water-warped squeal ripped through the pool. Now free, she lunged to the surface and swam with all her might, stabbing straight down, splashing and kicking to escape.

After nearly a minute, her sword hit something solid. The pool had grown shallow, allowing her to stand in waist-deep water. As she walked, the depth gradually lessened—thigh-deep, then knee-deep. Soon, only her feet and ankles pushed through the stream, but an extra weight dragged with her.

She sat down in the current, a little swifter now, and felt her right ankle. Something hung on, apparently the creature's severed appendage. She peeled away a snakelike section, popping suction attachments from her skin and clothing as she pulled. Once free, she slung it back toward the pool, whispering, "I drew first blood. You lost."

When she rose to her feet and resumed her stride, her ankle throbbed with every step. She glanced back into the darkness. Had that creature stung her? Injected her with poison? Maybe it followed, waiting for her to succumb to the venom and float back into its clutches.

Limping, she picked up her pace. Who cared about splashing noises? She had to get away.

Soon, her head scraped the ceiling. As she bent over and pushed forward, the current grew ever swifter. The passage had to be narrowing, and it seemed to be sloping upward now, a good sign. Maybe it would break through on the surface, preferably on the opposite side of the wall. But would she be able to crawl through? Or would she have to give up and go back the way she came, including swimming through the pool again?

Shaking her head, she muttered, "Retreat is not an option."

When the ceiling forced her down to hands and knees, she slid the sword back into her strapped-in scabbard and crawled. Her ankle ached horribly, and the sting began inching up her leg. Ignore it. Just ignore it. That was her only choice.

As she lowered herself to her belly, the water gushed. She waited through five surges, counting between each one, but the interval differed every time—five seconds, nine seconds, five seconds again, and three seconds. This wouldn't be easy.

She squirmed ahead, her nose barely above the surface. The stream gushed again, filling her nostrils. She sneezed, then inhaled just in time to breathe in the next surge of water. She jerked her head upward to cough and slammed against the ceiling, but it couldn't be helped. With her chin now above the surface, she coughed, spat out trickles of fluid, and coughed again, repeating the pattern several times. Soon, she expelled the last drops and lowered herself back to her belly.

Now taking a breath after each pulse of water, she pushed on. Her ankle felt like it was on fire, and the wound in her side stung. The bandage had likely stripped away long ago. Still, she wiggled ahead, progressing inches with every push. Would this channel never come to the surface?

After a few minutes, the blackness changed to gray. The rocky walls on each side became visible, as did her hands. With every push, a glow somewhere far ahead grew stronger. Could that be where the river poured into this underground channel? Might dragons be guarding the way out?

With light now making her path easy to see, she studied the passage. Only a few pushes ahead, the water surged to the ceiling for a moment, dimming the light, then lowered again without leaving enough room for a traveler to come up for air. Maybe this was the final exit, the gateway to the river's surface, but emerging into the light would expose her to any dragons that might be guarding the hole. She would have to take a deep breath, exit as quickly as possible, and dive back underwater until she could check for guards. And if she ran out of oxygen, retreating through the narrow passage would likely be impossible. It might be time to choose her poison—dragons or drowning.

After taking a deep breath, she charged ahead, wiggling and squirming with every muscle. The glow grew brighter, but the channel continued on, inches upon inches, feet upon feet. Her lungs ached. Her arms and legs burned. If she didn't find air soon, all would be lost.

Finally, her head broke the surface. She took in a silent breath of air and looked around. She had emerged in a cave. A wall stood only two body lengths in front of her with an opening that allowed the river and outside light to enter. The upper arch of the opening rose less than a foot above the river's surface, and the remainder of its circular shape, perhaps a body length wide, was underwater. A gate of crisscrossing wooden slats covered the opening, leaving gaps far too small to allow a human to pass through.

The river flowed in at a tranquil rate, and the tunnel sucked it in, slurping every few seconds as the level fell below the top of the tunnel before rising over it again. With the river being far larger than the tunnel, perhaps this outlet was just one of many.

Now in deeper water, she swam out to the cave's opening and pushed her fingers between the slats to hold on. Massive boulders framed the hole, stacked high and curving back over her head, an uneven surface made up of smaller stones and mortar. Had she come out within the wall itself, in a bubble of sorts carved into the stone to allow the river to exit?

Marcelle peered through the gaps in the gate. A dragon likely watched the river's exit. If not, a human on the other side could hold his breath, cut the slats, and escape through the tunnel. Still, such a feat was improbable. The tunnel to freedom was little more than a wormhole, and very few men were small enough to squeeze through. Certainly a warrior of Adrian's size and build couldn't have made it, and the slaves probably never considered sending a woman or a child.

She pulled the viper from the scabbard and began sawing through one of the slats just a foot or so below the surface. The water was clear enough to see several feet down, making her work easily visible, but with the pain in her ankle still growing, even the slightest effort seemed a chore.

Soon, the slat broke away, and she moved the blade to the one below it. It made sense to try an underwater escape, but how far could she swim upstream before coming up for air?

After several minutes, she had broken enough slats. It was time to squeeze through and face the dragons. She returned the sword to the scabbard and listened for any sign of their presence. Not a sound except for the intermittent slurping behind her.

A loud splash erupted from the river just beyond the cave's opening. A dragon flailed in the water, roaring and spewing flames. Blood poured from a gaping wound in its belly and spread throughout the water, tingeing it red.

Marcelle ducked under the surface and swam through the hole, then dove deep to get below the wounded dragon and avoid being seen. Whatever was happening up there, it had to be good. This distraction might be her only chance.

*　　　*　　　*　　　*　　　*　　　*

Zerath descended toward the wall, Adrian still dangling underneath. The flight had been fast and rough, and Cassabrie had said very little, only a warning to be submissive and to continue appealing for Arxad's aid. If more dragons heard his appeal, having witnesses might help his cause.

Below, two dragons stood on the wall's top, a wide road with a parapet on each side. When Zerath descended, Adrian touched feetfirst, but Zerath pushed his full weight on Adrian's back, forcing him to crumple. As Zerath stood on top of him, he dug his claws through Adrian's cloak and into his skin.

The other two dragons shuffled closer, and Zerath addressed them in a guttural drawl.

Lying on his belly, Adrian gasped for breath. Zerath's weight was bad enough, but those claws stung mercilessly.

"Here is the fire starter," Cassabrie said. "He signaled so that he could surrender."

"Are you translating?" Adrian whispered.

"Yes. Since they assume that most slaves know their language, they are not using it to hide their intentions. It's just easier for them."

The larger of the two dragons replied with what sounded like a series of clucks and then the lowing of a cow.

"Surrender?" Cassabrie said. "Does he not know the punishment that awaits him?"

As the dragons conversed, Cassabrie continued her translations.

Zerath shifted slightly, relieving some of the pressure. "I did not ask, but he immediately appealed to Arxad."

"Arxad?" The smaller dragon spat out a tiny ball of flames that splashed against one of the waist-high parapets. "That meddlesome priest is too softhearted."

"Yes, he is softhearted," the larger one said. "But that is to be expected. He has never had to deal with lazy, stubborn slaves."

"I heard he wants to close the cattle camp. How would we cull out the weaklings if we were to do that?"

The larger dragon bobbed his head as if agreeing, but his expression looked doubtful. "I have heard Arxad speak, and he is not siding with the humans. His reasoning is often sound. If the slaves think we are cruel to the children, they are less likely to work hard. They will do as little as possible."

"The sting of a whip will change that."

Zerath raised his voice, cutting off the other two dragons. "Save the political debates for later. If we all agree that he should be summarily executed, then we will not have to worry about protocol."

"Kill him," the smaller dragon said.

The larger one drew his head closer to Adrian. Adrian tried to look as innocent and friendly as he could, but with the clawing foot ripping his skin, holding back a grimace seemed almost impossible.

"Make him stand. I want to have a better look at him."

The weight lifted, allowing Adrian to breathe more easily.

"Get up," Zerath ordered, now speaking in the human language.

Cinching his cloak to keep it closed, Adrian rose slowly to his feet as he whispered. "I'll need your advice, Cassabrie."

"Ask them their names, and tell them you will speak highly of them in Magnar's presence, that they were vigilant, that their eyes were sharp, that no one can escape with them on duty."

Adrian bowed his head, then looked at the three dragons. "I hope to speak in Magnar's presence, and I wish to tell him the names of the sentries who brought me to his justice. I have already become acquainted with Zerath, and if I also learn your names, I can tell of your skill in finding me. Magnar will likely be glad to know that the boundary is well fortified by such vigilant dragons."

"I am Starmeer," the larger dragon said. "And my sentry companion—"he stretched a wing toward the smaller dragon—"is Ortmoll."

"If you allow me to live," Adrian said, "I will remember those names and speak highly of you to Magnar."

Starmeer drew his head close and sniffed Adrian. "Your odor is not like that of other slaves."

"Tell him you were in the Fragrance Fields," Cassabrie said. "The flowers have masked your normal stench."

Adrian sniffed the shoulder of his cloak. "The Fragrance Fields. I walked through the flowers, and they are hiding my stench. Humans need a splash of perfume every now and then, don't you think?"

Starmeer laughed while Ortmoll growled something in the dragon language, apparently speaking to Zerath.

"What did he say?" Adrian whispered.

"I will not repeat it. It was obscene."

"His cleverness amuses me." Starmeer stretched out his wings. "I will take him to Arxad myself."

Ortmoll stepped in front of Starmeer, again speaking in the dragon tongue.

"A clever slave is a dangerous slave," Cassabrie said. "Such talk is nothing more than condescension. While he plays at being humble, inside he is laughing at you. Humor is best squashed by executions. We cannot allow that poison to spread."

While the three dragons continued speaking, Cassabrie remained quiet for a few seconds. Then, as the discussion grew animated, she stretched out her words. "This is not going well, Adrian."

"What do you mean?" he whispered.

"They have decided to kill you, and they don't seem to care whether or not you know their intent. The only issue that remains is how to dispose of your body. I suggest that you consider a plan of escape."

Adrian looked at Zerath's belly. The legends said that every dragon had a vulnerable spot there. Indeed, the scales didn't quite meet at one point, but the exposed area was no bigger than his thumb. It would take a perfect sword thrust. Yet, even if he could slay the beast, the two other dragons would incinerate him before he could withdraw his blade from the first one.

He looked over the parapet on the river's side. The drop wasn't too far, maybe twenty feet, easily survivable, but could the dragons swim and follow him underneath? Even if not, he would have to come up for air eventually, and he would then be an easy target.

While slowly reaching under his cloak, he slid closer to the river side of the wall. Ortmoll stood within reach. This wasn't a great plan, but it was the only one he had. He withdrew the sword, drove the blade into Ortmoll's belly, and leaped to the top of the parapet.

With the sword still in his gut, Ortmoll flew at him, fire blazing from his mouth. Adrian ducked under the flames, grabbed Ortmoll's neck, and jumped toward the river, using the dragon's momentum to haul the huge beast with him.

Screaming wildly, Ortmoll clawed at Adrian and whipped him with his wings, but Adrian hung on. The moment they splashed into the river, he let go and dove deep into the warm, clear water. Above, the dragon flailed. Blood spewed, clouding the view.

Adrian glanced in every direction. Which way? The fall had spun him around. He stared straight ahead. The wall stood there. Wrong direction. But what was that shadow passing over his head? Someone swimming? A woman? Marcelle!

He swam up to meet her. Did she know about the other two dragons? She carried a sword, but that wouldn't be enough. He had to warn her.

He reached up and grabbed her free hand. In a flurry of swinging limbs and jetting bubbles, she attacked. Her blade, slowed by the water, swiped by his cheek, missing by less than an inch. She drew back, a hand on her chest. As another stream of bubbles flew from her nose, she shouted, "Adrian!"

An enormous splash erupted nearby. Zerath! The dragon looked at his fellow guard briefly before scanning the area. His red eyes gleamed. Above the water level, a shadow passed over, likely Starmeer waiting to scorch any head that appeared.

Adrian shed his saturated cloak and jerked out his hatchet. It was time to fight, futile though it seemed.

Zerath began a slow swim toward them. As he opened his maw, jagged teeth and a darting tongue appeared. Marcelle grabbed Adrian's arm and pointed at the wall. They paddled furiously toward it, Marcelle leading the way. She slipped through a hole in a wooden grate and disappeared.

After swimming through the hole, Adrian turned and, still under water, hid behind the wall, ready with the axe. The dragon's head darted through. Adrian slashed at its eyes, but the water slowed the axe too much. He couldn't make a dent.

Zerath snapped at Adrian, barely missing his face. Adrian thrust backwards. The dragon's body couldn't break through the hole, but his neck was long enough to bring those sharp teeth within range.

"Adrian!" Cassabrie called. "Trade weapons!"

Trade weapons? He looked up. Marcelle swam toward him, a sword extended. The dragon snapped again. His teeth tore Adrian's trousers and ripped away a long strip.

Adrian shoved the axe into Marcelle's hand and snatched her sword. With the next dragon lunge, Adrian stabbed at Zerath's face. The short blade pierced between two facial scales, deep enough to make his attacker flinch and recoil.

Marcelle chopped at Zerath's neck, though her blows did little good. Adrian's lungs burned. Dizziness flooding his mind, he continued to jab, aiming at Zerath's eyes. Finally, Marcelle grabbed his arm and hauled him to the surface.

Air! Adrian sucked in deep draughts. It never tasted so good.

Marcelle pulled him to the opposite side of the wall, but they could go no farther. They paddled in place, both gasping for breath. "I don't think ... the hole's big enough," Marcelle said, coughs interrupting her words. "The dragon ... can't get through."

Adrian slowed his breathing. "His head can get pretty far."

Zerath's head popped above the surface. Two lines of steam blasted from his nostrils and splashed against the wall between Adrian and Marcelle.

Marcelle lunged with the hatchet and hacked at his eyes. Adrian joined in with the sword, forcing Zerath to shield both eyes with his scaly lids. Now unable to see, he blew a stream of flames from his mouth but missed badly.

Zerath drew back, blinking. Marcelle surged ahead and hacked again, this time landing the hatchet's blade in the dragon's left eye. Fluid spurted. Zerath roared. Fire erupted from his mouth and both nostrils, spraying wildly.

Adrian lunged for Marcelle and dragged her below the surface. Zerath's head slid under with them and then back through the hole. After a savage swipe at the grate with his tail, he swam away.

Adrian and Marcelle resurfaced, again gasping.

"Now what?" Marcelle asked.

"Do you still have the hatchet?"

She shook her head. "I think it's embedded in its eye."

"We should go. One dragon's dead. Another is half blind. Maybe the third will be distracted. We'll just swim underwater as far as we can, come up for a gulp of air, and then keep going. If we stay here, they'll figure out how to break through and fish us out."

"Give me just a second." Marcelle inhaled and exhaled three times before nodding. "I'm ready."

Leading with Marcelle's sword, Adrian ducked underwater and glided through the hole. When Marcelle caught up, they swam side by side through a cloud of red and under Ortmoll's carcass, now floating with half its body submerged.

Adrian thrust himself up, pulled his sword from the dragon's belly, and hurried back down to rejoin Marcelle. He returned the viper to her and, after finding his cloak at the river bottom, scooped it up and tied it around his waist.

Once he reached clear water, he surveyed the scene. The north-flowing river seemed to be about twelve feet deep at the center, and the channel spanned about thirty feet, getting steadily shallower on each side. The current streamed into his eyes, bringing with it an occasional fleck of algae he had to blink away, and dozens of silvery fish, most no longer than a finger, darted about in seemingly choreographed moves.

He kept glancing up, looking for a shadow. Starmeer was out there somewhere, probably waiting for a chance to scorch their hides or pluck them from the water, like an eagle snatching a fish with its talons. Surely he was able to follow their trails. The water stayed clear, and every motion sent a line of bubbles streaming toward the surface.

Ahead, the river narrowed and grew shallower, presenting more problems. For now, an immediate danger demanded their attention. They had to breathe.

He tightened his grip on the sword. If that scaly eagle swooped down, he would get the fight of his life.

Looking at Marcelle, he pointed upward, hoping to signal his intention. She nodded. It was time. Jabbing with swords as they surged toward the surface, Adrian blew out all his reserves, getting ready to heave in another gulp. When they splashed into the open, he stabbed empty air.

Marcelle, her own sword also uplifted, sucked in deep breaths. She swung her head from side to side, slinging droplets. "Where is he?"

"I don't know." Adrian looked back at the wall. At the top, a dragon staggered, holding a wing over his eye, roaring mightily. "I see Zerath," Adrian said, "but Starmeer's nowhere in sight."

"If you looked in the correct direction, you would find Starmeer."

Adrian twisted toward the voice. At the eastern bank, Starmeer sat on his haunches, strings of black smoke rising from his nostrils. A growl rippled through his words. "Since you have slain a dragon, I have the right under the law to kill you. You cannot appeal to Arxad."

Still breathless, Adrian paddled hard with one hand to stay in place. "But the only reason I killed Ortmoll was because of your refusal to heed my earlier appeal to Arxad."

Starmeer breathed a long, "Hmmm."

Cassabrie whispered. "Well done, Adrian. Now ask him to grant you free passage. You will not mention his earlier mistake to anyone."

Adrian took in another deep breath. Hearing Cassabrie again took him by surprise. She had stayed silent for quite a while.

"Starmeer." Adrian tried to inject legal propriety into his tone, though treading water made it much more difficult. "Since I surrendered, surely you know that I trusted in your sense of justice. I was shocked that a trio of dragon guards would bypass such a noble and merciful law and resort to taking the law into their own ... uh ... grasp. Yet, I could tell that you were torn, that you were pressured into joining the other two. So, I appeal now to your integrity. If you will allow us free passage—"

"Stop the gibberish!" Starmeer extended his neck and eyed Marcelle. "Who is this woman? A conspirator in a plot to assassinate dragons?"

"Not at all," Adrian said. "We did not conspire to kill anyone. With your sharp eyesight, you must have noticed that she was already in the river when I fell. She had nothing to do with Ortmoll's death."

"Was she attempting an escape?"

Marcelle spoke up. "If you wish to learn of my activities, why don't you address me?"

The dragon spat a ball of fire. Adrian and Marcelle ducked under water just in time. The flames sizzled on the surface above them and vanished. When they resurfaced, Adrian whisper shouted at Marcelle, "Let me handle this!"

She glared at him. "Suit yourself."

"As you can see," Adrian said, turning back to Starmeer, "we are at a stalemate. You cannot harm us from there with your fire breathing. And if you choose to enter the water …" He lifted his sword and flexed his muscles. "You have seen my skill. My companion's skill is equal to mine. We will not die easily."

Starmeer continued puffing lines of dark gray smoke. "I am no fool, slave. I see through your façade, but I also see that granting your request is the better option." He waved a wing toward the bank. "Come out over here. If you want to live, you must hurry. Zerath still has a good eye, and when his pain eases, he will hunt for you without mercy."

Gesturing for Marcelle to follow, Adrian swam toward the shore. As they climbed to dry ground, their clothes heavy and dripping, he looked upstream. Of course, he had no idea which way to go, but that direction led away from Zerath, and Cassabrie would be sure to guide them later.

He pushed back the cloak, still tied at his waist, and slid his sword into its scabbard, then gestured for Marcelle to sheathe hers. "We thank you, Starmeer, and—"

"Spare me the guile, you deceiver, and be on your way. Do you think I care nothing that you killed my fellow guard and wounded another?"

"Say no more, Adrian," Cassabrie whispered. "Do not even look him in the eye. Turn upstream and walk quickly away. I will tell you where to go."

Taking Marcelle's hand, Adrian marched as fast as he could, but Marcelle lagged, walking with a pronounced limp.

"What's wrong?" he asked.

She grimaced but tried to keep pace. "Something stung my ankle. I don't know what it was, but it had a tentacle-like appendage."

He looked at her ankle, but her trouser leg covered it. "Does it hurt a lot?"

"Yes, but I can handle it."

"If you broke your leg, would you use a crutch?"

"If a crutch was available, I'd use it now."

"It's available." He swept his arms under her and lifted her into a cradle.

She tried to jerk away, but he tightened his grip. "What do you think you're doing?" she hissed. "I'm not an invalid. I can—"

"Shush!" He stepped into a lively march, trying to ignore the pain in his own leg. "You heard what Starmeer said about Zerath. We have to hurry or risk getting scorched."

With his back turned to the dragons, he imagined a barrage of flames blasting across his body. The thought made his skin crawl. When he finally put a hundred paces between himself and Starmeer, he let out a long breath.

"Tired?" Marcelle asked, a coy smile dressing her wet face. "You make a handsome crutch, but the ones I've used never breathed that hard."

Adrian gazed at her. With her hair slicked back, her face looked different. Maybe it was her forehead, usually veiled somewhat by her hair. Fully exposed, her uplifted brow animated her usually stoic expression. This new aspect was hard to read, less serious than her usual appearance. She seemed younger, perhaps even playful, almost like the little Marcelle he used to roam the woods with so long ago.

"Yes, I'm tired," he finally said.

"That took long enough to decide." Two lines dug into her brow. "What's wrong?"

He tried to shrug, but her weight kept his shoulders in place. It was definitely warmer here, causing him to break a sweat. "This is a strange world. I slept on a river raft last night, at least for a while, so I shouldn't be too tired. I think so many shots of adrenaline have taken their toll."

Part of him wanted to mention Cassabrie and her indwelling presence, but that would be like admitting to insanity.

Shifting herself higher, she extended her arm farther around his neck and smiled. "You should be tired. We had quite a battle back home and another one here. And you even killed that dragon. I'm impressed."

He nodded. "I took a big chance." As he walked close to the river, the trees thickened to his left. He related the story—signaling the dragon with the fire hoping to gain easy entry, getting flown to the wall where two other dragons patrolled, and attacking one dragon after they decided to kill him. Of course, he left out Cassabrie's involvement, including her ability to interpret the dragon language. Fortunately, the language question never came up.

When he finished, he looked back. The dragon and the wall were now out of sight, hidden by the forest. He stopped and lowered her to the ground, helping her sit. She rolled up her pant leg, revealing circular marks, red and swollen, from her ankle to her knee.

"That looks painful."

She nodded. "Something grabbed me in a pool."

"A bastra," Cassabrie said. "We have to neutralize the poison."

Adrian cleared his throat. "It looks like some kind of poison."

"I agree," Marcelle said. "I think it's spreading."

"Then we have to find something to neutralize it."

She looked up at him. "Strange poison in a strange world, Adrian. Nothing we know will help."

"Bastra poisoning is easily cured," Cassabrie said. "There is an herb that grows practically everywhere near the river. This time of year it has a yellow flower and black nodules around its base. You need the fluid in the stem. Put it on the wounds, and her skin will soak it in."

Adrian searched the area. Yellow flowers abounded in the ground cover. He stooped and plucked several, noting the black beads falling to the ground as he pulled. "Let's try these," he said as he broke open a stem.

She squinted at him. "A stab in the dark?"

"Just trust me." He poured sticky green liquid from the stem and rubbed it into one of the red marks.

"Ouch!" Marcelle jerked her leg back. "It burns!"

He looked at the thick juice in his palm. It stung quite a bit, probably worse on her raw skin, but not enough to rattle a warrior. "I never expected you to be squeamish."

"Squeamish? Adrian, I've stitched up my own wounds with a sewing needle. I'm not scared of a little burn, but I have to know it's not going to make things worse."

"It won't."

"How do you know?"

Adrian sharpened his voice. "If there's anything you should know about me, it's that I would never do anything to hurt you."

She stared at him. For several seconds, neither said a word. Finally, Cassabrie broke the silence in Adrian's mind. "Tell her it's called milk balm. It binds with the poison and neutralizes the toxin."

Adrian reached for her leg. "It's called milk balm. It will bind with the poison and neutralize the toxin."

"Oh." Giving him a look of surrender, she pushed her leg closer. "Why didn't you tell me you knew what it was?"

As he rubbed the tacky syrup on her wounds, heat radiated into his fingers. She grimaced tightly but said nothing.

Cassabrie whispered, "Aren't you going to answer her?"

Adrian shook his head. When he finished applying the balm, he wiped his fingers on his tunic.

"How long will it take to work?" Marcelle asked through clenched teeth.

"I don't know." He rolled her pant leg down. "I hope we can afford to wait."

Cassabrie laughed gently. "It works quickly. She will be back on her feet in a few minutes."

Adrian looked into Marcelle's hopeful eyes. She wanted reassurance, but if he told her more about the balm's properties, her interrogation might be too pointed to avoid.

"Adrian?" Cassabrie said. "Aren't you going to tell her?"

He coughed. "Can you feel any difference?"

"I do." She pulled up her pant leg again and looked at her skin. The wounds had already faded to pink. "That balm is amazing."

"Adrian, why aren't you talking to me anymore?" Cassabrie asked.

He rose to his feet and helped Marcelle to hers. "Can you walk?"

"I think so." She pressed her weight on the stricken leg. "It feels much better."

Cassabrie's voice spiked. "Adrian?"

Still holding Marcelle's hand, he looked at the river. "Now I have to ask our guide where to go next."

"Our guide?" Marcelle asked.

He nodded. "I don't know how to tell you this. You'll think I'm really strange."

She laughed gently. "Adrian, I have thought you strange ever since you were five years old and you beat up Saul Berryman for sticking his tongue out at me. Nothing's going to change that now."

Heat flowed into his cheeks. "Well, this is a lot stranger than a punch in a bully's nose. You see …" He looked at their hands, still touching in a loose clasp. "I don't know how to say this. I respect you too much to expect you to believe what I need to tell you."

"Go ahead," Marcelle whispered, a tear now glistening in her eye. "I'll believe anything you tell me."

Cassabrie's tone softened. "I now understand your dilemma, Adrian, and I apologize for my impatience. Maybe you can tell her that ever since you arrived, you have heard an inner voice that has been completely accurate about everything."

Adrian heaved a sigh. "Marcelle, like you said, this is a strange world, and ever since I've been here …" He pointed at his head. "I hear a voice, and it tells me what to do, including how to get milk balm for the poisoning. In fact, I even know what kind of creature stung you. The voice said it's called a bastra."

She blinked at him. "A voice? Like an audible voice? Like me talking to you?"

"Not exactly. It's audible, but it feels like it comes from inside my body."

"What does it sound like? A man? A woman?"

Adrian closed his eyes and concentrated on Cassabrie's presence. "I don't have any choice, do I?"

"Do what you think best, Adrian," Cassabrie said. "I am your—"

"I know. I know. You're my guide, not my mistress."

"Adrian," Marcelle said. "What are you talking about?"

He opened his eyes again. "Marcelle, it's Cassabrie."

She cocked her head, her brow furrowing. "What?"

"Cassabrie is inside me." He laid a hand over his chest. "In here. She is a spirit, a disembodied soul, and she's dwelling inside me.

She guided me from the Northlands, she suggested the idea of signaling the dragons, and she told me about the bastra and milk balm. She's my guide."

Marcelle stared at him for a long moment. She then dipped her head, averting her eyes as she pulled her hand back. "Okay."

"Okay?" He tried to catch her gaze, but she turned away. "Is that all?" he said. "Just *okay*?"

She swung back around, fire now blazing in her eyes. "I told you I would believe you. What else do you want from me?"

He held up his hands and backed away a step. "I'm sorry. You're right."

She crossed her arms over her chest and turned toward the river. "Let's just get going. We have slaves to rescue."

Adrian lifted a hand. Should he touch her shoulder? Give her assurance? If so, assurance of what? He let his arm droop at his side. "You're right again. We have to go, but I have no idea where."

Keeping her back turned toward him, she pulled a hair band from her pocket and looped it around her hair in the back. "Then ask your spiritual guide what to do next."

He nodded. What else could he do but press on? "Cassabrie? What now?"

"We will follow the river upstream. I will take you to the closest slave operation, at least the closest one I remember. We have to stay in the forest to the east of the river. We need to avoid all dragons from this point forward."

"Understood." Adrian looked to the east where a deeply forested area grew just beyond an alluvial plain, rising up like a green wall at the edge of the river's flood zone. Dark and foreboding, it offered both protection and potential danger. Yet, if Cassabrie said it was safer than the alternative, then they would have to take their chances with the unknown mysteries therein, rather than the certainty of fire from above.

FIFTEEN

D REXEL stood with Cassandra near the mesa's exit and looked out at the gathering of dragons. The beast the slaves had called Ghisto lay at the clawed feet of two others that were much bigger and more rugged looking. With the other children safely huddled deeper in the tunnel, he would be able to assess the situation without risking harm to the precious ones he had come to rescue. Yet, keeping Cassandra close made sense. She could provide information about this strange world without asking too many questions.

The biggest dragon looked up at the sky. The column of smoke rising above the mesa had blown toward him. Although the fire had died out, the men's bodies and some of the equipment still smoked. The extane continued to build, so any spark could ignite another eruption. Time would tell.

One of the two bigger dragons ambled closer to the mesa's entry. Drexel grabbed Cassandra and ducked with her behind an outcropping in the wall. He peeked around the edge. If they saw him and realized there were survivors, all would be lost.

A dragon's head slid into view. With pulsing red eyes, thick scales, and smoking nostrils, it was a sight to behold. No wonder Orlan seemed so worried. If this dragon was half as powerful as it appeared, even a photo gun likely wouldn't faze it.

The dragon called out. "Are there any survivors?"

Its rumbling voice echoed once and died away.

Holding Cassandra close, Drexel tightened his crouch. Would the other children heed his warnings to stay quiet? So far, so good.

The dragon's head withdrew. Two draconic voices drifted in, but they spoke in odd roars and rumbles.

"There is no one near the entrance," Cassandra whispered, "but it is difficult to see farther in. Shall I light up the passage?"

"Is that what the dragon said?" Drexel asked.

She nodded. "And the other one just said, 'No. We do not want to risk another explosion.'"

"Keep translating, but very quietly."

After each sentence the dragons uttered, Cassandra breathed the human equivalent.

"We could send a slave."

"I will see if we can spare one from the other mine. In the meantime, post a guard. Ghisto's death means that something evil is afoot. Someone has a sharp weapon."

"Perhaps the murderer died in the explosion."

"Perhaps. If we cannot spare a scout and no one emerges by evening, we will set a trap at the exit and check it in the morning."

"Consider it done."

The sound of shuffling dragons drifted slowly away.

Rising from his hiding place and holding Cassandra's hand, Drexel peered at the exit. No sign of a dragon. "Come," he whispered.

Holding his sword against his leg with one hand and clutching Cassandra's hand with the other, he hurried back to the pit. The children had gathered near the surrounding wall, out of view of any dragon that might fly over the extane exhaust hole above. Orlan stood while the other three sat in a huddle near a small pile of shavings that resembled manna bark.

Cassandra joined the trio, grabbed a pinch of shavings, and began chewing as she whispered excitedly with the other children.

Drexel swiped a sleeve across his sweaty forehead. "The dragons have withdrawn for now."

"I'm thirsty," the youngest boy said, looking up at him with a glistening face. "It's so hot in here."

Drexel let out a low "Shhh." He touched Orlan's back. The dirty shirt he had put on felt hot and sweaty. "Where do you get water while you're working?"

"The miners take flasks down into the pit. We drink from the stream."

"Then we'll just have to endure." He looked at the children. They were slaves. They were accustomed to suffering.

He crouched next to the thirsty boy and pushed back his wet hair. "Take courage, young man. Soon you will have all the food and water you could ever hope for. You will splash happily in water flowing from springs in which you will never lift a finger in labor. You will laugh with the other children and forget the harsh labors of this nightmare of a world."

"No dragons?" he asked.

"No dragons, not ever again."

"No whips?"

"If anyone ever raises a whip against you, I will personally shove it …" He glanced at all the wide eyes staring at him and cleared his throat. "I will personally shove it up his nose."

Cassandra covered her mouth and stifled a giggle.

"Now," Drexel continued in a whisper, "I know it's early, but it would be best if you try to go to sleep. It will help you forget your thirst, and you will need your energy for tonight's journey."

The four younger children reclined on the stone floor, curling their bodies into comfortable positions. A cooling breeze swept in from the tunnel, caressing their sweaty bodies and carrying the rising smoke more swiftly through the hole in the ceiling.

After they all appeared to be dozing off, Drexel grasped Orlan's arm. "The dragons will either send in a human to investigate or set a trap so no one can leave."

"That makes sense," Orlan said, chewing a piece of bark he held between his finger and thumb.

"Do you know what kind of trap they would use?"

Orlan withdrew the bark from his mouth. "They bury ropes in the grit just outside and place a thin mesh over the opening. The mesh is invisible in the dark, so if you don't know it's there, it's impossible to avoid. When you walk through, the mesh triggers the snare. Loops in the ropes grab your ankles, and barbs in the loops inject poison that can put you to sleep or kill you, depending on whether the dragons want you to live or die."

"A cruel device, to be sure." Drexel looked up at the hole in the ceiling. Gray and black smoke partially shielded the view. "Do you think they will set a trap up there?"

"Not likely. Who would try to go out that way if they think it's safe to walk out the exit?"

"Of course." Drexel imagined himself trying to jump up and grab the lip of the hole above. Since it was only eight feet or so from the floor, a good leap would span the gap. In his vision, he managed to grasp it for a moment before slipping and falling into the pit. There had to be an easier way. "I assume the ladders will go that high, won't they?"

"If they haven't burned up."

Drexel looked at the miners' hole. The top rung of the ladder no longer protruded beyond the rim. "Yes, that might be a problem, but we will have to wait for the approach of night to investigate. We can't risk being seen."

Orlan sat and leaned his head against the wall.

"Are you going to sleep?" Drexel asked.

"Maybe. Maybe not." He pointed his bark fragment at Drexel. "Someone has to keep an eye on you."

Drexel pulled off his sword belt and sat down next to him, crossing his legs as he set the sword and scabbard on his lap. "You are wise not to trust a stranger, young man, especially under these circumstances, but it seems that you don't have much choice."

Orlan stared at the sword. "I still have a choice."

"Is that so?" Drexel fingered the embossed design on the scabbard, an eagle with its wings outstretched in full flight. "What choice might that be?"

"Since you're a stranger here, you need my help, and as long as you need my help, I have choices." He let his eyelids droop but left one open a crack. "I suppose that means I can go to sleep."

"Yes, sleep," Drexel said. "And I applaud your cunning. Even if I were evil, I could never slit your throat as you slept, for in effect I would be slitting my own."

Orlan's eyes closed fully. "That's my way of thinking."

"Where did you learn such shrewdness?"

"Watching and listening to the dragons," Orlan said, his eyes still closed. "They are shrewd negotiators."

"I understand." Drexel pulled out his blade a few inches and ran a finger along its shiny surface. No, cutting Orlan's throat would be a fool's error. This boy was smart, experienced, and strong. His skills might mean the difference between success and failure.

He looked at the other children, now sleeping. With their little bodies bent into fetal positions, they seemed so innocent, so vulnerable, so trusting. Slitting one of those tender throats would make a lot more sense, less baggage, less whining, less chance of getting caught.

He pushed the sword back. Now that would be an option worth thinking about. Yet, when he marched triumphantly home, having a little girl in his company would help engender sympathy for the slaves and elevate his heroic platform. Cassandra would be a perfect choice to play the role of the pathetic waif, and Orlan could articulate the horrors of slavish strife, while he, Drexel the deliverer, stood in heroic silence, taking in the wordless worship of his wide-eyed admirers.

He settled his head back and closed his eyes. Yes, that day was coming, the day when his years of planning would finally reach fruition. Now to extend those plans. How could he escape to the other mine with just the two he needed in order to seal his place in history, while at the same time disabling the other children from revealing his whereabouts? That would take a dose of cunning a child like Orlan could only dream about.

*   *   *   *   *   *

Adrian and Marcelle marched southward through the woods, careful to raise as little noise as possible. A warm breeze dried their clothes and cast off the chill, while the occasional sound of running water to their right reminded them that the river flowed nearby. Many new aromas drifted in from every direction. A sweet scent emanated from thumb-sized flowers with hairlike petals of purple and gold. They grew on leafy vines clinging to trees bearing broadleafed fronds that shaded nearly every step of the journey. As their footfalls stirred the long-undisturbed debris underneath, a musty odor blended in, strong at times, but not unpleasant.

While they walked, Cassabrie offered a few bits of information about how the slaves transported rocks on rafts, much like the one Adrian had built, and how the dragons used the stones for building the wall and for decorating their courtyards. This practice started when the pheterone miners began excavating stones with vibrant colors and intricate patterns, perfect for ornamentation around the caves of the more self-important dragons, and once the slaves established the raft-transport system, the dragons decided that larger stones could be quarried from the mountains and shuttled to the wall for construction purposes. Soon, the mining of stones became so important, the gas the laborers were unearthing seemed like a by-product of the operation rather than the other way around.

After several minutes, Cassabrie whispered a long "Shhh."

Adrian grasped Marcelle's arm and halted. They peered through the gaps in the trees toward the river. At the bank, a dragon sat on its haunches, a long, thick whip in its clawed hand. At least four teenaged boys hauled hefty stones from a raft to a wooden cart, each boy skinny and bare-chested with sweat trickling down his bronzed skin.

"This is as far north as they allow them to unload," Cassabrie said. "One of the boys will push the cart to a dragon laborer who takes the stones to the boundary. They don't want any humans near the wall, supposedly to prevent any possibility of escape."

Adrian crouched and gestured for Marcelle to join him. As they watched the boys work, a tingle crossed his skin. Here they were, the Lost Ones, under the watchful eye of a dragon taskmaster. After all the years of ridicule from those who scoffed at the "myth," now that he beheld them with his own eyes, he could hardly believe it himself.

Marcelle withdrew the black sword from her scabbard and gave him a questioning look.

"No," he whispered. "There might be other dragons around."

"The cart's almost full," Cassabrie said. "One of the boys will come this way with it. See the path?"

Adrian scanned the ground in front of him. A narrow strip of trodden leaves cut through the forest only a few steps away. He lowered his whisper further. "Cassabrie, you saw that without me seeing it?"

"You saw it. It just didn't register in your mind. I suspect that will happen quite often as I observe things you don't know about."

Adrian touched Marcelle's shoulder and drew her close as he whispered, "Cassabrie says one of the boys will come this way."

She nodded her understanding and slid the sword back to its scabbard. Soon, the smallest of the boys drew closer, shoving the loaded four-wheeled cart with all his might. His wiry arms strained at the cart's rear handles, and sweat poured. He looked no more than twelve years old. Yet, he pushed a load that most sixteen-year-olds in Mesolantrum couldn't budge.

Adrian stepped out of the underbrush and onto the path a few paces in front of the boy. "Excuse me, young man. May I speak to you for a moment?"

He dropped the handles and backed away, his eyes wide. "Who … who are you?"

Adrian touched himself on the chest. "I am a friend. My name is Adrian. Don't be frightened."

The boy squinted. "You're dressed strangely, and your skin is so pale."

"That's true, but it would take too long to explain right now."

"Tell him you need to speak to the closest patriarch," Cassabrie said. "He will know what you mean."

"I need to speak to a patriarch. Will you tell me where to find the closest one?"

"No." The boy set his hands on the cart handles again and pushed. "If I'm late, they'll beat me."

After he passed, Adrian looked at his back. Reddish brown stripes crisscrossed his skin diagonally from shoulders to hips. They didn't appear to be fresh, but at one time the lashes must have been pure torture.

"Follow him," Cassabrie said. "You and Marcelle both. Just stay in the forest when he goes into the clearing."

Adrian waved for Marcelle to join him. They followed several steps behind the boy, keeping their heads low and their footfalls quiet. Soon, the boy passed into a clear grassy area, and Adrian signaled for a halt. Crouching behind a leafy shrub, he and Marcelle watched.

The boy stopped the cart on top of a dark circle that looked like a blanket or a tarp. He lifted a corner and drew it over the cart, then repeated the process for the other three corners and attached them to a metal hook.

As he held the hook above his head, he stared at the sky. After nearly a minute, a dark shadow swept overhead. A dragon swooped down, grabbed the hook with his rear claws, and hoisted the cart into the air. His powerful wings beat the air savagely. He struggled against the weight, but he soon lifted the cart over the treetops and flew away to the north.

The boy brushed his hands together and hustled back to the path. As he tried to hurry past, Adrian caught his arm. Marcelle caught the other. "Now can you tell me where to find a patriarch?" Adrian asked.

The boy glanced at the scabbard on Adrian's hip then at Marcelle before shaking his head. "If you don't know where a patriarch is, maybe I shouldn't tell you."

He tried to run, but they held him in place. Adrian whispered a stretched-out call, "Cassabrie?"

"He is being rather discourteous," she said, her voice carrying an annoyed tone. "Tell him that you've been relocated, and you beg for the grace due a stranger."

Adrian lowered himself to one knee, keeping his gaze fixed on the boy. "Young man, I know you see us as strangers. It's true, for we have been relocated. Is it not your custom to show grace to such strangers?"

The boy bent his brow low. "It is our custom to watch out for deceivers, especially those who falsely appeal to our kindness."

Adrian drew his head back. How interesting! Boys this age rarely spoke with such eloquence back home. "Why are you so suspicious of us?"

"You're too strong to be an inside worker, unless you're a miner, but you're too clean for that, and you're too pale to be an outside worker." He nodded at Adrian's scabbard. "No human is allowed such weapons, and"—he then pointed at Marcelle—"ever since Zena betrayed us, no one dresses all in black. Your wife reminds me of Zena, except shorter."

Cassabrie laughed but quickly stifled it. "Remind me to tell you about Zena later, but since this boy knows the legends, tell him that you have come from the Northlands to avenge Cassabrie. If he knows the Starlighter's final prophecy, he will understand."

Adrian pondered the word. Cassabrie had said she was a Starlighter and demonstrated her powers with supernatural storytelling, but the full meaning still seemed elusive.

"So," the boy continued, "are you going to let me go or shall I shout for the dragon?"

Adrian pulled the boy closer and whispered, "Listen carefully. I have come from the Northlands to avenge the Starlighter's death. If you know her prophecy, then your skepticism, though proper in its place, should be put to rest."

The boy's muscles relaxed. "But ... but the raven. There is no raven."

"I will explain," Cassabrie said. "Repeat the prophecy as I say it, so he will realize that I am with you."

She continued in a singsong cadence, and Adrian echoed each line.

Although I burn and light is spurned,
I shall return with freedom yearned;
Within another vessel strong,
I live again to sing my song.

A raven perched upon my wing
Will help us fly, will help us bring
My freedom's call to slaves in cords
And break their bonds with sharpened swords.

When Adrian finished, the boy looked at Marcelle and whispered reverently, "Is she the raven?"

"She is," Cassabrie said, "though I just realized it myself when the boy mentioned her garb."

Adrian nodded. "And the Starlighter is within me, like a spirit. She even recited the prophecy as I spoke it."

The boy let out a low whistle.

"Now that you understand our weapons and her manner of dress," Adrian continued, "will you lead me to a patriarch?"

The boy began heaving shallow breaths as he hurried his words. "I am Scott. I will take you to a patriarch, but I don't know how to get you into the dragon village. You will look like a purple vog."

"Vogs are purple?" Adrian asked.

Scott gave him a curious stare. "Of course not, and strong slaves are tanned and dirty. Most of us work without a shirt on."

"I see your point." Adrian looked down at his tunic. The top two buttons had been torn away, leaving much of his upper chest exposed, including the edge of the glowing patch. "If I take off my shirt," he said, shifting the material to hide the glow, "my pale skin will be even more obvious."

"Gwillen root," Scott said. "Go ahead and remove your shirt. I'll be right back. This is worth taking a beating for." He ran toward the river and disappeared in the brush.

As Adrian untied the cloak at his waist, still damp from the river plunge, he looked at Marcelle. "Gwillen root?"

Marcelle shrugged. "A skin dye?"

"Yes," Cassabrie said. "We used it for tanning leather. If it spilled on our skin, it would leave a brown mark that would take a season to wear off. The boys probably use it to seal gaps in the rafts that the heavy loads create."

Adrian nodded. "Cassabrie says it's a dye."

An irritated glare flashed across Marcelle's face, but it quickly vanished.

"Well, that gets *you* in," she said, "but what about me?" She crossed her arms loosely in front. "If they don't wear black clothing, then what do *I* do? Even the shirt I have on underneath is black."

"We'll have to ask Scott for an alternative." As Adrian unbuttoned, he turned to the side, hoping to hide the skin patch for as long as possible. When he slid the tunic off, he glanced at Marcelle.

Her arms still crossed, she had turned, apparently keeping an eye on the path leading to the river. Her profile displayed a scrunched brow and tight lips. Something was bothering her.

With Marcelle staring off into the woods, obviously not wanting to converse, the wait seemed interminable. How long might it take for Scott to find this gwillen root and prepare it as a dye? And the thought of dragons patrolling the skies or the forest paths increased the tension in the air.

Adrian looked up through the canopy. No sign of dragons. Of course, he could talk to Cassabrie while they waited, but that would likely drive a thicker wedge between him and Marcelle. Every word he spoke to Cassabrie seemed to infuriate Marcelle, as if she viewed Cassabrie as a wicked fairy or a seductive nymph who might carry him to destruction. Of course, nothing could be further from the truth, but how could he convince Marcelle? How could he communicate a feeling? She would just have to learn by experience. When Cassabrie's guidance proved trustworthy, then Marcelle would know.

Finally, Scott scampered toward them, swinging a wooden bucket at the end of a tightly flexed arm. Brown water sloshed out as he hurried. When he stopped, he dipped a brush into the slurry and rubbed it across Adrian's arm. He pushed hard, making the bristles sting.

"Your skin will absorb it better," he explained, "if I rough it up a bit. With your muscles, we'll have to say you've been hauling boulders. Even with your shirt on, the dragons will notice. And I have to make sure you're the same all over. An obvious change in color might give you away."

When Scott moved to brush his back, Adrian looked at Marcelle again. She kept her focus on the path, the same aspect casting her in a dark mood.

Adrian turned his attention to Scott. "One piece of information will help me greatly. I am searching for a man named Frederick. He might have been carrying a weapon similar to mine and possibly wearing a tricornered hat with a purple feather in it. Have you seen him?"

"Frederick," Scott repeated slowly. "I don't remember anyone with that name. Some of the women wear hats during the hot seasons, and a few of the older men, but I have not heard of one with three corners or a feather."

"Well, then maybe the patriarch will know."

When Scott shifted to the front, his eyes shot open as he pointed at the glowing skin patch. "What's that?"

Marcelle turned. Her eyes also grew wide. "Adrian, that looks awful! It pulses!"

Adrian touched the patch. "It's a sign that Cassabrie is inside me. The pulse is like her heartbeat."

"It's the Starlighter," Scott said as he moved the brush to Adrian's lower torso and continued working.

Marcelle stepped slowly closer, as if hypnotized, her stare fixed on Adrian's patch. Leaning over Scott, she touched it with her fingertips. "Does it hurt?"

He nodded. "Sometimes quite a bit, depending on Cassabrie's passion."

Marcelle's eyebrows lifted. "Her passion?"

"Excuse me." Scott pushed the brush higher. "Maybe this will cover it up. If the dragons see it, they'll send you to the Separators. That would be the worst thing that could happen."

Adrian repeated the word in his mind. *Separators.* It sounded ominous, wicked. Should he ask what it meant? Maybe Scott thought he was already supposed to know.

Scott let the brush drip over the palm-sized patch. The sepia drops drizzled across the glow and sloughed off into the skin underneath. "It's not absorbing," he said.

"I have an idea." Marcelle picked up Adrian's cloak and, using her sword, cut out a long strip. "I don't think you'll need your cloak in this weather."

After a few more slices, she fashioned a bandage and wrapped it around Adrian's chest, covering the glow with a thick patch of material. "I'm sure the slaves here get injured from time to time."

"One of the river rats bit you!" Scott said with a grin. "Your skin looks perfect now, but I could add some red for blood."

Adrian laughed. "I hope it won't be necessary. I'm planning to wear my shirt, but it'll be good to have the bandage. My top two buttons are missing."

"I agree." Marcelle laid her palm over the bandage and pressed down lightly. "Keep it where it belongs."

As her hand lingered, he looked into her eyes—still concerned, still anxious. Her warning meant so much more than the simple words implied.

He laid his hand over hers. "I'll be careful."

She pulled her hand away, her expression unchanged. "What's our next step?"

"Wait for evening," Scott said. "When the other men quit for the day, Adrian and I can enter the village with them, and I'll take him to Lattimer. He's the closest patriarch."

"What about Marcelle?" Adrian asked. "She can't go into the village dressed in black, can she?"

"She will have to wait here until I can come back with some normal clothes. There is another slave in Lattimer's home who is about her size."

Marcelle winced. "I assume I'll have to wear a dress."

"Well," Scott said, stretching out the word, "that is our way. Is something wrong with wearing a dress?"

"I haven't worn one since I was nine. Dresses are unsuitable for battle."

"They're really skirts that wrap around," Scott explained, demonstrating with his hands at his waist. "Most girls take them off while working outside, and they wear short trousers underneath."

Marcelle sighed. "I can live with that."

"So should we hide here in the woods while you finish your labors for the day?" Adrian asked.

Scott pointed at his foot. "I gashed it on a stone, so I'm done." Blood oozed from a cut between his two biggest toes, and the slice extended along the side of his foot and up to his ankle. "I had to make it big enough to be excused, and I faked a limp and cried a lot. The dragon wasn't very sympathetic, but at least I didn't get a beating."

Marcelle dropped to one knee and dabbed the cut with a shred of Adrian's cloak. "You did this to yourself?"

"Officially ... no. I slipped while pushing the cart. Unofficially ..." He withdrew a sharp stone from his pocket. "This adventure is worth a lot of pain."

"Then what do we do until evening?" Adrian asked.

Scott shrugged. "You're the prophesied one. I thought you and the raven would tell *me* what to do."

"The cattle camp," Cassabrie said. "Ask him to take you there."

Adrian touched Scott's shoulder. "Can you take us to the cattle camp?"

Scott's mouth lowered a notch. For a moment, he just stared, then swallowed. "I ... I will do as you ask, of course, but ..."

"What's wrong?" Marcelle asked as she straightened. "Is it dangerous?"

"Very dangerous, especially for the little ones who live there." He lowered his head. "If you can call that living."

"You must go," Cassabrie said. "When you do, you will understand why I sent you."

Adrian set a hand on Scott's sweaty back. "Take us as far as your courage lasts, and we will go the rest of the way."

Scott looked up at him. His voice dropped to a whisper. "I will take you there." Without another word, he tromped into the woods, choosing a narrow trail Adrian hadn't noticed.

Marcelle tossed the remains of the cloak to Adrian and followed, her sword again in the back scabbard.

With the wadded remnants of the cloak in one hand and his tunic in the other, Adrian fell into line. Fronds and leaflets brushed against his bare torso, tickling his skin, already itching from the drying dye. He put his tunic back on, buttoned it as high as he could, and pushed through the brush. The shirt's damp coolness felt good, a guilty pleasure, a soothing sensation that perhaps many of the slaves here rarely experienced. Yet, who could tell how much they suffered or how often they felt relief?

A cold dread washed over his body. Soon, it seemed, he would learn more than he wanted to know.

When they reached a denser portion of the forest, Scott slowed, finally halting in front of a vine-covered wall. He looked at Adrian and Marcelle, a pained expression on his face. "It's on the other side."

Adrian pushed a finger through a gap in the thorny vines and touched the stone wall. It rose to twice his height, and a tangled line of dry, twisted thorns sat on top.

Marcelle pinched one of the thorns and broke it off. "Poisoned?" she asked.

"No," Scott said. "Sharp, though. They will rip your skin off."

"Have you ever climbed to the top?"

"I used to climb every day and look into the camp, but after a while it wasn't worth all the cuts, because I couldn't see her anymore, so ..." As his voice trailed off, new tears filled his eyes.

"Her?" Marcelle asked.

He let his head droop. "My younger sister, Tamara. She was a poor rock carrier, so the Separators sent her to the camp maybe forty days ago."

"The camp is punishment?"

Scott shook his head, still hanging low. "I'd rather not talk about it anymore."

Marcelle whipped out her sword and began sweeping it across the vines, chopping off the exposed thorns. Soon, the wall looked more like a twisted ladder than a prickly barrier. "Now we can climb it easily."

Adrian looked up at the sky. The sun had long passed its zenith and seemed to be heading toward the western horizon. "What time of day is it? Mid to late afternoon?"

"We are in our cooler season," Scott replied. "The days are getting shorter, so evening will be upon us in about two hours."

"What's the safest time to enter the cattle camp?"

Scott shrugged. "I can't be sure, but if you wait till closer to the end of labors, the dragons will be less vigilant. They get bored and sleepy."

"How many dragons are in there?" Marcelle asked.

"Usually two, one to guard the stream's entrance, and one to guard its exit." Scott pointed toward the river. "It's a raft conveyor that flows into the river where I work."

Scott explained the system, repeating some of the details Cassabrie had provided earlier. The miners in the plateau area, usually in the heart of a mesa, drilled into the ground and cut out stones. The stronger children, also working at the mines, piled them on a raft and sent it floating on the stream. Then the raft entered the cattle camp through a gateway in the wall, opened by a dragon guard. The weaker children stopped the raft, collected the stones in pails, and, as the raft floated along, the children hauled the stones to the stream's exit from the camp. There they dumped the stones back onto the raft. Then the raft would leave through another gateway.

Of course, it was useless labor, but the dragons wanted to strengthen those who could survive the rigors and cull out those who couldn't. At the same time, they could sift through the rocks in search of crystals. Apparently Magnar craved a specific crystalline stone and promised a great reward to anyone who found it, complete freedom with safe passage to the Northlands.

After that step, the rafts floated to the main river where the older boys collected the stones to be delivered either to the wall or to the village for various building or decorating projects.

When Scott finished, Adrian looked at the sun again, considerably lower now. "I think it's time. I'll go first." He ripped the remainder of the cloak into four pieces, gave two to Marcelle, and wrapped the other two around his hands. "Scott, can you whistle?"

He nodded and let out a shrill warble.

"Good. Stay here, and use that as a warning if there's trouble. We'll be back as soon as we can." Adrian grabbed one of the wall's thick vines and scrambled up. Once at the top, he drew his sword from his hip scabbard, cut the thorny branches lying along the crown, and dropped them between Scott and Marcelle. "Listen for my whistle. That will mean it's safe to follow."

SIXTEEN

ADRIAN looked into the cattle camp's enclosed area, a flat expanse of pebbly terrain and dry grass. The wall extended to the left and right about a mile before curving to form an ellipse, with the wall on the opposite side sitting several thousand feet across the way.

A few trees dotted the area, especially near a stream that cut vertically through the right-hand third of the ellipse, flowing from the far wall to the near one and exiting well to Adrian's right. A dragon stood near the stream's exit, but his distance made his size and other details impossible to determine. Vines covered the wall's interior side, similar to the exterior except thicker and thornier near the ground.

Holding his sword away from his body, Adrian leaped down. After looking both ways, he let out a short, shrill whistle. Seconds later, Marcelle appeared at the top, vaulted over, and landed with a graceful bend of her knees. When she straightened and gave him a nod, he pointed his sword at the dragon, whispering, "If we stay near the wall, maybe he won't see us."

"Something else is moving there," Marcelle said. "Could it be the children?"

"Maybe." He marched ahead, hugging the wall as closely as the thorns would allow and looking back every few seconds to see how Marcelle fared. Apparently the Bastra poisoning had been neutralized. Even after that leap, she displayed no noticeable limp. His own pain had also diminished, a fact he hadn't noticed earlier.

"Cassabrie," he murmured, "you're the one who wanted us to see this place. What should we do now?"

"Get as close to the dragon as you dare. You heard about the children, but when you see them, you will understand."

As he continued, the movements near the dragon grew clearer. Children walked back and forth along the stream, each one carrying a pail. When Adrian came within a stone's throw, he stopped at a skinny tree and crouched behind it, signaling for Marcelle to crouch with him.

The children appeared to range from four to eight years old, marching from left to right toward the dragon, separated by time intervals of about a minute. Others shuffled away from the dragon, their pails apparently empty as they swung freely at their sides.

The older children tromped with their heads dipped low, their skinny chests bare, and their bodies leaning to one side, each with a dirty arm weighed down by a rock-laden pail. They wore ragged short trousers and no shoes, exposing bruised and bloodied feet, and their sluggish gaits revealed a weariness of mind and body.

Some of the younger ones wore nothing but loin cloths, while a few shielded their bodies with only the bucket they carried. When they reached the dragon, the children dumped their pails of stones onto a raft near the wall, then trudged back upstream, their heads now higher, though their faces carried vacant expressions.

The dragon held a long whip in his clawed hand and swung it from side to side, as if matching the rhythm of the slavish march. With his back turned toward Adrian and Marcelle, they couldn't gauge his attentiveness. If he was bored, as Scott suggested, he showed no sign of it. He appeared to be considerably smaller than the dragons at the river wall, but still formidable.

Marcelle showed Adrian her sword. "It's just one dragon," she whispered. "If we surprise him, the two of us can slay him easily and get these children out of here."

"Maybe." Adrian scanned the river upstream, far to the left. It seemed that the children with empty pails stopped near the opposite wall, probably the station where they collected stones. Something large loomed over them, a dark shadow that swayed with the breeze. Was that the other dragon, or just one of the nearby trees?

"Adrian?" Marcelle set the dark blade near his eyes. "His back might not be turned this way for long."

"I think I see another dragon. If we kill this one, the other might be on us in a flash. Who knows how many children will get hurt if we can't get them out?"

"We'll get them out," Marcelle said. "The stream has to exit this place somehow. If they use the same kind of wooden gate as they did at the river, we can chop it open, get the children out, and hide in the forest."

"And then what? Do you know where to go or how to keep them away from the dragons? They'll eventually be recaptured and punished. We won't do them any favors by acting rashly."

"Rashly?" Although Marcelle kept her reply at a whisper, it sounded like an angry shout. "Isn't slaying dragons what we came here for? Are we going to miss this opportunity because there *might* be another dragon watching?"

"We should talk to the patriarch first and make a plan. If we can set them all free without hurting—"

"Oh!" A girl stumbled, spilling her pail. She fell into her stones and rolled to the side, her forehead bleeding as she lay with her face toward the sky.

The dragon flew at her. The whip snapped across her bare chest, leaving a red welt. She grimaced but didn't cry out. With her eyes clenched shut, she just lay there while the dragon lashed her again and again. While the other children marched upstream, one girl stood nearby, watching with her pail hanging at her side. "Only five more, Shellinda," she called. "Be brave."

Marcelle's arms shook with fury. "How can you stand to watch this?"

Before Adrian could say a word, she leaped up and dashed toward the dragon, her sword extended. Adrian jumped up and sprinted behind her. It was too late for planning now.

With the dragon still facing away, Marcelle ran straight up its back, hopping over the short spines that lined its backbone. By the time Adrian arrived, she had straddled the dragon high on its neck. She hacked savagely at its eyes, blow after blow raising a spray of fluid.

The dragon roared and tried to sling her off, but she locked her legs in place and hung on. When it reared up, exposing its underbelly, Adrian charged and thrust his sword into its vulnerable spot, a larger target than on the previous dragon. After driving the blade in up to the hilt, he twisted it and jerked it back out. Dark green liquid gushed forth, spilling over his boots and raising a horrible stench.

Adrian backpedaled. The dragon lurched from side to side, then toppled forward. Still riding on its neck, Marcelle waited through the fall. Just before its chin slapped the ground, she released her leg lock and let the momentum push her into a run that sent her stumbling into Adrian.

He caught her with one arm, while pointing the sword at the dragon with the other. It didn't budge. After a few seconds of silence, he whispered, "I don't think we have to worry about this dragon anymore."

Marcelle's eyes darted from side to side. "Any sign of another guard?"

"Not yet." Adrian looked upstream. The dark form he had seen earlier hadn't moved, and the children continued their march, the tail end of the line still in view. "I wonder where the children are going."

"To feeding time," Cassabrie said. "No one wants to be late for that. You should let them go. They won't be easily persuaded to do anything else right now."

After Adrian relayed Cassabrie's explanation, Marcelle hurried to Shellinda. The other girl had already helped Shellinda sit up and now knelt beside her.

Marcelle pulled both girls to their feet. With several welts painting red stripes across her chest, Shellinda wobbled, nodding as Marcelle spoke softly and gently brushed grit from her back.

"Adrian," Cassabrie said, "your danger has not passed. I suspect that the other dragon has not already attacked because the workday is over. Yet, another dragon will arrive soon for feeding time. Either climb back over the wall, or ask the two girls to take you to their hole. You will be safe there for the time being."

"Safe?" Adrian looked at the dead dragon. "But this was an easy kill. He never even used fire. If the other one attacks, we shouldn't have any trouble."

"This one was a drone, a castrated male, much weaker than all other types. It is doubtful that they would allow two drones to work together. The cattle feeder will likely be a guardian who will check the perimeter before nightfall. When he finds the slain dragon, he will kill at least five children."

"Five? How can you know that?"

"It is the dragons' way, but I will speak no more about that now. The girls will want to go to the feeding, so attend to them as quickly as possible."

Adrian joined Marcelle. When Shellinda noticed him, she crossed and uncrossed her arms, apparently hoping to hide her wounds but not wanting to touch them. Finally, she just looked at the ground, trembling. With brown, matted hair tied into a rope that fell halfway down her back, and ribs clearly outlined in her emaciated, prepubescent torso, she appeared to be about seven years old.

"What's wrong?" Adrian asked.

The other girl, a waif a little smaller than Shellinda, spoke up. "Shellinda thinks you will steal all the food when it comes. You're so big, no one can stop you."

"Steal all the food?" He bent over and set a finger under Shellinda's chin, lifting it so he could look into her eyes. They were brown and bloodshot, dry and vacant. "I would never deprive you of the smallest crumb."

Marcelle touched the other girl's shoulder. "What's your name?"

"Erin."

"How old are you?"

"Six years. Shellinda is eight. She is the oldest girl. If no one buys her on the next trading day, she will go to the breeders."

Shellinda scowled at Erin. "Someone will buy me. I will kill myself before I go to the breeders."

"The breeders?" Adrian asked.

"Of course." Shellinda squinted at him. "Who are you, and why are you here?"

"My name is Adrian, and ..." He nodded toward Marcelle. "And this is Marcelle. We're from a faraway land, and we were told we should see this place before speaking to a patriarch."

Shellinda grasped her hair rope and twirled it in her fingers. "What dragon would allow you to travel on your own?"

Adrian glanced at Marcelle before answering. "The King of the Northlands."

Shellinda spat on the ground. "If there is such a beast, then curse his name. If he lets us suffer like this, then he must be a monster." She turned and strode along the stream's bank. "Come on, Erin. Nancor will be here soon, and you didn't get any bread yesterday."

Adrian hurried after her, Marcelle close behind. They caught up with Shellinda and Erin and walked with them. "Is there a place for us to hide while you're eating?" Adrian asked.

Shellinda kept her focus straight ahead. "You can go to our hole."

"Where is that?"

"I will show you."

As they walked four abreast, Adrian glanced at the sky every few seconds, always wary of any changes—birds flitting by, a tree's undulating shadow, or a cloud briefly hiding the setting sun. Soon, they came upon the other children. They had gathered in a cluster between the stream and a dirt mound that rose ten feet from the ground and spanned a circle about a hundred feet in diameter. With several holes punched into its walls, big enough for the children to crawl into, it appeared to be an enormous anthill.

The children, perhaps forty in number, milled about, almost shoulder to shoulder, sometimes nudging one another to gain a little space, sometimes shoving deliberately, especially the older boys trying to gain an advantage over the younger. They all focused on the sky most of the time, looking at each other only to scowl, their faces becoming increasingly menacing with every glance. Apparently Nancor would be there soon.

Shellinda stopped and pointed at the mound. "Go through any hole you want, but mine and Erin's is the one with the red rocks."

Adrian led Marcelle to the mound. Four reddish stones protruded from the hard clay around one of the holes, as if marking up, down, left, and right.

Adrian peered inside, but it was too dark to see anything. "Any fear of tight passages?" he asked.

"Trust me," Marcelle said as she pushed her feet into the hole, "I can handle it." She slid quickly out of sight.

Adrian copied her entry and stepped down onto a hard surface. Bare rock enclosed them in a dim hovel, perhaps two paces across. Piles of grass lined the curved wall, and pieces of broken pottery lay here and there. The hovel smelled clean, though quite stale.

Stooping because of the low ceiling, he peered out the hole, now at waist level. He and Marcelle pressed close to each other, nearly cheek to cheek, as they watched.

Outside, a dark form overshadowed the children. They jumped in place, their arms stretching upward. An older boy pushed down a younger one and stood on his back. A girl grabbed the bigger boy and wrestled him to the ground, clawing at his face while he slapped her savagely. More children shoved, tripped, and pulled hair until the scramble looked like a mass of bronzed flesh, flying hair, and flailing limbs.

Bread began raining down in various sized morsels. The taller children snatched the larger pieces out of the air while the little ones scrounged along the ground, gathering up tidbits, like dogs licking droppings from a dining table. After getting two fistfuls of bread, the bigger children began devouring, alternating between their handfuls. One girl kicked a small boy, barely older than a toddler, took away his morsel, and quickly shoved it into her mouth. The tiny boy squawked and bit the girl's leg, but the girl just slapped him down and ran toward the mound.

Marcelle pushed an arm through the hole as if ready to climb out. "Someone has to put a stop to this."

"Not this time." Adrian pulled her back and looked into her angry eyes. "They've probably been doing this every day for years. No sense in interfering now."

Soon, something indistinct dropped from the sky. The children went into a frenzy, some shouting, "Fish!" though the falling offerings sounded more like stiff planks when they struck the ground.

After a few minutes of free-for-all skirmishes, Shellinda and Erin appeared at the hole and slid inside, each clutching bread in one hand and a fish plank in the other. Two other girls followed. Both pushed their empty hands against their gaunt bellies.

Shellinda plopped down on a pile of grass and ate her bread greedily. Erin sat next to her and did the same, while the other two girls, both about Erin's age, looked on, their stares cold and wanting.

Marcelle clanked her sword against the stone wall. "Can't you two share with the others?"

Shellinda spoke with her mouth full of bread. "They ate yesterday." She then puffed out her pitiful chest, apparently no longer bashful. "I have to get some meat on my bones. Otherwise no one will buy me on trading day."

Marcelle took a heavy step toward her, but Adrian grabbed her shirt and pulled her back. "Patience!" he whispered.

She spun toward him, every muscle in her face taut. "If you think I can stand idly by while this injustice goes on right in front of me—"

He covered her lips with his fingers. "Think long-term. We'll solve all their problems if we just stay patient and plan an escape for everyone. We need to buy time and meet the leaders."

She grasped his wrist and jerked it down. "My way has bought us a dead dragon, and there have been no repercussions."

"Not yet," Adrian said. "You have no idea what will happen when they find the dead body."

Marcelle huffed. "As if *you* do."

Cassabrie's words knifed back into Adrian's mind. Five children. How would it happen? When would the dragons exact their punishment? Should he let Marcelle know what to expect?

A boy slid into the hovel, faced Adrian, and scowled fiercely. "Who are you?"

Still hunched over, Adrian bowed lower. "Adrian Masters, a stranger relocated from a faraway land."

With shaggy hair overlapping his ears, and blue eyes that seemed brighter and clearer than those of the other children, he pressed a thumb against his chest. "I'm in charge here. Adults aren't allowed in the camp, so you'd better leave."

"He's Thad," Erin said as she chewed on her fish plank. "He's eleven. The dragons put him in charge of the rest of us, 'cause he's the biggest."

Thad spun toward her. "Shut up, if you know what's good for you."

"You don't scare me, bonehead. I'll tell Nancor that you stole Tamara's trousers."

"Did you catch that?" Adrian whispered to Marcelle.

She nodded. "Scott's sister. We'll have to check on it."

"Then I pick you," Thad said, pointing a finger at Erin. "I was going to take Shellinda, but now I pick you." He grabbed Erin's wrist and jerked her to her feet.

"For what?" Erin shouted as she tried to break free. "I didn't do anything."

"Someone killed a dragon, so Nancor says I have to pick five of us."

Erin's eyes widened with terror. "Not the burning!"

"You should have kept quiet." Thad pulled her toward the exit hole. "This'll teach everyone not to sass me."

Adrian blocked his path. "Wait!"

Thad stopped and glared at him. "You'd better leave, or I'll tell Nancor you're here."

"Did you say Nancor plans to kill five children?"

"The price for a dead drone. We didn't do it, but the dragons think killing us will stop the adults from meddling." Thad's scowl deepened. "Did *you* do it?"

Adrian stared at the angry boy. Cassabrie was right, as usual. Killing the dragon would cost the lives of five children. Too many. One was too many. Somehow, he had to stop the slaughter. "Let's say I did do it. Does it really make a difference? Nancor has to know these children couldn't kill a dragon."

"All he knows is that Millence is dead. No matter who did it, everyone will find out that five of us got burned to death. The dragons think that will keep the adults in line."

Marcelle pulled Erin free and drew her sword. "Adrian and I killed the lizard. We will face Nancor ourselves."

Thad looked up at her. For the first time since he arrived, a streak of fear crossed his face. "You don't understand. Nancor isn't like Millence. He is a guardian. His fire is a blazing flood from hell itself, and his scales are stronger than granite. If I don't bring five to Nancor, he will burn me alive and choose four others himself."

Adrian leaned close to Marcelle. "I want to kill that monster, too, but we're the only hope these children have. If we die, who will rescue them?"

While leaning, his shirt opened further, revealing the bandage that hid his glow. Marcelle laid her hand over the frayed material. "Where is the heart of the warrior I once knew? Where is the passion that burned like an inferno when you battled Darien and his henchmen? Has the spirit of a girl living within softened you that much?" She pushed him away. "Stay here and babysit. I'm the one who attacked Millence. I'll fight Nancor myself."

Adrian looked at the glow, the top edge exposed again by Marcelle's touch. It still pulsed with Cassabrie's heartbeat. Was Marcelle right? Had he lost some of his passion, the warrior's drive to protect every innocent life? Yet, the truth was the truth. This battle to save five would be noble, but might it risk destroying their purpose for coming here?

"No!" Thad blocked Marcelle's path to the hole. "If you lose …" His voice shook with fear, forcing him to swallow before continuing. "If you lose, they will kill five anyway. If you win, they will bring a dozen dragons and maybe kill us all. If you let me take five, then no more will die."

Adrian looked at Marcelle. Her downcast expression said it all. Thad was right. Win or lose, at least five children would die. A battle would cost more lives, more suffering. But how could they possibly hide in safety while a dragon burned innocent children to death? It was unthinkable!

Adrian grabbed a fistful of his own hair and paced in a tight circle. "There has to be a way! There just has to!"

"If we fight," Marcelle said, a new determination steeling her jaw, "at least we'll give them a chance. We'll take them all out of here and hide them in the woods."

Thad shook his head hard, his eyes growing wilder. "And then what? Yarlan, the fierce one, comes every evening on patrol. Because of the dragon murder, he will demand a count. If we're missing, he will bring the greatest dragons, even Maximus, to find us. If they don't find us, they will kill other slaves, our parents, our brothers and sisters. They never let anything go unpunished. And if they do find us, who can tell how many of us they will burn?"

As a tear dripped from Marcelle's eye, she lowered her head. "I will say no more."

Adrian stopped pacing and stared at Marcelle and Thad, then at the four half-naked girls, each one looking at him with wide, frightened eyes. The stripes on Shellinda's chest spoke volumes. The dragons were cruel and heartless. They wouldn't hesitate to inflict the worst of tortures.

His heart thumped. What could he do? Every option seemed too horrible.

"Adrian," Cassabrie said. "There is one chance, but it is a very risky one."

He bent lower, as if listening to a whispering mouse. "Let's hear it. I don't like the options we have so far."

Thad looked at the girls, a curious expression wrinkling his brow, but he stayed quiet.

"Is Cassabrie talking to you?" Marcelle asked.

He nodded and clamped his hands over his ears. "Go ahead, Cassabrie."

"Remember what I said before? Learning where great faith and brutal practicality meet might be your only hope. Great faith overcomes the fear of high risk when the goal is valuable enough."

"Yes, I remember."

"Then prepare for a difficult decision." Cassabrie seemed to let out a sigh, though she had no breath of her own. "The dragons permit bargaining. In fact, they rather enjoy it. Allow Thad to select the five, and when he leads them out, you go with them and tell

282

Nancor that you're a negotiator. He should then allow you to offer an alternative to the punishment he wants to impose."

"Alternative? What alternative?"

Her voice rose to an entreaty. "Oh, Adrian, we are at a line I cannot cross. I have guided you to this place, to the terrible hell where your people abide in misery, and now you have seen their wretched state with your own eyes. What you are able to offer must be in keeping with how you judge their worth, their rescue, their freedom. I cannot decide for you how to value these little ones or what risk you should endure for their sakes."

Adrian absorbed her words. Although they appeared at first to be avoiding his question, soon everything became clear.

"Let's do this," he said to Thad. "Go ahead and select the five, and I will face the dragon with you. I will explain to him that I delayed you."

Thad grabbed Erin again and pulled her toward the hole. "No!" she cried, jerking wildly. "I don't want to burn!"

Marcelle wrenched Adrian's arm, whisper shouting, "What do you think you're doing?"

Pointing at her, he spoke in a firm tone. "You stay here."

She tapped her chest with her thumb. "But *I* attacked the dragon. *I* should be the one risking my life."

"Trust me. Our only hope is for you to stay out of sight. When it's over, go back to Scott and find the patriarch."

Shellinda jumped up. "Let Erin go! Take me instead."

"Are you crazy?" Thad asked. "You've heard the screams. Nobody volunteers to burn."

Shellinda broke her fish plank in half and handed the pieces to the two other girls. "No one is ever going to buy me. Dying is better than being here, and a lot better than the breeding rooms."

Erin shook free, leaped to the opposite side of the hovel, and cowered against the wall, sobbing. "Oh, Shellinda! Oh, my poor friend!"

Thad nodded at Shellinda. "Let's go." As he crawled out the hole, she followed, glancing back briefly before disappearing.

Adrian unbuckled his sword belt and let it drop to the floor. "Listen." He took Marcelle's hand and stroked it tenderly with his thumb. "I'm going to offer myself in their place. I have no idea how it will work out, but if I die, saving the children is all up to you. You will be their only hope. That's why you can't come with me. Do you understand?"

She nodded, her chin trembling. "What do you want me to do?"

He set a finger on the side of her head. "Think before you act. Your heart is right. You're desperate to rescue the Lost Ones. We both are. But they need you to be calm and clear thinking. Killing every dragon you see won't help them."

Tears dripped to her cheeks, and a tremor rattled her voice. "And now you're going to die because of me? You'll be dead, and I'll have to rescue all these poor souls by myself?"

"I don't think we have any other choice. You're smart and courageous. Just go with Scott and learn what you can from the patriarch. Remember our priorities. First, you have to find Frederick, and maybe the patriarch can help you. Cassabrie told me a story that might give you a clue. There's a wilderness area of some kind where runaway slaves try to go, and I think Frederick might have set up a refuge for them. If you can find that refuge, you might find Frederick."

"A wilderness," she said, her voice still trembling. "I will find it."

Laying his hands on her cheeks, he kissed her forehead. "Pray for me. I'm going to need a miracle."

He pushed through the hole and into the waning daylight. Several paces away, Thad knelt next to Shellinda, tying a rope to a stake in the ground. The rope wrapped around her ankle in a tight knot and led to the ankles of three boys and another girl. The other children crouched, shaking and crying, each one no more than six years old. Shellinda stood upright, hands on her hips and her eyes dry.

A huge dragon sat on its haunches in front of the victims, half again larger than Millence. His scales were darker red and clearly thicker, and smoke pouring from his nostrils gave evidence that a hot fire burned within.

Adrian nodded. Seeing Nancor's size and constitution confirmed Thad's warnings. Even with Marcelle's help, defeating him would likely have been impossible. Leaving his sword behind was the right move.

"Who are you?" Nancor bellowed.

Taking a deep breath, Adrian strode toward him. "I am Adrian Masters, and I have come as a negotiator to offer an alternative to the punishment you have prescribed."

"Is that so?" Nancor's head swayed back and forth, his eyes glowing scarlet. "By what authority do you take the negotiator's role? You are not their foreman."

"They have no adult supervisor, so I am here at the behest of a close relative of one of the children." Adrian straightened his body to show resolve. Indeed, Scott had asked him to come for his sister, so that much was true. "Shall we negotiate?"

"I am interested, but I must ask a simple question." He shifted his gaze to Thad. "This adult was with you in the hole. Why did you not report him?"

Thad stood and sidestepped away from Shellinda, trembling. "I ... I ..."

"I am the cause," Adrian said. "He knew that if he reported me, I would oppose him. He likely feared for his safety."

"I find that excuse to be inadequate. He knew the rules, so I will have to appoint a new leader." Nancor opened his mouth and shot a blast of fire at Thad. The flames covered his bare chest, instantly melting his skin. Thad screamed, but the fire raced up to his face and smothered his cries.

Adrian lunged toward him, but the dragon sent another blast of fire, blocking his way. As Adrian backpedaled, the dragon growled. "If you interfere, you will suffer the same fate, as will the five sacrifices."

While Nancor blew a new stream of fire at the boy's chest and head, Adrian panted, sweating, heaving. Criminal! Damnable! But what could he do?

Thad dropped to his knees. Buried in flames from his waist up, he choked and gagged while slowly turning black. Soon, his body toppled forward, and the flames withered.

The odor of burning flesh assaulted Adrian's nose. He bent over and wretched, but nothing came out. Tears poured forth and dripped to the dusty ground.

When he straightened again, he glared at the dragon. Nausea knotted his stomach. Grief tightened his throat. He couldn't say a word. He heaved quick breaths, trying to calm himself. He had to save the other five.

"Now," the dragon said, turning to Adrian with a toothy smile, "I am ready to hear your offer."

While Adrian tried to slow his breathing, Erin ran from the hole and dragged Thad's body several feet away. She began stripping off his trousers, mumbling, "I'm giving them back to Tamara."

Adrian fought against emerging tears. Marcelle would have to check on Tamara. One way or the other he wouldn't be able to do anything more for these children.

"Well?" Nancor said. "Are you going to negotiate or not?"

Adrian cleared his throat and forced his voice into a bass range. "I know who killed the dragon you call Millence." He nodded toward the children. "In exchange for the lives of these five, I will deliver the killer to you."

"Is that so?" Nancor drew his head closer. "What guarantee do I have that you will present him before me?"

"What guarantee do I have that you won't punish me when I do?"

Nancor let out a throaty chuckle. "An adult comes into a forbidden zone, carrying an arrogant swagger in his gait, and expects immunity."

"I assume delivering the dragon killer is valuable to you, so immunity is a fair trade."

"You have already requested the lives of these vermin. Are you requesting both?"

Adrian resisted the urge to glance at Marcelle. She was likely watching from the hole. "The assassin you seek," Adrian said, "is a mighty warrior with a sharp sword that could kill many dragons."

Nancor snorted. "If a rash of dragon deaths occurs, then every murder will be matched tenfold with the deaths of slaves."

"Perhaps you would like for me to pass that warning on to the assassin, but for now I suggest that we continue our negotiations."

"Very well. I will grant your immunity and spare the lives of three slaves of your choice. The other two will join the overseer in a pile of ashes."

Adrian raised a finger. "Since you have already executed one child, we should be negotiating over four children. You should be setting one free without question."

"Different crime, different punishment. Since these are cattle vermin, I am free to do as I please. You will have to find another offering to gain the other two."

Adrian kept his stare on the dragon, hoping to display confidence, though he was running out of leverage. Still, one item remained. "Then I take back my request for immunity and ask that I be allowed to retain Arxad as my counsel and be given a trial, and you will let all five children live."

"Hmmm." Nancor's head swayed again as if rocking like a pendulum. "That is a desirable token, but only if you will not contest the fact that you have trespassed the camp walls."

"I will not contest it. The number of witnesses is overwhelming."

"As if the vermin could be reliable witnesses." Nancor looked at Erin, now standing over Thad's naked corpse, holding his trousers in her grip. "Untie the others," he growled.

While Erin worked on the knots, Nancor shuffled closer to Adrian. "Now, intruder, you will present the assassin to me. If you do not, the bargain is broken, and your life is forfeit, as are the lives of the ones you have purchased."

Adrian spread out his arms. "I am he."

"The assassin?"

He nodded. "The same."

"Then show me the weapon you used."

"That was not part of the bargain." Adrian crossed his arms over his chest, trying to keep a confident stance in spite of the situation.

A deep rumble sounded from within the dragon's throat. "You will die!"

"You cannot kill me!" Adrian shouted. "You granted my appeal to Arxad!"

"You deceived me. You did not tell me you were the assassin."

Adrian raced through his words. "You neglected to ask, but your failure doesn't change the bargain. If a dragon's word is ever to be honored above a human's, then you are obligated to keep it. Otherwise, you will be forever scorned by all, for just as vermin skitter from rubbish heaps and spread disease from body to body, so will the news of a dishonest dragon spread from ear to ear, and your integrity will be destroyed among your own kind, and your claims of superiority over those spreading the news will be bankrupt. You would have to kill every child here to assure that your lie remains a secret."

"Oh, bravo!" Cassabrie shouted. "That was masterful!"

Adrian concealed a swallow. Not exactly masterful. That last statement was stupid. No sense giving the dragon any ideas.

Nancor grumbled under his breath. "I concede your point. Yet, granting your access to Arxad is a trivial matter. Even he will not defend a dragon killer."

"Then take me to him," Adrian said, spreading out his arms again. "I am ready."

"Very well, but you have no idea what awaits you."

Shellinda ran to Adrian, wrapped her arms around his waist, and leaned her head against his stomach. "Thank you for saving us!" she cried.

Adrian patted her on the head and spoke in a gentle, low tone. "You are worth saving, precious one."

She looked up at him, her eyes brighter than before. "But I'm not worth anything. I'm skinny and weak, and I fall a lot, and—"

"Shhh." He pushed his fingers through her tangled hair. "You're human. That's all that matters to me. I gladly give my life for you."

He kissed her on the forehead, and, as he pushed her gently away, she kept her stare fixed on him, whispering, "I will save you, kind sir, no matter what it takes."

With a beat of his wings, Nancor took off, flew in a quick circle, and swooped down. He dug his claws into Adrian's back and shoulders and lifted him into the air.

"Augh!" Adrian arched his back, biting his lip to keep from crying out again. Below, dozens of children had emerged from the mound, and they all looked up. As Nancor flew away, Shellinda trotted underneath, apparently trying to follow, but she soon fell behind and gave up.

With horrific pain stabbing his shoulders and ripping down his spine, Adrian could only watch. He was a mouse in an owl's talons, being taken to a court with owls for judges. Did a mouse ever win such a trial? Would Arxad really help? He was a dragon, and, as Nancor said, he likely wouldn't want to give counsel to a dragon killer. All seemed lost, at least for him. Yet, not for the children. They still had hope. They had Marcelle. And maybe Frederick was still around somewhere, ready to help once she found him. And maybe their father would journey from the Northlands and lend his expertise and his sword.

Adrian sighed. Yes, there was still hope for the children, but apparently very little hope that he would be around to witness their liberation. So he might never know if those precious lambs escaped from their torture. If the Code's promise of an afterlife proved true, maybe he would be able to see their escape from a distant shore, but it wouldn't be the same as marching the precious ones to freedom in person. To be in their presence, to see their tears of sadness transform into tears of joy, to dance with them in the streets of liberty—Oh, that would be true paradise. Yet, it was not to be.

As the pain in his back heightened, the sky turned darker. This journey to the world of dragons was about to end.

✸ SEVENTEEN ✸

MARCELLE scrambled out of the hole, now wearing Adrian's sword and scabbard on one hip and the viper blade on the other. She looked at the sky. Nancor clutched Adrian's shoulders with his rear talons and let him dangle. Blood streamed down his arms as the dragon pitched him into a sway.

Thad lay dead on his stomach. With his body charred from the waist up and his buttocks exposed to gathering flies, he seemed to be a symbol of the slavish tragedy—humanity reduced to chattel, bearing value only insomuch as they served someone more powerful than they, easily disposed of when that value diminished in the sight of the conqueror. Human life had become nothing more than a decorative bauble that could be cast away whenever convenient.

Cold sweat dampened Marcelle's brow. Clenching her teeth, she rolled her fingers into a tight ball. The beast! The sick, twisted monster! Before this journey was over, that dragon's heart would be skewered at the end of her sword!

She rushed to Shellinda and Erin. "Where will the dragon—" She hushed herself. That was a shout. She couldn't afford to get caught now.

Looking Shellinda in the eye, she lowered her voice. "Where will Nancor take Adrian?"

Shellinda pointed toward the dragon's shrinking form. "Adrian asked for Arxad's counsel, so probably to the Zodiac. It's in the dragon village."

"If I get you out of here, can you show me the way?"

Shellinda nodded. "It's not real far."

Marcelle looked back at the mound. "Where is Tamara?"

"Tamara?" Shellinda repeated, tilting her head up at her. "Why are you asking about her?"

"I want to tell her brother how she's doing."

Erin held up the trousers. "Come with me."

As the three hurried to the other side of the mound, the remaining children scattered to various holes, the boys and girls separating into gender lines before climbing into the dim burrows. When they reached the opposite side, Erin slid into a hole and disappeared.

Shellinda tugged on Marcelle's sleeve. "Nancor has a big head start. We have to help Adrian right away."

"We?" Marcelle set a hand on Shellinda's head. "Once you show me this Zodiac place, I'm going to find you a safe spot to hide. Or maybe you should come back here. When the dragons discover that you're missing, won't they look for you, or maybe kill some of your friends?"

Shellinda pulled away from Marcelle's touch. "If one of us escapes, they don't care enough to kill anyone. We're not valuable. Whenever the count was down by one, Thad searched every hole to see if someone was sick or dead, and he dragged that person out, dead or alive, to show Nancor. If a missing slave couldn't be accounted for, Nancor would whip Thad, so Thad made sure we didn't wander off anywhere."

"So since Nancor isn't here," Marcelle said slowly, "and you don't have an overseer …"

"Now is the time to escape." Shellinda pointed downstream. "Yarlan might be guarding that exit in Millence's place, and no one can climb the thorny vines, so they think we can't get out. And for most of us, that's probably true, but maybe one sneaky little girl like me could manage it."

Marcelle looked upstream. "What about that way? The water gets in here somehow. Is there a gate?"

Shellinda nodded. "Metal bars. It's—"

"Aren't you two coming?" Erin had poked her head out of the hole. "Tamara has her trousers on now."

Marcelle gestured for Erin to slide back into the hovel, then lowered herself inside, followed by Shellinda. When her feet touched the floor, she tried to straighten, but her head bumped against the ceiling. Even Erin had to stoop to walk around.

On the opposite side of the circular room, about two steps away, a body lay on a haphazard pile of straw. As Marcelle's eyes adjusted to the dimness, the view clarified. A girl, maybe seven years old, lay curled in a fetal position. Her torso bare and calf-length trousers hanging loosely on her narrow hips, she heaved shallow breaths.

Marcelle knelt at her side and tried to push her fingers through Tamara's hair, but it was too tangled and matted. She touched Tamara's ribs, clearly outlined in her emaciated frame. The little girl trembled at the touch. Yet, her eyes stayed closed. Might she be asleep? Unconscious?

As the odor of urine drifted into Marcelle's nostrils, she swallowed down a gag reflex. Apparently no feces littered the straw, so someone had been keeping her area somewhat clean.

Marcelle turned to Shellinda and Erin as they crouched nearby. "How long has she been here?"

"Not real long," Shellinda said. "She got sick maybe twenty days ago. Thad dragged her out to show Nancor and then brought her back and left her to rot. A little while later, Thad ripped his trousers, so he took hers. He decided that as long as she wasn't going to work, she didn't need them."

"Twenty days!" Marcelle said. "How could she survive?"

Erin picked up a handful of straw. "We girls have been chipping in to help her stay clean ... well, sort of clean. But no one wants to give up her food, so she doesn't get much to eat, just a few crumbs a day. Good thing she was well fed before she got here."

Marcelle muttered under her breath. "A few crumbs. Pitiful."

"I gave her all my food a couple of times," Shellinda said. "She'd be dead by now if I didn't."

"But you never washed her or cleaned her straw," Erin countered.

"I did so! I even—"

"Hush! It doesn't matter." Marcelle slid her hands under Tamara's back. "Help me get her out of here."

"Are you going to take her out of the camp?" Shellinda asked.

"Like you said …" Marcelle lifted Tamara into her arms. "With Nancor and Thad gone, now is our best chance. They won't miss her."

After exiting the hovel, Marcelle stood with Erin and Shellinda near the stream, cradling Tamara. Although the girl's arms and legs hung loosely, she felt no heavier than a sack of bones.

Twilight darkened the sky. With the dragons thinking they had the assassin in their grasp, the timing was perfect. "We'll go over the wall," Marcelle whispered to Shellinda and Erin. "I might need both of you to help me get Tamara to the other side. I'm hoping her brother is still there to help us."

Marcelle marched across the pebbly field, leading the girls straight to the point where she and Adrian had scaled the wall earlier. With darkness shrouding their advance, even if a dragon guarded the stream's exit, he likely wouldn't see them.

When they reached the wall, Marcelle scanned the thorns on top, searching for the bare spot. A light shone from somewhere, aiding the effort. Might a moon be rising?

After a moment or two, she found the gap in the thorns and let out a whistle, trying to copy the one Adrian had used, but it sounded weak and raspy by comparison.

Another whistle sounded from beyond the wall, shaky and shrill. Seconds later, Scott's head appeared at the top. "Where have you been?" he whisper-shouted. "I've been waiting and waiting!"

Marcelle lifted Tamara higher. "I brought you your sister."

"My sister?" Scott vaulted over the wall, landed on his feet, and staggered toward her. He laid a hand gently on her cheek. As he stroked it with a finger, his chest heaved. "Is she ..."

"She's alive." Marcelle shuffled toward the wall. "Help me get her out of here."

Scott's voice quaked. "What do I do?"

She nodded at the hip scabbard that sheathed Adrian's sword. "Take my sword and shave off the thorns, just like we did before."

Scott slid it out and began slicing away at the twisted vines, careful to leave enough intact to maintain a way to climb. After returning the sword, he scrambled back up, squatted at the top, and reached down as far as he could. "If you can get her hands this high, I can lift her.

With Shellinda climbing on one side of Marcelle and Erin climbing on the other, both grasping one of Tamara's wrists, Marcelle pushed Tamara's body upward. Scott snatched an arm and hoisted her the rest of the way. His hardened muscles rippled in the light of the rising moon.

Now holding Tamara in his arms, he smiled at Marcelle. "Going down will be easy, but what will happen when the dragons find out she's gone?"

"Don't worry," Marcelle said, clutching a vine. "They won't know. Just get her home. She needs food and water right away. And if you can let the patriarch know we're coming, it might help."

"I can do that." Holding Tamara under one arm, Scott turned and descended without a sound.

Marcelle climbed to the top and looked down, pointing at each girl in turn. "Shellinda, follow me. Erin, stay here and cover our tracks."

While Shellinda climbed, Erin's face wrinkled. "When are you going to come back for me?"

Marcelle sat on the wall's bare crest and raised her hand. "I swear to you that I will free everyone in this hellhole, even if I have to kill every dragon on the planet to do it."

A weak smile broke through. "Okay," Erin said. "But please hurry. It will be lonely without Shellinda."

When Marcelle and Shellinda dropped to the forest side of the wall, Scott was nowhere in sight. "First, show me the Zodiac," Marcelle whispered, "and then we need to find Lattimer."

"He's a night watchman in the dragon village." Shellinda looked around as if trying to get her bearings. After a few seconds, she pointed northward. "We have to go that way and then follow the bend in the wall. The dragon village is about a half hour away."

Marcelle touched her shirt. "Will I be conspicuous in this?"

Shellinda blinked at her. "Con … what?"

"Conspicuous. Will dragons notice that we're out of place?"

Shellinda dabbed one of the oozing stripes on her chest. "More me than you. Girls wear shirts everywhere unless they're cattle, like me."

"You're not cattle!" Marcelle barked. She quickly covered her lips with her fingers and whispered between them. "Sorry. I tend to lose my temper easily."

"Don't worry about it. You're a stranger here, so you don't know how we live. Since the Separators put me here, I will be cattle until someone buys me or I get sent to the breeders. If they don't want me, when I turn thirteen, I go to the mill."

"The mill?"

Shellinda nodded, using her hands to explain. "They put a reject in a big hopper. She slides down to a rolling stone that smashes her body and grinds her meat and bones into a messy glob. Then they feed the glob to the wolves to keep them away from the slaves."

Marcelle set her hands on her hips and gave her a skeptical frown. "That sounds like a fairy tale."

"A fairy tale? What's that?"

"A made-up story someone uses to either encourage people or else scare them."

"The mill scares me, but not as much as the breeding rooms." Shellinda shivered. "Do you want me to tell you what happens there?"

Marcelle waved a hand. "I'd rather you not, but it can't be worse than how I picture it in my imagination."

"Don't be so sure."

Marcelle tried to read Shellinda's expression, but with the forest canopy blocking the moon's glow, shadows veiled the little girl's face.

"Here's what we'll do," Marcelle said as she stripped her outer tunic over her head. "You can wear this. It's big, but it will be less noticeable in the dark than having nothing on at all."

While Shellinda put it on, Marcelle straightened her remaining shirt and checked the buttons. Everything seemed intact, and it was finally dry.

Marcelle looked Shellinda over. As a breeze swept through the woods, the shirt billowed like a canopy. Marcelle tied the tail into a knot, tightening the shirt over the girl's narrow body. "That should do it."

"Let's go." Shellinda scampered ahead, dodging trees and bushes as if following a path illuminated by three moons hovering in the sky. Marcelle forced her body into a swift run to keep pace with the surprisingly energetic girl. Her own legs ached, revealing her exhaustion. Yet, the image of Adrian hanging from the dragon's clutches flashed in her mind, spurring her forward. Somehow she had to find him, rescue him, bind his wounds. Right now, nothing else mattered.

She bit her lip, hard enough to sting. She had been such a fool! Why couldn't she control her temper? Sure, her attack had brought about the death of a dragon, but at what cost? Adrian's life? And he had taken her place, given himself up as a sacrifice. He trusted her to free the slaves in his stead.

A new image entered her mind, Adrian bowing as he forfeited the tourney match, and his words followed, barely a moment after she had parroted his usual forfeiture. *"Let it be as you have spoken."*

Now her heart ached. She had mocked him! And even when she offered an apology, it rang hollow, a noisy gong that he rightfully rejected with a simple, *"Tell it to the crowd. Then I'll believe you."*

And, of course, she had kept silent, too proud to risk her esteem in the eyes of the nobility. Yet, Adrian risked his. No, he obliterated it. And why? Because he refused to break his code of honor, his belief in protecting women and children, no matter how insolent and prideful they were. He never allowed them to suffer. Never. Even if it meant being dragged away to execution by a scaly beast.

Marcelle took in a cleansing breath and let it out slowly. She wrapped her fingers around the hilt of Adrian's sword. She would make everything right, or die trying.

*   *   *   *   *   *

As Nancor flew, his claws ripped at Adrian's nerves, forcing his shoulders and back to tighten. Spasms clenched his muscles. Pure torture. The sadistic dragon offered no pity. In fact, he frequently forced Adrian into a sway, tightening his grip with each swing. Malice. Evil malice.

Bullets of pain shot up and down Adrian's spine and into his head. His vision blurred. His thoughts fogged. Even his memory of why this strange creature was carrying him seemed too difficult to hold in the forefront. Survival. That instinct constantly pushed through as his only clear thought. Somehow, he had to escape.

A soothing voice drifted through his mind. "Adrian, I am with you. I cannot purge the pain from your body, but I can spread balm across your spirit."

Like the strengthening light of a newly lit lantern, Adrian's senses began to clear. Cassabrie. He wasn't alone. Someone loved him. Someone cared.

"Cassabrie," he whispered, his words shattered by the pain. "Any help … you can offer … "

"Shhh, dear Adrian. Spare your strength. When we come to Arxad, I will try to gauge his state of mind. He is not exactly predictable. In the meantime, I will do what I can to distract you from your suffering."

As the wind whistled in his ears, deep within his mind a new sound emerged, Cassabrie's singing voice, yet not that of the youthful songstress who serenaded during their journey through the flowers. Her tone deepened to a mature alto as she crooned a haunting melody.

> The claw of bondage
> Penetrates
> Mutilates
> You share their pain
> Deep within
> Feel the sin
> That binds their wrists, their legs, their hearts
> And pierces souls with angry darts
> Deflating hope and ceasing prayer
> To God above who doesn't care
>
> Or isn't there
>
> Is life unfair?
>
> Yet this I swear
>
> If heroes march into the square
> Their swords withdrawn, their courage bared
> Then hands unbound will fill the sky
> And hope restored will make them fly

To lands of freedom, chains asunder
To clap and worship, hearts in wonder
That God in mercy heard their cries
And sent a friend who dried their eyes

And now my friend
Cry with me
Bleed with me
You share my pain
On your back
Feel the rack
That stretches souls till faith is bare
And shackles hearts and sows despair
For slavish strife and brutal bonds
Destroy all hope in life beyond

This darkened pond

Will you respond?

And bring our dawn?

Cassabrie repeated the refrain, this time with passion unmatched by any fiery prophet in any world.

When heroes march into the square
Their swords withdrawn, their courage bared
Then hands unbound will fill the sky
And hope restored will make them fly

To lands of freedom, chains asunder
To clap and worship, hearts in wonder
That God in mercy heard their cries
And sent a friend who dried their eyes

Finally, Cassabrie's voice faded away, but her words continued to echo. "Will you respond? ... Will you respond?"

Adrian's pain, so intense, so piercing, had become profound. Pain was a thief. It stole hope and replaced it with despair. And his own pain had lasted only minutes, enough to stretch his faith to the breaking point. What had years of toil and torture wrought in the slaves of this land? Surely, despair and misery beyond comprehension had shaken their foundations and ripped the heart of hope out of many.

Adrian relaxed his muscles. The spasms subsided. As the pain diminished, he whispered, "Thank you, Cassabrie. I understand now."

The voice of the teenaged Cassabrie returned. "I sang it, Adrian, because I believe in you."

Adrian took in a deep breath. *I believe in you.* Such beautiful words. Ah, what solace! An infusion of energy. He would respond. This journey wasn't over. Not yet.

Soon, a group of buildings came into view, a few tall edifices along with one-story structures nestled in between. The dragon orbited a building that boasted at least ten glass-like spires encircling a central dome with a hole at its apex.

Nancor dove toward the hole. The claws dug in deeper. Adrian held his breath. No crying out. No groaning. A display of courage and resolve might be his only hope.

They descended through the opening and into a circular room bordered by beds of smooth stones and cacti. Irregular black tiles covered the floor, making the surface look like cracked coal. Lanterns lined the perimeter wall, providing undulating orange light, enough to illuminate the courtyard in the deepening twilight.

Swooping low, Nancor released Adrian. He tumbled over the slatelike tiles, then slid, the blood on his shirt providing lubrication. When his feet struck something solid, he finally stopped. Bending his neck, he looked up. A dragon stood there, bigger and more muscular than Nancor, yet wounded. Cuts and scratches marred his wings, but no blood dripped anywhere. It appeared that he had suffered recent injuries and had already tended to his wounds. An ovular bundle sat next to him, something wrapped in a dark sheet. The dragon glanced at it before training his stare on Adrian.

Adrian blinked, trying to focus as he breathed out, "Cassabrie?"

"This dragon is Arxad," she said. "We are blessed. Yet, he appears to be hurt. I have never seen him like this."

Adrian tried to smile, but spasms in his shoulders overwhelmed his relief at seeing Arxad. He settled his head against the tiles and tried to relax his muscles as he whispered, "Any advice is welcome."

"If Arxad detects my presence, there is very little I can do. My gifts are not as effective over someone who is prepared to resist them, but I will do what I can."

As Nancor landed next to him, his wings cast a breeze across Adrian, cooling his skin. Arxad and Nancor spoke in the dragon language, and Cassabrie translated immediately, making the conversation easy to follow.

"Why have you brought this human?" Arxad asked. "Are not the children in the cattle camps enough of a responsibility?"

Still breathless from carrying his load, Nancor replied. "He intruded ... killed Millence ... confessed his crime and asked for your protection."

A low growl rumbled in Arxad's throat. "If he confessed to killing a dragon, then you are not required to grant access to me. You had the right to execute him immediately."

Nancor's voice settled. "Yes, I know, but he tricked me in the bargaining process. I granted him access in exchange for his confession."

"That is an odd bargain. He is still a prisoner and will be condemned. Why would he settle for that?"

"There is more. In order to punish the humans for killing Millence, I had chosen five children to die. He bargained to spare their lives."

Arxad's ears flattened. "So we have only this single human in exchange for the death of a dragon? Do you think a dragon life and a human life are equal?"

"No, Arxad. I killed the overseer who neglected to tell me of his presence." Nancor lowered his head. "I hoped that was enough, but I see now that I was wrong. Allowing him to deceive me will surely be a bad mark on my record."

"Perhaps we can avoid that mark." Arxad looked at the hole in the curved ceiling. "Tell Magnar that we have a dragon killer in custody and that I have requested a trial with him alone. Pray that he does not ask you questions that will reveal your mistake. Then you may fly back to your post."

"Thank you for your mercy." Nancor spread out his wings and vaulted toward the hole. Within seconds, he was gone.

Adrian sat up slowly and exhaled. "Whew! I'm glad to be free from his clutches."

"Free?" Arxad shouted in the human tongue. He swung his tail around and smacked Adrian across the face, knocking him back. "You are a fool! How dare you kill a dragon and then ask for my protection? Do not think for one moment that I will do anything to set a dragon murderer free."

"Adrian!" Cassabrie said. "Arxad doesn't know who you are. Introduce yourself, but exercise humility, not familiarity."

Adrian propped himself on an elbow and rubbed his stricken cheek. "Right. He doesn't. I thought—"

"You thought?" Arxad's head shot forward and stopped within inches of Adrian's nose. "You did not think! If you want to help the cattle children, then stay away from them!"

"Arxad," Adrian said. "I am Adrian, from Darksphere."

"As if that matters! If you had a particle of sense in your biped brain you would have discerned that killing dragons is not the way to free your kind."

"I didn't want to kill him. You see, Mar—" Adrian bit his tongue. Implicating Marcelle would be the worst move possible. After staring at the dragon's fiery eyes for a few seconds, he let out a sigh. "I had no choice."

"No choice?" Arxad drew back and thumped his tail against the floor. "Then will you be satisfied if we have no choice but to put you to death?"

"I was hoping you would defend me."

"Defend you?" Arxad's nostrils flared. "Did you kill Millence in self-defense? Did he attack you first?"

"One of the little girls tripped and spilled her pail of rocks, so Millence started beating her. Of course, I wanted to stop him, so—"

"Do you think a few stripes on the back of a cattle child should result in the death of the one inflicting them?"

"How was I supposed to know that he wasn't going to kill her?"

Arxad roared, and smoke billowed from his mouth and nostrils. "Stranger from another world, how dare you assume that we would kill a slave for such a trivial mistake! Are you so arrogant that you believe your species is the only one with an understanding of justice? Are you so self-absorbed that you believe humans to be the only species of worth? That you can take the life of a dragon because you assumed that a cattle child's life *might* be in danger?"

Adrian looked away, aching to explain his desire to free the slaves by stealth rather than by direct force, that someone else had made the fatal decision. He breathed another sigh. "I see your point."

"And you see it too late." Arxad looked at Adrian, apparently focusing on his chest. "Stand, human."

Grimacing with every movement, Adrian struggled to his feet.

Arxad stepped closer, smoke still streaming from his nose. "Cassabrie is with you."

Adrian glanced at the patch on his skin, exposed by his open shirt. The bandage had shredded and fallen off. Now glowing reddish orange instead of yellow, the patch stung, but only a little. "She has been very helpful."

"Yet not helpful enough to advise you to spare Millence."

"She didn't have time. It all happened too fast."

"Too fast?" Arxad's ears rotated halfway around, an angry-looking posture, but his smoke dwindled. "Would you have been so quick to kill a human?"

"If he was attacking a defenseless little girl?" Adrian firmed his jaw. "Without a doubt."

"Your attitude is most interesting." Arxad stared into his eyes again. "Cassabrie, come out. You must not be within him during the investigation."

Adrian's lips moved, and his voice passed through. "Yes, my lord."

He touched his mouth. This was new, Cassabrie using his body to speak out loud.

"Adrian," Cassabrie said in his mind. "Remember what I told you about our closeness. This separation will likely be very painful."

A cold sensation erupted within his chest and radiated toward his skin. The glowing patch burned, like a fire-heated poker plunging through. Both icy cold and scalding heat knifed into his breast. He arched his back. It seemed that someone was peeling his heart with a dagger and drawing the membrane out—cutting, tearing, pulling.

The pain was too horrible. He couldn't hold it in. Like an explosion, he cried out in a long, loud wail. It seemed that a claw was ripping his soul from his body.

A shimmering ray of light poured out from the skin patch. As it flowed, it collected in a rising column on the floor, and the patch shrank and cooled.

The pain eased. Adrian relaxed his muscles and exhaled. The light formed into Cassabrie's familiar shape, a girl of pure radiance. With her hands folded at her waist and her head dipped low, her countenance contradicted her radiant persona—sadness, disappointment, and pain seemed to dim her glow until she faded into transparency.

Adrian set a hand over his heart. The patch had disappeared. The warmth had fled, and a sense of cold washed through his body. He shivered. Cassabrie, the indwelling furnace, was gone. And with the cold, emptiness filtered in—loneliness, darkness, solitude. A dungeon.

He swallowed through a tightened throat. His wounds ached. His arms and legs felt limp. Had she energized him that much?

Cassabrie's form reappeared for a moment as she dipped into a graceful curtsy. "I am at your command, Arxad."

"Be ready," Arxad said. "I will require your talent while I am conducting my investigation." He touched a support column with his tail. The lanterns began winking out one by one. As the light dwindled, the ovular bundle glowed with a purple aura, as if the object inside possessed an energy source.

"Excuse me for a moment." Arxad lifted the bundle with a claw, then half-walked, half-flew to a darker area in the chamber. When he returned, he no longer carried the bundle. He shuffled toward the center of the courtyard, his eyes aimed upward. With darkness now almost complete inside the room as well as out, the opening above appeared to blend in with the surrounding black ceiling.

When the final lantern died away, a low grinding sound descended. The hole shrank and disappeared.

A slight glow emanated from the center of the room. A sphere sat atop a head-high crystalline column embedded in the floor, casting just enough radiance to reveal its presence. Dots of light appeared on the ceiling, like stars in the sky.

Arxad set his clawed hand on the sphere. A shadow in the shape of his draconic hand covered the stars. "Since Nancor agreed to bring you to me, I am obligated by the duties of my priestly office to investigate," he said. "But if I can find no defense for your actions, I cannot be your counselor. It would be a charade and a waste of time."

Adrian gave him a submissive nod. "I understand."

When Arxad lifted his hand, the stars reappeared. "I have watched humans for a long time, and I have learned to be an excellent judge of their character. I know when they lie, when they hide truth, and when they speak with hidden meanings. Most do so to prevent their backs from being flayed, their self-preservation instincts trying to keep their skin intact. Yet, I have not learned why a few individuals hide truth at their own hurt, as you are doing now."

Adrian pointed at himself. "As I am doing? What makes you say that?"

"I know you are withholding information from me, and your reason cannot be for self-preservation, because at the present course, your death is the only possible end."

Adrian took a few steps closer to the glowing sphere. "Would it be strange for a person to withhold information in order to protect someone else?"

"It is strange, indeed. With the exception of parents protecting their children, it is extremely rare for a human to choose a sacrificial death." Arxad extended his neck and studied Adrian's face. "Judging by your age and the fact that you have embarked on a nearly suicidal quest, my guess is that you are childless."

Adrian nodded. "I am not even married."

"Oh, yes. Married. I nearly forgot that humans are required to do that on Darksphere."

Adrian pondered the comment for an instant but let it pass. Whether or not he understood made little difference now. "May I ask you a question, good dragon?"

Arxad appeared to smirk, but only for a brief moment. "Whether or not I am good, I will leave you to judge, but feel free to ask. I do not promise an answer."

"On one occasion when Cassabrie visited my world, she left a tricornered hat and a video tube. The hat belonged to my brother Frederick, and the tube recorded part of his actions here. What do you know about these things?"

"I know a great deal about them." Arxad's wing bent around, and the tip pressed against his chest. "I have met Frederick myself, and I was very impressed with his valor, integrity, and passion. I gave Cassabrie the hat and video tube to leave on Darksphere in order to draw more humans into contact with us."

Adrian's heart raced. "Where is he now?"

"This I cannot answer, because I do not know. He rescued at least one of the cattle children and escaped to the wilderness. I have not heard from him since."

"Is there a refuge in the wilderness, a safe place for runaway slaves?"

"If there is," Arxad said, "I wish not to know about it. It is better for all if I remain ignorant. Yet, it is doubtful that such a place exists. No slave has ever returned from those forests. The dangers are too great."

Adrian gazed at the dragon's countenance. Although he had experienced only a few dragons, it seemed clear that Arxad was being truthful. Learning more about Frederick's location from him seemed unlikely, but now that Arxad was ready to provide help, Adrian felt a surge of hope. "Why did you draw humans into contact? Why did you want the extane?"

"I will not speak on that issue, and the time for your questions has ended. You are accused of murdering a dragon, and I have already extended you more privileges than you deserve. I must conduct the investigation."

Adrian bowed his head. Testing this dragon's patience probably wasn't a good idea. "I am ready."

"Because of your odd behavior," Arxad continued, "I have decided to probe your brain, and I will use the Reflections Crystal to learn what I need to know."

Adrian stared at the glowing sphere. Apparently, this was the Reflections Crystal. Was it a torture device of some kind?

As if reading Adrian's mind, Arxad waved a wing, speaking softly as he gestured for him to come closer. "The process is not painful. It will merely help me discover whether or not there is more to your story than you have revealed."

Adrian took three more steps, bringing him within reach of the orb, clear and white. It seemed that the glow created a cloud of light that hovered above the clear surface, like a sparkling mist floating over water. With swirls of radiance mixing with sparkling points, the sight dizzied his mind. Whatever this thing was about to do to probe his thoughts, he had to resist. Marcelle's life might be at stake.

"Now," Arxad said, "we must provide a baseline lie. Stare at the crystal and say something you know to be false."

Adrian shook away the fog. "Okay." He cleared his throat and spoke slowly and clearly. "I feel no remorse for killing Millence."

The crystal faded to gray, then black.

"An intriguing choice," Arxad said, his brow lifting. "And a wise one."

Cassabrie glided within reach of the globe, her radiant body visible as she moved. "If I may vouch for his character, my lord, I—"

"If he cannot vouch for his own character," Arxad said, "then who are you to play the role of advocate?"

She bowed, her head and torso the only visible parts of her body. "Yes, my lord."

Adrian nodded toward the crystal, now white again. "So it turns black when I lie and stays white if I don't?"

Arxad glared at him. "You have a firm grasp of the obvious. If only your wisdom had been as well developed."

Adrian maintained eye contact with Arxad. If he were to avert his gaze, that would make him look all the more guilty. Integrity never has reason to be ashamed.

"Cassabrie," Arxad said, "While I question him, I want you to tell me what happened."

"Very well." Cassabrie's hands appeared, and as she reached down, the sides of her skirt materialized, sparkling white. "I assume you want a Starlighter's tale."

"I do, indeed."

Cassabrie twisted, making her entire body radiate, and as she twisted back, her cloak fanned out, and streams of sparkling light flew from the hem, like shining droplets cast away from the petals of a daisy. She lifted her hands, creating an aura around her, and her features clarified. With shining green eyes, flowing red hair, and pinpoint freckles scattered on pearl-like skin, the cadaverous body she inhabited in the woods of Major Four seemed like a fossilized shell compared to the radiant beauty spinning in place here in the world of dragons.

She spoke with a lovely, lilting voice. "I was dwelling within this man of honor, peering through his eyes. The children paraded before us, each one leaning with a heavy burden, a pail of stones that would decorate a dragon's luxurious home, allowing him to glory in his wealth, eating lambs, drinking wine, and sleeping on soft pillows. All the while, the pitiful urchins who supplied the stones scrabble for crumbs before crawling into their holes and sleeping on rocks, hoping that the pangs in their bellies will allow them to sleep. They beg for the spasms in their muscles to ease so that they can once again gather stones the next day and avoid the dragon's cruel whip."

As she spoke, the raft and stream appeared in front of her, and a line of children walked next to it, each one carrying a pail. Although semitransparent, their details grew clear enough. They were the same children Adrian and Marcelle had seen in the cattle camp.

Marcelle came into view, hiding behind a tree, and Cassabrie crouched next to her, taking Adrian's place in the tale. Now a dragon stood over the children, a whip in its hand.

While Cassabrie and Marcelle watched from their hiding place, Arxad touched a wound on Adrian's neck with the tip of a wing. "Why do you choose punishment when the truth might well set you free?" His voice was deeper now, more resonant, and the statement sounded like a command rather than a question.

As Adrian stared at the ghostly scene, the globe's radiance brightened at his side, casting light over Cassabrie and the children. They seemed more real than ever, solid bodies with naked torsos and streaming sweat.

The mirage drew closer, as if he were walking into its glowing envelope, yet his feet never moved, and the globe remained stationary at his side. Now the descending sun shone over the cattle camp, and everything appeared to be as real as when he stood there only hours ago. Yet, Cassabrie still crouched in his place next to Marcelle, and the crystalline sphere continued to sparkle.

As if time had reversed, the pain in his shoulders eased. The dragon had not yet clawed his back and carried him away. In fact, every worry melted. The loneliness crumbled. All was well.

"Adrian."

The dragon's voice seemed far away, like an echo in a canyon. What was his name again? It started with an *A*.

"Adrian, why do you choose punishment when the truth might grant your freedom?"

As if summoned from deep in his chest, his voice filtered out unbidden—calm and smooth. "I am a man, so I must protect a woman."

The orb at his side glowed white, perhaps even whiter than before.

"Did you, in fact, kill Millence?"

"I did."

The radiance dimmed a shade.

"Yet, there is more to the story. There is something you are not telling me."

A girl tripped and tumbled to the ground, spilling her pail. The dragon lashed her chest with its whip—once, twice, three times.

Marcelle leaped from behind the tree, ran up the dragon's spine, and hacked at its eyes with a sword. Cassabrie, her body sparkling, dashed ahead. A sword appeared in her hand, and she stabbed the dragon in the belly. It vanished, as did the children, except for the girl the dragon had whipped. Cassabrie and Marcelle knelt at the girl's side.

"Marcelle attacked the dragon," Adrian said. "I thought it was a foolish thing to do, but I was afraid she would be killed, so I ran to her aid."

The orb's original glow returned, sharp and bright white.

"Are you certain Millence would have killed her had you not joined the battle?"

"I wasn't sure, but I couldn't wait to find out."

The sphere remained white.

"Why could you not wait?"

"Because if it became clear that she would lose, it might be too late for me to help."

"So was your motivation pure chivalry, the code of a gentleman warrior?"

Adrian swallowed. The question seemed strange, not a simple factual query, but rather a question of the heart. "I have been taught chivalry since I was a little boy. It is part of my being, so I react accordingly, sometimes without thinking."

The glow dimmed several shades until it turned a smoky gray.

"That is likely a true statement when not in context, Adrian, but it does not answer the question in complete truthfulness."

"I ... I don't understand."

The globe turned even darker, now a mass of coal.

"You do understand. You have other reasons for protecting this woman, but there is no need to pry that information from your mind. I have learned all I need to know."

Something grasped Adrian's arm and drew him away from the black sphere. The pain in his shoulders roared back, throbbing, aching.

"Cassabrie," Arxad said. "That is all."

Cassabrie rose from her knees. The aura shrank. Marcelle and the girl dissolved, as if drawn into the dwindling light. Finally, Cassabrie grew transparent until she disappeared.

The crystalline sphere slowly shifted to gray. Adrian touched his chest. The patch was still gone, and the chill returned to his bones. What had happened?

Arxad set a wing on Adrian's arm and turned him around. "You and I will speak to Magnar, the leader of all dragons. If it is his will that you die for killing Millence, then so be it, but I will do what I can to plead for a lesser punishment."

"Did I …" Adrian set a hand on his head. His mind seemed clogged. "Did Cassabrie tell you what happened?"

"She did. I saw what you saw. Cassabrie's talents put you in a trance, so you were unaware of your surroundings. I now know that Marcelle is the true culprit in this murder."

Adrian's words spilled out in rapid-fire fashion. "She knows better now. She won't kill any more dragons. If you let us get together again, I'm sure I can control her."

The globe turned dark gray.

Arxad's brow dipped low. "Your level of certainty is greatly lacking."

Adrian glared at the lie-detecting sphere. It seemed infallible. "What will you do about Marcelle?"

"I am not sure. Perhaps it would be best to allow her to decide her own fate. If she controls herself and attacks no more dragons, she will be difficult to find even if I send out a search party. Yet, if she continues attacking dragons, she will not survive very long. For her sake and those of your fellow humans, you had better hope she has learned to keep her sword in its scabbard. The mission on which you have embarked is already in great peril."

Cassabrie walked toward Adrian, every step giving light to her presence. When she stopped at his side, she disappeared again. Sparkles of radiance spilled from her mouth as she spoke. "I will stay with you, no matter what happens."

Adrian smiled at her, though it seemed no one was there. He then turned to Arxad. "So is the investigation complete?"

"It is."

"When will the trial begin?"

"As soon as I hear that Magnar is ready for a trial, but I must take you to the Basilica immediately. I have something that I must deliver there as soon as possible." Arxad entered a darker portion of the chamber again, returned with the ovular bundle, and set it down. "When my delivery is complete, we will come back here."

"And will Cassabrie come with us?" Adrian asked.

"Her presence will be indispensable. I will need her for a number of reasons that I care not to explain at this time."

Adrian set a hand on his chest, letting his touch linger. "Will you permit her to dwell within me?"

"Only while you are being transported to the Basilica. She must not be seen until the proper time. Yet, I confess that I am confused. From the reaction I observed when she departed from you, I wonder why you want her to reenter."

"I can't explain it," Adrian said as he lowered his hand. "I suppose it's a human phenomenon. Once we have tasted the pleasure of perfect union, we don't want to be alone again, no matter how much the pain of the next separation rips at our hearts."

Arxad dipped his head. "So be it."

Cassabrie's hand appeared, reaching toward Adrian's chest. She touched the place where the glowing patch had been. As if absorbed by his skin, her fingers passed through the membrane, then her hand and wrist. The entry point stung, fiery hot, and the warmth spread across his skin and deep within.

A river of light formed at his feet and flowed into his chest, every second pure torture, yet also pure pleasure. Her presence had returned—the joy, the companionship, the warmth of embrace.

A girlish sigh passed into Adrian's consciousness. Cassabrie was home.

"I am glad, too," Adrian whispered.

She spoke in a faint whisper. "Yet, if you are found guilty and are condemned, all will be lost. You will die, and I will again be disembodied. As wonderful as it is to serve the dragon king, living as a ghost without you will be a torture I cannot bear."

"Arxad," Adrian said, "what will happen to Cassabrie if I die?"

"There is no need to discuss hypothetical questions, but I can tell you this. Whether you live or die, I can arrange for you to be together." Arxad's brow lifted. "Yet, is she the female with whom you wish to spend eternity?"

As warmth again spread throughout Adrian's body, the pain of his wounds eased. He spoke as if in a dream. "I have no other female. No wife. No intended. Cassabrie is my only love."

"Although she appears to be younger than you," Arxad said, "Cassabrie is actually considerably older, though rather ageless in her current state. I am confident that there are other females of your age who would find you to be an attractive mate. I saw one in Cassabrie's tale who appears to be quite suitable."

Adrian blinked. The dragon's words seemed odd, distant. He wasn't making much sense at all. "All is well," he finally said. "As you indicated, she is ageless."

Arxad drew his head close to him and looked into his eyes. "Cassabrie, if you love this man, do not violate his trust. You cannot keep forever that which is not freely given."

Adrian's voice passed through his lips but not by his command. "I understand, my lord. It is my love that heals his mind and body and allows him to endure his trials, but I will release what is not rightfully mine at the proper time."

"Very well." Arxad touched the ovular bundle with a wing tip. It still pulsed, but with less energy than before. "Remember, Cassabrie, Magnar is vulnerable, and if Adrian is sentenced to die, you will be present at the execution. Perhaps your love will be used in another way."

"Again, my lord, I understand."

✸ EIGHTEEN ✸

WITH moonlight illuminating the mine, Drexel knelt and shook Orlan, hissing quietly. "Wake up! Something terrible has happened!"

Orlan blinked before staring at Drexel. "What?"

"Come. I'll show you." He rose to his feet and pointed at Cassandra, now sleeping alone. "Wake her and bring her along."

While Drexel waited, Orlan scrambled to his feet and roused Cassandra. As she stretched and yawned, Orlan looked at Drexel. "Where are the others?"

"You'll see." Raising a finger to his lips, he tiptoed into the passage between the mining pit and the mesa's exit. As they traveled away from their source of light, darkness closed in, but moonlight from the exit guided their way.

When they arrived, Drexel pointed at the skirt of pebbles and sand around the opening. Three vague small bodies lay motionless, two with legs ensnared by one rope and the other similarly caught in another rope.

Orlan lunged, but Drexel caught his arm and whispered, "They're not moving. I'm pretty sure they're dead."

Orlan spun toward him, his face streaked with pain. "What happened?"

"They went to sleep early in the day, so it was to be expected that they would awaken. I can only assume that they went out in search of water and fell into the dragons' snare."

"But why? They should have known it was dangerous!"

Drexel stroked his chin. "Now that I think about it, I'm sure they were asleep when we talked about the trap. They had no idea it was there, and thirst must have driven them to risk the danger of being seen. They probably thought darkness would keep them safe."

Orlan's face twisted. Heaving shallow breaths, he dropped to his knees and covered his face. Cassandra crouched and leaned against Orlan's arm. Both children wept softly.

Drexel stooped in front of them and spoke with a sympathetic tone. "Come, my sorrowful friends. Now is the time to do what we must to avenge their deaths. When we escape to freedom, we will return with a thousand warriors and defeat those evil dragons. You'll see. Those child murderers will be the ones locked in chains and cowering under our whips."

Orlan brushed away tears and rose to his feet while helping Cassandra rise to hers. Looking at the quiet bodies outside, he nodded. "Let's go."

With Cassandra's hand in his grip, Drexel led the way, again tiptoeing. As he stepped on the mesh that triggered the snare, now lying flat and dormant, his shoes crunched the gritty surface underneath. He paused at the girl's body, lying prostrate with a tight loop around her bare ankle, and felt her neck. It was cold and still. Orlan held a hand over the mouth of one of the boys. After waiting for a moment, he looked at Drexel and shook his head sadly.

After checking the other boy, also lifeless, Drexel gestured for Orlan and Cassandra to follow and strode confidently toward the portal, retracing the path that led him to the mine. Four moons shone in the sky, three near one horizon, and a larger one just beginning to rise on the other. The nearby stream raised the comforting sound of running water, muffling their own noises—nervous breathing, crunching gravel, and Cassandra's leftover sniffles. At times, it meandered away, only to return again with its soothing rhythms. At a point where the stream drew nearest, Drexel allowed the children time to stop and drink, but he hurried them through the process. The need for safety, of course, outweighed the need for hydration.

Every few seconds, Drexel scanned the purple sky. No sign of dragons. Very strange. Before coming here, the image of dozens of dragons patrolling the air and ground had fostered the idea of obsessive control, that every moment in the slaves' lives passed under a dragon's watchful eyes. Yet, it seemed that they were supremely confident in their power, having subjected their underlings to such cruelty that a less vigilant approach to captivity sufficed. Perhaps no one dared step out of line, knowing that death or brutal beatings would surely follow.

When they reached the other mesa, Drexel pulled out Blackstone's journal and turned to the page showing where he hid the portal-opening crystal. After angling it toward the moonlight, he read the entry and searched the base of the mesa for a gap in the solid rock. Supposedly, Uriel had dug out a hole and hidden the crystal deep within, but he had also tied a rope to it so he could fish it out when necessary.

"This is odd," Orlan whispered, pointing toward the ground.

A skinny rivulet ran from the stream to the mesa where it struck a boulder that appeared to have been placed there to direct the flow away. Water coursed around the boulder and branched off in several directions, fingerlike runnels heading back toward the stream.

Drexel walked behind the boulder and crouched at the mesa's base. A hole had been excavated, and the surrounding grit and sand was damp, as if the rivulet had at one time been channeled into the hole. Using his fingers, he dug through the wet silt and found a thin rope, exactly as Uriel had described. He pulled it toward himself, hand over hand, until he found the end, an empty loop tied with a knot.

He cursed under his breath. The crystal was gone! Someone must have known it was here and used the water from the stream to flush it out. Now there was no way to open the portal from the dragon world.

Leaning to the side, he peered around the boulder. Orlan and Cassandra were looking at the rising moon, oblivious to the catastrophe. Only one chance remained. Maybe someone left the portal open.

He rose to his feet and whispered to the children. "Stay here. I will return very soon." Walking in long strides, he hurried to the exit hole where he had emerged from the mesa and hustled down the staircase leading to the portal. Now in darkness, he knelt and rubbed his hands along the floor. After a few seconds, his fingers came upon one of the crystalline pegs. He followed the line of crystals until one fingertip dropped into an empty hole. It wasn't there.

Mumbling a stream of profanity, he hurried up the stairs and stalked back toward the children. What could he do now? Kill them and try to blend in with the slaves, hoping to get information about the crystal? Maybe a slave discovered it and didn't know what it was for. If he could locate it, encouraging some other pitiful waif to accompany him to freedom would be easy enough.

As he closed in on the children, who were now standing in the shadow of the boulder, he withdrew his sword. Killing these two would be an ugly business, but, of course, necessary for the long-term goals. The cost of a few lives paled in comparison to the reward of freedom for hundreds.

Orlan stepped out of the shadow and pointed toward the moon. Drexel glanced that way. The silhouette of a dragon crossed the glowing disk.

When Drexel drew near, Orlan eyed the sword and whispered, "Good. You already saw him."

"I did." He pulled Orlan back into the shadow and stood between him and Cassandra. He laid a hand on a shoulder of each child, the sword still in his grip as he rested it on Orlan. "It would be better not to fight such a beast in the dark."

"What about our escape?" Orlan asked.

"Bad fortune has come upon us. The door to freedom is closed and locked, and I cannot find the key."

Orlan pulled away. "What? I thought you said—"

"I said I knew how to find our way to freedom. I know the path, but the way is blocked, at least for now."

Orlan looked at the sky again. "I don't think he's coming this way, but we'd better hide soon."

"What are our options?"

"This mesa or the other one, but those hiding places won't last long. Someone will find us eventually."

"Are there uninhabited areas?" Drexel asked. "Mountains? Forests?"

Cassandra piped up. "The wilderness!"

"Yes," Orlan said. "There *is* the wilderness. Some slaves run away there, but it's probably too dangerous. No one has ever returned."

Drexel watched the patrolling dragon. It had passed them by, but it appeared to be swinging around for another sweep. "I wouldn't expect runaways to return to their chains."

"True, but we thought they would at least try to get a message to us."

"And risk their freedom? Not likely." Drexel looked out over the terrain, flat except for the other mine's mesa and a few boulders and stunted trees. "Tell me how to get there."

"After that dragon flies by again, the way should be clear. I'll lead you to it."

"Just give me directions. I assure you that I can find it."

Orlan shook his head. "I'm making sure you still need me. And once we get there, you'll probably need help figuring out which vines will give you a rash, where the forest vipers hide, and which fruit is poisonous."

"Ah, yes, my cunning little friend. You are correct in your assumptions of my ignorance." Drexel slid the sword away and bowed. "I acquiesce to your plan."

After waiting a few minutes for the dragon to fly out of sight, Orlan led Drexel and Cassandra into the arid field. They crossed the stream twice, wading up to Drexel's thighs and Cassandra's waist, but, with a firm grip on her hand, Drexel whispered constant assurances. Of course, picking her up was out of the question. He had to save his strength for the wilderness.

They traveled up a barely perceptible incline. To the left, mountains loomed, and to the right, a line of lights danced in the breeze, perhaps lanterns in a distant village. About an hour later, the trees grew taller and more densely packed. The canopy above provided a comforting umbrella but also dimmed the forest floor. Soon, the path disappeared, and thick underbrush blocked their way.

"I have never been past this point," Orlan said, his voice now at a normal level. "You could use your sword to cut a path, but then we could be followed."

Drexel peered at the obstacles in the dimness ahead—thick ferns, vines draped from tree to tree, and moss-covered logs. "You mentioned vipers."

"I did, but everyone says they only come out in the daytime."

"Everyone says that? I suppose 'everyone' includes all the runaways who never came back to report what they saw here."

Orlan glowered at him. "I'm just telling you what I've heard."

Drexel withdrew his sword and pointed ahead. "Lead on. We'll try not to leave much evidence of our whereabouts, but I assume after we are deep within the wilderness we will be freer to cut a path."

"I think so." Orlan bent a thorny bush to the side and held it while Drexel and Cassandra passed. They ducked under hanging vines, stepped over knee-high ferns, and squeezed between trunks where the trees grew as thick as grass.

After another hour, Drexel began slashing with the sword— slicing vines and hacking off thorny protrusions from any bush that dared to get in their way. With grunts and snapping vegetation, he raised quite a racket, but the surrounding jungle seemed to absorb every sound.

Soon, Orlan stopped and pointed at the forest floor. "A path."

Drexel bent over. Indeed, the underbrush appeared to end abruptly at each side of a narrow strip of trampled ground. "What do you think it means?"

"Runaway slaves. Some of us think they set up a place to live."

Something sharp poked Drexel's back. He stepped forward to move clear of the thorn or whatever it was, but it stayed in place.

"Drop your weapon." The voice was deep and commanding. "And raise your hands."

Drexel spread out his fingers. His sword fell and thudded on the ground. As he raised his hands, he looked at Orlan and Cassandra. Both children stared with wide eyes.

The stinging point pulled back. "Now turn around slowly."

Sliding his feet, Drexel turned. A man stood before him, dressed in clean but tattered clothes. His tunic, dark olive with thick material and perfectly sewn trim, was surely a modern garment from Mesolantrum. No slave would have access to such clothing. Drexel studied the stranger's face. A thick beard covered chin and cheeks, hiding his features.

"Well, if it isn't my old friend, Drexel." The man slid the sword into a hip scabbard. "What brings you to this God-forsaken planet?"

The stranger's voice finally pricked his memory. "Is that you, Frederick?"

"The same." Frederick bent over, picked up Drexel's sword, and pushed the hilt into his hand. "You'll need this. I'll explain later. First, tell me your story."

Smiling, Drexel leaned the blade against his shoulder. "Well, of course, ever since you disappeared, the Underground Gateway has searched for a way to follow you into this world. A dragon delivered your courier's tube to us, so we knew you might still be alive."

Frederick stroked his hairy chin. "A dragon. Must have been Arxad."

"Perhaps. I never learned his name. In any case, I overcame many obstacles and found the secret." Drexel patted his tunic. "I came into possession of Uriel Blackstone's journal. Although there were many puzzles, I managed to solve them."

Frederick tilted his head to the side. "You came alone? Why?"

"As a test. Because very few believe in the existence of this world, the Gateway needed someone to prove that the journey was possible, so why not me? My idea was to rescue one or two slave children and then return." Drexel touched Cassandra's head. "Who better to rouse the passions of our soldiers than an undernourished little girl?"

Frederick nodded. "I can't argue with that, but why are you here in the wilderness?"

"It seems that my plans have run into an obstacle. Uriel's book tells of a crystal that opens the portal, but it is missing from its hiding place. Because of other unfortunate circumstances, we have run afoul of dragon laws and are now fugitives."

"That's putting it mildly," Orlan said. "He killed a dragon and blew up mine number two."

Frederick laughed. "Blew it up? How did you manage that?"

"Yes, well I ..." Drexel replayed the events in his mind, including the killing of the miners and guiding three children into the dragons' snare. What parts could he tell without risking the loss of Frederick's support? "It's like this. You see—"

Frederick waved a hand. "Never mind. You can tell me all about it later." He grasped Drexel's arm. "Come. I have something to show you."

Leading with his sword, Frederick marched down the path. Drexel and the two children followed. At one point, a coiled snake rose up and struck at Frederick, but in a flash of metal, he sliced off its head before its fangs reached his leg.

A minute later, a low, catlike growl sounded from deep in the forest. Frederick paused and listened. "Only one," he said with a sigh before marching again. "Good fortune is with us."

After a few minutes, the path narrowed and disappeared. A primitive cabin stood nestled in a dense stand of trees, shaded by a network of branches and vines in the forest canopy above. The single moon, now rising higher into the sky, barely shone through and coated the roof with dappled light. A breeze filtered down and rustled the roof's huge leaves. Tied together with thick vines, they wore a slick, dark green skin, apparently waterproof.

Frederick laid a hand on one of the cabin's exterior walls, a stack of logs with thick, mudlike paste wedged in the gaps. A proud smile spread across his face. "How do you like it?"

"A wilderness lodge?" Drexel asked as he drew closer.

"You might call it that, and from above it's practically invisible." Frederick pulled open a knob-less door, a collection of bark and thick leaves apparently glued together by the same mortar used on the logs. "If you don't mind sharing floor space, there is plenty of room."

"Who else lives here?"

"Just me and four children, two boys and two girls." Frederick walked inside and beckoned them to follow. "They're under eight years old, so they don't take up much room."

When all had entered, they sat on the floor, an assortment of leaves, similar to those on the roof, covering an uneven foundation. With no windows and just a hint of moonlight entering the door, the interior gave away only the outlines of the four sleeping children.

"Are you hungry?" Frederick asked. "Thirsty? It's dark, but I'm sure I can find something."

Drexel waved a hand. "We can wait until morning. I am much more interested in hearing about your situation here."

"Well ..." Frederick rubbed his fingers along the rough floor. "I decided to build this little house so I could rescue a few of the children from slavery. Every once in a while, I journey into the dragon village at night and try to get more information about portals while I forage for supplies. After learning nothing over all these months, I had nearly given up trying. But now that you tell me of my tube's appearance—"

"And your hat, the tricornered one." Drexel raised a pair of fingers. "Two separate events."

Frederick laughed. "Well, it seems that old Arxad knows more than he was letting on when I last saw him. I'll have to pay him a more forceful visit."

While the two continued talking, Orlan and Cassandra lay down and listened. Drexel absorbed Frederick's words and asked question after question about this strange, new world. Maybe if they put their knowledge and experience together, they could find a way back to Major Four with six children in tow.

He looked at Frederick's sword, now unhitched from his belt and lying on the floor. Of course, it wouldn't do for him to come along. Sharing the glory simply wasn't part of the plan, and Frederick would never agree to Drexel's assumption of the throne by threatening the people with the specter of another dragon coming to steal more slaves. He would not understand that the people, nobles and peasants alike, needed a strong yet benevolent hand guiding their destiny. Only fear, and his assurance of protection, would elevate such a ruler.

While Frederick rambled on, sincerity and trust in his eyes, Drexel smiled. Yes, this would work. Although the plan might be delayed by many days, establishing an alliance with this valiant warrior would be the next step, for only fools and close allies are vulnerable to a stab in the back.

* NINETEEN *

WITH three moons setting and a single, larger moon rising on the opposite horizon, Marcelle skulked up a rocky hill, following Shellinda. The little girl had slowed quite a bit. Her poorly fed muscles had likely spent their last morsel of energy while running through the forest.

When they reached the top, Shellinda squatted and pulled Marcelle down. She pointed toward a series of flickering lights in the distance, probably lanterns with wicks turned up to illuminate the way for evening travelers. After catching her breath, she whispered, "The grottoes."

"Caves in the hillside?" Marcelle asked.

Shellinda nodded and shifted her finger to the right. "Lattimer lives in the cave closest to the dragon village. As the night watchman, he will go on duty, but not real soon."

Marcelle let her gaze drift to the right, beyond the cave Shellinda had pointed out. Brighter lights raised a glow over a series of buildings in the distance, some tall and oddly shaped. "Which one is the Zodiac?"

"See the spires?" Shellinda asked, pointing again.

Marcelle followed a line from the girl's finger to the village. A series of tall spires rose high above a domed building, creating crisscrossing shadows in the light of the moons.

"So that's where Adrian is," Marcelle said. "How do we get in?"

"Lattimer can probably help with that, but it will be difficult to contact him without getting us all in trouble."

"Unless Scott gave him the word. He knows to look for us, so maybe he will come. We can wait for a little while." Marcelle sat down fully and looked up. It seemed strange to gaze upon so many moons, especially with a backdrop of familiar constellations. Apparently she was still in Major Four's planetary system, and the stars were the same ones she had watched since childhood, shifted only slightly from their usual formations.

She pointed at one of her favorites—four stars in a vertical line and five arcs sprouting from the top, each arc consisting of three stars. "The Tree of Life," she whispered.

When Shellinda looked up, the moons' glow highlighted the smudges on her face. "The one with the long straight line and then curved lines?"

"Um-hm."

"The Dragon's Whip."

"Oh." Marcelle frowned. What a sad existence. Not even the simple pleasures of sky-gazing could—

"Psst!"

Marcelle grasped her sword's hilt and shot to her feet. "Who's out there?"

"It's me. Scott."

Bending low, Marcelle scooted toward the voice. Scott emerged from the shadow of a boulder, sweat glistening on his bare arms. He took a deep breath. "I have bad news. Lattimer is dead."

"What? How?"

"Maximus, guardian of the Basilica, killed him last night. There are many rumors about why."

"Then what do we do?" Marcelle asked. "Is there another patriarch?"

"His wife will speak with you. She is just as knowledgeable, but I fear that you will not get very far."

"Why is that?"

"You will see."

Shellinda pulled on Scott's trousers. "How is Tamara?"

He pushed her hair back from her eyes. "She is doing better. Thank you for asking."

Marcelle sighed. Such a tender display. This young man knew how to treat a little girl. "I'm sorry. I should have asked about your sister."

"She is not the worse for your lack of asking." Waving an arm, he bent low and hustled toward the grottoes. "Follow and stay quiet."

Marcelle and Shellinda hurried to keep pace. When they reached the cave on the right side of the hill, Scott slowed. A woman carrying a lantern waved frantically from the entrance.

"Come," she hissed. "My master, Hyborn, is occupied, but I do not know for how long."

Scott dashed ahead and waited at the cave's yawning entrance. When Marcelle and Shellinda caught up, he whispered, "I will leave you in Daphne's care." With that, he sneaked away into the night.

Daphne grabbed Marcelle's arm and croaked in a low, gravelly tone. "If you will have pity on a poor widow, you will not say a word until I speak again."

Marcelle gazed into her sad eyes, glistening in the light of the moons. Deep lines etched her face with grief. Her husband had perished only the night before, yet she was willing to take a risk for the sake of strangers. Marcelle nodded and touched her own lips, then Shellinda's, signaling their silence.

Curling her finger, Daphne ducked into the cave. Marcelle took Shellinda's hand and followed. Inside, a high and wide tunnel with a rocky, uneven floor led past a series of wall-mounted torches. Undulating light cast a trio of hunched-over shadows on both walls, making it seem as if six trembling ghosts mimicked their stealthy march.

The sounds of emptiness filled Marcelle's ears, like air whisking through the expanse. She took in a quiet breath through her nose. Unlike other caves, this one lacked any hint of mold or must. With the scent of cooked meat and something spicy in the air, it smelled more like dinnertime at Grandmother's house than an empty hole in the side of a mountain.

Marcelle glanced at Shellinda. The smell of food seemed to have no effect. Maybe months of stale bread and fish had desensitized her. She probably didn't remember what real food smelled like. Still, she needed to eat and drink. The long run had been enough to wear anyone out.

They breezed by a dark room on the right with a door big enough to accommodate a dragon. A loud rumbling sound came from within, like troubled breathing. It bounced off the opposite wall and sent tiny tremors across the floor.

Daphne seemed unconcerned. She just marched on.

Marcelle looked back. Could Daphne's master be in there, asleep and snoring? No wonder she wanted complete silence.

As Daphne led them further in, the rows of lanterns ended, leaving them in darkness. A hand grasped Marcelle's, strong and cold. She followed its pull to the left. The snoring diminished, as did the buzz of emptiness. This corridor was likely narrower with a lower ceiling, explaining the muffled sounds.

After a few seconds and a turn to the right, the pull eased, and the hand let go. A scratching sound interrupted the silence. Sparks flew, and a wick sprang to life. Daphne turned a lantern's wheel, heightening the flame. The glow spread throughout the room. Three mats lay side by side, their combined widths taking up nearly all the floor space, save for a desk and chair at the foot of the rightmost mat. A girl, perhaps Shellinda's age, rested cross-legged on the mat. Wearing a thin nightshirt that covered her body to halfway down her thighs, she leaned against a wall that curved into an arched ceiling. She blinked at the sudden light. In contrast to the cattle child, this girl's shoulder-length hair, light brown and shiny, was clean, as was her rosy face. Although somewhat thin, her cheeks showed none of the hollowness that Shellinda's and her workmates' displayed.

Across the room on the left side, another girl lay on her mat with a gray sheet covering her from the waist down. Likely about twelve years old, she, too, blinked.

Marcelle eyed the second girl. With darker and shorter hair, her expression seemed pensive. She tightened and loosened her grip on the edge of the sheet and kept her gaze averted from the visitors.

"Now," Daphne said, her voice again low and rasping, "we can converse in safety." She sat down cross-legged on the center mat and gathered her long skirt into her lap.

Marcelle and Shellinda joined her at the foot of her mat. "Thank you for your time," Marcelle said. "I am sorry about your tragic loss."

Daphne sniffed. "Lattimer was a good man. Although we disagreed on everything from dragons to dreams, he was a very good man. We were lucky. The dragons allowed us to share our final months together. He was dying. He knew it. We all knew it. So Arxad requested that the Separators put us together. Still, no one knows why Lattimer aggravated Maximus enough to provoke his wrath. Maybe he wanted to end his life before the suffering stage became worse. Since the dragons won't tell me, I will likely never know."

"Again," Marcelle said, "I am sorry. I can't imagine the pain."

"Life is suffering. That much is sure. But this tragedy teaches us once again that we are better off submitting to the authorities over us. Resisting them is futile and foolish." A weak smile appeared, and Daphne let out a mechanical laugh. "Scott was so excited about the arrival of strangers, he babbled a stream of nonsense about travelers from another world. So I'm looking forward to hearing your story to see what reality he twisted into a fable. Boys that age tend to have wild imaginations, you know."

Marcelle forced a smile. Daphne's little speech about submission pricked her sense of wariness. "Yes, boys are like that." She nodded at Shellinda. "Before I begin my story, may I request food and water for my traveling companion? She is in great need of nourishment."

"Yes, of course. I should have offered, but my mind was fixed on getting you safely inside." Daphne touched the older girl's hand. "Penelope, please fetch a dish for each of our guests. I restocked our cache while Hyborn was away, including some dried lamb strips. Let us hope he doesn't sniff them out."

"Yessim." Penelope pushed away the sheet and rose slowly, keeping her eyes on Daphne. She traversed the gap to the desk in two steps, picked up a wax taper from the desktop, and returned to the mats. Bending over, she pushed the short wick into the lantern's flame.

While Penelope waited for the candle to light, Marcelle scanned the girl's legs. She wore a nightshirt that fell to midcalf. Red stripes ran from that point to her ankles, clearly the marks of a whip, fairly recent wounds.

"You poor girl." Marcelle touched the hem and lifted it, revealing the bottom cuff of short trousers underneath.

Penelope quickly batted her hand away. "They don't hurt," she said as she pulled the skirt back into place.

After dipping her knee toward Daphne, Penelope padded out of the room in silence.

Marcelle stared after her. She was hiding something, but what? The short trousers? If so, why?

"Don't be troubled by her curtness," Daphne said. "She is a good girl, and I never have any trouble with her, but she's disappointed about exam scores she recently received. You see, she is rather slow. Try as she might, she is always far behind in her studies."

Marcelle looked at the desk. Three books lay in a stack, a thick tome on top opened to somewhere near the middle.

"Vanna, on the other hand …" Daphne nodded at the other girl. "Vanna is a bright child. She will be a scholar."

Marcelle imagined the little girl combing through the pages of the huge book. "The dragons allow you to become scholars?"

"Oh, they insist that we study from cradle to grave." Daphne cocked her head and gave Marcelle a curious stare. "You really must be from another land. How far have you traveled?"

"I'm not sure. Very far, I think. I couldn't keep track of the distance."

Daphne looked at Shellinda. "This girl isn't a traveler. I'm sure I have seen her before."

"Shellinda," Marcelle said, touching the girl's shoulder. "And my name is Marcelle. She didn't come from my land, but she is traveling with me now."

"Have others visited here from your land?" Daphne asked.

Marcelle's heart pounded. This was a great opening. "In fact, yes. A man named Frederick journeyed here some months ago and never returned. I would very much like to find him."

Daphne formed Frederick's name on her lips three times before replying. "The name is familiar, but I can't place it." She turned to Vanna. "Do you know of a man named Frederick?"

"Broderick sounds a little like it," Vanna said. "He is a miner at number two, but I don't know any Frederick."

"And Broderick is certainly not from another land," Daphne added with a laugh. "We played cactus tag together as children."

Once again padding softly, Penelope returned and set a pottery plate in front of them along with two clay mugs. Strips of dried meat lay across the plate as well as a small loaf of fresh bread and two oblong objects that looked like some kind of fruit.

Marcelle imagined a hidden door in a cave wall that housed the clandestine collection of food. In spite of Daphne's sermonette about submission, she seemed ready to slide through convenient loopholes, including hiding secretive travelers.

When Penelope sat again on her mat, Shellinda looked at the food hopefully. "May I?" she asked.

"Of course," Daphne said. "Help yourself."

Shellinda grabbed the loaf, tore it in half, and began stuffing it into her mouth, chewing as fast as she could.

Daphne leaned forward and touched Shellinda's oily hair. Her eyebrows lifted. "A cattle child?"

"I need someone who knows your land and your ways," Marcelle said. "And she seems quite adept."

"*Our* ways?" Daphne's brow tightened. "Your words continually remind me that you are not one of us. From where exactly do you hail?"

Marcelle studied the woman's probing stare. Telling her everything at once could be too much of a shock. "Before I answer that, do you mind if I ask you a few more questions?"

Daphne spread out her arms. "I am the hostess, and you are my guest. Who am I to interfere with your business before you are ready to reveal it?"

"I will reveal it soon." Marcelle glanced at Shellinda. She had already wolfed down half the bread and one of the fruits and now guzzled from her mug.

Marcelle took a drink from her own mug. It tasted like water with a hint of something sweet. Honey, maybe? Apparently these slaves enjoyed many more benefits than did the cattle children, yet, Penelope's stripes proved that life here included brutal discipline.

"We received word," Marcelle said as she set down her mug, "that Frederick might be hiding in a refuge in the wilderness. Do you know of such a place?"

Penelope coughed. Covering her mouth as her cheeks flushed, she coughed several more times.

"Did you get something to eat as well?" Daphne asked as she patted Penelope on her back. "Stolen food carries the bite of a rat."

Marcelle cast a wary glance at Penelope. What had brought about that reaction? Frederick's name? The mention of a wilderness refuge? Should she ask Penelope directly or rather probe for other information first? With Daphne's apparent loyalty to the dragons, albeit a duplicitous one, later would probably be better. Maybe they would have a chance to speak about the refuge in private. "I found Scott's fable interesting," Marcelle said. "What is this tale about travelers from another world?"

"Myths. Ghost stories concocted to give hope to the hopeless. Supposedly, we humans came to Starlight from a planet called Darksphere only a hundred years ago, transported through space by Magnar himself. Utter nonsense, of course. It's not enough that the simpletons believe that a dragon could fly that far; they even reject hard evidence."

"Hard evidence?" Marcelle asked.

"Well … the prophecy of the black egg, for example, is hundreds of years old."

Penelope slid back against the wall, her eyes wide. Vanna lay down and pulled a thin pillow over her face.

Marcelle took note of their frightened postures. Sheer terror. "So this prophecy is dark and foreboding?"

"Indeed it is. The dragons have a bard named Tamminy, and whenever he sings the prophecy, we jest about it, but our nervous laughter is merely a sign that we fear the truth behind it. In fact, starting at the change of seasons, rumors began buzzing that the egg has already been laid and is now incubating. Lattimer chided such pessimistic chatter, but I think the gossip shook even his confidence."

"Perhaps you should tell me this prophecy so I can understand your fear."

"It is in the dragon language," Daphne said with a strange tongue click, "so I cannot sing it. Lattimer translated and memorized the human language version, but I know only a bare summary. You see, the dragons are awaiting a new ruler who will hatch from a black egg. At first, he will be weak and perhaps crippled, but he will grow into the most powerful dragon of all. Because of a unique gift, he will be able to find all the pheterone the dragons need, and then the dragons will kill all the slaves. Why keep them around if they are no longer needed?"

Marcelle drummed her fingers on her thigh. This was getting more interesting all the time. "So the main reason you are enslaved is to get pheterone for the dragons."

"Of course, but an entire slave industry has blossomed. Many dragons find us useful as house slaves and menial laborers, and they buy and sell us like common trinkets. If not for the Separators making the final decisions about where we should go and what price should be set, the slave trading could easily get out of hand. We could be bartered and traded every day if they had the mind." Daphne shook her head. "A terrible prospect, I think."

"Okay," Marcelle said, "now I understand the talk about the other world, but why was Scott so enthralled with the idea that I had come from there?"

"The believers in that myth, and they are small in number, mind you, expect that warriors will eventually find their way here to rescue us and take us home." Daphne chuckled. "Imagine that. No one living now was even alive back then, neither in this world, nor on the mythical planet, and yet some fools believe in something ridiculous that no one has ever seen. Their whippings have led them to conjure hope-filled dreams that will never come true."

"I believe they will come," Vanna whispered, her head now poking out from beneath her pillow. When she noticed everyone looking at her, she quickly hid herself again.

"Oh, here is Miss Know-it-all giving us her well-informed opinion." Daphne reached over and jerked the pillow away. "Pray tell, O intelligent one, why would anyone on Darksphere come here when every witness of this mythical transport is long dead? Who told them about us, and how would they still be alive?"

Vanna hid her face with her hands but peeked between her fingers. "Uriel Blackstone went back and told them. They're trying to come here, or maybe their grandchildren are trying. They just haven't figured out how yet."

Marcelle looked at Vanna. She knew about Uriel Blackstone's escape. Apparently the slaves passed that story down through the generations, most likely considering it another hopeful myth now.

"You and your fanciful imagination." Daphne tossed the pillow at her. "If you keep your head in the clouds, you'll never get a promotion."

Vanna buried her head under the pillow again. "I don't want to be promoted."

"You see?" Daphne said, gesturing toward Vanna. "You see what I put up with? One girl works as hard as she can and still can't pass her exams, and the other sings through her studies like a songbird, receives the best scores, and still is unable to tell a dragon from a dream. At least Penelope is smart enough to want a Promotion."

Penelope spoke up with a mousy voice. "I got one."

"Got one?" Daphne said. "Got what?"

"A Promotion." Penelope's eyes glistened in the lantern light. "Your late husband, bless his soul, told me after exams. A Separator was there, and he chose Natalla and me."

"Natalla?" Daphne turned the wick, heightening the flame. "Her scores are barely better than yours."

"I know. We had the lowest scores again."

Daphne reached out and caressed Penelope's knuckles. "It stands to reason, child. You and Natalla are hatched from the black egg. The Separator knows this and expects you to grow into an elegant lady who will serve the King of the North with beauty and grace."

"The King of the North?" Marcelle repeated.

"The promoted slaves go to the Northlands to serve the dragon king there." Daphne leaned over and whispered in Marcelle's ear.

"A few of the foolish say that the King of the North is the myth and that the dragons eat the promoted slaves. That's why they choose the ones of weaker mind, to 'cull the herd,' as some phrase it."

"I heard you," Penelope said. "Natalla thinks the same way, and she's scared. So now I'm scared, too."

Daphne clucked her tongue. "Foolish fears beget needless tears. Reject the lies and be known as wise." She rose to her feet, picked up the open book on the desk, and brought it back to the mat. After sitting once again, she flipped the pages to the front of the book and withdrew a folded parchment. "I do this for the sake of our guest," she said as she opened the parchment and showed it to Marcelle. "Or perhaps also for Penelope, since she seems to have lost every vestige of common sense."

Marcelle took the page and scanned it. It appeared to be a letter written in hastily scrawled script. "What is it?"

"It is a letter from my sister when she was promoted more than fifty years ago. She wrote it from the Northlands and sent it to me, proving that she is there with the dragon king."

"And this is her handwriting?" Marcelle asked.

"Indeed, it is. Rondi's penmanship was never very legible. She was twelve when she left, plenty old enough to know what she was doing."

"The dragons made her write it," Penelope said. "Then they ate her. That's why you never got any other letters."

"Why you continue chittering that nonsense is beyond me. Rondi's letter said this would be her only communication. Servants of the king have no time to dwell on relationships of the past."

"Or they are unable to," Marcelle added.

"Unable to?" Daphne narrowed her eyes. "What do you mean?"

"I have been to the Northlands, and I have been inside the dragon king's castle and seen one of the servants there."

For a moment, Daphne just gawked, her mouth agape. Then, shaking a finger at Penelope, she said, "You see? Absolute proof. An eyewitness."

Penelope looked at Marcelle, her brow rising as a timid smile appeared. "Did you see Rondi?"

Marcelle shook her head. "That's why I suggested they were unable. The King of the Dragons is served by invisible spirits that can be seen only when they move, so grabbing one and having a conversation wasn't easy. And I think they change their names when they arrive. The one I met went by Deference, but she said she had a choice of names, so I assumed she had another name before."

Daphne and Penelope glanced at each other, then stared at Marcelle. Vanna also stared, now sitting up with her pillow in her lap. Shellinda swallowed a mouthful before letting her jaw go slack.

Finally, Daphne clapped her hands and laughed. "Oh, I see! You're a jester! You're mocking those who make up wild tales and report them as truth. Deference, indeed! Very clever." She leaned over and pushed Marcelle's knee. "I am impressed. You had me convinced for a moment, and I am not easily fooled."

Marcelle let out a nervous laugh. Should she let them believe it was a joke? Would it do any good to try to convince them of such an impossible story? Probably not. Maybe it would be better to stay quiet and let them believe what they wanted to believe, at least for a while.

"Now we must hear your story," Daphne said. "Where are you from? Are there places in this world where humans are free to travel? If so, why did you come here and risk becoming enslaved?"

Marcelle looked at the four pairs of eyes, again staring at her. What should she say? How much should she reveal? Probably a little at a time, but they needed enough of a spark to ignite their passion. "I do come from a land where humans are free, and I traveled here to rescue the slaves and take them to my home where they, too, can be free." Marcelle took in a breath. The next statement would be a huge gamble. "I am the raven."

Daphne's brow shot up. Penelope looked at Vanna, and a wide grin spread across the face of each girl.

"The raven!" Daphne reached out and touched Marcelle's black sleeve. "Then is the Starlighter within you?"

Marcelle studied Daphne's countenance, bent and wrinkled. Was she asking this out of curiosity? She seemed disappointed, or perhaps even angry. Maybe she was asking so she could report her to the dragon authorities. Still, the issue was now out in the open, and the question couldn't just lie there naked and exposed.

"Cassabrie the Starlighter is within Adrian," Marcelle said, "my traveling companion. I am the raven perched upon his wing. The dragon guardian of the cattle camp captured Adrian and took him to the Zodiac, so I need to go there to rescue him."

Every face in the room turned downward. "The Zodiac?" Daphne asked. "There is only one reason humans are ever allowed in there."

"To witness an execution." Vanna quickly clapped her hand over her mouth. "Sorry."

"Not the only time," Penelope said. "Promoted humans go there before being transported to the Northlands. The Separator himself told me I would go there when Trisarian rises toward its zenith."

Marcelle nodded, pretending to know what Trisarian was. Since she had gone along with their idea that she had come from another place on their world, she couldn't ask. Was it the name of one of the moons? Perhaps it was a star. "I have lost all track of time." She reached for the remaining bread, hoping she appeared nonchalant. "How long until Trisarian reaches that point?"

"About four hours," Penelope said. "I have been commanded to be at the gates of the Zodiac an hour before its peak."

Daphne swung toward her, a scowl forming. "Why didn't you tell me?"

"I …" Penelope looked at each face in the room. "I hoped to leave after you fell asleep, so I wouldn't have to say good-bye."

Daphne gave her a one-armed hug and set her gray head against Penelope's dark brown locks, but her scowl persisted. "Oh, I understand, dear girl. It is very hard to say good-bye, but you need to tell me these things. We could have pulled a few extra treats from the food cache and given you a farewell meal."

Marcelle glanced at Penelope's hands. Her fingers twisted nervously in her lap. The poor girl wasn't a very good liar, and apparently Daphne was more easily fooled than she thought. The short trousers meant that she planned to run away, perhaps with the other promoted girl. Natalla? Yes, that was her name. Since runaway slaves tried to find refuge in the wilderness, maybe the mention of that destination really did provoke her coughing fit.

While studying Penelope's facial structure and frame, Marcelle imagined her own image in the mirror as she made ready to speak to her father. Yes, there was a resemblance, perhaps close enough. Could she execute such a deception? *Should* she? And if so, whom could she trust? Maybe not Daphne, but there was a way to find out.

"So," Marcelle said, "have you slaves ever thought about organizing a rebellion? There are many more of you than there are of them, and they need you to survive. You have numbers and leverage."

Daphne waved a hand. "Oh, there have been rabble-rousers who have tried, and they have brought about suffering and death for themselves and our children. The wise among us realize that we are put under the dragons for a reason, so we must surrender to that fate. Everything is determined. Nothing is left to chance. To rebel would be to criticize the choice of threads in the grand tapestry. We who sit under the stars would be fools to question where he who stands above placed them in the heavens. Yielding to what is, is the only option."

"What if rebellion is a thread in the tapestry?" Marcelle asked. "Perhaps the grandest of designs is to allow the threads to choose the pattern. To watch the weaving of a living tapestry, I think, would bring the greatest satisfaction of all. Perhaps the one who places the stars enjoys an adventure with fire and heat and vibrant colors, a tapestry that surprises and delights. Perhaps he prefers a flying carpet to a floor mat."

"Oh, nonsense. If we are destined to be floor mats, that is what we will be. There is nothing we can do to change it, and if we defy authority, judgment will follow. The sooner we learn to accept it, the better our future, and the easier it will be to avoid dragon fire."

Marcelle tossed the bread into Daphne's lap. "And the bite of a rat."

Daphne's scowl returned, deepening in ferocity every second. She got the message. She who would hide the prophesied deliverer and steal food to feed the enemies of the dragons had proven herself a hypocrite.

"Your tongue is sharp." Daphne rose to her feet and stepped toward the door. "Perhaps you will find you have stabbed yourself with it."

"Wait!" Marcelle jumped up and grasped the viper's hilt. "What do you mean to do?"

Daphne halted and turned back. "What every good citizen must do."

"I suggest otherwise." Marcelle slid out the black blade. "Need I say more?"

Daphne glanced at the sword. "Is murder a chosen thread, Miss Raven?"

"It is not murder to prevent the death of the innocent." Marcelle set the point against Daphne's throat. "Yet, why fear? No matter what I do, it is already determined. Yielding is your only option."

"What …" Daphne swallowed. "What do you want from me?"

"Just sit in the corner and be silent." Maintaining a warning glare, Marcelle put the sword away. "Do you think you can do that?"

Nodding as she backed away, Daphne laughed nervously. "As you said, yielding is my only option." She leaned against the room's left rear corner and slid down to a seated position.

Marcelle waved toward Penelope. "Stand next to me."

Trembling, Penelope rose. "What are you going to do to me?"

"Whatever it takes to keep you safe from the dragons."

Penelope glanced at Daphne, then at the sword, but quickly retrained her eyes on Marcelle. "Okay. If you say so."

Marcelle waved for Vanna to join them, then pulling the girls close together, she whispered, "I'm not going to hurt Daphne. I just need to make sure she doesn't get in the way. Do you understand?"

Both girls nodded.

"Good. I need you both to be brave. I have an idea that might work." Marcelle turned Penelope and set her back to back with herself. "Are we the same height?" Marcelle asked, looking at Vanna.

Vanna stared at the tops of their heads. "Very close. Why?"

Marcelle removed the band that held her hair in place and shook out her tresses. "And our hair. Does it match?"

"Not at all," Vanna said. "Penelope's is darker and shorter."

"Then we will need hair dye and shears." Marcelle looked around the room. "What is a promoted slave supposed to wear?"

"Her normal clothes," Penelope said. "The Separator said I would be provided with a ceremonial dress when I arrive."

"Then let's see if your clothes fit me."

"I see your plan." Vanna wrapped her fingers around Marcelle's waist as if measuring it. "Her skirt will probably fit you, and you're about the same height, but your body shape isn't the same."

Marcelle looked at Penelope's torso. Vanna was right. Penelope's bust was still that of a preadolescent.

"Her tunic is loose-fitting," Vanna continued, "but even a dragon will notice the difference if you wear it. They're not stupid enough to think you're a twelve-year-old."

Marcelle glanced at her own chest. "A little binding should take care of that."

"True, and the looseness will hide your muscles." Vanna took a step back and surveyed the two, tapping her finger on her chin as she studied them. "It might work, but we'll need gwillen root dye and shears for your hair and bandages to flatten your chest."

"Good," Marcelle said. "Let's get started."

Vanna's brow furrowed. "We have a blade but no gwillen root."

"I can get that," Shellinda said, now standing. "I remember where it grows."

Marcelle touched Shellinda's black tunic. "You're dressed for stealth, but be careful. With all that's been happening, the dragons will probably be watching for anything unusual."

"I will lead her to the entrance," Penelope said.

Vanna nodded. "Then come right back with a sharp knife from the kitchen. I'll need you as a model while I cut Marcelle's hair."

"I will." Penelope, now smiling, took Shellinda's hand and led her into the dark corridor.

"Can we do anything while we're waiting?" Vanna asked.

Marcelle picked up one of the three bed sheets. "Just to be safe, help me tie up your mistress."

"Oh, I could never do that." Vanna turned away from Daphne and suppressed a grin. "Unless, of course, you forced me."

Marcelle grasped her sword's hilt and faked a threatening glare. "Consider yourself forced."

"Since you insist," Vanna said, taking the sheet. "I know a really good knot."

TWENTY

STRADDLING Arxad's neck as they glided over the dragon village, Adrian held on to a spine that rose between his thighs. Just before they left the Zodiac, Arxad promised a short trip to a building he called the Basilica. Even as he spoke, he kept a wing draped over the ovular bundle, as if petting it. And when they took off, he picked it up with both rear-leg claws, carefully, almost motherly, and carried it with him.

Adrian scanned the ground quickly, trying to memorize the layout. Although the dizzying height and whistling air brought a rush of exhilaration, there was no time to enjoy the ride. He had to get all the data he could in a hurry.

Below, several humans walked from building to building, some carrying lanterns and others striding confidently in the moonlight. Unlike the cattle children, clothing covered them from ankles to neck, though not in rich apparel, more like the peasant class in Mesolantrum, at least that's how it appeared in the dimness.

Adrian clutched the spine more tightly. Arxad had said he would ascend and descend at sharp angles in order to avoid revealing his passenger, and he had just leveled out, so ...

Arxad's body tilted forward. Then, he folded in his wings and dropped. Cassabrie squealed with delight. Adrian held his breath. What was she so happy about? The trial lay ahead, then possible execution. Yet, he couldn't ask. The whipping wind took his breath away.

Arxad fell past the top of a bell tower, thrust out his wings, and caught the air. The sudden deceleration forced Adrian's backside against the scales underneath, but when the dragon flapped his wings twice and slid through an opening in the roof, the pressure eased.

They glided downward and entered a huge chamber where a healthy fire licked a stack of logs at the center of the room. The flames created a dome of orange light, vibrant and steady in the center, and fading toward the edges.

After setting the bundle down near the flame, Arxad landed next to it and spoke in a quiet tone. "You may dismount now."

Adrian slid down the dragon's scales and looked around. In front of him, a chest-high stone pedestal stood within reach, a lectern of sorts, upon which a large open book lay, a page rattling in a gentle breeze. Three feet beyond it, a platform filled half of the room, a stage big enough for performing dragons.

He pivoted toward the opposite half, now facing the fire. Open floor space backed up to a curved wall, as if the space had been planned for an audience. Perhaps dragons gathered there to watch proceedings on the stage, and the firelight provided illumination for the actors.

"Cassabrie," Arxad said, "Zena keeps a selection of human clothing in her dwelling place. I assume you remember where that is."

Her reply again came through Adrian's mouth and voice. "I do, my lord."

"Withdraw yourself from him and retrieve appropriate clothing. It will be better for all concerned if Adrian wore a more suitable tunic than the torn one that exposes your presence."

As before, a cold sensation erupted in Adrian's body, and a stream of light poured forth from his chest, but this time the pain was less severe, though it still felt as if a swarm of angry bees stung his heart.

Cassabrie again appeared in a column of light before disappearing in transparency. "What shall I do if Zena detects my presence?" she asked, sparks once more giving away her position.

Arxad petted the bundle with a wing. "Since I have not yet returned her master, she will likely be waiting for him at the incubator. Stay away from that place. Although I know what you wish to do, it is better to avoid conflict."

She bowed her head and glided away, her form again coming into view. Although her legs moved in a normal gait, she seemed to float above the floor. She entered a corridor and began to rise, as if drawn by a vacuum. A few seconds later, she faded out of sight in the upper reaches of the chamber, and her aura vanished.

"She climbed a rope leading to a bell," Arxad explained. "Since she has almost no weight, she did not activate it."

"Why did you send her away? Is covering a glow that important?"

"The main reason is to let you know your options. You are already so hypnotized by her, it would not be just to allow her presence to persuade you. The choice is too vital."

"Hypnotized by her? What do you mean?"

Arxad lowered his voice to a barely audible whisper, glancing at the bundle as if concerned that it might be listening. "Cassabrie is a Starlighter. Her power is beyond your grasp, and her influence is beyond your ability to withstand. It was for this reason that Magnar put her to death years ago in an unspeakably cruel manner. When she sees Magnar again, her reaction might well be an eruption of her gift that I cannot predict. Since you have been under her spell, you will likely be swept into her influence once again."

Adrian flinched. The pain in his wounds throbbed worse than ever. "I am not hypnotized by her," he said, also whispering. "I am in my right mind."

Drawing his head back, Arxad raised his voice. "How can you know? Your mind is unable to judge its own state. If you are under her influence, your ability to recognize that influence would be impaired. If it is handicapped by a mesmerizing host, then its self-judgment is also handicapped. You cannot trust your self-evaluation."

The words, spoken in the low, rumbling voice of a dragon, echoed in the massive chamber. With every reverberation, they pounded Adrian's brain. *You cannot trust your self-evaluation. Under her influence. Handicapped.*

The flames sizzled and popped, as if newly fed by green wood. The page on the book rattled again. Adrian peered at the book. On the left-facing page, odd, indecipherable text covered the parchment. On the right, normal words had been written in flowing script that seemed impossible for a dragon's clawed hand to produce. A centered headline announced the topic, The Starlighter's Curse, and the first two sentences began the description:

A Starlighter is a human possessed by dark powers we do not yet understand. Legends from Darksphere describe these creatures as "witches," though the description of a witch does not truly match the characteristics of the one Starlighter we cooked at the stake.

Adrian turned away. Cassabrie. Sweet, beautiful Cassabrie. These foul dragons killed her! Cooked her! Of course, he already knew that, but seeing the truth spelled out in their book, a self-confession of murder, sent a shock wave through his body.

Breathing heavily, Adrian clenched both fists. He had to control himself. A flying rage would serve only to hasten his execution. But one truth became clear—trusting this dragon would be foolhardy. Even if Arxad had nothing to do with executing Cassabrie, he still didn't prevent her torture. He let it happen. A creature of integrity would never allow it, no matter his species. His chatter about hypnosis and self-evaluation amounted to nothing more than another attack against a poor girl who couldn't hurt him even if she tried. With every command he uttered, she always bowed in reverence and said, "Yes, my lord." There was no hint of deceit or rebellion in her soul. This dragon, ally of the murderers, could not be trusted.

"You have had ample time to consider my words," Arxad said. "When the Starlighter returns, you must prepare yourself and guard your mind. For now, you have another decision to make. If you are sentenced to death, I can rescue your spirit and take you to the Northlands, just as I did for Cassabrie. The process is extremely painful, but it has never failed. Another alternative is to be executed without my help, and your spirit will go to wherever your god directs it. A final option is to fight for your life so that you can join Marcelle and help her rescue your fellow humans. As it stands, she is on this journey alone and has little hope of success without you."

Adrian firmed his jaw. "If you remove my spirit, will I be with Cassabrie forever?"

"Yes, if that is your wish. I will be able to arrange it."

Adrian pictured Marcelle skulking through the forest, guiding a line of children out of the cattle camp. With her intellect and warrior skills, surely she would be able to lead them home. Wasn't she always the supremely confident sword maiden? Didn't she strut into the tourney ring and mock him in front of everyone? Such unbridled bravado could accomplish anything. And her actions proved that she cared for only one person—Marcelle. Her subsequent apologies had been private. So far, nothing she had done made up for the shame she had cast upon him. She hadn't sacrificed her position or her status in the eyes of the people. Let her get the glory for rescuing the slaves. She could have it.

Besides, without a weapon, fighting for freedom would be impossible. Surviving to live with Cassabrie seemed to be the only viable option.

He took in a deep breath. "Then I choose to—"

"Shh!" Arxad's neck stretched out, and his head drifted past the book. He sniffed the stage area several times. "This is good, exactly what I was hoping for. It is the traditional time for a Separators' meeting, but I was not informed of the schedule because I have been away."

"What is a Separators' meeting?"

"A meeting of the dragon elders. You will soon learn more." Arxad nodded at the ovular bundle. "Pick up the egg and bring it with us, and do be careful."

Adrian looked at the bundle, still glowing slightly. The egg? He slid both hands under it, sheet and all, and carried it at his waist. It was heavier than he expected, about the weight of his fishing boat anchor, and it was warm to the touch, quite warm, in fact.

Using a wing, Arxad guided him toward the bell rope. After Adrian set the egg down, the two stood in the midst of the shadows and peered out at the stage, pedestal, and fire. With a low whisper, Arxad said, "Perhaps what you learn here will help you with your decision. It is why I came to this room in the first place."

A dim light shone from above, Cassabrie climbing down the rope and carrying a dark shirt with long sleeves. With her body appearing and vanishing, it sometimes seemed that the shirt floated next to her shining form. When she set her feet on the floor, she bowed her head toward Arxad. "All is well. I did not see Zena."

Adrian removed his old shirt and took the replacement. As he slid an arm through a sleeve, Cassabrie touched his chest, her fingers now the only visible part of her body. "Let me come into you first."

Adrian stopped and looked at Arxad. The dragon gave him a quick, noncommittal glance and turned away.

"Let's wait," Adrian said. "There's a dragon meeting coming up, so—"

"All the more reason for our union. I can translate in your mind." She rubbed her finger along the spot where the pulsing skin patch used to be. The touch felt like a warm mug filled with something sweet—comforting and promising pleasure. The outline of her face appeared, and her eyes glowed soft green. "So may I come into you now?"

"Well, I do need to hear what's going on."

Arxad whispered, "You will understand all you need to know even without translation."

Adrian slid his hand under her fingers. "Let's wait. I should ... well, it's hard to explain."

The glow in her eyes dimmed. "Adrian, I will abide by your wishes, of course. Just let me know when you decide you need me."

"Quiet," Arxad warned. "They are coming."

Adrian quickly put the shirt on and turned to watch.

From a wide entryway at the opposite side of the room, a big red dragon flew in and settled on the stage. As soon as his wings folded and he sat on his haunches, five other dragons followed through the entry, shuffling along instead of flying. They took places in the audience area, each one quiet and somber.

Arxad's voice dropped to a barely audible whisper. "The dragon on the decision platform is Magnar. Stay here. There is no way of escape." He extended a leg as if to join the other dragons, then pulled it back. His expression seemed filled with curiosity, though Adrian wasn't sure. Dragons' faces weren't as readable as those of humans.

A glow appeared at Adrian's side. Cassabrie's body shimmered, hot and bright, giving clarity to her form and face. Her brow knitted deeply, her eyes blazed green, and her hair turned bright red, flapping as if whipped by a breeze.

Arxad wrapped her in a wing, hiding her glow. She offered no resistance, but the wing's trembling membrane proved that her rage burned on.

When the dragons in the audience settled, Magnar spoke in a low tone, a series of guttural rumbles and growls. With each pause in his speech, the five in the audience nodded and murmured.

Then, from the same entrance, another dragon, a smaller one that resembled Millence, used an uplifted whip to herd a line of four humans—a man, a woman, and two female children. Staring straight ahead as if dazed, they ambled slowly until they reached the front of the stage and stopped between the pedestal and the fire. They gawked at Magnar, their mouths partially open. Drool leaked from one of the girls in a long strand that nearly reached the floor.

As Adrian watched the family, a medicine-like aroma trickled into his nostrils. These people had been drugged.

The family continued to gape in a stupor, each one a portrait of perfect compliance. The smaller dragon rifled through the book and set a claw on its chosen page. Then, after reading the text in the dragon language, he passed the whip to Magnar.

With a loud crack, Magnar snapped the whip over the drooling girl's shoulder. "On your knees!" he shouted in the human tongue. "All of you!"

The dark-haired girl, maybe nine years old, flinched but didn't cry out. The four lowered themselves to their knees, their eyes and mouths still wide.

Adrian reached for his sword but swiped across empty air. No hilt, no scabbard, no hatchet. Here he was, the rescuing warrior with no way to do anything about the injustice occurring right before his eyes.

"Krelin, what are their past placements?" Magnar asked, still speaking human.

The smaller dragon replied in a higher pitch. "The husband was a logger, and the wife was a seamstress. They lived together in the logging camp. These girls worked as cooks and maids in Lelor's home."

"And why are they being moved?"

"With the recent loss of the miners, we are recruiting new ones. This man is strong and has proven himself a good worker. The woman has pleaded to attend him at the miners' camp and to bring their daughters along, but we already have a woman and her daughter there who do an adequate job at cleaning and providing meals. Lelor, however, would like to use this opportunity to his advantage. He heard about a redhead coming available, a cattle camp child who has survived the rigors well, so he is willing to give up the two girls for the right to acquire the redhead."

"How old are the girls?" Magnar asked.

Krelin touched the smaller one with a wing. "The younger is eight, and the older is thirteen."

"If all are in agreement," Magnar said, "then let the man be taken to the mining camp and allow Lelor to acquire the redhead, but bring her to me for examination first. We want no more Star-lighters to arise."

"And where should these females go?"

Magnar scanned the other dragons. "Are there any petitions for such as these?"

A dragon on the left of the line spoke up. "The breeders are hoping to continue their experiments on younger girls, so the older of the two will be welcome there. Her frame is strong, and she appears to be well into adolescence. The younger one can join the new mine laborers."

"And the mother?" Magnar asked. "Is she still fit for breeding?"

Krelin's ears rotated toward her. "She is too old, but she can be trained as a midwife. The oldest midwife is ill and close to death."

"Very well. Let it be so."

"One moment." The dragon in the middle raised a wing, a strange expression on his face that resembled a grin. "Shall I assume Arxad's role?"

A ripple of rumbling laughter spread across the dragons.

"Do you have a point of order?" Magnar asked.

"I do." The middle dragon glanced at the others, his grin still apparent. "You need to obtain permission from the head of the family.

Is that not why we explain these assignments in their language in the first place?"

Magnar's brow lifted. "Oh, yes. My favorite way to waste time, especially in light of the crises at the mines. But we cannot leave this step incomplete. Arxad would not be pleased."

Another wave of laughter passed through the dragon audience, this one loud enough to echo in the chamber.

Adrian glanced at Arxad. His ears drooped, and his wings sagged. Rather than angry, he seemed sad, disappointed, perhaps even heartbroken.

Magnar extended his neck and drew his head close to the man. "You have been transferred to the mines. Do you understand?"

With his eyes still wide, the man nodded blankly.

"Do we have your permission to move your wife to the breeding rooms where she will care for pregnant women and deliver their babies?"

Again, the man nodded.

With a hint of a smile, Magnar looked at the other dragons briefly before continuing. "We will move your older daughter to the breeding rooms where she will be impregnated by a man of our choosing. Do we have your permission to send her there?"

The man hesitated. Sweat glistened on his forehead, and his jaw trembled.

"Is he sufficiently medicated?" Magnar asked Krelin.

"A double dose, my king, but a little persuasion might help."

As Magnar refocused on the man, his toothy smile widened. "The breeders will take good care of your daughter. Such a beautiful girl will be a sacred vessel, cherished throughout her time there, and the children she bears will be your honored legacy. Your love for her cries out for this position, and a father would never refuse her the opportunity. Am I correct?"

Adrian clenched a fist. This was absurd! This poor man couldn't think straight. His fuzzy mind was being cruelly manipulated!

Finally, with a boyish smile, the man nodded.

"And your other daughter will go to the mines."

Again, he nodded.

Magnar turned to the dragon in the middle. "Thank you, Arxad's surrogate. I hope you enjoyed that display of comedy."

While laughter again flowed from the audience, Magnar waved a wing at Krelin. "Take them away."

With rage burning within, Adrian turned to Arxad. A tear shimmered in his eye, and his expression stayed morose. Was there anything he could do to stop this madness?

The dragons, except for Magnar and Krelin, shuffled toward the entryway. When they had sufficiently spread apart, they extended their wings, jumped into the air, and flew through the opening. Krelin herded the slaves toward the same exit, while Magnar stayed put, his ears straight up and rotating in half turns.

Arxad stepped farther into the shadows, pulling Cassabrie with him, still coiled in his wing. Adrian followed. Magnar glanced their way, sniffing. After a few seconds, he, too, took to the air and left the room.

Arxad let out a long breath and unwrapped Cassabrie. Her body had faded to a bare shimmer, and her face gave no indication of her mood.

"Come," Arxad said. "We have another errand before we can return to the Zodiac. If Magnar has received my request for a trial, he will be there soon."

Adrian pointed at the egg. "Is that the errand?"

"It is. When I take it to its nest, I will have to carry you by claw, for the egg's mistress would be appalled otherwise." The dragon's gaze probed deeply, as if searching for something that lay beyond the issue of transport.

Offering a nod, Adrian turned away. Arxad wanted some kind of response to what they had witnessed. This strange dragon, although ready to put him on trial for his life, had brought him here to learn something profound. And this family of slaves and their trials certainly carried a jolt. They were herded like cattle and separated into labors of muscle, sweat, and reproduction. The poor father was cajoled into giving his daughter away to suffer humiliation in a degrading manner. Will that father see his daughter's tears the first time she is forced to copulate with a man she might not even know? Will her father be there to comfort her when she pushes out a baby, though she is not much more than a baby herself?

Yet, he nodded in agreement. Drugged and pliable, he gave away a precious treasure in exchange for ... for nothing, for an empty promise, for a lie.

"It is time to go," Arxad said softly.

Cassabrie laid a hand on Adrian's chest, and her eyes glowed green again. "Now will you let me come in?"

The warmth instantly soaked through his shirt and began to penetrate his skin. Her presence drifted closer, already bringing an intoxicating effect—exhilarating, mesmerizing, dizzying.

Adrian heaved in a breath. No. He couldn't let her. No matter how good it felt, he had to keep out all influences, at least until his mind cleared.

Smiling, he gently pushed his hand under hers. "Not yet. I want some time to think about it."

As her fingers caressed his knuckles with soothing warmth, her voice stretched out in a songlike cadence. "Adrian, you know how good you feel when I'm inside. Your pain eases, and my passion sends delight coursing throughout your body. Why turn away pleasure and invite pain when there is no need to do so? Let me come into you, and all will be well."

"There is a need," Adrian said, this time stepping away. "I just can't explain it right now."

Her eyes faded to pinpoints of green, and the song in her voice died away. "Very well. I am able to ride on Arxad, so I will see you in the Zodiac soon."

Arxad stretched out his wings. "Then mount my back, Cassabrie. We must go."

As the lithe, glowing phantom climbed the scales, the image of the father pulsed in Adrian's mind—confusion, perplexity, a boat without an anchor. The dragon twisted this man's love into blind acceptance, to the point that his actions allowed the worst kind of cruelty. It was almost as if love had transformed into hatred, and he had no idea that he had poured out his daughter's soul.

Arxad lifted into the air, catching the egg bundle in one claw and Adrian's shirt in the other. As they shot upward, the material rubbed against Adrian's wounds. It hurt … a lot. But somehow the pain was comforting. Free from Cassabrie's anesthesia, every sense seemed to come alive—spiritual vision, duty, love for the Lost Ones, danger—and pain came with the package.

As Arxad flew through dark corridors, lit only by an occasional lantern on the side walls, Adrian heaved a sigh. He had to hang on to this clarity, this new sense of purpose. Maybe he could survive. Maybe he could save the Lost Ones. And Marcelle. Yes, he had to help Marcelle. She would never give up.

Still, shouldn't he also learn to overcome the effect of Cassabrie's presence? He had the strength of purpose, the will power, to suppress her charms. It seemed that pushing her away conceded defeat, a silent confession that he lacked the inner constitution to withstand a mesmerizing influence. Obviously, she never intentionally hypnotized him. Her gift came along with her presence, so if he had any hope of being with her forever, he needed to learn to compensate and stay in his right mind no matter what.

Arxad entered a brightly lit oval-shaped chamber. From the center of the room, a woman dressed in black hurried toward them. As Arxad made a quick orbit around the room, beating his wings to decelerate enough to set down his load, the woman turned with him, her stare fixed and her hands wringing.

Arxad deposited Adrian on the floor tiles in an upright position, then set the bundle down gently before running to a stop. The woman ran to the bundle, scooped it into her arms, threw back the sheet, and began kissing the shell of a black egg. "Oh, dear prince! You have returned! I will never let you out of my sight again!"

She turned to Adrian and stared at him. Tall and slender, she wore a form-fitting black sheet tied at the shoulder. With a strong, yet silky voice, she said, "Who is this stranger?"

Arxad rose up high on his haunches, apparently trying to conceal Cassabrie's presence. As she did while in Magnar's company, Cassabrie began to shimmer, though not as brightly as before.

"Zena," Arxad said. "This man is a prisoner who will soon stand trial. I had to bring him along or else be delayed further in delivering our prince to you."

After setting the egg down gently, Zena crossed the few steps that separated them and stood nearly toe-to-toe with Adrian. She stared. Blue paint smeared her lids and dripped to her cheeks, mixing with dark pink blush. Her black eyes housed oval pupils of a slightly darker shade of black. They wandered, as if unable to focus, making her appear to be blind. "I sense something familiar. He is very much like the young man who rescued the Starlighter. What was his name?"

"Jason," Arxad said.

Adrian froze, unable to breathe. Jason was here? What had happened? He stared at Arxad, hoping he would reveal more information.

As if reading Adrian's mind, Arxad continued. "That young man is now far from the dragon realm, as is the new Starlighter. After I retrieved the prince from their clutches, I sent them into exile, as Magnar ordered, so you need not be concerned about them doing us any further harm."

"What is this man's crime?" Zena asked.

"He killed a dragon."

Every facial feature stretched out as she screamed, "He what?"

His body relaxing, Adrian nodded. "I did, but it was—"

Zena slapped him savagely, her long nails dragging across his cheek and lips as she followed through. "The prince and I will come and witness your termination, and he will absorb your energy for himself!" She heaved shallow breaths, her black eyes pulsing.

"You will not!" Cassabrie leaped off Arxad, her body now ablaze in yellow and white. With her fists clenched and her brow low, she stomped toward Zena.

Blocking with her hands, Zena staggered backwards. "Stay away from me, Starlighter! My quarrel is not with you."

"Well, my quarrel is with you." Cassabrie halted an arm's length from Zena. At least a head shorter, she looked up at the woman draped in black and pointed a finger. "You betrayed me! You sent me to the cooking stake!"

"Your own actions were your downfall. I am not at fault for exposing your crimes."

"Crimes!" Cassabrie's hair flamed, shooting out scarlet flares. "It is not a crime to pursue freedom for my fellow humans. Yet, you sided with the dragons and—"

"Enough!" Arxad growled. "I will not allow a battle. If the prince is harmed, then all will be lost."

"The prince!" Zena hurried back to the egg. Again cradling it in her arms, she marched to the center of the room and set it in a marble basin, padded inside with white pillows and sheets. She stroked it tenderly. "He will likely hatch by dawn," she crooned, "and we will see what he thinks about the survival of this Starlighter and the schemes of those who concealed her."

Adrian stared. What was this black egg? Who was the prince? This woman's obsession seemed like madness.

Zena reached into an open floor panel. Jets of fire spewed from the tiles and splashed against the stone ceiling, thin fountains set so close together, no one could pass in between. Narrow sections of

Zena's body stayed visible between them as she continued petting the egg.

Adrian breathed the word Arxad had mentioned earlier. "The incubator." Whoever this prince was, Zena wasn't about to let any harm come to him. Yet, if he was so important, why did Arxad decide to show him the Separators' meeting before taking the egg to the incubator? It didn't make sense.

Zena stepped through the flames and stood with her arms crossed, apparently unharmed. "The prince is well and he thanks you for the safe transport."

Arxad bowed his head. "Then all is in order in spite of the recent mishaps."

"We shall see very soon, won't we?" Zena pivoted and reentered the circle of flames.

As Arxad unfurled his wings, he turned to Adrian and whispered, "We must go. I will carry you in my claws again. Magnar might already be at the Zodiac, so your posture as a potentially condemned prisoner is important."

"Why didn't Zena burn?" Adrian asked.

"Her story is not yours, and I don't choose to tell it now." Arxad stretched out his wings fully. "Come."

Cassabrie, fading once again, climbed onto Arxad's back. Adrian straightened his shirt, making ready for another pain-filled journey. As he smoothed out the material on his chest, his hand passed over the area that used to glow. Deep within, an emptiness throbbed, like a hole begging to be filled. Yet, more important issues flooded his mind.

"Arxad," he whispered, "Jason is my brother. I didn't even know he was here. Is he safe?"

"He is for the time being. I sent him to the Northlands with a new Starlighter named Koren, a living girl who will be of great help to him."

Adrian breathed a sigh of relief. "Then he will probably find my father there. Maybe they will come back together."

"The possibility did enter my mind."

With that issue settled, another surfaced in Adrian's thoughts. He glanced at Zena, once again within the circle of fiery jets as she knelt close to the egg. The whoosh of flames acted as a good sound barrier, allowing him to speak freely. "Do you think Cassabrie will react when she sees Magnar again?"

"Cassabrie's gift causes her emotions to vent in uncontrollable ways. She can be a passion volcano."

"Will you be able to hide her this time?"

"It will be difficult. I need her to stay close at hand for a purpose I cannot divulge, so I will have to think of a way to conceal her once we arrive. Since Zena knows she is back in the land of dragons, Magnar will soon learn of it."

"And if Magnar sees her?"

"He will surely attack her," Arxad said. "She is vulnerable to heat. That is why she must abide in the Northlands during the hotter seasons. Although she feels no change in temperature, I think a blast of fire from Magnar could destroy her spirit."

Adrian took in a deep breath. With his mind clear, now he could try again to withstand her presence. "Okay, I guess she should come inside me, then. Magnar will never see her—"

"Oh, yes!" Cassabrie slid down Arxad's side, ran to Adrian, and threw her radiant arms around his waist. "I knew you still loved me! I knew it!"

Arxad gave him a sideways stare. "Even after all you have experienced, will you risk such an unpredictable consequence?"

"It's like jumping into a chasm to save a friend. I don't know how deep it is, but I'm willing to take the risk. That's what love does."

"I see." Arxad eyed him for a moment before muttering, "Humans are a strange lot."

Cassabrie's hands lifted the hem of Adrian's shirt. Her light energy crawled underneath and penetrated his chest, once again bringing the surge of warmth and passion. Yet, this time, Adrian resisted the pull, the yearning to join in the celebratory explosion of emotional ecstasy. Like a man treading water in a deep pool, he kept his head above the surface while tentacles wrapped around his legs and tried to drag him under.

Taking another deep breath, Adrian lifted his chin. "Let's go."

Arxad took to the air, made a wide orbit around the fountains of fire, and swooped down, picking up Adrian as he flew by. He rocketed out of the chamber and then nearly straight up. Above, a wide hole in the roof opened to the sky.

As before, the claw wounds in Adrian's back burned and ached. Cassabrie whispered into his mind. "Allow me to massage your pain away, dear Adrian. That's why I'm here."

Adrian said nothing, choosing instead to close his eyes. *Resist. Just stay focused. Recognize the influence and fight it.*

"Adrian ..." Her voice was as soft as velvet. "Your pain is obvious. Let my love flow within. I will soothe all your woes, your pain, your worries, and your heartaches. You cannot face this trial without me. If you are sentenced to death, I will be there to welcome you to my eternal state. But you have to allow our union—one heart and one mind. You know how good it feels. Let me give you that pleasure once again."

Gasping for breath, Adrian shook his head. "If you love me, Cassabrie, stop seducing me."

"Seducing you? Is that what you think I'm doing?"

"I'm not sure. I don't have another word for it right now. Just stay hidden and stay quiet."

"Of course, Adrian." Her voice sounded hurt. "I would never force myself upon you."

After circling once over the Zodiac's open dome, Arxad flew close and peered into the hole as he passed. He extended his neck down and spoke to Adrian. "Magnar is already there. Prepare for a landing suitable for a dragon killer."

Arxad dove into the hole, dropped Adrian roughly on the slate tiles, and landed near the crystal sphere. Folding in his wings, he turned to Magnar and spoke in the draconic language. Cassabrie translated immediately and continued as the conversation went on.

"I apologize for the delay," Arxad said. "I had to return the prince to Zena, and I could not leave the prisoner here without supervision."

Adrian rose to hands and knees and stayed in that position. Humility was likely the best posture.

"Understood," Magnar said. "But I have not waited long. We had a Separators' meeting a short while ago, so I, too, was delayed."

Arxad waved a wing toward Adrian. "The prisoner has confessed to the crime, but he sought my protective counsel, so I have brought him to you. Because of the confession, the law requires no assembly."

Magnar's neck extended, drawing his head within Adrian's reach. His eyes seemed deeper and redder than those of the other dragons, perhaps even wiser. "Does this murderer have any defense at all?"

"Yes," Arxad said. "I will present it at the proper time."

"Then, let us get on with it. You have promoted humans to prepare in a few hours, and I need to make ready for the morning's banquet. Still, the timing is good. The murderer can be included in the festivities."

"Very well." Arxad turned toward Adrian and spoke in the human tongue. "Get up, dragon killer."

Adrian struggled to his feet. As he looked at Magnar, he felt Cassabrie glaring at him. Her stare burned, and her spirit boiled within. Heat radiated to his skin, raising droplets of sweat. "Calm down," he whispered.

Her voice hissed. "He is the butcher of the Basilica. The emperor of executions. His list of atrocities against the innocent is an assault upon heaven itself. The blood he has poured from the veins of women and children cries out from the ground to stop this foul fiend who dragged us from our homes, locked us in chains, and forced us to serve him with our limbs, our life's blood, and our loins."

Like a flood, Cassabrie's passion washed over Adrian's mind. His legs trembled. His heart pounded. She had broken through his wall of resistance, and her energy radiated throughout every part of his body.

He tilted his head back and let out a long breath. Her presence felt so good! Every pain eased. Every fear of death at the hands of the dragons melted away. Even if the worst happened, he would be with her forever.

Magnar glanced at the crystalline sphere atop the stake in the middle of the room and then stared at Adrian. "You have been accused of killing a dragon. Is this accusation true?"

Adrian looked him in the eye. "It is true. I plunged a sword in the belly of Millence. I killed him."

The sphere glowed white but slowly faded to light gray.

Magnar looked at Arxad. "What is the meaning of this ambiguous result?"

"He has told the truth, but he has held back part of it."

"As I suspected." Magnar shifted to Adrian, hatred burning in his eyes. "I heard a report about a human murdering a dragon at the barrier wall and severely injuring another. Are you the culprit?"

"I battled the guardian dragons," Adrian said, "but only because they refused my appeal to Arxad. They were going to kill me."

When the sphere turned white again, Arxad growled. "I knew nothing about this. The human withheld this information from me."

"Such is the substance of his character," Magnar said. "Let us hear the case and get this over with."

Arxad gave Adrian a long stare, anger obvious in his countenance. Would he proceed with the defense in spite of the new revelation? If this priestly dragon was still obligated to help, he would probably tell Magnar about Marcelle's attack on Millence in order to mitigate the crime. But that would reveal the presence of another dragon assassin in their midst. Since he faced certain death, protecting her was the least he could do.

"No," Adrian said. "There is no defense. I killed both dragons intentionally, and if I had the opportunity under the same circumstances, I would not change what I did."

The sphere stayed bright white.

Arxad lowered his head. "So be it."

"A waste of time," Magnar said to Arxad, "but I understand. You have to do your duty."

"And your verdict?" Arxad asked, his eyes aimed toward him.

"Oh, yes. The formalities." Magnar turned to Adrian. "You are guilty of murdering two dragons and maiming a third, so I sentence you to death. When Trisarian reaches its peak, you will be cooked along with the others."

Adrian looked at Arxad. The others? The dragon priest had to know what Magnar meant, but he stayed silent.

Magnar stretched out his wings. "Keep him in chains here. We will bring in witnesses for the execution, as usual, and then process the promoted humans as soon as the others leave."

Cassabrie flamed again, sending a new wave of heat through Adrian's body, but her voice stayed low and steady. "Process the promoted humans. That cowardly serpent. If only he knew what the king has in mind for him."

After Magnar flew through the hole in the roof, Cassabrie's passion mellowed. Adrian drew in a quick breath, again feeling as though he were treading water. He had resurfaced and survived another onslaught of her influence.

Arxad settled to his belly and laid his head on the floor, his long neck in the shape of an S and his snout aimed at the crystalline stake. He closed his eyes. Thin curls of gray smoke ascended from his nostrils, so weak they were barely visible.

Cassabrie whispered through Adrian's lips, "Arxad? What's wrong?"

His eyes still closed, he lifted his head just enough to speak. "You will find a fire poker in a box near the wall. It is locked, but Cassabrie knows how to open it. Use the poker to slay me. I will not resist. I am the worst of hypocrites, and I deserve to die." He turned to his side, exposing his underbelly, and tucked his head under a wing. "If you pry loose one of my scales, you can use it as a key to exit this chamber. Cassabrie will teach you how to employ it."

Adrian looked at the crystalline sphere. It glowed bright white. "Cassabrie," he whispered. "What's going on?"

A lamenting tone spiced her reply. "He is sacrificing himself, Adrian. The law won't allow him to set you free, but if he is dead, he can't stop you."

"Why would he do that?"

"I think he wants you to find Marcelle and free the slaves. He is despondent. You heard how they mocked him in the Separators' meeting."

"I heard." Adrian walked closer to Arxad and, bowing his head, gazed at the wondrous sight, a huge beast splayed on the floor, once the enemy, now a sacrificial ally. "Does he have a family?"

"A mate, Fellina, and a daughter, Xenith. They are a model dragon family, as dragons go. They have slaves who act as cooks and cave-keepers, but Arxad treats them with respect. They are never beaten. At least that's what he has told me."

Adrian continued staring at the dragon, humbled and vulnerable. Why would he be willing to leave his family bereft? Maybe the great shame he felt from the Separators' mockery sucked out his will to live. Maybe the disregard for law and propriety among his dragon peers had left him without hope for the dragon race.

Still, he was a dragon. At the very least he had submitted to a culture that enslaved the innocent. While children suffered brutal treatment in the cattle camps, Arxad enjoyed the fruits of their back-breaking labors. The stones in this very courtyard were borne in the pails of little boys and girls who carried bleeding stripes along with their physical burdens. Every morsel of food he ate came to him from the hands of humans who longed to be free from their chains.

Adrian marched toward the perimeter, scanning the curved wall for a box.

"Adrian, what do you mean to do?"

He stayed silent. This was no time to converse with her. No matter what he planned, if she objected, her overpowering presence would likely prevail.

He found a low wooden box next to a stack of hewn logs. An old padlock similar to those back home fastened the latch. "Arxad said you know how to open it."

"He has a master key to all padlocks in the Zodiac."

"Where is it?"

"Adrian, I don't think—"

He growled as he spat out his question again. "Where is it?"

"In the cactus bed," she said, her voice shaking. "Under the stones near the edge."

Adrian followed the perimeter, passing three columns spaced by abstract murals on the wall, until he reached a bed of cactus and river rock, mostly pebbles with a few larger stones mixed in. He stooped and ran his fingers through the smooth pebbles.

"A little to the right, I think," Cassabrie said.

He shifted over, found the key, and hurried back to the box. After unlocking the latch, he slid the key into his trousers pocket. As he lifted the hinged lid, a powerful rush of heat flowed into his cheeks and ears.

"No, Adrian. You can't kill Arxad. That would be murder."

Inside the box, a long poker lay among several other fire-tending implements—a blower, a small shovel, and a broom. He grasped the poker's handle tightly and marched toward the dragon.

Again, heat surged, stinging his skin. Sweat trickled down his back. Every step seemed like a journey through desert sand—scalding, draining. His throat dried out, and the muscle aches roared back.

Cassabrie's voice grew to a commanding shout. "You will *not* kill Arxad! I forbid you!"

Adrian stopped, now within a few steps of the dragon. Looking straight ahead, he spoke as clearly as his parched throat would allow. "You said, 'I am to be your guide, not your mistress.' What happened?"

"I ... I ..." As she fell silent, the heat tempered.

Regripping the poker, Adrian walked up to Arxad's belly and found his vulnerable spot, a gap no bigger than a fingertip between two scales. He stooped close enough to speak softly. "You talk a lot about choices, Arxad. You asked me if I would be satisfied if you had no choice but to put me to death. Are you satisfied that you have given me no other real option but to put *you* to death?"

"We always have options," Arxad muttered from beneath his wing. "Some are more desperate than others."

"Understood. You also gave me the option of dying and staying with Cassabrie or dying and going to meet my maker. Those choices were rather limited."

Arxad drew his head out from under his wing. "I also gave you the option to fight your way to freedom."

"Yes, you did. How many dragons will be at my execution?"

"As few as two or as many as five or six, depending on the interest. With the human witnesses present, I doubt we could fit any more in here."

"Even with two, my probability of survival is very low, especially if I'm in chains and without a sword."

"As I said, some options are more desperate than others. You seemed unwilling to exercise that option, so I have taken your risk upon myself." Arxad tucked his head again. "You need not fight to secure your freedom. Drive the poker and be on your way."

A soft feminine voice echoed in his mind, as if Cassabrie was speaking again, but it seemed more like a memory than murmuring. *Your mission is very nearly impossible, and learning where great faith and brutal practicality meet might be your only hope.*

She had reminded him before, and he had surrendered himself to Nancor as a result. He was ready to sacrifice then, to give his life for the sake of the children. What happened? To what hiding place had his resolve flown? Would he now slay another dragon, one who had provided transport to this land in spite of the risk to himself? Would he pay back this dragon's counsel with a rod of iron and leave a widow grieving with her daughter?

Adrian dropped the poker. It clanked loudly on the tile. With his arms dangling loosely, he shuffled to a column near the perimeter and sat down hard, his back against the cool marble. Whom was he trying to fool? This mission truly was impossible. How could two humans, the size of rodents in the eyes of the dragons, possibly liberate hundreds of slaves right from under their masters' scaly snouts? It would take an army of well-armed soldiers, and Prescott would never agree to send them, not without proof positive that the slaves and the dragon planet really existed.

"Unless," he whispered out loud, raising a single finger. Unless he could take one slave back, someone who could testify to the cruelty here, someone like Shellinda. She was articulate and perfectly pathetic. The stripes on her rail-thin body would rally dozens of men with sharpened swords ready to cut dragons' throats. The sight of a brutalized little girl would be enough to make every father in Mesolantrum foam with rage.

He shook his head. No. Even Shellinda wouldn't be enough. Prescott would just deny it all. He would accuse them of making up the story, including bribing the girl to endure the lashes and spread her lies. That would bring the fathers' swords swinging at Adrian's throat.

What could possibly be irrefutable evidence?

Adrian looked at Arxad, still on the floor, his head hidden from view. Of course! A dragon! And not just any dragon. Arxad was the only one who could do it. With his sympathy for humans, he could be trusted to tell the truth, and there would be no risk that he would hurt anyone on Major Four.

"But ..." Adrian raised a finger again. "Prescott's soldiers would try to kill him."

He leaned his head back on the column. So tired. Just sleep. Everything will be clearer after a few hours. If he decided to fight for his freedom, he would need every ounce of energy possible, especially without a weapon.

He opened one eye and looked at the rod lying on the floor. The poker. Arxad would likely return it to its box when he finally decided to get up. The box was unlocked, and both he and Arxad knew it. When execution time came around, the poker might be his only chance.

Closing his eyes again, Adrian let out a long sigh. "Good night, Cassabrie."

"Good night, brave warrior."

He raised his eyebrows. "Brave warrior? I didn't do anything brave."

"Oh, but you did. It took a lot of courage to drop your weapon. I am so proud of you, I could—"

"No. Please don't burst with passion again. I need to sleep."

"Very well," she said, laughing. "I will just sing you to sleep." Cassabrie began humming a sweet tune, and after a few seconds, she added words.

The dragons found in danger's lair
Cannot withstand my hero's stare;
He trusts in courage, not in steel,
In sacrifice's golden seal.

His words become his weapons bared.
His faith transforms to shields prepared.
Defending those forsaken souls,
He soothes, protects, sustains, consoles.

And now my hero needs his rest,
For midnight brings his greatest test.
His spirit soon will join with mine,
Embraced forever, hearts entwined.

As her song swam through his mind, a sense of dizziness took over, and her words brought a new touch of soothing energy— *brave warrior, hero, embraced forever*. Less than a minute later, her gentle pull drew him into sleep's embrace.

TWENTY-ONE

VANNA held a palm-sized mirror and moved it from side to side and up and down while Marcelle followed it with her eyes, using the light from a lantern sitting on the desk. With each new angle, a different part of her altered appearance came into view. The darker hair tied into short pigtails looked foreign around her familiar face, and the light gray tunic covering her flatter chest made her look like a prepubescent girl again, especially when combined with the skirt, a darker gray garment that fell just past her knees.

At one angle, Daphne came into view, still propped in the corner with her hands tied behind her back. She stared with sleepy eyes, blinking frequently and staying quiet.

"Does everything fit?" Shellinda asked from the desk chair. "Better make sure."

Marcelle lifted her knees in turn. The short trousers underneath fit perfectly, so running wouldn't be a problem. Yet ... She inhaled deeply and felt a twinge. The binding around her chest restricted her breathing. That might be a problem, but the appointed hour approached, the time for the charade to begin. A little pain wasn't about to stop her.

She spread out her arms. "What do you think?"

"You could be her twin!" Vanna said. "The dragons won't be able to tell the difference."

"What I'm hoping ..." Marcelle reached for the viper blade lying on one of the mats. "I'm hoping I can conceal this."

"That won't be a problem." Penelope, now dressed in Marcelle's clothes, picked up her sheet. "I'm supposed to bring my possessions with me, including the slip I wear at night. The dragons say we will need all the protection we can get in the Northlands. It's a lot colder there."

"So if I wrap the sword," Marcelle said as she slid the blade under the sheet, "they won't notice, because—"

"Slaves don't have weapons," Vanna finished. "And who would suspect that an innocent little girl would come prepared for battle?"

Marcelle looked at the mat again. Adrian's sword lay there, much longer than the viper blade, too obvious to include under the sheet. "What will Adrian battle with?" she asked under her breath.

"If you find him at all," Daphne said from the corner. "If you don't, how long will you play out this deception?"

Marcelle turned and met Daphne's defiant stare. "At least until I learn what they really do with promoted slaves."

Daphne let out a tsking sound. "Once the dragons take you to the Northlands, you will have another long hike back here."

"Ah, that might be true," Marcelle said, "but if everything has been determined, then the fact that your warning is insufficient to overcome my stubbornness is also unavoidable." She copied Daphne's tsks. "Such is life."

Shellinda picked up the remaining sheet. "Maybe *I* could bring Adrian's sword. I could hide it and pretend I'm delivering something to the Zodiac."

Daphne shook her head. "You would be delivering yourself to death. Is that what you want?"

"No," Shellinda said. "I want to help—"

"Psst! Are you girls dressed?"

Marcelle turned toward the familiar voice coming from the corridor. "Is that you, Scott?"

"Yes. I have important news."

"Come in. We're dressed."

Carrying a weak lantern, Scott walked in and glanced at Daphne briefly, apparently not noticing her bound condition. "Have you heard? The dragons are calling the villagers to attend an execution at the Zodiac."

"The cooking stake?" Penelope asked.

Scott looked at Penelope, then back at Marcelle. "Wait a minute. Which one of you is—"

"I am the raven," Marcelle said. "This disguise is part of the rescue plan."

"You had me fooled." He looked at Daphne and nodded toward the corridor. "Hyborn is already on the way to the Zodiac. He saw me on the street and told me to come and tell you to hurry."

"Yes," Penelope said. "He called for me earlier. It's a good thing he's too big to come all the way into our quarters."

Marcelle patted Scott on the back. "Thank you. We will meet you outside in a moment."

Scott hurried into the corridor, taking his lantern.

"It is now clear," Daphne said in a derisive tone, "that finding Adrian won't be a problem for the black-feathered bird, but she should be a bit more concerned about the chance that she, too, will suffer his fate. The Zodiac has a central room with a domed ceiling, and the one being executed is chained tightly to a crystalline stake. The crystals capture the light from the sun or moon and begin cooking the victim slowly, ever so slowly, unless the dragons decide to have mercy and adjust it so that it works more quickly."

Marcelle stared at Daphne. New retorts about destined events bubbled in her mind, but she let the subject drop.

Shellinda picked up Adrian's sword. "This is my chance! Now I can go to the Zodiac with a weapon."

"The dragons will turn you into a fried minnow in two seconds," Daphne said. "I absolutely forbid it."

Shellinda set a hand on her hip and glared at Daphne. "Who are you? My mother?"

Marcelle took Shellinda's hand. "Maybe you'd better think about it. Conceal the sword and bring it with you, but you don't have to take it into the Zodiac." She gave the girl a stealthy wink. Since Arxad said dragons learned winking from humans, these slaves likely knew that signal.

As the two stared at each other, Shellinda suppressed a smile, her eyes widening ever so slightly. She understood. She would be there with Adrian's sword. With freedom as her prize, the risk was worth it.

Penelope touched one of Marcelle's pigtails and watched it sway. As her eyes watered, her lower lip quivered. "You're doing all this for me?"

Marcelle pulled her into an embrace and caressed the back of her head. "For you and all the other slaves. Everything will be all right. Just try to get some sleep while we're gone."

"I will." Penelope pulled back and nodded toward Daphne. "When may I untie her?"

"Not until Vanna comes back with news." Marcelle set a finger on the lantern's handle. "Vanna, if we leave this here, will you be able to lead the way in the dark without it?"

"I have wandered these halls in the dark many times." As Vanna walked into the corridor, Marcelle followed, holding the viper in front with both hands. Concealed in the sheet, it truly felt like a serpent ready to strike.

"I have seen other promotion processionals," Vanna said as they entered the dragon's living area. "We're supposed to be quiet. It's a time of grieving for those left behind. But since this one is coming at the same time as an execution, I don't think many people will pay attention."

Marcelle looked back. In the flickering light of Penelope's lantern, Shellinda was wrapping Adrian's sword in a sheet. The brave little girl had a lot of spunk.

Heaving a sigh, Marcelle strode on. Now she would have to save Adrian and protect Shellinda at the same time. Would it be possible? How many dragons might there be in the Zodiac? Yet, if Shellinda could arm Adrian with his sword, maybe they stood a chance, however small it might be.

She reached under the sheet and gripped the viper's hilt. At least maybe they could save Shellinda and die together in a literal blaze of glory. Their example as martyrs for the sake of the slaves might give them courage to continue on in spite of their cruel captivity. After all, Edison was still out there somewhere. Maybe he would find Frederick, and the two of them could muster an emboldened army of slaves. And maybe they could make up for her stupid, stupid mistake. They could lead the slaves to freedom and—

Marcelle bit her lip. Tears welled in her eyes. Her stupid mistake. If not for her impatience, none of this would have happened. She and Adrian might have led every child from that horrible cattle camp by now. They might have found Frederick's refuge in the forest. They could be marching to the Northlands with a host of rejoicing slaves in their company.

As the tears began to flow, she slid her hand away from the hilt. No, her death wouldn't be a blaze-of-glory exit. She would be hiding in a shroud of shame, a death shroud made by her own hands.

Sniffing back a sob, she lifted her head high. So be it. There was nothing she could do about it now. At the very least, Adrian wouldn't die alone.

*　　　*　　　*　　　*　　　*　　　*

Adrian blinked his eyes open. The Zodiac's domed chamber was darker now. The crystalline sphere gave no light at all. Only a withering flame on a nearby lantern provided any illumination. Arxad no longer lay on the floor. Everything was quiet, deathly quiet.

From his seated position at the column, he looked up through the hole in the ceiling. A single moon neared the apex of the sky and cast its glow into the room. The middle of the night approached, perhaps his final night on this or any other world.

"What troubles you?" Cassabrie asked.

"Endings."

"Oh … endings. Fear of jumping into the unknown."

He clasped his fingers together and allowed his thumbs to spar. "Not that so much. It's the fear of leaving things undone. Lost opportunities. Unfortunate circumstances. Crumbled hopes."

"Yes, it was unfortunate that Marcelle lost her temper. Much damage has resulted."

"I can't argue with that, but she's not the only female I know whose passions flare."

"Adrian, your point is sharp, and the cut deserved. I *am* a woman of passion who boils at the sight of evil, but I did not attack Zena, and I kept peace in Magnar's presence. What makes such a woman honorable is the way in which she deals with her passions, the manner in which she tempers her response."

"Like not attacking a dragon alone?"

"You said it. Not I."

"But you were thinking it."

Cassabrie stayed silent for a moment. Adrian listened to the sounds in the chamber's drafty air, a rustling somewhere in another room in the Zodiac. Human footsteps? Wings beating? Had dragons and slaves begun gathering to witness his execution? Probably. He would be a spectacle, an example set for any human who dared oppose authority.

With a sigh in her voice, Cassabrie finally replied. "I do not deny my thoughts. I am not ashamed of my opinion of Marcelle. She made the foolish choice that has caused you great harm. Now she is free, and you will die. When she returns home with liberated slaves, she will receive the glory due a hero, while the true hero perishes in agony. I am justified in my opinion."

As her soothing warmth flowed through his body and mind, the image of Marcelle attacking the dragon appeared, and not just in his thoughts. It played out on the floor in front of him, just as it had done when Cassabrie related the tale to Arxad. Was this her doing? Or was this a product of his tortured mind?

Marcelle slashed the dragon's face with her sword. Her courage was amazing, her skills unquestioned. But her judgment? Apparently nonexistent.

Cassabrie's voice melded in with the scene. "Have you decided? Will you go to be with your maker, or will you allow Arxad to join us together for all eternity? I bring pleasure to your soul. I remove every pain, even the memory of its cause. I fill the longings of your heart. I am your Starlighter."

"Those aren't my only choices," Adrian said.

"You are correct again. Will you then choose to fight for your freedom? Do you wish to find Marcelle and restore her as your warrior companion? Will you accept all her faults and tempers, or will you continue to be at odds with her, battling her pseudonobility and her refusal to accept public shame for her foibles?"

"Now who has the sharp point?"

"Ah, but it's sharp for a reason. Whomever you choose, you have to decide to bear the problems as well as the joy."

A hinge creaked. Adrian climbed to his feet and looked for the source. Double doors at the perimeter swung open. Arxad shuffled in, his head low. When he arrived under the partially open dome, he looked at Adrian. "Your execution is at hand."

Adrian squared his shoulders. "I know."

"We have an unusual circumstance. Magnar has ordered you to be cooked at the stake, which happens to be the same crystal that divines truth and falsehood. The problem is that we also have a Promotion ceremony, and those being promoted always come to the Zodiac first to be prepared."

"Not that it's any of my business, but what is involved in the preparation?"

Arxad's head drooped closer to the floor. "I give them a drug that makes them compliant, the same drug you saw working in the separated family. Then they each write a letter to a relative describing their joy at being in the Northlands. When Trisarian rises higher, I chain them to the stake. At midnight, Trisarian sits directly above this ceiling, and its beams combine with the crystal's energy to draw the spirit out of anyone touching the sphere. The spirits are absorbed into the crystal, and after their bodies are removed, I can capture their spirits and transport them to the Northlands where they will be safe."

Adrian imagined the process, a girl writhing in pain and a misty light streaming from her body and into the sphere. Then, she slumped, her agony ended. His breaths coming a little faster now, he stared at Arxad. "What do you do with the bodies?"

"They are still alive in one sense. Their brains continue to coordinate their normal functions, but they have no awareness, no sentient thoughts. Even when the drug wears off, they act as if they are still under its influence. Then, while I am flying their spirits to the Northlands, their bodies are led to a banquet with Magnar as the host."

"A banquet? Why would they be invited to a banquet? I don't understand."

"I am glad to hear that. In this case, Cassabrie's influence over you is beneficial."

Adrian squinted at him. Cassabrie's influence? She was still within, but he had resisted her. He was in his right mind now. Everything was crystal clear.

"So," Arxad continued, "the promoted slaves will have to witness your execution along with other humans who are ordered to watch your suffering, which is unfortunate, because I will have to give them a stronger dose of the drug in order to allay their fears."

"That much I can understand."

With a quick beat of his wings, Arxad drew closer and set his head directly in front of Adrian's. The normal rumble in his voice smoothed to an almost humanlike softness. "Now that I have told you about the process of removing your spirit, have you decided what you want to do?"

Adrian closed his eyes. Again Marcelle came to mind, an image of her battling dragons and leading slaves out of this world, but as quickly as it entered, a sense of warmth pulsed and washed it away. It felt so good, so soothing. All was well. There was no reason to try to escape. How could he possibly battle multiple dragons without a weapon? It was impossible. And Marcelle was strong and brave. She could survive without him.

He took in a deep breath and nodded as he exhaled slowly. "Draw my spirit out and send me with Cassabrie. Nothing else makes any sense."

"Then so be it. You will find chains and padlocks near the stake. If you would be so kind, allow me to wrap the chains around your body and the stake. My hands are not equipped to do it if you struggle. The padlock will engage without need of a key, so I can manage that."

Adrian spread out his hands. "Why chains? I am going willingly."

"Magnar will not be pleased to see a condemned prisoner free of chains. Not only that, intense pain might influence you to alter your willingness. Once the sphere glows, you will understand. Its heat will scald your brain, and no lie you tell will darken it. You are not powerful enough."

"Do you plan to drug me?"

"There is no need. You are already fully drugged."

Adrian narrowed his eyes. "What?"

"Never mind. Let us proceed. The promoted humans will be here at any moment."

Adrian walked up to the sphere, the crystalline orb atop the cooking stake. Behind it lay a pile of chains he hadn't seen the day before. Perhaps Arxad put them there earlier in the night.

He set his back against the stake, and his head against the sphere. As Arxad wrapped the chains around him and the stake,

Cassabrie whispered, "All will be well, Adrian. I withstood thirteen days of suffering before my spirit entered the sphere. That was before Arxad knew about Trisarian's power or even that a spirit could be captured. But I will save that story for another day. Just be comforted in the fact that someone else has endured much more than you will have to endure. You are brave and strong. There is nothing to fear."

After Arxad tightened the chains, he fastened the two ends together with the padlock. When it snapped in place, he looked at Adrian and spoke softly. "I tried to show you, but your eyes were blind."

"What do you mean?"

"You are not in a state that will allow you to comprehend, but perhaps pain will clear your mind, albeit too late to make a difference." Arxad turned away and began shuffling toward a double doorway. The rising moon peering through the hole above had brightened the room, allowing Adrian a good view of the dragon's progress. When he reached the door, he stopped and looked back. "Magnar is now entering with the promoted ones. Prepare for suffering."

❋   ❋   ❋   ❋   ❋   ❋

As a huge moon rose toward the top of one of the Zodiac's spires, Marcelle stood at the front of a crowd of about fifty humans— restless humans, shifting, shuffling, mumbling humans. What were they expecting to see? Death? Pain? Why would the dragons put their cruelty on display? To incite fear? Didn't they also risk planting the seeds of rebellion, or had the threat of murdered children drained courage from even the most stouthearted men in the land?

As the image of Thad burning in agony came to mind, Marcelle winced. Yes, that had to be the case. Men who hoped to defend the innocent would surely pause when scorched and blackened children haunted their nightmares. Witnessing an execution likely reminded them of the horrors the dragons were willing to inflict.

The slavers were calculating, brutal, cold. A human child meant little more to them than a piglet that could be replaced by choosing from the next litter in the breeding rooms.

She blew out a sigh. So what were the slaves feeling now as they waited for the next brutal act? Perhaps they hoped for a miracle, the victim's escape from bonds that would foreshadow their prophesied liberation. Then again, maybe they had no expectations at all. The dragons said they had to come, so they obeyed, and even now a dragon paced in front of the Zodiac, Penelope's master, Hyborn. As the dragon in charge of one of the promoted slaves, he had been assigned to lead them into the Zodiac, but, as some of the slaves whispered, with the added dimension of a pending execution, maybe plans would change.

A breeze tossed Marcelle's altered hair, reminding her once again of the danger. She was an impostor, an infiltrator who would soon walk into a den of dragons and battle impossible odds. Death seemed certain, but death was better than leaving a friend to suffer alone.

She scuffed her too-tight sandals against the pebbly outer courtyard. Penelope's feet had to be at least two sizes smaller than her own, but they couldn't afford to overlook any detail. From the sheet and nightshirt, still wrapped around the viper and cradled in front of her, to the pigtails in her hair, to the crimping corset that pinched her into a prepubescent frame, she not only had to look like Penelope. She had to *be* Penelope.

A preteen boy stood next to her, Bron, she had learned earlier. He clutched his own bundle tightly against his chest as he rocked back and forth on his feet. His face expressionless, he appeared to be the model for promoted slaves. Maybe he had seen this procession before. It would be a good idea to copy his manner.

Behind her, a variety of opinions buzzed. Some said the execution victim was a laborer who blew up mine number two. Apparently, an explosion had occurred there earlier in the day. Others believed him to be a murderer or a kidnapper. Some children had died at mine number one, and others were missing. A few believed that he was guilty of both. It was hard enough to believe that one person would be so stupid, but two? Out of the question.

All spoke with contempt. How dare this human stir up such trouble? His crimes would cause every dragon master to crack down on his slaves and add heavy labors with harsh penalties. Surely he deserves to die.

Trying to keep her head still, Marcelle glanced to her other side. Shellinda stood in the second row of people. She had draped her body with one of the sheets, and the excess material dragged the ground behind her. Somewhere underneath the loose garment, she had hidden Adrian's sword.

Marcelle looked away. Good girl. Now she just had to remember her instructions not to reveal the sword until Adrian was set free. Otherwise, it might be used as a weapon against the humans. She rotated slightly and scanned everyone in her field of vision. Scott and Vanna were nowhere in sight. No use looking for them now.

Refocusing straight ahead, Marcelle tried to take in a painless breath but to no avail. With shuffling steps, Hyborn blocked her view of the building as he passed. Then, he stopped and eyed her. Smoke trickled from his nostrils and drifted slowly upward.

"Penelope," he said. "You look … different."

Marcelle froze. What could she say? He hadn't even asked a question. She cleared her throat, hoping to mimic Penelope's higher voice. "My countenance is fallen. Leaving my home brings sorrow, even in a time of joy for myself."

"Well spoken." The dragon's head drew closer. "Where is Daphne?"

"She's …" Marcelle swallowed. "She's unable to come. She didn't say why."

"Very well. I will ask her myself later." Without another word, Hyborn drew back and continued his pacing.

Marcelle exhaled. That was close. But she passed the test. Hyborn thought she was the real Penelope.

Ahead, a massive pair of doors swung inward. A huge dragon flew from within and landed gracefully between the building and the people.

As if guided by a conductor, the slaves bowed. Marcelle quickly did the same. As she kept her torso bent, she looked around, waiting for the others to pop back up. Had anyone noticed her hesitation? A few whispers of "Magnar" floated about, some surprised in tone, some reverent.

"You may rise," Magnar said.

When everyone had straightened, Magnar spoke again, this time with the fervor of a fiery prophet. "Hear this! You are about to witness the execution of a dragon killer. As you know, punishments for disobedience rarely rise to this level. We are merciful, limiting the severity of your penalties to lashes. Even their count and their ferocity are strictly measured. But when a human dares to murder a dragon, there can be no other consequence, and this public viewing will remind you of the value of a dragon's life in comparison to your own."

Magnar looked directly at Marcelle and then at Bron. "Why do we have only two promoted slaves?"

Hyborn glanced back and forth between Marcelle and Magnar. "Natalla has escaped. We assume she has fled to the wilderness."

"Yes, yes, I know that." Magnar's ears flattened. "Could we not find a replacement?"

"Maximus killed the examiner. We do not know where the exam records are."

Magnar snorted. "Very well. Let us proceed. I will take the promoted humans first so they can be prepared. You fly a patrol around the village. With all that has happened lately, I want this area to be free of further trouble."

"As you wish," Hyborn said, bowing.

As Magnar led the way, Bron marched forward. Marcelle jumped into a similar gait, glancing at him to read his body language—shoulders back, head erect, eyes forward, lips firm. She copied every feature. She would be the image of the solemn, proud slave who yearned to travel to the Northlands to meet the King of the Dragons, yet found sadness in her departure from those she loved.

When they passed into the cavernous building, Marcelle glanced around. The room, long and rectangular, like a huge hallway, lay very nearly empty. The floor reflected their sandals and legs as they walked over the polished surface. Murals decorated the walls at each side, and a line of lanterns mounted on protruding rods in front of each mural focused beams of light on certain portions as if highlighting an important scene.

On the left wall, a dragon, larger than life, blasted a barrage of fire at a radiant sphere, as if attacking a moon. Maybe it *was* a moon. The dragon seemed to be flying across a dark background with stars behind him. Yet, the moon had no craters, no sign of flaws that most moons displayed. It just shone with an ivory glow, likely painted with a phosphorescent oil. In fact, flecks of shiny paint made the entire mural sparkle.

A woman cowered behind the moon, as if hiding from the dragon's fury. With long auburn hair and petite frame, she looked familiar somehow. The lantern cast a beam on a name etched underneath the moon, written in the human language. *Laurel Blackstone.*

Marcelle let the name seep in. Uriel Blackstone's wife? The legends say she died in childbirth while he was in captivity, and she had blonde hair, not auburn. And how would the dragons know anything about her, much less what she looked like?

On the other wall, a redheaded girl in a long white dress spread out her arms, her head angled upward and her mouth open. A lantern focused on her green eyes, making them shine. A brilliant aura, much like the moon's glow on the opposite wall, wrapped the girl in a halo, as if she were inside a semitransparent moon herself. A woman dressed in black approached her from behind, a dagger in her thin fingers. With a gaunt pale face and black eyes, she looked more phantom than human.

Another set of double doors lay ahead. Magnar pushed them open and continued walking slowly. Marcelle and Bron followed him into a dim circular chamber with a domed ceiling. As the dragon's wings stretched out to help him balance, he blocked most of the view in front. Something stood at the center of the floor. It moved slightly, making a clinking sound, but the dimness obscured any details.

Magnar stopped, swung around, and faced Marcelle and Bron. "Halt," he said in a low tone. "It is time for your preparation."

Marcelle tried to see around him, but his body still blocked her view of the center of the room. Another dragon walked toward them from the shadows on the right. As he approached, a grinding noise sounded from the ceiling. A hole grew in the center of the dome and continued expanding until the entire room became an open courtyard. The light from Trisarian washed over the area, revealing the other dragon's identity—Arxad.

Marcelle stiffened. If any dragon could recognize her, he would be the one. He seemed intelligent and attentive, but the moonlight might not be enough to reveal her identity. Maybe this promotion procedure was routine for him, and he wouldn't pay much attention. She kept her head low, hoping to shade her face. The moment of truth had arrived.

"Sit," Arxad commanded.

Bron dropped to the floor cross-legged and set his bundle in his lap. Marcelle joined him but laid hers to her left, out of Arxad's view. She risked a glance at him. He looked so different. Wounds covered his wings and face, and his expression seemed despairing, like that of a bereaved father. Something terrible must have happened.

Arxad carried sheets of parchment in one clawed hand and a pair of quills in the other. He set the parchment down at Bron's right and flipped a quill into each of their laps. "Write a letter to your closest relations," he said without a hint of emotion. "Tell them you are happy in the Northlands and serving the King of the Dragons with contentment. Because of your duties there and your desire to keep them from heartache, this will be the only letter they will receive. When you are finished, I will read it and deliver it to the people you indicate."

Bron picked up the parchment and handed one sheet to Marcelle. He set the page on the floor in front of him and immediately began writing.

Taking care not to look at Arxad, Marcelle leaned forward as well. Inside, she fumed. Obeying without question just wasn't in her nature. How could anyone write a letter about something she hadn't really experienced? Penning a lie was worse than speaking one. At least a verbal lie eventually withered on the vine. A written lie lasted forever.

As she set the quill close to the paper, Arxad placed an inkwell between their letters. "Do be quick about it," he said. "We have much to accomplish tonight." He then turned and disappeared into the shadows.

Magnar sat on his haunches, his huge body still blocking whatever stood at the center. With fiery red eyes rocking back and forth with his swaying head, he watched closely.

Marcelle touched the parchment with the quill. She and her conspirators hadn't discussed this part. To whom should she address it? What should she say? Did Penelope have a mother? A sister? Would writing to Vanna be believable? And since Penelope was one of the poorer students, might that mean that she also lacked good penmanship, spelling, and grammar? Not necessarily. Besides, faking mistakes would be harder than writing correctly.

After taking a deep breath, she wrote in decent but inelegant script:

Dear Vanna,

As we thought, it is cold in the Northlands, but I am sufficiently warm here in the ivory palace. The King of the Dragons is a kind master, and I am pleased to be in his service. I hope someday that you, too, will be free so we can be together again.

Because I am so busy here, this is the only letter I will write to you, and I also wish to spare you the heartache of hearing from me.

With much love, Penelope

She laid down the quill and looked at Bron. He continued writing, dipping his quill in the well from time to time. His writing reflected a deliberate hand, perfectly formed letters and heartfelt words to a beloved mother.

Arxad returned, this time carrying a mug. "Drink half of this," he said, extending the mug toward Bron. "The journey to the Northlands is long and difficult. This elixir will allow you to endure the hardships. We will provide you with ceremonial clothing in a little while."

Bron took the mug with both hands, raised it to his lips, and tipped back his head. His throat muscles moved up and down twice before he passed the mug to Marcelle.

While Arxad collected the letters, Marcelle took the mug, wrapping her fingers around the warm, glazed pottery. Inside, a thick liquid sent a sickly sweet aroma into her nostrils. A drug, no doubt, something to make victims powerless to resist the next step.

Resisting the urge to glance at Arxad, she copied Bron's motions and let the liquid pass around her upper lip without letting any drain into her mouth. After moving her throat up and down to mimic swallowing, she lowered the mug and passed it back to Bron who then set it on the floor.

Holding Marcelle's letter, Arxad looked at her over the edge of the page. "Who told you about an ivory palace?"

Marcelle steeled her body. Another mistake, and a big one. "I heard rumors. Someone said a man journeyed from the North-lands only yesterday, and he described the palace."

"Interesting." Arxad stretched out his neck and looked inside the mug. His brow scrunched for a moment. He cast a glance at Bron and then Marcelle before returning to Marcelle's letter. "Who is Vanna?"

She kept her head low. "My friend. We serve together with Daphne. She is like a sister to me."

"That will do." Arxad turned toward Magnar. "Let us proceed with the murderer's execution and conduct it quickly. I would like the human witnesses to be gone before midnight, so I can finish the preparation for these two in the usual way. By then, the elixir will have had time to take full effect."

"Excellent," Magnar said. "No need to stretch out this one. He is nothing special."

"My thinking as well. In fact, let the two of us be the only drag-ons in attendance. It would be better if Hyborn did not see Penel-ope in this state. I think he has grown fond of her."

"Easily done. I already sent him on a patrol assignment." Mag-nar stretched out his wings and took to the air, flying toward the doors he had entered while calling back. "It might take a few min-utes to get the vermin organized."

With the dragon's body out of the way, Marcelle looked at the central object on the floor, a man chained and padlocked to a stake with a sphere on top, apparently made of some kind of crys-tal. The sphere reflected the moon's glow and created a white halo around the man, veiling his features. She squinted and studied his face—square jaw, firm chin, light brown hair. Yes, the man was Adrian. Even in the dimness, who could mistake him for anyone else? He stood up straight with his shoulders back, his eyes wide open. His lips moved. Was he praying? Or was he whispering to Cassabrie?

At the thought of Cassabrie, a surge of heat flashed across Marcelle's skin. Trusting that girl was a bad idea. Since the time she went inside Adrian, he had become softer, more passive, less decisive.

She looked at her bundle on the floor. Could she grab her sword and free Adrian? Should she threaten Arxad and demand the key to unlock the chains? He had already proven his ability to defend himself as well as his lack of fear of her sword. A swipe with his tail was all it had taken to disarm her in an embarrassing fashion.

As they waited for the witnesses, Arxad raised up on his haunches. Marcelle eyed his underbelly. The vulnerable spot was there, small but easy enough to see in the moonlight. She let her gaze drift to the dragon's face. He stared right at her, a deliberate stare.

She looked away. What could that mean? If she leaped for him and pressed the sword against the spot, would he acquiesce and provide the key? But how could she keep the sword in place while unlocking Adrian's chains? Could Bron do it?

She glanced at her fellow promoted slave. His head wobbled, and his shoulders slumped. No. He was already under the drug's influence. He would be more likely to stick a key in his nose than in the padlock.

Marcelle lifted the bundle into her arms and rose slowly to her feet. Arxad didn't flinch. His stare stayed focused. As she pushed a hand under the sheet, she again broke eye contact. He likely noticed her lack of response to the drug, and her letter had made him wary. If he knew who she was, why didn't he say so?

She listened for the sound of footsteps. Time was running out. Maybe it would be better to wait for Shellinda and Adrian's sword. With all the people around, some of the men would surely help her.

But help her do what? No plan came to mind. Relying on instinct would have to work. Just react and trust in her training.

After another minute, the clatter and shuffle of many feet filtered into the courtyard. A line of humans passed through the doorway at intervals of about two steps, most with their heads low. A middle-aged man led the way, followed by two women. Shellinda walked in next. With the tail of a sheet dragging the floor behind her, she held one arm over her waist while the other arm stayed hidden.

Barely visible far to Marcelle's left, someone walked through a smaller doorway in the perimeter wall, a woman wearing a black dress and carrying a bag of some kind. Several people gasped when they looked her way. The woman withdrew something from her bag and knelt behind it, but the object was too dark to distinguish.

After everyone had filed in, Magnar flew over their heads and landed next to Adrian. As the dragon settled, he scratched Adrian's ear with a claw on his wing. Adrian grimaced but said nothing.

Marcelle pressed her lips together, fuming. Those scaly fiends used every opportunity to deliver pain. They would soon get a taste of it themselves.

Flapping his wings, Arxad glided to Adrian's opposite side. Both dragons now stood about an arm's length away from him.

"The time has come," Arxad called to the witnesses. "By this execution of a dragon murderer, all humans will learn once again that the lives of their masters are sacred."

Marcelle tightened her grip on the viper's hilt. The time had come all right. Live or die, she and Adrian would be together.

❋ TWENTY-TWO ❋

ADRIAN straightened his body and stood tall. With a crowd of people gathered in a semicircle and two young teens watching from close range, he had to show courage. The girl, in particular, seemed very interested. There was something familiar about her—a strong face, square shoulders, and confident stance. Who could she be? A relative of someone he knew on Major Four? Maybe. Surely such relationships existed, cousins a couple of times removed, so features could be similar even to this day.

Two other familiar faces appeared at the front of the crowd, Shellinda's and Scott's. Dressed in bulky sheets, Shellinda looked ready to make a bed. How had she managed to escape from the cattle camp? Might that mean that Marcelle lurked somewhere in the crowd?

A dark slender form emerged from a narrow door to Adrian's right. He squinted to get a better look. No, not Marcelle. It was Zena. With long, deliberate strides, she sashayed toward the right side of the crowd. She carried a bag with a strap over her shoulder and hugged the bag itself close to her black dress. Breathing hushed murmurs, the people on that end drifted away, leaving her in an island of space.

She stooped and pulled the black egg from the bag. A new round of murmurs rose from the crowd. One woman began crying, and several shushed her with strong oaths. Once Zena had propped the egg with the bag and a nest of padding, she knelt behind it and watched.

Magnar flew in and, beating his wings furiously, landed at Adrian's left. With the last flap, Magnar clipped Adrian's ear with a claw at the end of his wing. Adrian flinched but refused to cry out.

As warm liquid trickled down Adrian's neck, Magnar spoke in a rumbling whisper. "You will soon pray for pain of such low degree."

With his wings pushing him along, Arxad skittered across the floor and stopped at Adrian's right. After facing the crowd and waiting for them to settle, Arxad spoke in a commanding voice. "The time has come. By this execution of a dragon murderer, all humans will learn once again that the lives of their masters are sacred."

"Be calm," Cassabrie said. "They are planning a quick execution, so the pain will last only a few moments. I will help you through it."

Adrian nodded. No sense in talking now. Soon, death would come, and he and Cassabrie would be able to talk all they wanted, and maybe they could work together to figure out how to help Marcelle, wherever she was.

"Penelope?" Arxad called.

Adrian followed Arxad's line of sight. He spoke to the girl, the young teen who seemed so familiar. She stood next to a teenaged boy who sat cross-legged, his head drooping low.

Penelope held a hand under a bundle of clothing in front of her. "Yes?" she said in a timid voice.

"If you feel dizzy during this execution," Arxad said, "then feel free to sit on the floor."

Magnar growled. "Why are you delaying? Let us proceed."

"I am following protocol," Arxad countered, his voice too low for the others to hear. "We always pamper the promoted humans in public."

Penelope glanced around before directing her gaze at Arxad. "Um … thank you. If I get dizzy, I will sit."

Adrian focused on the girl's face. Her voice sounded strained, too high to be natural. Somehow her eyes and brow seemed older than her frame.

"You must have a strong constitution," Arxad said, again speaking to Penelope. "It is clear that your labors have given you muscular forearms and hands, especially for a girl your age."

Penelope looked directly at Adrian. Adrian stared back at her. Who was this pig-tailed girl? So familiar, so strong in body and in countenance.

She cleared her throat before answering. "My labors have been hard. They have made me as strong as most boys my age."

Adrian let her words echo in his mind. Her voice was lower now, more mature.

"How do you know this to be true?" Arxad asked. "Have you had skirmishes with the young males?"

"Arxad!" Magnar bellowed. "What is the meaning of this inexhaustible query?"

Arxad stretched his head around Adrian and whispered to Magnar, barely loud enough for Adrian to hear. "I always question the promoted humans. It allows me to know when the drug has taken effect. This one is quite resistant."

"Very well." Magnar waved a wing. "She may answer, but this is the last question."

Keeping her eyes locked on Adrian, Marcelle shook her head and spoke in an even lower tone. "No skirmishes. The boys always ask me to consider it a forfeit."

Adrian sucked in a breath. What did she say? A forfeit?

Penelope dropped the clothing bundle and whipped out a black sword. She lunged at Arxad and pushed the tip of the blade against his vulnerable spot. "And now," she shouted, "I demand that *you* forfeit and let the prisoner go!"

The crowd gasped. Several women screamed. A loud buzz carried throughout the courtyard, spiced here and there with profanity.

Adrian stared at the girl's stern profile. Marcelle!

"What?" Magnar roared. "How dare you!"

Marcelle glared at him. "I am a daring person. It's what I do."

While Arxad stood high on his haunches, completely still and stoic, Adrian fought the chains, rattling them loudly as he grunted, "Got to … get loose!" He jerked, twisted, and wiggled, but the chains wouldn't budge.

"Arxad!" Magnar shouted. "Just knock her away like the annoying fly she is, and I will turn her into ashes."

"If you do—" Marcelle pushed the sword, piercing Arxad's belly. Liquid trickled around the point. "You will find that I am like lightning! He will be dead!"

Cassabrie screamed in Adrian's mind. "You witch! Don't kill Arxad!"

Adrian gulped. Yes, Marcelle would do it … in a heartbeat. Only one chance. He looked down at his pocket. "Cassabrie," he whispered. "The key is still there. Arxad said it worked on every lock in the Zodiac. Leave my body and unlock me."

"First I have to save Arxad."

Adrian's voice burst out without his command. "Marcelle! Look out!"

"What?" Marcelle spun toward him. "Where?"

Magnar leaped and slapped her with a wing. She flew across the room and slid along the tiles, forcing the crowd to scatter. Magnar launched a blast of fire in her wake, but she rolled out of the way and into a throng of scrambling legs. The people didn't bother to help her up. They just ran to the perimeter wall and watched.

Summoning all his strength, Adrian lunged against the chains. They loosened a little but not enough. He thrust his hand toward his pocket. No chance. With his arms pinned, he couldn't reach.

Marcelle leaped to her feet. Magnar shot another stream of flames and swept it toward her. She jumped, flipped over the river of fire, and landed upright on the other side, the sword still in her grip. "You will have to do better than that!" she yelled. "Come to me in close combat, and I will introduce you to the pain your whips inflict on my people."

"You are such a fool!" Magnar waved a wing toward the crowd behind her. "Men, capture her and bring her to me. For every minute that she continues to defy my authority, one of your children will die."

"Cassabrie!" Adrian hissed. "Get the key!"

Cassabrie said nothing.

Adrian growled through clenched teeth. "Cassabrie! Do what I tell you!"

"Patience, Adrian. Patience. More decisions are yet to be made."

Adrian clenched his teeth. What did that mean? Had she gone mad?

Four men stepped from the crowd, each one trembling, perhaps fathers who feared for their children's lives. They formed a ring around Marcelle and closed in.

"No!" Adrian shouted at the men. "Now is the time to loose your chains. If you work together, you can be free!"

Magnar shot a fireball at Adrian's arm. The flames splashed across the chains. Although the metal acted as a protective sleeve, one of the tongues scorched his hand.

"Augh!" He tried to shake his arm, but the chains held him fast.

Arxad leaned closer to Adrian. "Now you know why we consider Starlighters so dangerous. The way they use their power is unpredictable. She has become much more than a guide, has she not?"

Marcelle turned slowly, her sword extended as she barked a challenge. "Just because you're human, do not think I will spare any of you. For the sake of liberty for all, I will shed the blood of a few."

The men halted and looked at Magnar as if asking what to do now.

"Kill the murderer," Magnar said to Arxad. "The girl will be next on the stake."

Arxad reached a hand toward the sphere and spoke to Adrian in a soft tone. "This is the choice you made. I fear that I cannot alter your course now. Yet, when it is over, you will be free to do as you please."

"Yes," Cassabrie said. "When we are joined in spirit, we will be invisible to the dragons. We can work together to free the slaves. Once you are in my condition, you will understand how much more powerful you can be."

Shaking his head hard, Adrian yelled. "If you would betray Marcelle, I don't want to be with you! Get out of me! Now!"

Her warmth caressed his body. "Adrian, take care what you say, for I am not betraying Marcelle. I am following a plan that is greater than you can perceive. Soon you will understand that what I am doing is necessary for the good of all."

Arxad set his hand on the sphere. Above, Trisarian's glow cast a narrow beam into the crystalline surface. It burst into a dazzling globe of radiance. Heat shot into Adrian's head and knifed into his spine. Scalding pain roared from limb to limb.

He cocked his head back and bit his lip, but the agony burst through in a gut-wrenching scream. His voice rose into the dark sky until he ran out of breath, exhausted.

Gasping, he looked at the courtyard. Sweat poured. It was so hot, so terribly hot. How much longer could he stand it? Arxad said that a lie wouldn't work, but he had to give it a try. Panting heavily, he breathed out, "I want Marcelle to die."

The sphere flickered but not enough to alter the searing radiance. Arxad was right. He lacked the power.

Marcelle dove headfirst and somersaulted between two of the men. Magnar blew another jet at her. She leaped to the side. This time, she slipped and smacked her head against the tile. As she rose to her feet, her legs wobbled. Blinking, she staggered from side to side.

The sphere continued pouring heat into Adrian's body. His eyes burned. His tongue dried out. He couldn't breathe a word. It wouldn't be long now. Death was closing in.

Magnar blew yet another ball of fire. With a quick step to the side, Marcelle dodged again, but the fire in her eyes had vanished.

"Zena!" Magnar shouted. "Let us end this spectacle. Disarm the girl and have the men bring her to the stake. I will guard the prince." He flew to the egg and settled next to it.

As if gliding across a stage, Zena walked with graceful steps, her long lines evident. When she drew near, Marcelle spun toward her and pointed her sword. "Back away," she growled, "or I will give you a good reason to look like a corpse."

"Very clever." Zena stopped just out of reach. "But you have no idea who you're dealing with."

"A corpse, I think. You look more dead than alive."

"You are very perceptive." Zena lunged toward her. Marcelle thrust the viper and plunged it through Zena's midsection. Zena halted and looked down at the blade, then, with a savage swing, slapped Marcelle across the face. Marcelle staggered back and fell to her bottom.

Zena grasped the viper's hilt and drew it out of her body. Then, with a nonchalant toss of her head, she called to the men. "Take her."

The four men rushed toward Marcelle. With two on each side, they grabbed her arms and hoisted her to her feet.

Zena pointed at the stake. "She is next. Take her to Arxad."

As they dragged Marcelle, she struggled mightily, kicking and biting. One man let out a yelp, but their slavery-hardened muscles kept her in check.

While Zena returned to the egg and Magnar shuffled toward the stake, Marcelle looked directly at Adrian and began screaming as she thrashed. "I will slay every dragon in this sick and twisted land, and then I'll go back to the world of humans alone! You spineless slugs deserve your chains! No one who is too cowardly to fight for his freedom deserves anything more than the marks of a whip on his back and the disdain of the tyrants who drive them to despair. If all it takes is a verbal threat to your little ones to turn your backbones into butter, then you can just die and rot here! A real man would fight! A real man would charge into battle! A real man knows that freedom is a greater gift to his children than safety from an oppressor's threats. If a woman has to put on a man's trousers to shake you from your cowardly delirium, then so be it! I will die fighting for that cause!"

As the horrible torture purged his brain of all other thoughts, Marcelle's words stabbed Adrian's soul. What had he been thinking? How could he possibly give up this fight now? It was time to draw a sword!

Battling the chains with all his might, he squeezed out a desperate cry. "Cassabrie, I beg you. Let me go! Don't let me die a coward. Let me fight at Marcelle's side!"

"Do you want to be her partner," Cassabrie asked, "no matter what?"

"Yes! No matter what!"

A wave of cold washed through his chest. Streams of light poured from underneath his shirt and collected in a feminine shape in front of him. The crowd began to buzz, some pointing. When Cassabrie appeared, Adrian spat out another plea. "I have to help Marcelle!"

"Shh! We must work quickly and quietly." Visible as she moved, she pushed her hand into Adrian's pocket, withdrew the key, and inserted it into the padlock, now dangling from a link near his stomach. With only her hands evident, no one else would notice, especially with every eye focused on Marcelle as she set her feet and continued her tirade.

"Men! Summon your courage! Dragons who would burn your children don't deserve your allegiance! They are devils, I tell you, the worst kind of devils!"

As Magnar neared, Arxad stepped in front and spread his wings slightly, further shielding Cassabrie's efforts. Adrian tried to see around him but to no avail. Only Marcelle's shouts gave him any clue to what was going on.

The lock clicked open. While Cassabrie quietly unwound the chain, Adrian wiggled, trying to loosen the coil and let it slide down his body. Scorching heat still raged from head to toe, but the hope of escape spurred him on.

Cassabrie guided the last loop to the floor, set it down gently, and helped him step away from the stake. Rising to tiptoes, she kissed him on the cheek. "I hope to see you again someday." With that, she disappeared.

Adrian shook his head. Hot waves still pulsed inside. He side-stepped around Arxad and looked for Marcelle. One man had grabbed her throat from the side, squelching her voice. Another followed with the viper at her back.

"The dragon murderer has escaped!" Adrian turned toward the shout. Zena had risen and was now carrying the egg toward the stake. "Capture him and chain them together! The prince craves the sphere's energy flow!"

"Adrian!" Shellinda threw a sword low across the floor. It spun as it skidded across the tiles before stopping near Marcelle and her captors.

Adrian dashed ahead and dove for it. Sliding as he grabbed it, he sliced the leg of the man carrying Marcelle's viper. He then leaped to his feet and looked for the black blade. It lay next to a man who writhed on the floor, holding his bleeding ankle.

"Stay where you are," Magnar shouted, "or I will incinerate her immediately!"

"She'll die anyway!" Adrian bent his legs to leap again, but a wave of fire surged past his eyes, blocking his path.

Magnar hurtled toward him, wings spread, mouth wide, teeth bared. Adrian dropped to the floor and let him fly overtop, snapping his jaws as he passed. He thrust the sword at the dragon's belly but missed the soft spot. The blade clanked against armor.

His momentum unchecked, Magnar slammed into the crowd. Slaves toppled into each other. As he pivoted, Magnar spied Shellinda and shot a ball of fire at her. The sheet burst into flames. Screaming, she ran through the doorway. Scott and a girl hurried after her, and the doors closed behind them.

Adrian strangled his hilt. Not Shellinda! The poor child!

"Surrender," Magnar roared, "or I will choose another child to kill."

"Never!" Adrian charged. Magnar turned to the side and batted Adrian with his tail, sending him flying across the room. He crashed into a column. His head smacked the marble, and he toppled to the side.

Blinking to clear his blurry vision, Adrian looked at the glowing sphere. Trisarian's beams had strengthened. A bell gonged from the direction of the Basilica. Was it midnight?

With the egg again in the bag strapped to her shoulder, Zena picked up the chain. While the men held Marcelle against the stake, Zena wound the links into place, binding Marcelle's arms. She struggled again, but as the radiance pulsed, she stiffened. Her eyes clenched shut. Even the men holding her grimaced.

Zena clicked the padlock and backed away while pulling the egg from the bag. She held it in front of her with both hands as if warming it in the sphere's glow. "Now we will see Trisarian's full power. The prince will hatch, and a new era of dragon authority will dawn."

Bending her neck back, Marcelle gasped and panted. She let out a pitiful wail. "Adrian! Oh, Adrian, I'm so sorry for everything I did. It was all my fault! Save yourself. Free the slaves. They're more important than me!"

Still clutching his sword, Adrian pushed a hand against the floor and climbed slowly to his feet. His head throbbed. Shades of black pulsed in his vision. Magnar stalked toward him again, his mouth open and smoke pouring forth.

Marcelle cried out. "Adrian! I love you!" Then, with a final breath, her head drooped to her chest.

Fire gushed from Magnar's mouth. Adrian dodged the blast and charged toward the stake, screaming an elongated, "No!"

Another loud cry reverberated throughout the courtyard, feminine, youthful, and desperate. "Adrian! I hate you! And I never want to see you again!"

The sphere turned dark. A stream of black fog poured forth and hovered over the courtyard, blocking out the moon.

Adrian skidded to a halt. The entire chamber had turned dark. Leading with an extended arm, he groped toward the stake. One way or another, he would find Marcelle.

A grinding noise sounded from above, and the ceiling began to close.

"Open it!" Magnar shouted. "The crystal must be reignited!"

The feminine voice returned. "Listen to my story, O dragons and humans, for it is a tale of heartbreak and woe. Slaves driven by whips and claws are forced to bear loads that break their backs, children burned by fire and the elements are forced to fight for crumbs and shatter their innocence, and girls thrown onto beds of despair are forced to uncover their loins for men unknown, and they weep at the loss of their maidenhood."

The sphere brightened, revealing Marcelle's slumped body. The glow spread slowly across the chamber, like the earliest rays of dawn.

Feeling dizzy, Adrian pushed his leaden feet forward, as if slogging through a swamp. Everyone in the room looked like statues, petrified and staring at the sphere. Arxad stood near the stake, his wings spread, as if guarding Marcelle. Magnar had propped himself high on his haunches a dozen or more paces away, his draconic mouth wide open.

Adrian pushed onward, inch by inch. Cassabrie's gift worked all too well. The hypnotizing effect of her tale left no one untouched.

"Behold, the victims!" Cassabrie shouted.

The black cloud overhanging the courtyard streamed to the ground and reshaped into childlike beings, as black as coal and semi-transparent. Carrying pails with their backs bent, they formed a line that led from the sphere to where Magnar stood.

One by one, they dumped the contents at Magnar's feet. Glittering gems poured out, each bursting into flames and dwindling as it struck the floor and bounced around.

"Oh, the tragedy!" Cassabrie cried. "Trust betrayed. Virtue squandered. Innocence lost. The gems of youth spoiled by the greed and cruelty of wicked taskmasters."

Adrian threw his body forward with all his might. He stumbled into the stake, stopping his momentum by wrapping an arm around Marcelle and hanging on. His hand swiped across the lock at her chest, but where was the key now? Zena didn't need it to snap the lock closed, so maybe …

He laid down the sword and dipped his hand into his pocket. Yes! Cassabrie had put it back! After fishing it out, he tried to push it into the lock with stiff fingers, glancing at the hypnotized dragons as he worked. He set his ear close to Marcelle's mouth and listened for a hint of life. Nothing. No breaths at all, but maybe they were too shallow to hear.

When the lock finally popped open, he frantically jerked at the chains.

Arxad stretched out his neck and drew his head close to Adrian. "Your brother and his female companion were more fortunate. It was strange to witness a near repeat of their experience here, but this time the outcome leaves a casualty." The dragon's voice was strained, as if each word required every ounce of energy he could muster. "Marcelle is gone. Leave her here. I will care for her body. You must escape while you can. The Starlighter is doing this for your benefit. She cannot keep Magnar entranced for long."

"Dead or alive," Adrian said as he slid the chains down Marcelle's body, "I am taking her with me. I will not leave this treasure in your clutches."

"Human from another world, I urge you. She is not there. The body will be an anchor."

Adrian hoisted Marcelle over his shoulder and wrapped an arm around her legs. "Maybe so, but she's *my* anchor." He stooped, picked up his sword, and pointed it at Arxad's snout. "I will bury her in the soil of a free world, not in dirt polluted by tyranny and the cowardice of those who support it by their silence."

The sphere brightened further. Arxad's eyes glittered, like a fire rekindled. "Go! Find Frederick. He might be your only hope. Hurry, before it is too late."

Magnar shook his head as if awaking from a deep sleep.

Cassabrie's voice again swirled in the air. "Adrian, you are a weak coward. You hate Marcelle and let her die. Because of your faithlessness, you will never see her again."

The sphere turned black once more. Darkness filled the room. A stream of tiny sparks flowed near his eyes, Cassabrie's whispered voice. "Follow me."

Like a glowing ghost, she walked away, her body now visible as her cloak fanned with her movements.

"Where is he?" Magnar roared. "Ignite the sphere! The murderer must die!"

Zena shouted. "Light the lanterns!"

Adrian shifted Marcelle's body higher on his shoulder and, bending low, skulked after Cassabrie. While he weaved through the people, the loud buzz of frenzied conversation muffled every sound.

A lantern flickered to life far to his right, not enough to give him away to Magnar, but enough to reveal the slaves' worried faces and the bare outline of the door at the perimeter wall.

As he pushed on, his body shook. His calf muscles cramped. Despair stormed through his brain. Marcelle was dead. She had given her life trying to save him. It wasn't supposed to happen this way. He had sacrificed himself to save her so she could rescue the slaves. But now no one would be rescued. He had to run for his life and hide, somehow find Frederick or maybe the portal leading home where he could recruit reinforcements. But would they believe him?

Cassabrie stopped at the exit and faded out of sight. His legs still cramping, Adrian hurried to catch up. As she pulled a door open, her body brightened again, and her face clarified. With a furrowed brow and thinned lips, she spoke in a firm tone. "You must hurry. I will keep the dragons here as long as I can, but I have expended so much energy, I'm not sure what I have left."

He ached to reach out and caress her cheek, but then again, hadn't she contributed to Marcelle's death? Was she even now hypnotizing him? Why hadn't she told the lie to darken the sphere before Marcelle died? She must have had good reason, but there was no time to ask.

Giving her a nod, he slid through the opening. As it closed softly behind him, he looked into the long corridor ahead. A light shone in the distance, maybe indicating an exit to the outside.

Ignoring the pain, he pushed on. Something moved within the light. Humans? They had to be small, maybe children.

As he drew closer, the forms grew clear. Scott stood face-to-face with Shellinda on the Zodiac's front portico, wiping her cheek with a sheet. "The burns are minor," Scott said. "I think you'll be all right."

Shellinda grimaced at his touch. "They don't *feel* minor."

When Adrian arrived, he lowered Marcelle's body to the marble floor and knelt beside her.

Scott spun toward him. "Adrian? What happened?" He dropped down and joined him at Marcelle's other side. "Is she dead?"

"I'm not sure. I couldn't check while I was in there, and I can't stop for long." He pressed his ear against her chest and set a hand over her lips. A series of thumps sounded, weak and irregular, but no air touched his fingers.

"She's alive but not breathing." Adrian slid his arms under her body. "Is there a doctor anywhere? We need someone who can open an airway."

"Wait," Shellinda said, reaching a hand toward him. "Give me your sword."

"What? Why?"

Her tone sharpened. "Just give it to me!"

Adrian passed her the hilt. Kneeling between Marcelle's legs, Shellinda lifted the hem of Marcelle's tunic and pushed the sword underneath. Peering at the hidden blade as she pushed and pulled it in a sawing motion, she explained. "Part of Marcelle's disguise was to look like a twelve-year-old, so—" Something popped under her shirt. "There!" Shellinda withdrew the sword. "Now she should be able to breathe."

"Come on, warrior!" Adrian whispered while watching Marcelle's chest. "Show me that fighting spirit!"

Marcelle heaved in a breath, then, with her eyes still closed, her chest rose and fell in an even rhythm.

"That's better," Shellinda said as she rose to her feet with the sword in hand. "Let's get moving."

A spasm tightening his throat, Adrian lifted Marcelle into his arms and stood. As tremors rippled across his limbs, he took in deep breaths. He had to hurry. "Scott, can you lead me to the wilderness?"

The boy nodded. "I was already going there. Shellinda is in trouble, and Penelope can't show her face in public, so I'm taking both of them as far as I can."

"Penelope?" Adrian asked.

"The girl Marcelle pretended to be," Shellinda said. "Vanna went to get her ready."

Adrian nodded. "Then give the sword to Scott, and let's go."

With Scott and Shellinda leading the way, Adrian marched quickly along the street. The buildings lay dark, and not a soul stirred. Trisarian, now past its zenith, cast their hurrying shadows to the side.

Adrian walked and watched Marcelle at the same time. She lay motionless, save for her steady breathing. When they reached a cave at the outskirts of town, Shellinda ran inside while he and Scott waited.

"How is she?" Scott asked.

Adrian looked. Her eyes were now open, staring straight at him. "Marcelle," he said as loudly as he dared, "how are you feeling?"

She said nothing. Her expression completely blank, she continued staring. What might be wrong? Arxad had said something about people with no awareness, but what was the context? It seemed that his own mind had gone through a time of fuzziness, fogging his memory.

Scott laid a hand on her forehead. "Might she have brain damage from lack of air?"

"Maybe." Adrian shifted her higher in his arms. "It might take a while before we know."

Soon, Shellinda returned hand in hand with another girl dressed in men's trousers cinched at the waist with a rope. Adrian glanced back and forth between the newcomer and Marcelle. Yes, the resemblance was plain enough. She had to be Penelope.

"Are you ready?" Adrian asked.

Penelope tucked a water flask under her arm and pulled her trousers higher. "I hope so. I had to borrow these from a boy I know."

Adrian nodded at the flask. "Do you mind if I have a little?"

"All you want," Scott said as he reached for it. "We'll refill it on the way." He lifted the spout to Adrian's mouth, and after Adrian drained the contents, Scott waved the sword. "Let's go. I see lantern lights coming toward us." He hurried away from the village and into the shadows cast by cliffs that housed a row of dragon caves. Penelope and Shellinda joined him, again hand in hand.

After stepping into the darkness, Adrian looked back. Bobbing lights followed on the path, still a good distance behind. Another light glided toward them through the air. Might it be a dragon patrol?

Scott picked up the pace and ran into a forest, disappearing from sight. When Adrian and the girls plunged in, Scott grabbed his arm and pulled him against a wide tree trunk. Penelope and Shellinda huddled close, shivering.

"Shhh." Scott looked up. A winged form passed overhead. Trickles of fire fell through the canopy and draped over the path, like sections of flaming rope.

"Search lines," Scott whispered. "They help the dragons see what's below. We'll have to leave the path and go straight through the forest."

Adrian's shoulder muscles cramped. "How far?"

"About two hours by the path. Probably more through the underbrush."

Adrian blew out a sigh. His arms would just have to hold out. "Lead on."

Scott set down the sword and extended his arms. "You've been through a lot. Let me take a turn."

"Can you handle the weight?"

Dappled light from Trisarian illuminated Scott's grim expression. "For a while. I'm sure she's a lot lighter than a cartload of stones. But when we get to the wilderness boundary, I have to leave. You'll be on your own."

Adrian made ready to lay Marcelle in his arms, but then pulled her back. "No. I'd better carry her."

409

"But you're wounded and exhausted," Scott said. "I'm fresh."

"I know." Adrian lifted Marcelle higher and kissed her cold cheek. "I think I need to hold her close for a while."

Scott picked up the sword and, gripping it firmly, marched into the underbrush. "Okay. Let's go."

Adrian followed, looking at Marcelle as often as he could. She blinked but said nothing. Her wide eyes seemed to focus on the moon, partially veiled by branches.

Pain stabbed every part of his body, but it didn't matter. Only Marcelle mattered now. The slaves could wait. Freedom could wait. He would find his way through the wilderness and locate Frederick. Maybe Jason and their father would arrive from the Northlands, and they could mount an attack together.

While Scott paused to cut away an obstructing branch, Adrian pulled Marcelle close again and whispered, "Thank you for coming to save me. I will never forget your love and courage for as long as I live."

*　　　*　　　*　　　*　　　*　　　*

Light filled Marcelle's vision, a cyclone of radiance, swirling around her ... swirling, ever swirling. Soon, darkness streamed in and painted horizontal stripes across the radiance from the top of her field of vision to the bottom. As the cyclone contracted, the stripes drew closer and wrapped around her body, like a snake squeezing its prey.

She glanced to the side. A twin cyclone spun through the same process. Dark lines coiled around another victim, apparently female, but in the mix of light and darkness, her identity remained unclear.

After a few seconds, her own vortex slowed and finally stopped. Marcelle staggered for a moment, trying to gain her balance. She looked down and patted her body, once again dressed in her black warrior's garb. "How strange!" she whispered.

The other cyclone formed into a girl in a white dress and blue cloak. When her spinning halted, she looked at Marcelle and smiled. "We made it. You did magnificently."

"Magnificently?" Marcelle looked at her hands. They were ghostly pale. "What did I do?"

Cassabrie laid her palm on Marcelle's head. "Your memory will come back soon. After you do this a few times, you learn how to resist the brain scrambling."

Marcelle blinked at her surroundings. She stood in a forest clearing with the sun breaking through low in the trees. A bird chirped somewhere in the branches, a familiar song. Dew covered the grass, and a shallow depression spoiled the pristine turf.

She pointed at the spot. "The gas tank was there."

"That's right," Cassabrie said. "Very good."

Marcelle lifted each foot in turn, sending new feeling into her tingling legs. "I was away, but now I'm home."

"Excellent! Do you remember where you went?"

Marcelle closed her eyes. A flood of memories stormed through her brain—dragons, slave children with pails, Adrian chained to a stake, Zena pulling a sword from her own belly, the horrible pain at the cooking stake, and even vague memories of flying with Cassabrie.

"I was being executed," she said. "I had chains wrapped around me, and I couldn't escape. Adrian tried to save me, but I blacked out. I don't remember anything after that except for flying with you."

Cassabrie nodded. "Of course your memory is stricken. It's such a frightening experience, very few of the promoted slaves remember. Some remember Arxad's transport to the Northlands, as you have, but little else."

Marcelle patted her torso again. "At least I survived."

"In a way." Cassabrie laughed. "If you could see your face, you might have a different opinion."

Marcelle touched her cheek. "What do you mean?"

"Let's just say that you don't have your usual rosy color. When absorbing the elements to gain a body here, it's hard to get a blush without real blood flowing through our veins." Cassabrie touched Marcelle's sleeve. "You did a great job with your clothing, though. You must have a powerful mind to get it right the first time. It's too bad you lack experience or else you could have created a sword as well."

"I ... I don't understand." A chill ran along Marcelle's skin. She wrapped her arms around herself and shivered. "What are you talking about?"

"Just as with the promoted slaves," Cassabrie said, "the reflections sphere drew your spirit out of your body. Since Arxad was less vulnerable to my storytelling, he sneaked out before Magnar recovered. Then he carried us to the Northlands, and we helped you transport back to your home planet. Before we left, I explained how to reconstitute your body when you arrived here, and you followed my instructions beautifully."

More fuzzy memories filtered into Marcelle's brain, including Cassabrie's serious expression as she explained the reconstitution process only moments ago. Marcelle rubbed her hands up and down her arms. "So this isn't my—"

"Real body?" Cassabrie shook her head. "Adrian rescued your body before the dragons could eat it. That's what they do to the others once the spirits are removed. You are dwelling inside the body your mind conjured, and now that you're on your home planet, you constructed it from the materials here."

Marcelle shivered harder and pressed her hands against her stomach. All the amazing revelations seemed to pour acid into her gut, if there really was a gut in there. "So Adrian has my corpse?"

"I'm not sure if your body survived or not. I couldn't be certain, but it didn't appear to be breathing. If it did survive, it would be no more than living flesh hanging on bones. It might walk and respond instinctively to stimuli, but the real you wouldn't be there. I wonder if Adrian would even know the difference." Cassabrie lifted a hand to her mouth. "Oh, I'm sorry. That came out wrong. I mean Adrian might think it's the real you and that your brain has been damaged."

Marcelle frowned. This girl was quick, real quick. "Why did you bring me here?"

"To get help. Now that you have seen how powerful the dragons are, you must realize that you and Adrian can't do this alone. Go to your governor. Tell him what you have seen. Perhaps your ghostly appearance will be convincing enough."

Marcelle tapped her chin with a finger. "Prescott might believe, but I'll have to avoid Orion. If he sees either one of us, he'll think we're witches of some kind."

Cassabrie backed away a step. "I am not going with you. Adrian is still in great danger, so I have to return to see if I can help him. His father is well now, and he and I will venture out to search the wilderness for Adrian. Without my help, I don't think he will make it."

"I understand," Marcelle said, nodding, "but how will I return once I get an army together?"

"The portal will remain open." Cassabrie turned toward the gas tank's former position. As she extended an arm, her hand disappeared. "It is very dangerous to leave it this way, but I think we have no choice. Take note, however. When you return to the Northlands, you will again be a spirit. Your army will have to march behind a ghost; prepare them for that."

Marcelle pushed her own hand through the portal. Hers, too, disappeared. She looked into Cassabrie's eyes, so loving, so sincere. But was she? With her ability to hypnotize someone as strong as Adrian, might she be spinning a tale even now? Once they both went on their way, would she close the portal, trapping Marcelle in a world where she could be only an animated corpse? Did this Starlighter consider her a rival for Adrian's heart?

Marcelle drew an image of Adrian in her mind, standing tall, then bowing in his typical chivalrous fashion. Of course, Adrian was a wonderful friend and the greatest of warriors, but would he ever see her as anything but a hot-tempered she-devil?

"I perceive doubt," Cassabrie said. "Am I the reason?"

Marcelle nodded. "There's no use lying about it. I know what you did to Adrian."

Cassabrie looked at the ground. Her voice became soft and gentle. "I make no apologies for my actions. I have reasons for what I did, and I cannot tell them to you now." Setting a hand over her heart, she focused again on Marcelle. "Yet, I vow not to indwell him again. You and I are now in the same condition, spirits without bodies. Nothing matters more than rescuing our people. With all my heart, I long to be your partner in the war against the dragons and their cruelty."

Marcelle looked into her eyes again. She was so passionate, so convincing. Either her words were truly sincere, or this gift carried more power than even the most ardent skeptic could resist. "Adrian needs our help," Marcelle said, extending her hand, "and I will be your partner."

Cassabrie slid her hand into Marcelle's and formed a gentle grip. "Until we meet again on Starlight." Her smile as sweet as ever, she pulled away and glided into the portal. In a brief flicker of light, Cassabrie was gone.

Marcelle stood still for a moment. The birds stopped singing. Everything seemed as quiet as death itself. She eased closer to the portal and pushed a finger through. It disappeared. Yes, the door to Starlight remained open.

She frowned. Was it wrong to doubt? Did Cassabrie deserve complete trust? Maybe, maybe not. Her possession of Adrian seemed so self-serving at times as she turned his passion toward herself. Yet, at the end, he escaped and battled the most powerful of dragons alone. And why? To rescue the woman whose hot temper put him there in the first place.

Yes, that was true heroism. When he dropped his sword belt and walked out of the hovel to give himself up for those children, that was the most noble act of all—more chivalrous than a tourney forfeit, more courageous than battling two warriors at once, and more loving than any romance Mesolantrum had ever seen. And Cassabrie was with him all along. Maybe there was a lot more going on inside his mind than she would ever know.

Mimicking Cassabrie's voice, Marcelle spoke into the warming breeze. "I make no apologies for my actions."

Then, touching her hip where a scabbard should have been, she spun and marched into the forest. "Now if I can just find a good sword."

Cassabrie's Song

Arranged by Jessica Coleman

Piano and soft pad

Cello

1.The claw   of bond-age
2.And now,   my__ friend

penetrates,____   mutilates,_   you share   their pain.   Deep within
cry   with me   bleed with me   you share   my pain.   On your back

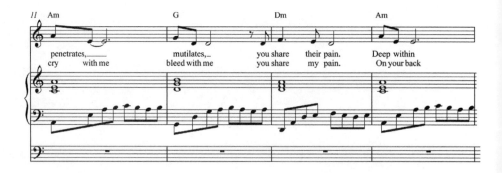

Feel the sin, that binds their wrists, their legs, their hearts, and pierces____ souls with
Feel the rack, that stretches____ souls til faith is bare and shackles____ hearts and

angry____ darts. Deflating____ hope and ceasing____ prayer to God above who
sows____ despair. For slavish____ strife and brutal____ bonds destroy____ all hope in

doesn't____ care or isn't____ there. *Is life* *unfair?____*
life beyond this darkened pond. *Will you* *respond____*

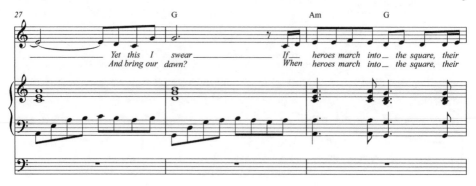

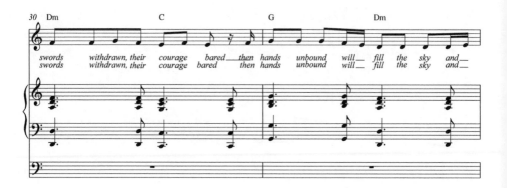

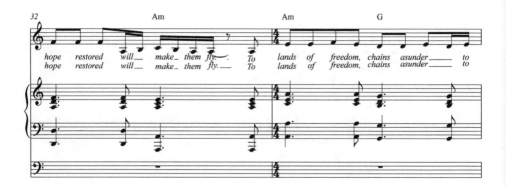

4

clap and worship, hearts in wonder that God in mercy heard their cries and
clap and worship, hearts in wonder that God in mercy heard their cries and

sent a friend who dried their eyes.
sent a friend who dried their eyes.

Will you respond

Will you respond.

419

Coming in 2011 from Living Ink Books

THE THIRD STARLIGHTER

(BOOK 2 IN THE <u>TALES OF STARLIGHT</u> SERIES)

Bryan Davis

Adrian and Marcelle continue their quest to free the human slaves on the dragon planet of Starlight. While sword maiden Marcelle returns to their home planet in search of military aid, Adrian stays on Starlight to find his brother Frederick, hoping to join forces and liberate the slaves through stealth. Both learn that reliance on brute force or ingenuity will not be enough to bring complete freedom to those held in chains.

For purchasing information visit

www.LivingInkBooks.com

or call 800-266-4977

Coming in 2011 from Living Ink Books

SONG OF THE OVULUM

(BOOK 1 IN THE CHILDREN OF THE BARD SERIES)

Bryan Davis

While in battle against demonic forces, brother and sister Joran and Selah, teenaged children of Methuselah, escape the great flood by transporting to a desolate world. Pursued by Tamiel, a seductive demon, Joran and Selah must reconstruct the portal through which they traveled, and each piece of the puzzle provides them with a glimpse into the post-flood world. Using their talents, they are able to influence events on their home planet, including the stories that readers know so well from the Dragons in our Midst and Oracles of Fire series. Because the demon constantly stalks them, every moment is filled with excitement and adventure.

For purchasing information visit

www.LivingInkBooks.com

or call 800-266-4977

The **Dragons in our Midst®** and **Oracles of Fire®** collection
by **Bryan Davis**:

RAISING DRAGONS

ISBN-13: 978-089957170-6

The journey begins! Two teens learn of their dragon heritage and flee a deadly slayer who has stalked their ancestors.

THE CANDLESTONE

ISBN-13: 978-089957171-3

Time is running out for Billy as he tries to rescue Bonnie from the Candlestone, a prison that saps their energy.

CIRCLES OF SEVEN

ISBN-13: 978-089957172-0

Billy's final test lies in the heart of Hades, seven circles where he and Bonnie must rescue prisoners and face great dangers.

TEARS OF A DRAGON

ISBN-13: 978-089957173-7

The sorceress Morgan springs a trap designed to enslave the world, and only Billy, Bonnie, and the dragons can stop her.

EYE OF THE ORACLE

ISBN-13: 978-089957870-5

The prequel to *Raising Dragons*. Beginning just before the great flood, this action-packed story relates the tales of the dragons.

ENOCH'S GHOST

ISBN-13: 978-089957871-2

Walter and Ashley travel to worlds where only the power of love and sacrifice can stop the greatest of catastrophes.

LAST OF THE NEPHILIM

ISBN-13: 978-089957872-9

Giants come to Second Eden to prepare for battle against the villagers. Only Dragons and a great sacrifice can stop them.

THE BONES OF MAKAIDOS

ISBN-13: 978-089957874-3

Billy and Bonnie return to help the dragons fight the forces that threaten Heaven itself.

Published by Living Ink Books, an imprint of AMG Publishers
www.livinginkbooks.com ✦ www.amgpublishers.com ✦ 800-266-4977